CRASHING DOWN

Carrie wondered if she were invisible, standing here in the shadows no less than fifteen feet away. She did feel herself straining to become invisible, all her muscles tensing as she tried to squeeze herself into a tiny ball, the way she had as a child.

At the same time, she acknowledged that she would not run now, even if she could. In spite of herself, she felt magnetized to the spot by the high energy that emanated from Breen as he proudly showed the men about the room, pointing out the large-screen television and the VCR, the books, the craft supplies, the state-of-the-art music equipment.

"We've done all of this so far with private donations," he said at one point, "but you can see why federal backing would help. We'd like to expand without losing quality."

As he gave his pitch, Carrie studied him. He might look somewhat different—he might have reinvented himself in many ways—but he was, she thought, the same monster she had known as a child.

MEG O'BRIEN
CRASHING DOWN

MIRA®

ISBN 1-55166-516-6

CRASHING DOWN

Copyright © 1999 by Meg O'Brien.

All rights reserved. Except for use in any review, the reproduction or utilization of this work in whole or in part in any form by any electronic, mechanical or other means, now known or hereafter invented, including xerography, photocopying and recording, or in any information storage or retrieval system, is forbidden without the written permission of the publisher, MIRA Books, 225 Duncan Mill Road, Don Mills, Ontario, Canada M3B 3K9.

All characters in this book have no existence outside the imagination of the author and have no relation whatsoever to anyone bearing the same name or names. They are not even distantly inspired by any individual known or unknown to the author, and all incidents are pure invention.

MIRA and the Star Colophon are trademarks used under license and registered in Australia, New Zealand, Philippines, United States Patent and Trademark Office and in other countries.

Look us up on-line at: http://www.mirabooks.com

Printed in U.S.A.

For my children...
Kevin, Katherine, Amy, Greg, Robin

And for my grandmother Ethel Corson Fisher,
and my newfound niece, an unexpected gift...
Peggi Fisher Gosha

As a book is being born, nothing is more important to an author than having a good editor. I would like to thank my editors, Amy Moore-Benson and Dianne Moggy, for their faith in this book and in me.

I would also like to thank my son, Greg, for his excellent editorial skills, and for being with me every step of the way.

"Through the long night watches
May thine angels spread
Their white wings above me
Watching round my bed."
— "Now the Day is Over"

Words by Sabine Baring-Gould (1834-1924)
Music by Merrial, Joseph Banby (1838-1896)
Public Domain

Author Note

The most frequent question an author hears is: Where do you get your ideas? Generally, we haven't a clear answer. Ideas are gifts; they seem to float in on the wings of the dawn, and I for one have always felt richly blessed to have an idea at all.

Most of the events in *Crashing Down,* however, took place in my own childhood. Though current-day characters are fictional, nearly every word, feeling and incident of abuse experienced by Carrie in childhood was experienced by me. Carrie's grandmother—as to character, if not each fictional incident—was mine, and her father and mother were mine. Each of these people, indeed my entire birth family, has long since passed on, and though I began this story fifteen years ago, it is only now that I feel it can be told.

Crashing Down takes place in a semi-fictional town called Holly Beach, New Jersey. Semi-fictional because, though the town has grown and changed, I write from memory of the way it seemed when I was a child. It was then, and is now, the city of Wildwood, at the southernmost tip of New Jersey.

My grandfather was a Baptist minister who literally built, with his own hands and the help of his parishioners, the First Baptist Church of Wildwood. I spent many childhood hours in this church, playing in the pews and the Sunday school rooms, and behind the huge pipes of the organ. At about age six, on my grandfather's anniversary, I was persuaded to sing on stage for him. In a nervous, whispery voice I managed to squeak out, "Blest be the tie that binds..." I was very shy, and held a little basket in my trembling hands filled with cash gifts for my grandfather, from parishioners. When I finished singing I was so relieved, I walked off the stage with the basket instead of presenting it to my grandfather. Everyone laughed; a natural enough reaction. It is, perhaps, the sign of an abused child that for many years I remembered only the laughter, not the fact that I was hugged afterward by those same people and told I'd done quite well.

Though I have moved on both in faith and life, the First Baptist Church of Wildwood will always be an integral part of who I am today. It is of this church I write, from memory, in *Crashing Down*. A certain amount of poetic license has been taken in relocating my grandfather's church to Anglesea, at the northern end of the island. And, of course, names have been changed to protect the innocent.

I began to write *Crashing Down* many years ago, and throughout its labor and birth, much healing as well as much pain has taken place. Early readers have told me that while *Crashing Down* is a true suspense novel, complete with twists, turns and plenty of intrigue, it also helped them heal. If I have been able to do that by reliving the difficulty of those long years, then I am gratified. This is all an author can hope for when sitting before a computer in a rumpled robe, sipping at a cold cup of coffee as she waits for that one true story, the one that must be told.

Grateful acknowledgment is made to George F. Boyer for his book, Wildwood: Middle of the Island, which helped me to refresh old memories. I would also like to acknowledge a few old childhood friends, lost over the years through my many Gypsy-like moves and the fact that sadly, women lose their friends through marriage and last-name changes. My best to Janet Boyer, Barbara Blake, Eleanor Hess, Mary White, Georgie Moore, Howard "Putt" Palmer, Billy Deaver, Harold "Howdy" Hamilton and Jerry Ludlum, with whom I spent my early years at school. They were years spent in silence, as I was afraid to speak the truth. What more can one ask, in times like that, than a kind word, a friendly face, a "How's it goin', kid?"

It's goin' pretty well, thank you—now. And what about you?

Finally, I would like to thank Oprah Winfrey for giving those of us whose voices were muffled far too long the courage to speak out.

Meg O'Brien can be reached by mail through MIRA Books at 225 Duncan Mill Road, Don Mills, Ontario M3B 3K9, Canada. She would love to hear from all readers, and especially old friends. Along with your return address, please include an e-mail address if you have one.

Part 1

From *Webster's Dictionary:*

To crash: to break or go to pieces.

1

Holly Beach, New Jersey, 1971

The man was coming at her. Carrie knew what would happen next. It had happened once before, and she had tried to stay away from him since then, had tried to squeeze herself into a tiny, invisible ball every Sunday since then.

Outside in the church courtyard there were voices, other children laughing as they arrived. Here in the dim cold basement of the church everything was silent except for the steady drip of a rusted pipe and the slow, deliberate breathing of the man who was moving toward her, blocking her path to the door.

"You came back," he said, and he smiled.

But she hadn't come back. Not on purpose. It was a mistake. Carrie began to cry quietly, the tears still way in the back, making her throat feel like there was something stuck there, something huge and hard.

"I left my doll," she said, swallowing.

"You mean this?" He held Christy, her doll, beyond her reach...her beloved Christy, her best friend, the only one she could talk to about the things he had done to her. He said, "I found her for you, Carrie."

"Thank you," she whispered.

He held the doll farther away. Laughing, he pulled Carrie toward him, a hand that smelled of shaving lo-

tion tugging at her head. Carrie's whole body was stiff with fright, her neck a hard, unbending column. But he was stronger, and he pulled her closer and closer. "You give me a little kiss," he said, his voice sounding funny and thick, "right here...and I'll let you have your doll."

She heard Christy drop to the floor as both of his hands held her head, and he moved it back and forth so her cheeks were forced to rub against the stiff, dark material of his trousers. Carrie tried again to pull away, but he held her fast. "Oh, yes," he moaned.

Carrie cried harder, not making any sound, the tears flowing fast and wet down her cheeks. She couldn't breathe. She was shaking so much she lost her balance, and without thinking she reached out to steady herself with both hands around the man's thighs.

His breath quickened; his hold tightened. "That's right, Carrie, that's right."

Carrie stood like a statue, a tiny, six-year-old statue with dark blond hair and bangs, in her best Sunday dress—the only evidence of her pain the tears that streamed down her face. She heard the sound of his zipper, and then, "Good girl, Carrie, that's a good girl." He said it the way her daddy did when her piano lesson went well.

After he had finished with her he warned her not to tell her daddy, because Daddy would be mad and he wouldn't believe her. He made her rinse off her face at the drinking fountain, the one for little kids like her, the one she could reach, and then he wiped her face with a paper towel from the janitor's bathroom across the hall.

"You'd better get upstairs now," he said, smoothing his hair and blotting spots on his suit that her tears had made. He was like another person suddenly, his

face a little red, but more as if nothing had happened, like Mommy after she had spanked Carrie for being bad. She would say, "For God's sake, Carrie, there's nothing to cry about now," as if once the spanking was over, there wasn't any reason it should hurt anymore.

Carrie grabbed Christy from the floor and backed away, then turned and stumbled up the stairs to the Sunday school rooms. They were empty, and the bells were ringing in the steeple. She ran down the hall toward the big church, forgetting that she wasn't supposed to run, wasn't supposed to make noise when she came in late. She looked through the door from the hallway and saw her Sunday school class, everyone standing with hymnals in their hands. She saw her daddy sitting at the organ, and heard him start to play the song about daring to be a Daniel, and she didn't know who Daniel was but she wished she were like him, wished she were brave.

Instead, she felt dirty and sick as she looked at her friends. She didn't belong with any of them. Turning, she ran outside and down Atlantic Avenue, passing old Mrs. Baker along the way, seeing her outraged face as Carrie almost knocked her down, running as if the devil were at her heels. That's what Mrs. Baker would say to Carrie's mother, Alice, after church. She'd say it on the phone, because Carrie's mother didn't go to church, and her tone would imply that everything bad that happened to the Holder family happened for that very reason. She'd say, "You'd better do something about that child, Mrs. Holder. Six years old, and out on the streets when she should be in Sunday school! And Mr. Holder giving all his time to the church the way he does, you'd think there would be more discipline in the home. Almost knocked me down and didn't even stop to apologize...like the devil was at her heels, don't you know.''

Carrie would get spanked for that when she got home. For upsetting Mrs. Baker and embarrassing her mother, mostly, and for not being in Sunday school. ''It's the second time you've pulled that, young lady, and it had better be the last.''

But she didn't know that now. Now she was running, running toward home, running to where she thought her mommy would hold her, where she thought she'd be safe, stopping only once at the big old house on the corner of Nineteenth Street to use the hose under their high front porch to wash her mouth out, over and over and over, even though it didn't do any good, didn't wash any of it away. She wished the water were a wave, that a wave would come up from the beach and wash right over her, wipe her out, drown her, so this would never happen again.

But the wave never came and Carrie didn't drown, and it did happen again. And again. And again. So that by the time she was ten and he would find her, no matter how hard she tried to hide, when he would come up behind her and press himself against her, a hand slipping into her summer halter to squeeze her tiny beginning breast, she felt nothing so much as numb.

She thought that this was simply the way life was. And it never occurred to her to wonder, until much, much later, why that should be so.

2

This is crazy, the grown-up, thirty-four-year-old Carrie thought. *I'm* crazy.

She was sitting in a makeup chair at WPPH-TV, in Philadelphia, allowing herself to be pouffed and powdered, sprayed and arrayed. She felt bogus, an illusion. No sooner had the makeup artist hidden the fine lines around her eyes than he'd added more, circling the upper and lower lids with thick, black, greasy strokes. "You have absolutely gorgeous green eyes," Randy, the hairstylist, argued. "You don't want them disappearing on camera, dear. And that blond hair? My goodness, what I wouldn't give for that."

Carrie smiled. She had written a book titled *Winter's End,* and when it miraculously hit the bestseller list the third week out, her publisher had sent her on tour. Starting in her hometown of San Francisco, Carrie flew east from city to city, sometimes signing books in two and three cities in one day. This was the last stop, an in-depth interview, twenty minutes, all hers.

Which was great. The more exposure for the book, the better. And if she sometimes felt weary and longed to be at home in her familiar robe and slippers, in front of the old computer, there was also an almost overwhelming excitement to all this at times. She had worked hard to get to this point, and the success of *Winter's End* was a personal win, as well as a professional one. In truth, she was flying high.

Sharon Smith, the bright, perky assistant to Teddi Marx, the host of *Today in Philadelphia,* had stuck her head in the door a few minutes ago. "Everything going all right? Good. By the way, I've read your book. It's wonderful."

Another miracle, Carrie thought. They almost never read your book. I am blessed.

Sharon had handled the preinterview with her when she first arrived. Then she'd brought her here to makeup.

"You're not nervous, are you?" she had asked. When Carrie confessed she could hardly think straight at the moment, swinging between weariness and pumped-up exhilaration, Sharon had patted her shoulder. "You'll do fine. Teddi loves you. I swear, she's read every article you've written since 1988. She particularly loved that humor piece you did on dating a few years ago."

Carrie remembered the article. By the time she was twenty-six, she had stumbled through several uneasy relationships. Finally she chained herself to her Royal portable and swore off men, swore to stick to something she knew. Which, in an age of failed relationships, with eighty percent of the male population married and the rest seemingly gay, was to tell women how best to live without a man. The article Sharon most likely had referred to was *Someday My Prince Will Come...And With My Luck He'll Be A Queen.* It was published in *Ms.* magazine and led to Carrie being dubbed the "new Fran Lebowitz." The piece was cutting and witty and fun to do, but Carrie didn't want to be a new anyone. She'd moved on to more serious works, writing about almost every women's issue: welfare, day care, AIDS, the utter futility of one-night stands.

The only indication that her past hadn't entirely healed was that she had changed her last name from Holder to Holt, in an attempt to distance herself from her childhood, and she had carefully skirted the issue of child abuse in her writing. If she thought about what had happened to her at all, she thought, *Well, it wasn't all that bad. Not like what happens to some kids.* There had been terrible stories in the papers lately, stories of babies being raped, left in Dumpsters and worse. Carrie thought about them, agonized for them. She had just never felt, until recently, that she could write about them.

All that had happened to her long ago, however. And in four days she would be back in her hometown, Holly Beach, to speak at the Children's Festival of the Arts there. The invitation had come six months ago, and Carrie had hesitated at first. Last year she had begun making frequent trips to the Pines Convalescent Home in Holly Beach to visit her grandmother. The Pines was at the far tip of the seven-mile-long island, and Carrie had traveled quickly from airport to cab to the Pines, never connecting in any way with the town itself. Holly Beach was a place with too many bad memories, and becoming familiar with either its past or current inhabitants was the last thing she needed or wanted.

Therefore, when the invitation came to speak at the festival, she didn't know what to say. The Children's Festival of the Arts was being held at Anglesea, the old church where so many painful things had happened. Could she do that?

She wasn't sure. But she would give it her best shot. It helped that the church was a conference center now. It also helped that it had been twenty-two years since she'd even been near it. It was unlikely old ghosts would still inhabit its walls.

Besides, as her agent, Molly Blair, had pointed out, it would be great PR for the book. "This is a big deal, Carrie. The festival was put together at the request of the President, as a positive step toward building children's self-esteem. There will be major stars there, CEOs, politicians. The media will single you out for interviews because it's a small town, and you're a local-girl-makes-good. You've got to do this, Carrie."

It hadn't taken much to talk her into it. She rather liked the idea of returning to her old hometown a success for a change, someone who had risen above a difficult childhood to not only make it good, but very good.

If only my mother were alive to see how things have turned out, she thought now, shifting in the makeup chair and smoothing the silky green skirt of her suit. *Alice would have been proud.* As it was, only her grandmother was left. And Elizabeth would not be well enough to attend.

An AD poked her head into the room, holding up both hands, fingers splayed. "Ten minutes! She should be in the green room by now."

Carrie's stomach twisted. The first moments before a camera were always hard. But if there was one thing she'd learned over the years, it was to "act as if." Whistle in the dark. Though she'd started out being terrified to speak in public, she could now hold her own at a podium and shake hands afterward as well as any Amway salesman.

She smiled into the makeup mirror at sea green eyes and even white teeth. Her hair fell in sun-streaked waves to her shoulders, not a frizz or strand out of place. *Hey, I'm good,* she told herself, sticking out her chin.

No—I'm great!

"Five minutes," Randy called out to the AD, gesturing widely with a spray bottle that gave Carrie's hair, the mirror and everything else within a three-foot area a final silica sheen. "I need five more minutes!"

Carrie grinned. *It's tougher than I thought making me look good.*

"Your book, *Winter's End,* has been receiving excellent early reviews," Teddi Marx said, referring to her notes. "I hear it hit the bestseller list this week—number five and climbing."

"That's right," Carrie answered, leaning forward in the chair, in a manner she had been told would make her seem more engaged. The image consultant in San Francisco, who gave lessons to authors and others appearing in public, had also told her to keep her face mobile. Smile, laugh, raise eyebrows, grin. She hoped she didn't look like Carol Channing.

"You must be thrilled." Teddi Marx's smile was tremulous. She was young, new to being host of a morning show, Molly had told Carrie in advance. Nervous about meeting her first "real live author." The crew was nervous, too. Worried about whether Teddi might screw up, no doubt, making their own jobs more difficult. The entire studio felt tight, as if filled with so many tensions there was no empty corner, no room left to move or breathe.

"I'm just happy that *Winter's End* is reaching people," Carrie said. "It's a book that's meant a lot to me."

She went on to tell that *Winter's End* was the true account of a woman who had escaped slavery in Virginia via the Underground Railroad, to become one of the most powerful and wealthy landowners in Pennsylvania. Carrie had worked furiously on the book, nearly every night for five years, while supporting herself with magazine articles written days. She had been driven, living in the emotions and on the strength of Hannah, her protagonist, rather than her own. Hannah, abused by her owner as a child and then by several men as a young woman, had fought her way free.

"That was the important thing about her story, as I saw it," Carrie said, "not her eventual fame or wealth."

The host of *Today In Philadelphia* nodded, smiled, said, "That's wonderful," and wet her lips again. With a hand that visibly shook, she glanced down at her list of prepared questions. Valiantly, she continued, asking the same questions that were asked on nearly every interview show. *When did you start writing, how did you know you wanted to write, how long did it take to get published....*

Carrie answered each query brightly, doing her best to soothe the woman's nerves. But she could see that wasn't helping. Well, she hadn't expected it would. That's why she'd come prepared. There would be one question—one that was always asked; it never failed.

In the next moment, it came. "Writing, I hear, is

lonely work," Teddi Marx said. "What do you do to relieve stress?"

Carrie smiled. Reaching down beside and a little behind her chair, she brought forth a Bloomie's shopping bag she had asked an assistant to put there. As Teddi Marx watched, curious, she pulled out a large, red plastic bat, the kind for kids one finds in drugstores. Then she pulled out a large, white plastic softball.

"I do this," Carrie said, standing. She held out the hollow ball and whacked it hard with the bat.

The bat made a loud cracking sound. The ball sailed well over the heads of the shocked crew and bystanders, who nevertheless ducked as one, eyes widening and mouths falling open. The white plastic missile smacked against a wall at the far end of the studio, where it fell with a soft thud to the carpeted floor.

Carrie turned to Teddi Marx, whose jaw had dropped along with everyone else's. "Try it," she said, handing her the bat. "Can somebody get that ball?" she yelled, cupping her hands around her mouth.

The astonishment of both host and crew lasted a long moment before anyone moved at all. When they did, it was as if every tension in the studio disappeared in one fell swoop. Teddi broke up, her laughter loud and relieved. Everyone else in the studio followed suit.

"I've never had a guest like you," Teddi said, wiping tears of laughter from her eyes with the tips of her pearl pink fingernails. She held up a hand that no longer shook. "Look at me. I'm not even nervous anymore."

Carrie grinned. She had used this same icebreaker on a cable interview show in California, and that show had won an award as the best of the year. It was the only one where people were laughing and having a good time, instead of simply sitting around like talking heads, pondering impossible-to-answer questions like *Where do you get your ideas?*

"When I was in high school here in Philly," Carrie explained, "we played a lot of softball."

Teddi passed on batting practice, but the surprise interlude had worked its charm. It took only a few moments to get back to the interview, and by then, both Carrie and the host were relaxed and enjoying themselves.

"I did see from your bio," Marx said, "that you once lived in Philadelphia. Was that right here in the city?"

Carrie nodded. "Just a few blocks from here."

She began to tell about moving up here from the Jersey shore when she was twelve, about loving the docks where the ships came in, and the first thrill at seeing the Liberty Bell. But then Teddi asked, "You lived here with your mother and father?" and Carrie answered, "No, just my mother..."

As she continued to talk, she could feel her mind running in two directions—part of it remaining in the present, the other part lost in the past.

"The apartment in Philly doesn't have any frills," her mother had warned as they packed hurriedly for the move. They had to be gone, Alice said, before Carrie's father got home.

Forget frills! Carrie had thought with her first stab at the humor that would sustain her over the next difficult years. The first summer was a monumental blister. There was no air-conditioning, and the temperatures often ran into the hundreds, with the humidity nearly as high. There were no more cool ocean breezes as in Holly Beach, no swimming in the ocean or long, lazy days on the sand. Alice Holder was working now, and there were chores to do. Carrie would stand in the kitchen feeding clothes through the old wringer washer with one hand, a book in the other, her hair rolled up in orange juice cans for a bouffant look—sweat streaming down her face.

"For God's sake, Carrie, don't catch your fingers in that wringer!" The panicky words would tumble out, her mother standing with both hands against her cheeks, her mouth a horrified O as Carrie forgot for a moment what she was doing, lost in a world of words. Mistress of Malloby, The Darkening Moors—mostly gothic romances, they were all the rage, but she liked the old detective pulps her mother read, too. Blondes Don't Cry ran a close second to No Bed of Her Own as favorites.

Reading was a whole new plane without pain.

"Life isn't like those books, and it's time you found that out, missy," her mother would say time and time again.

And indeed, Carrie never could seem to get a handle on the chores. Often, she would scorch the clothes, and once she plugged the frayed cord of the iron in and fire shot from it in a stream, scaring her half to death. There were outlets screwed into the ceiling lights that occasionally did the same, and a water heater that you lit with a match, then had to be sure and turn off before it got too hot and exploded.

It seemed that life in Philadelphia was fraught with a whole new set of fears. Don't go out at night alone. Don't hang out on the corner. Don't swim in the public pool, you'll get germs. And for God's sake, don't talk to strange men.

A bit late in the day for that one, Carrie thought.

Still, there was no longer a man in the house to worry about. None who stayed around, at least.

Now and then her mother would come home from Tony's Bar and Grill on the corner a little tipsy, with a man. Carrie would hear Alice giggling as they came up the wooden apartment-house stairs, and moments later Carrie's bedroom door would open and the ceiling light flick on. Hot with embarrassment, she would quickly pull her worn army surplus blanket up to her chin, while her mother said, "This is my little girl, Carrie. Carrie, say hello to Tom." (Bob...Charlie... whoever.)

If Carrie complained about these nocturnal introductions, her mother would say, "It's the only way I can get rid of them, honey. You know, they buy you a drink and then they want you to pay up. Once they find I've got a kid to support, they lose interest, but you gotta show them—you know?"

Carrie was thirteen at the time this began. Old enough to understand that, although her mother didn't want men staying overnight, there was something wrong with saying "no." It confirmed everything she had learned up to that time.

This was the same year her mother started making Carrie use a tint from a capsule to lighten her darkening hair. "It's an Italian neighborhood, honey, and Italian boys love blondes."

It was a mixed message she constantly received. On the one hand, make yourself as attractive to men as possible. Be all the things men admire in a woman. Make them like you and want you. But don't, for God's sake, let them touch you.

At times it would seem her mother was playing the part of Victorian pimp to Carrie's virgin prostitute.

Still, every now and then her mother would be the other person—the one who laughed and sang old songs around the house, who told Carrie stories about the past and her dreams for the future. "We'll have a big white house with blue shutters and an English rose garden. A pool. A horse."

As a child, and even a teenager, Carrie had few dreams of her own. She never saw herself as growing into the kind of woman who had a fascinating career, or even having the kind of intelligence it took to become a professional. Other people did those things; they were way beyond her reach. It wasn't till Berkeley and her stint on the college paper...

Carrie came back just as Teddi Marx was thanking her. She had a smile on her face and looked pleased as she shook Carrie's hand warmly.

"Thanks so much," Teddi said. "You were great."

I've done all right, then. Whew. It's over.

Randy stood beside her in the makeup room, his mouth a disappointed thin line. "I simply don't understand why you want to ruin all my hard work."

"It's not that I don't like what you did," Carrie soothed as she brushed the spray from her hair. "I just like it a bit looser for everyday."

He clucked with his tongue and turned away, flipping the channels on a small TV on the corner of the dressing table. Carrie finished with her hair and took a bite of the turkey sandwich Sharon, the assistant, had brought her. "Early lunch," she had said, smiling. "I, uh...your story touched me. And it was great, what you did for Teddi. I just wanted to do something for you."

Carrie wondered what in the world she had said to touch this woman so. She could barely remember.

"Thank you," she said, grateful for the woman's kindness.

The sandwich had come with a pot of tea. Carrie poured a small amount of the fragrant Earl Grey into a cup and asked Randy if he had something she could remove the heavy makeup with.

He rolled his eyes and pointed to a large jar of cream. "Help yourself."

"Thanks." She tried not to smile. If she hadn't done all right with the interview, she might have been slinking away, afraid to make waves. As it was, she felt wired and high, the way she usually did after a good appearance. She took a bite of the sandwich. The food, she knew, would have a sedative effect. It would help to bring her down to where she felt more like a writer than a fighter pilot.

Wiping the almond-scented lotion onto her face, she watched the television screen idly. A public service commercial was running, something with two little girls talking about being kind to each other and all living things. Carrie, who seldom had time to watch TV, sipped at her tea and took another bite of sandwich as the words *The Christopher Show,* came onto the screen.

Randy made a sound like a snort. "Not that guy again." He clicked the remote, changing the channel.

"No, wait," Carrie said.

He paused, then went back.

There was a song playing over the opening credits, one Carrie remembered vaguely from childhood. The song wasn't why she watched, however. She watched because there was something oddly familiar about the man who stood at the center of the stage, a man surrounded by children who looked up at him with glowing faces. The man seemed perhaps thirty-five. His blond hair was casual and ruffled, his face boyishly handsome. Clever lighting created a halo, giving him the look of an angelic Peter Pan.

Then the music began a crescendo and the camera zoomed in for a close-up. Carrie saw that the man was older than she'd thought. There were deep grooves around the eyes, and the blond hair, graying at the temples, had been styled to make it seem to recede less than it actually did. The man whispered to a little girl who knelt leaning against his knee. Carrie saw the child—about seven, with golden curls—respond with a look of adoration as the man reached behind her head with one hand, smiling affectionately and tugging the child's head closer. A voice-over announced, "And now *The Christopher Show,* with Christopher Jamison Breen."

Carrie paled. Bits of turkey sandwich stuck in her throat. She choked and forced herself to swallow hard, grabbing for the tea. Her hands shook as she washed the sandwich down. Her cup rattled back to its saucer as she stared at the screen.

Randy was saying sarcastically, "He's got the fastest-growing show on the East Coast, bigger than *Sesame Street* when that began. What a joke."

Carrie looked at him blankly.

"He'll be at that festival in Holly Beach this weekend, that one you're going to? Their keynote speaker. Like I said, the man's a joke. He's got 'em all bamboozled."

Then the music was down and the man named Christopher Breen was speaking in a soft, melodic voice that could, Carrie recalled all too well, charm birds off trees. "Remember, my friends, a little child shall lead them...." He gathered the children closer, lightly touching each one fondly on the head, a shoulder, a cheek. "In an age when adult greed for power and material wealth has led us to war and confusion, it is the children who offer hope. Join with me...."

Carrie heard no more. There was a roaring in her ears, and though he was older now, yes, and without the steel-rimmed glasses, yes, she was seeing him as he had been twenty-odd years before, and hearing, "Oh, yes, Carrie, yes, good girl, Carrie, good girl," and, "You'd best go upstairs now," straightening his clothes before he himself, a teaching assistant in her father's church, went up to join the others at the early service, smiling as if nothing had happened. And the hand behind the little girl's head now had been on her own head then, affectionately at first, just in Sunday school, all-innocence in front of her teacher, who was beaming at her assistant's "wonderful way with children," the adult validation making Carrie trust him, making her feel that whatever he told her to do was right, even when something inside her tummy kept screaming it was wrong...it was wrong.

And all the anger and pain she had been wrestling with her entire life became fresh new horror now, all happening again, over and over as she stared at the screen—all the indignities, the humiliations, the sick, sad feelings wrenching her apart, doubling her over with unbearable pain.

And she wanted to SMASH HIM
and SMASH HIM
and SMASH

Part 2

From the *Random House Dictionary:*

To smash:

1. to break violently into pieces.
2. to hit or strike with a shattering force.
3. to destroy...or be destroyed completely.

3

Holly Beach, New Jersey, 1999

Nicky D'Amico dragged his gaze away from the slender blond woman, the one who looked like she'd been chased in here to hide by a pack of mad dogs. This was his off-time, after all, and Neal's Holly Beach Tavern was the one place he could escape the demands of work.

Neal's was strictly a local joint, and a well-kept secret. Its simple fare and dark, quiet atmosphere hid behind plate glass windows that were tinted a cool dark blue. There was a TV, its volume low, above the bar. The set went off after four every day, and piped-in music came through, cool, quiet jazz from Atlantic City, easing the worries—and, for Nicky D'Amico, the bad thoughts—away.

Nicky liked having time alone here after work, using this hour to sort things out and get himself into a better mood before he hit home.

Taking a sip of ice-cold beer, he turned from the bar and leaned his tall frame against the rail, wincing as a small pain shot from a bruise on his arm. He had gotten the bruise that afternoon from a drunk under the boardwalk when he'd approached to help the beat cop take him in. The man wasn't violent, he just didn't know what the hell was going on. Nicky figured he needed a good night's sleep and a meal.

Nicky had changed out of his usual plainclothes attire, a neat pair of jeans, white tee and summer jacket, into worn jeans and a faded black tee—the closest he ever came to looking like a TV cop. Nicky had worked hard, in fact, to develop a reputation these ten years on the Holly Beach PD, as the antithesis of a TV or big-city cop. He hardly ever used force or drew his gun, depending on an air of steadiness and calm to hold people in line. Cops, after all, were originally called peace officers—"peace" meaning a state of harmony, a freedom of mind from fear, and "officer," one who dispenses same. It was what he tried, without making a big thing of it, to be.

There had been an interview in the local weekly about him a few years back when he'd broken up the drug ring that was trying to set up in Holly Beach at the time. The reporter had described Nicky, to his embarrassment, as "someone who looks beyond to where others can't see—to his own vision of how things should be."

"Nicky D'Amico," the article went on to say, "is just over six feet tall, with a solid build and clear gray eyes from his northern Italian grandmother's side. He seems guided not by a concept of right and wrong, but by a personal need for order—whatever, to him, that might be. D'Amico hardly ever follows standard cop procedure, but ambles through a crisis, and somehow things seem to turn out okay."

Good thing, Nicky thought now, that J. J. Perrione, that poet of the papers, hadn't been around on a certain June night last year. Nicky had broken a few things before that night was over. It had taken all of them— his mom, dad and even Uncle Mike—to hold him back.

His rage had turned him into 190 pounds of monster, something without thought that wanted only to kill.

He'd broken a few things since that night, too, when he was alone and the anger came tearing through his gut. But anger was normal, he'd been told. What hurt people and made them do self-destructive things was holding the anger in.

Nicky believed that. He'd learned it firsthand. And he'd begun, now, to watch for those people when he was out and about—the ones who were holding the anger in. If you ignored them, he'd found, they almost always gave you trouble down the line.

Which was why, he told himself, he could barely take his eyes off the agitated woman who'd walked through Neal's front door some time ago.

Attractive, Nicky thought, with an automatic tug at his loins. But her features were pulled tight, like she was under some intense strain. She had medium-length blond hair brushed back in a kind of soft, feathery look, and an intelligent face. From this distance it seemed that the eyes were green. She looked familiar, though he'd swear she had just hit town. One clue was the kind of clothes she wore: a green suit and silky-looking blouse, stockings and heels. A lot of people came down from the city dressed that way. Didn't take them long to get into summer togs.

Nicky toyed with his beer and sighed. *She's not your business, D'Amico.* This woman was hardly a fired employee out to gun down an ex-boss, or a spurned lover looking to shoot up a burger stand.

He hunched his long frame onto a stool, angling it so he could watch the tourists pass by. It seemed there were more tourists than ever in Holly Beach this year. Nicky didn't mind; he had been a summer visitor himself as a kid. His parents had moved the family down from Philly permanently in '66, when he was around five.

There was a lot of prejudice at first against the new entrepreneurs, the "Eyetalians," as they were called by some. But once begun there was no stopping the growth of motels and fast-food places. Pretty soon the Irish owned them as well, and the English, French, and God knows, maybe a reincarnated Huguenot or two—whoever could afford the skyrocketing prices of property in Holly Beach.

The town—so named for its exceptionally fine beaches lined with holly and pine—had been a family resort since the late 1800s, smaller and more conventional than Atlantic City. An island, technically, it was attached to the mainland of South Jersey by bridges at either end, and people drove here from New York and Pennsylvania, D.C. and Baltimore, all summer long. In the winter, icy waves crashed over the boardwalk, drenching abandoned concession stands. The town died.

In the old days the summer visitors had stayed in cottages and cabins or rooms in private homes. Now there were motels all over the place, some top-drawer like the glitzy Bahia, on oceanfront property at the southernmost tip of the island. At the other end of the scale were rooms that were not much more than a closet to wash off the sand between trips to the beach.

In the middle were the kind Nicky's family owned. The Crest Inn went back to the 1930s, a compound of neat white cottages with green shutters, surrounded by smooth green lawn. It was a few blocks up from the beach, but most of the people who stayed there didn't come to play in the sand. Nicky's father and mother had cut a niche for their business early on by respecting and catering to older visitors, rather than new. Some had been coming to Holly Beach every year since the thirties and forties, women who wore floppy sunhats and printed rayon dresses, who came to walk on the boardwalk in the cool of the evening and maybe have a "nice ice cream," listen to concerts on a Sunday afternoon. Most were living on retirement incomes that had shrunk with inflation over the years, like poor Dottie Corson, the retired teacher who had just canceled this year's reservation, when her sister died.

Nicky's father and mother knew the financial sacrifices their tenants made to get to Holly Beach every year, and how much the old routine and memories meant. They kept their prices affordable by doing most of the work around the place themselves. There was always painting, for one thing, and mowing the lawn so the old folks could play croquet. Sometimes, over the years, Nicky had tired of the constant repairs. He'd even wondered what life might have been like if he'd had his own bachelor pad and gone home to a three-thousand-dollar stereo at night, and to an answering machine with six calls on it from beautiful women wanting dates.

Well, in a few months he'd find out. About the bachelor pad, anyway. He'd started building his own place, south of here on the beach. Shoot, he might even have that stereo, and a beautiful woman or two. Nicky grinned to himself. And *at* himself. Trouble was, he hadn't even moved out yet, and he'd already started missing the family he'd be leaving behind.

Especially his uncle Mike, who, at eighty-two, smelled up the place cooking liver and onions every other day for lunch, but redeemed himself by making a homemade red that no eastern vineyard had been able to match. Nicky genuinely got a kick out of sitting at the kitchen table on a Sunday night, dunking almond biscuits into a cup of that red and listening to his uncle talk about the lives of the saints.

Of course, there'd been that difficult period when pantsuits came into fashion and all Uncle Mike talked about was how women who wore pants were whores. No amount of argument would make him change his mind. The saints never wore pants and neither did the Virgin Mary, and that was that.

Later, when Nicky was in his teens, he came to secretly believe that his uncle complained only because he missed seeing women's legs. Nicky had tested out his theory by bringing home one girlfriend after another in pants, watching as Uncle Mike grudgingly gave his approval.

"A nice girl, Nicky," Mike would say. "You gonna marry this girl?"

"I don't know, Uncle. She wants to wear pants to the wedding."

"*Tshish.* You be good to her, Nicky, she'll come around."

But Nicky never seemed to get around to asking that all-important question. The truth was, he liked things pretty much the way they were. And even though he was building his own house now, he still liked being at home with his uncle's statues on the mantel and the waxy scent of vigil candles, the whole family getting together once a month to make homemade sauce, dumping in meatballs with raisins, pork chops and chicken, the pot bubbling on the stove all day. Most of all, he liked being around to help his dad, Mario, who wasn't as old-fashioned and religious as Uncle Mike but still thought women were to be protected. Who, when his wife was pregnant with Nicky, then Sally Anne, had mopped the floors in their big old house in

Philly, scrubbing in the corners so she wouldn't have to strain.

Nicky loved, too, having morning coffee and talks with his mom. Helen D'Amico was a small, vibrant woman, still young. Not the stereotypical Italian mama of times past, but an artist of repute who would rather sit at her easel in the evenings than put dough through a pasta press.

A good family. The best, Nicky thought. If anyone asked, he would tell them he'd been blessed. As indeed he had. But he'd almost blown it all to hell last year.

"A rough day, Nicky?" the bartender asked as he wiped down the bar.

"Not too bad, Lou," he answered, coming out of his reverie.

He drank the last of his beer and straightened to ease a sore muscle in his back, then gave another professional glance at the blond woman, in a booth now, over by the wall. She was rubbing her forehead.

Even as he'd been staring out the window at tourists, Nicky's coplike peripheral vision had noted that she'd been going back and forth from booth to telephone for the past ten minutes, and with each trip she seemed more defeated and worn.

As he watched, trying not to be obvious, but splitting his attention between the TV at the end of the bar and her, the pen she had been using rolled to the floor. She was unfolding a newspaper, turning the page, and from Nicky's vantage point it looked as if she'd had just about all she could handle for one day. She didn't notice the fallen pen.

Nicky would remember later that he could have just dropped a tip on the bar and walked away. Could have, should have...what the hell, who knew? You climb on your charger and off you go in defense of fair maid, and sometimes it's good, while sometimes...

Sliding his full six-feet-one of muscle off the stool, he crossed over to the woman's booth and picked up the pen. "I think you dropped this." He nodded at the paper and smiled. "Classifieds?"

She jumped. Her eyes in that first second of contact were clouded with fear. Her shoulders hunched forward as if to protect her body from a blow. Then, with an obvious effort, she drew them back and stretched out a hand.

"Thanks," she said as she took the pen, giving Nicky a look of dismissal.

Nicky hung in. All of a sudden he wasn't so sure that his first instinct about this woman hadn't been right. There was a chill along the back of his neck, something that only came on him when there was trouble about.

"Is there something you want?" the woman asked curtly.

He shook his head. His thumbs were in his belt, his legs wide, a stance he knew could seem aggressive. Still, she shouldn't look so frightened as, underneath that cool surface, she did. One hand clenched and unclenched, while with the other she held the pen tightly, clicking its button open and shut, open and shut.

Nicky smiled. "I thought maybe you might need some help. Mind if I sit down?"

"As a matter of fact, I do...." she began. He was already easing himself into the booth.

Nicky leaned back, hoping to put her at ease. Even so, his arms had automatically folded across his chest in an attitude of protection. Odd, he thought, how the body intuits things, sometimes, that the mind overlooks.

"I thought I might know you from somewhere," he said.

The woman folded her hands on the table and sat upright, in the manner of a schoolteacher, or possibly someone on a witness stand. Like someone determined to tell her story in a way it would be believed.

Then she slumped, and said only, "I don't think so." She was obviously tired, and maybe even on the verge of losing control. Nicky felt a pang and thought, *She's just going through a bad time. I should have left her alone.*

That was the thing about white chargers and fair maids. One never knew when one's services were called for. A long time ago, there was that fiasco on the school playground with Turkey Bowen and Babs Lake. Turkey had yanked Babs's new winter jacket away. Nicky—hell, Babs was the prettiest girl in class—went careening after, not realizing at the time that sweet little old Babs was loving the whole thing.

Nicky had Turkey down in the dirt, had him yelling "Uncle," when Babs had sucker punched him. He went flying four feet, landed against the monkey bars, split his face open and tore the sleeve right off Babs's new jacket all at the same time.

She'd been furious. She'd kicked Nicky in the right shin, and nine years later had landed the final blow by becoming Babs Lake-Bowen. The incident had taught him not to be too quick to rush to the rescue of beautiful women.

Still, old instincts lingered on. Nicky sat forward and toyed with a small cocktail napkin the woman hadn't used. "It's pretty hard to find anything during the season here." Motioning toward the newspaper, he added, "I see you've crossed out some ads under Rooms For Rent."

"I'll manage," she said coldly.

"You've probably checked the motels and they're all out of sight. Summer…it's a short season, and they get what they can."

She stared, volunteering nothing.

"I'm Nicky D'Amico." He held out his hand.

She ignored it, but then he figured she would. He felt like the worst sort of intruder, and no amount of coplike excuse—"I thought she looked troubled, and people like that sometimes bring trouble"—would do. The woman had a right to her privacy.

He moved to get up, but as he did the classified pages slipped sideways on the table, revealing the first section of that morning's paper. The woman's photograph was there, with several others. A caption began, "Speakers at the Children's Festival of the Arts include…"

"I remember now," he said, touching the paper. "I saw this earlier. Carrie Holt. You're speaking this weekend at the festival."

"That's right," she said, turning away.

But he couldn't give it up. "Looks like a big one this year. Christopher Breen's the keynote speaker. You know him?"

"No." But something flickered in her eyes.

"You're kidding. Never heard of the famous Christopher Breen?"

"Of course I've heard of him," she said, obviously annoyed. "I thought you meant do I know him personally."

"And you don't?"

"Of course not. Why would I?"

"I don't know, I just thought all you people who talked at these things knew each other."

"Well, we don't."

He nodded. "Yeah, I guess that makes sense, when you come to think of it. Anyway, this Breen, he seems to have shot up pretty fast."

She didn't respond, but Nicky could swear there was more interest in her eyes than she was letting on. "Started right here in Holly Beach, that's the funny thing. He was a youth leader at one of the local churches. Then he went away for a while…no one really knows where. Suddenly he appears back on the scene with this children's program. It was a lot smaller then, of course. Local only. Didn't take him long, though."

"Long?" The woman's eyes met his.

"To build up to being a star."

"Oh."

"You're sure you don't know him?"

She frowned. "I said I didn't. Look, what do you want?"

He shrugged. "Like I said, I thought I might help. But I guess you don't really need a room. You'll be staying at the Anglesea Conference Center, won't you? Most of the out-of-town speakers at the conferences stay there."

"Actually, there wasn't a room left at the center. I signed up late."

"And now you're finding all the hotels have filled up, right?"

"Something like that."

"Tell you what," he said. Drawing his wallet out of a back pocket, he took one of the Crest Inn business cards from it, handing it to her.

"My family runs the Crest, and I think we've got just about the only reasonably priced room left in town this weekend. One of our tenants, who usually stays a month, canceled out when her sister died."

The woman took the card and turned it over a couple of times. After a long moment she looked at him. "This is some coincidence. You with a room to rent...and me looking for one."

Nicky shrugged, and she stared at him some more.

"I'll leave you alone now," he said easily, standing. "If you want the room, call that number and ask for my mom. Helen D'Amico. Tell her I referred you."

"Your mom?"

"She sort of runs the place."

The woman smiled slightly, and you would think that might make a difference, Nicky thought. But the smile didn't make it to her eyes.

"I'm sorry if I seemed rude," she said tiredly. "I've been calling places for what seems like forever, and I came in here because I—" She broke off, and her eyes took on a haunted look. "It seemed dark and cool in here. And I wanted to sit alone and think for a while."

"I hear you," Nicky said. "I hate bars where everybody you know hangs out and all they do is talk. I get enough of that at work all day."

He held out his hand and she took it this time, though hesitantly. Hers was cold and clammy, trembling a bit.

"Thanks for the referral," she said. "I'll call right away."

"Just tell my mom I sent you. Nicky," he added, in case she hadn't heard it before.

"Right. Nicky. I will."

He left her then, placing a tip on the bar and heading for the front door. Along the way, as if it were an omen, the quarter-inch scar on his cheek began to itch—the one left by his scuffle in fifth grade with Turkey Bowen. Nicky lifted a finger and rubbed it. Uneasy, he turned and looked at Carrie Holt.

She was holding the first page of the morning paper and staring at it blankly, unmoving.

4

Carrie looked up from the newspaper and watched the man—Nicky—push open the door of the bar and leave. She was tired, all nerves, and he had startled her, coming out of the blue that way. Well, she supposed he was harmless enough. And she wouldn't be likely to see him again.

In and out. She would visit her grandmother at the convalescent home, as promised. Then she would call Molly and tell her she was canceling her appearance at the festival this weekend. Today was Monday. That gave them four days to find someone else. Not much notice, but it would have to do.

Glancing at the paper again, she studied Christopher Breen's photograph just above hers. His appearance as keynote speaker for the festival was apparently a last-minute change in the lineup. It hadn't been in the brochure she'd received in San Francisco; she clearly remembered her contact person telling her, in fact, that the keynote speech would be given by Senator Alan Weiss. Weiss was currently working at establishing children's art, writing and music programs in the inner cities. His platform, in fact, had been that he would work to replace programs the previous administration, through cutbacks, had slashed.

What had happened to Weiss? And how in the name of God had Breen ended up as keynote speaker instead?

Carrie rubbed her eyes, which by now were stinging from lack of sleep. The important thing at the moment was that, in all likelihood, Breen would be staying at the conference center—a place she could not, now, go within miles of. The outrage she had felt in Philadelphia, at seeing him with those children, had dissipated into depression on the long drive down. She no longer wanted to kill, so much as to run.

Still, she could not—would not—let Breen's presence here make her miss her visit with her grandmother. Since Elizabeth had broken her hip a year ago, Carrie had made a point of flying in to Holly Beach as often as possible. This particular visit had been carefully scheduled between the end of the tour, today, and the beginning of the festival on Friday.

Not that Elizabeth would be likely to know her granddaughter was here. Carrie's bright, relatively active grandmother had fallen into a depression and withdrawn completely months ago, when her hip had failed to mend. It was wrenching to see how quickly, at only seventy-six, Elizabeth had deteriorated.

Regardless, Nan Martin, the owner of the Pines Convalescent Home, continually stressed that Carrie's visits were important. "We can't know how much she hears or is aware of, but she always seems better when you've been here."

Carrie sighed and looked again at the Crest Inn business card. She had lied to Nicky D'Amico; they were holding a room for her at the conference center, of course. She'd made a reservation. But that Christopher Breen still lived in the area, much less had a television show here, was something she'd never expected, not in a million years. Now—to possibly come face-to-face with Breen? Unthinkable. How had he become this…

this celebrity? The man was a monster. What could people be thinking?

What she herself had thought, of course, and her parents, as well as all the other adults who had known him when he was young. That he was quiet. Well-mannered. Good with children.

Dear God.

She picked up the remaining coins on the table. As Nicky D'Amico had said, every vacancy advertised was already gone. After only a moment more of hesitation, she slid the coins into her purse, holding one quarter out. Slinging the light summer bag over her shoulder, she went to the phone.

"Mrs. D'Amico, please? Yes, hello. I, uh…your son gave me your card. Nicky? I understand you have a room to rent."

"As a matter of fact," the woman said warmly, "it just came free. One of our regular people had to cancel."

"That's what he said. May I take a look at it? I'm here in town."

"Yes, of course. You have the address?"

They talked a few moments about price, which was more than reasonable, and directions. Then Carrie paid the tab for her coffee and left. Her rental car was at the curb and she noticed there were no longer empty spaces along the street. It was late in the afternoon, and people would be up from the beach and ravenous. Restaurants would soon be packed.

The rental car was hot and the air-conditioning on the blink. Her clothes were sticky within moments, and she couldn't wait to get them off, to lie on a cool bed and stare into space. She'd slept hardly at all before her appearance on *Today In Philadelphia*. And with all the summer traffic it had been a long, wearying drive down from there.

The Crest Inn was just outside the center of town and to the south. Carrie parked in a small, tree-shaded lot. Following Mrs. D'Amico's instructions, she crossed a wide green lawn to the rear of a large, two-story white house with green shutters. There were wings on either side, but the house was not pretentious. Rather, it rambled, in the way of beach homes that were added on to over the years.

Mrs. D'Amico answered the kitchen door with a smile and apology, saying, "Sorry to make you come to the kitchen." She was a small woman, with short dark hair that framed her face in soft curls. She wiped her hands on a rag and rubbed a spot of fresh paint from spattered jeans. "I'm an artist in my spare time," she said, "and I was working in my studio when you called. I sometimes forget to listen for the bell up front."

Her tone was friendly, but she seemed poised to run back to whatever project she had left, anxious to get on with her work. Her cheeks were flushed, her eyes quickly assessing Carrie.

"Sorry for the intrusion," Carrie said. She smiled, taking Mrs. D'Amico's extended hand.

Nicky's mother's grip was firm, not unlike that of her son's. She smiled, too. "The room's upstairs." Taking a key from a pegboard beside the door, she led the way outside again, to white-painted wooden stairs alongside a sunroom. At the top was a set of French doors and a landing that stretched along this entire wing. A breeze blew off the ocean, flapping green awnings over several windows.

"I hope Nicky warned you this wasn't one of the

cottages. We have two rooms like this, one on either side of the main house. You've got a separate entrance and bath, but those other doors there—'' she nodded toward a similar set of French doors a few feet along the landing ''—lead to my daughter Sally's room. She's sixteen, and sometimes her music can get loud.'' Helen smiled. ''Feel free to knock on your wall if you want her to turn it down. Or let me know, and I'll speak to her right away.''

Carrie stepped into the room and looked around. There were windows on an opposite wall for cross-ventilation, and gauzy white curtains billowed from the salty ocean breeze.

''It's a lovely room,'' she said, ''and the price you quoted on the phone is more than fair. I'll take it.''

Mrs. D'Amico nodded. ''Good. We're right downstairs if you need anything, but no one will bother you here.''

Carrie brushed her hair back from her forehead with a weary hand. ''Thank you.'' She took the key that Helen D'Amico offered. ''Let me give you a check now…in case I decide to leave when you aren't available. Would four days in advance be all right? That would take me up to the weekend.''

''That's fine. Just let me know soon if you decide you'd like it longer.''

''I will.''

Carrie wrote the check sitting at a small antique desk, then watched as Mrs. D'Amico moved swiftly down the stairs.

A nice enough woman, she thought. And a lucky break to find this room. But God help me…I'd rather be safe at home.

The word *safe* had slipped out without conscious

thought. But briefly—just briefly—another thought came with it. It was a thought that had been twisting in her head like an army of snakes since the moment she'd seen Christopher Breen with his hand on that little girl's head, and her oh-so-trusting head on his knee.

Kill him. You always wanted to, you know. Kill him and have done with it. Now.

5

Before unpacking, Carrie called her agent in New York.

"Molly? It's Carrie. I'm in Holly Beach, and I need you to do something for me. I need you to get me out of the festival this weekend."

"Out of the *Anglesea* festival? Carrie, are you crazy? This isn't the time to back out of anything. Look, I'm glad you called. I just got off the phone with your publicist. They're setting up another tour for you now that *Winter's End* is moving up on the bestseller list. Did you see? But of course you did. It moved up to number two in yesterday's *New York Times!*"

Carrie hadn't seen. She had been on a plane from Chicago to Philly, and the whole day had been a blur. Now she wondered how, in just twenty-four hours, she had gotten so far from her usual life. Where was the thrill and excitement she would have felt if this news had come at any other time?

"The tour will hit a lot of new cities," Molly Blair continued, without pausing for breath, "Boston, Atlanta, New Orleans...."

Carrie's heart sank. She felt overwhelmed with weariness, too tired to cope.

"I don't think I can do that," she said, knowing what Molly's reaction would be.

"What are you talking about? Carrie, this is *it* for

you! It's what you've worked for, the past ten years, struggled through rejection slips for. This is the biggest high cycle of your career, kid, and you've got to go with it or it'll pass you by. Listen, I didn't want to tell you this until it was firm, but your publisher is talking a three-book contract, with multi, multi bucks. Carrie, you can't back out on your commitment to them now. You've got to do this PR.''

Carrie rubbed at her temple with her fingertips. She sat huddled over on the bed, her eyes closed.

It was as if she had been transported into another world suddenly, and everything Molly said was alien now. Things that would have been of prime importance only a day ago—book contracts, publicity tours—what importance did any of those things have in a world where children were robbed of their childhoods, made to feel dirty and ashamed?

And how would she ever go back to that other world, to the tinny glitter of photo sessions and green rooms, of talk show hosts and cocktail parties with, for God's sake, caviar and Indonesian hors d'oeuvres? If she had thought of the future at all these past few weeks, it was in terms of *Soon, soon now I'll be able to go home and hide behind my computer. Do nothing but write and be alone for the next six months.*

A world that was foreign under the best of circumstances had become impossibly distant with all the old memories flooding back.

She began to cry, silently, raw inside with the newly reopened wounds of the past. She wondered if she would ever heal.

She heard herself say, "Listen, Molly, let me call you back, okay? I'm at a phone booth, and somebody else wants to use the phone."

God, she was lying so easily now.

"Where can I reach you later on?" Molly asked quickly.

She gave her the Crest Inn number.

"You will think about the tour. You will do it, right?"

"Please, Molly. Not now."

"Promise, Carrie."

"I'll call you tomorrow."

There was a pause. "Hey, kid, you okay?"

Carrie laughed—a tight, false laugh that said her life was on the verge of disaster and she didn't know what to do. The sound of it chilled her. "I'm okay," she said. "Gotta go now. Tomorrow."

She hung up. Then she sat on the bed and rocked, letting grief overtake her. All the things she'd thought she'd scuttled under a rug, all these years...

But she hadn't. Not entirely.

She thought of Esther Gordon, a psychologist and neighbor in her apartment building in San Francisco. Carrie had dropped in on her occasionally last year. She'd told herself she was only being neighborly, that she enjoyed the comfort of the motherly therapist and her large, colorful apartment with splashes of sky blues and golds. She enjoyed Esther's view of the fog batting up against the Golden Gate Bridge, and the calming jasmine tea Esther would brew in the Chinese porcelain teapot. More than anything, in the early days, she had appreciated Esther's own calming effect on her.

Eventually, however, Esther had begun to ask questions—pointed questions that told Carrie she had either said or done something that had clued the therapist into her troubled past. Esther had pried things out of her that Carrie had deliberately tried to forget: her father's lifetime of drinking and eventual death from a liver ailment; Alice's death, recently, of cancer. And some of the things, not all, that had happened with Breen. Finally Carrie had begun to feel invaded, as she always did when people came too close.

So, while she was wise enough to admit to herself that she visited Esther largely because she *was* a therapist, and Carrie had been feeling a need, finally, to talk about these things, it wasn't long before she drifted away. *Sorry I haven't been around. I'm on a deadline. I've had the flu. Gearing up for a tour.* The pain of remembering had become too much.

With an effort, Carrie stood and looked at herself in the dresser mirror, hardly recognizing the woman there. Her hair, usually pale, smooth and shiny, was tangled from Randy's lingering spray and from not having been combed in hours. Her face was drawn, her eyes dull.

She would have to pull herself together before seeing her grandmother. Exhausted, she removed her sticky clothes and showered. The shower did not revive her, however; it left her feeling enervated. A minute, she thought, that's all I need. A minute or two of rest.

Pulling a terry cloth robe about her, she stretched out on the bed. An ocean breeze drifted through the windows, playing with a single pink rose on her nightstand. Its scent mingled with salt air and was scattered about the room. Carrie barely noticed. Though she had hoped to nap, anger consumed her. She imagined what she might do if Breen stood before her at this very moment. She could see her hands wrapping around his neck, see them squeezing, squeezing... But as she touched him, anger swung to fear. Carrie could see him laughing at her, see her entire body disappearing into the powerlessness he had always so easily inflicted upon her.

Dammit, I need to get the hell out of here and go home.

Then she thought of the little girl on television this morning with Breen, her head against his knee. Don't I have an obligation to stay here now? Carrie asked herself. Isn't it time to break that hideous code that was forced upon me as a child—time to come forward, finally, and tell? So he can't ever do those things to anyone again?

Or am I assuming too much? Surely he can't still be molesting children. Not after all these years. He'd have been caught. Wouldn't he?

She could hear Esther Gordon's voice answering that same question last year in San Francisco. *They can go on through generations without being caught, Carrie. And even if they are arrested and put away, sex offenders are the most difficult to rehabilitate. Most come back and start right in again.*

It was a frightening thought. Still, Carrie had been helpless against him back then. What made her think she could do anything to stop him now? Even if she went to the police, surely no one would believe her. While she had been living with the pain of the things he'd done, the man had built himself up into a saint.

At the bar earlier, she had read that article about him in the newspaper. Breen was, apparently, well loved by children and adults alike. He had the admiration of politicians and celebrities in every field. From the time he had returned to Holly Beach with his "little production," as he described it to the interviewer, he had been on the fast track, winning friends and fans everywhere. Before long, he was on television up and down the East

Coast, then as far west as Chicago and St. Louis. *The Christopher Show,* it was simply called. Which explained why Carrie—who never watched children's TV, and had never seen the show—had not once thought of putting it and Christopher Breen together.

Even when I did see him on TV this morning, she thought, I didn't recognize him right off. He's completely reinvented himself. The makeup, the hair, the way he holds himself...

Breen was, according to the article, just short of becoming a national idol. He taught children morals through puppetry and storytelling, through music and dance. Adults urged their children to watch him, and by inference, to trust him. He had their trust.

That was what kept fueling Carrie's anger. He had their trust.

Glancing at her watch, she saw that there were four hours left before dark. Voices of children could be heard passing by on the sidewalk a hundred feet away. Now and then there was the familiar rattle of a sand pail and shovel, and Carrie pictured them clasped in a tiny hand, short stubby legs beneath a striped or dotted swimsuit, the hot sidewalk burning the soles of the child's feet.

Holly Beach was full of children in the summer, she remembered. Happy children, laughing and jumping in the surf, running from the waves. Their sounds, though muted by several large maple trees between her room and the street, kept dragging her into the past.

Grandmother, she thought. If only Elizabeth were aware enough that Carrie could talk to her about Breen. She, and Carrie's grandfather, too, had known Christopher Breen. They had all gone to the same church, and everyone knew each other in those days.

No—they hadn't just known him. Like everyone else, they had trusted him. Would her grandmother even believe, now, what Carrie could never bring herself to tell her, all those years before?

Forcing herself to rise, she dressed in white cotton shorts and a navy tank top. It seemed as if she had been awake forever this day, but the clock on the night table told her it was barely 5:00 p.m. With her nerves raw, and the rage she had brought with her from Philadelphia fast sliding into depression once more, she headed out.

The Pines Convalescent Home was at the south end of the island, only three miles from the Crest Inn. Carrie walked along a sidewalk toward the beach, deciding to follow the shoreline all the way. Chances were the beach would not be crowded at this hour, she thought, and she knew from the past that the farther south she walked, away from the boardwalk and concessions, the more the crowds would thin.

The sidewalk took her two blocks through a semi-residential neighborhood, and Carrie was astonished at the things she recalled from her childhood, the most minute details. She remembered trudging the hot side-walks in summer, carrying brown bags of groceries from the store. Always looking down. Afraid of seeing someone she knew, afraid that her secret was emblazoned all over her, as if she carried a sandwich board that said I'm Being Abused.

Not that she would have expressed it that way then. At the time she was aware only of feeling ugly and ashamed.

And because she had always looked down rather than around, the grass and weeds that grew in the cracks of the sidewalks were imprinted forever in her mind, along with other oddities, like the bubbles of tar on Surf Avenue. You could step on the bubbles and they'd crack, and then you could stick your finger in the hole and touch the black ooze.

If you weren't careful, you could also muck up your brand-new tennis shoes, and then you wouldn't be allowed to go to the boardwalk and ride on the roller coaster that Friday night.

When she was a child there were dozens of vacant lots in Carrie's neighborhood. Along the sidewalks she remembered wild roses, stalk after stalk of Queen Anne's lace with velvety purple centers, milkweed, hoptoads. And praying mantises everywhere.

"Progress" had done away with most of that, she supposed. But there were still hydrangeas here and there, scent-heavy, with blue and pink blooms as large as beach balls. They grew in front of the older houses, hiding the high-water-level foundations. Some were over fifty years old. But the wild roses were gone. Traded, like so many bubble gum cards, for motels with swimming pools and parking lots.

Now and again she saw one of the homes that had captured her imagination as a child; the siding a mixture of stone and tiny bits of colored glass. Like something from a fairy tale, she had thought when she was five years old.

She reached the boardwalk and kicked off her sandals to walk in the cold wet sand beneath it, where she used to search for coins that had fallen through.

"Don't ever play under the boardwalk," her mother had warned, wagging a finger. "You never know what can happen under there."

But nobody ever said what could happen. So, of

course, Carrie had to find out, and, of course, she did, the day the strange man was there and pulled down his trousers, flashed her, then took off running.

Was that all? she couldn't help thinking. Pale stuff ii. comparison to what was going on with Breen. Carrie had grown inured to most things sexual by then.

She had lived, summers, on the beach. The back steps of their house opened onto the sand, and she would take a big jug of iced tea with lemon and a bunch of peanut butter sandwiches down there early in the morning. Even when she was seven and eight she was allowed to go alone.

"Always stay in sight of the lifeguards," her mother, Alice, cautioned. "And keep an eye on the window. If I think you're going out too far, I'll hang a pillowcase out. And don't tell me later you didn't see it, young lady! That doesn't work anymore."

But Carrie knew there was nothing to fear from the ocean and thought it silly to be afraid of "going out too far." That was for city people, not her.

She had always thrilled at the first cold shock of salt water, then the battering of waves. It was them against her, and Carrie always won. She won by going under them and around them, by timing the swells, as she did with life, knowing that once beyond the breakers she was safe. She could float for hours that way, up and down, up and down, checking only now and then to see how far she had drifted from her block. Sometimes a rip would take her all the way to Nineteenth Street, where the boardwalk began.

There was never much money for clothes, but Carrie's mother would make bathing suits each summer, three or four, so that Carrie could change to a dry one several times a day. One year she made a two-piece suit with a Hawaiian print from a Simplicity pattern Carrie would always remember the name of: Aloha Moons. Her mother gave the skirt too big a hem, which became weighted with sand, and as Carrie walked out of the water one day the skirt fell to her knees.

She had crouched in two feet of water, pulling Aloha Moons up with one hand and dumping sand from the hem with the other, to the mocking hoots of kids she hardly knew but went to school with. She'd nearly died of shame. She didn't go to the beach again for several days. And then only in the evenings, when everyone else had gone home.

Now, at thirty-four, Carrie felt a rush of anguish and love for the mother who had struggled late at night over a sewing machine, running up clothes so that her daughter might "look nice." It couldn't have been easy for Alice, living with an alcoholic husband and trying to be a good mother, too.

Carrie stepped up her pace, walking south along the damp sand at the edge of the water. The beach had been crowded when she started out, but now there were black storm clouds moving in across the Atlantic. The sea had turned to slate, and people were picking up their umbrellas, blankets, coolers; calling for the kids— "Rinse the sand off in the water first!"—and starting to head for home.

Carrie knew all about summer storms. The water always seemed warmer when it rained, and she loved swimming beneath thunder and lightning, loved the slightly sulfuric smell of the ocean in a storm. She loved knowing that what she did was forbidden by her parents, whom she hardly ever disobeyed. But her mother and father were often not at home and didn't know.

She was totally without fear of nature's fury. People were what frightened her. Men. Women. Teachers. Neighbors. Shopkeepers. And what she loved most about Holly Beach in the rain was that when it rained, most of the people went home.

6

Nearing the Pines, Carrie headed up from the shoreline to the softer sand, her gaze drawn to the large, graceful Victorian with its white wraparound veranda. Where the sand left off, a well-tended lawn began, and on the lawn were lounge chairs for the residents, facing out to sea. Pines and imported palm trees dotted the lush gardens surrounding the Victorian. Along the perimeter of the gardens were tall hedges that partially blocked the sea view, warding off winter winds.

The Pines Convalescent Home was the best on the island. It was also the most expensive. Carrie's grandfather had died five years ago, leaving only a small amount of savings. He and Elizabeth had always had a fair amount of income, but in retirement their resources dwindled steadily. A year ago, when Elizabeth broke her hip, there was a scurry by the county to make her sell her home to pay for care in a questionable facility of the county's choice, on the mainland.

Rather than see that happen, Carrie had offered to pay for her grandmother's nursing care at home. With everyone else in the family gone, she had seen it as her responsibility to look after her grandmother. Not that she ever regretted that responsibility. Elizabeth was the one person she remembered from childhood with total love, rather than mixed emotions.

Elizabeth, however, protested that she didn't mind

selling the home in town, and even the farm. "You can't hold on to material things when you're my age," she had told Carrie, smiling. "They get too heavy. It's bad for the health."

So Carrie had come up with an alternative. No matter what she had to do, she would cover at least part of the cost of her grandmother's care in a good nursing home. She had thoroughly looked into the Pines and then helped Elizabeth to move in here, assured that not only her physical but emotional needs would be taken care of.

In the end, like a gift from the gods, the financial burden had been lightened. Only a third of the monthly fee, she learned, would be taken from the sale of her grandmother's property, thus making her "nest egg" last longer. Another third would come from an anonymous benefactor who donated vast amounts to the Pines because his own mother had died in poverty and without proper care, when he was young.

The final third, Carrie herself would cover. To do that, she had taken in extra work at home over the past year: technical writing, editing, critiquing...whatever she could scare up, she fit into her regular schedule, working long nights and longer days. At times she consoled herself that in providing for Elizabeth this way, she was doing everything she could for her.

There were, however, moments when she wondered. Should she have moved back here and nursed her grandmother herself, at home? Had being more or less alone, now, caused or added to her grandmother's mental deterioration?

Elizabeth had fallen into a deep depression within three months of coming to the Pines, and the depression failed to respond to treatment. At first her condition was thought to have been caused by post-surgical trauma. But when Elizabeth didn't come out of it, and her memory began to fail, Carrie had wondered if her grandmother would ever again be the same.

On her last three visits, Elizabeth hadn't known who she was. The nurses and aides had told Carrie there was nothing she could do that she wasn't already doing. "You needn't feel guilty," they'd said. Busy with her own life, Carrie had gratefully accepted that. At first, she was rushing to finish *Winter's End.* Then the book came out and the publicity tour began. It seemed there was always something.

Looking at her grandmother now, however, Carrie felt she had made a mistake in not coming more often. Elizabeth sat in a chair in her room, at the large bay window that looked out across the green lawn to the sea. She was wearing a soft, coral-colored shawl Carrie had given her for Christmas, and against this and the well-kept white hair, her grandmother's face, Carrie thought, was more beautiful than ever. Elizabeth had always been an attractive woman, but with age the planes of her face had become softer, her complexion more translucent. And though her eyes had paled from what her grandfather had called "cornflower blue," they still shone, now and then, with a certain bright light—belying the fact that the mind behind them had tragically lost its early, brilliant luster.

What bothered Carrie at the moment, however, was that her grandmother had lost weight. Not an enormous amount, but enough that it was noticeable to Carrie, who hadn't seen her in the past three months.

Nan Martin, a woman in her forties who had owned the Pines for ten years, had come with her to her grandmother's room. Carrie said sharply, "She looks so small. Isn't she eating?"

"We're doing our best for her," Nan said gently, drawing Carrie back into the hall. She gave her smooth dark hair a push, tucking one side behind an ear. "She simply hasn't much of an appetite. Your grandmother is, after all, seventy-six. As people get older, especially when they aren't as physically active as they once were, they don't require huge meals. But, Carrie, we do see to it that she eats well. Vegetables, fruits, small quantities of meat. All the food groups."

Nan smiled. "Personally, I'd have her on tofu. But we try to give our patients what they're accustomed to and what they like."

She touched Carrie's arm reassuringly. "You mustn't be misled by her size. Elizabeth has been having physical therapy several times a week, ever since she came here. And she's walking more than she did at first, with the help of an aide, of course. We usually have to coax her into it, but—" Nan smiled again "—whatever works."

"I'm sorry," Carrie said. "I didn't mean to imply you weren't taking good care of my grandmother."

Her accusatory tone, she knew, had sprung from her own guilt about not coming sooner. She had made friends with Nan on previous visits and had checked the rest of the staff out, as well. Carrie felt secure in the belief that they were all good caregivers.

"Her health is still basically good?" she asked.

"Her blood sugar is up a bit, but not seriously so. We do, of course, keep a close watch on it, and we gear her meals to it."

"What about her memory?"

"To be honest, I'm not really sure. As you know,

these things can't always be measured. I would encourage you, as you've done before, to talk to her about the past, try to nudge her into remembering. But gently. If she doesn't want to remember, you don't want to put too much pressure on—"

"Wait," Carrie interrupted. "*Want* to remember?"

Nan shrugged. "I've spent a great deal of time with Elizabeth. I like her. She's very sweet, you know, and there are times when she just brings me up short. She'll say a word, or a name, and she seems so lucid suddenly. I would swear she's recalling something. But then she's off again. It almost seems she's deliberately slammed a door on whatever it was she remembered."

Carrie felt her spirits rise. "But isn't that a good sign? I mean, if she's slamming that door deliberately, couldn't she open it again, just as deliberately?" *Could she open it to memories of Breen? Could she be of any help?*

"Anything's possible, of course. But I wouldn't want to get your hopes up, Carrie. I might have read more into these occasions than they call for, simply because I would like to—for Elizabeth's sake and yours. You should talk to Dr. Esmond."

Carrie rolled her eyes. "The last time I talked to him, he said my grandmother's condition was irreversible and declining with every breath she took. If he weren't her oldest still-living friend, I'd have kicked him off her case long ago."

Nan laughed. "He's not a truly bad doctor. Just not a great diagnostician. That's a skill very few have, I'm afraid. Still, your grandmother was adamant when she first came here. She would have the good Dr. Esmond and no other."

"I know. I tried to talk her into seeing someone else,

but she wouldn't listen. I've been wondering...has she tried to wander off again?''

''Not since the last time we talked. We've increased security, and we did fingerprint everyone this year, just in case, God forbid, we should lose anyone.''

''Good idea. But how did my grandmother take the fingerprinting?''

''She barely responded.'' Nan smiled. ''Though I might have seen a flicker of rebellion.''

Carrie laughed. ''My grandmother was what in the old days they called 'genteel.' A lady. If anyone had tried to take her prints then, she'd have brought them up on charges.''

''I can well imagine.'' Nan checked her watch. ''Carrie, I have to make some phone calls. Why don't we talk later, after your visit? I'll be in my office.''

''Right. I'll see you then.''

Before crossing the room to her grandmother's side, Carrie stopped at the nightstand beside her bed, slipping a twenty-dollar bill into the drawer beneath a notepad and pen. She sent spending money for Elizabeth on a regular basis, which Nan kept in the office safe. The aides used that money to buy Elizabeth sweet-smelling bath bubbles, light cologne and any other personal items she might need. Carrie usually left a few dollars in her grandmother's nightstand, as well, in case she wanted something when Nan wasn't readily available.

It touched Carrie now to see how few things there were in the nightstand drawer. In her nearly total withdrawal of late, her grandmother had shown little interest in the kinds of baubles and minutiae that had overflowed her bedroom drawers at home. Here she had a small package of Kleenex. A comb. One white notepad and a gold pen. That was all.

Carrie hadn't seen the gold pen on her last visit, however, and it looked expensive. Was that a hopeful sign? Had her grandmother asked an aide to buy it? Had something of her old life come through, reminding her that she was once a person of means—and filling her with the hope that she might still be one now?

Stifling a sigh, Carrie crossed over to the bay window and took a seat opposite her grandmother. Recent visits had been trying on some levels, but nothing like now. Before this she had had the patience to deal with Elizabeth's memory loss, the futile attempts to connect. Now, despite every effort to the contrary, she felt herself coming unstrung. Her grandmother was the one who used to sit on the floor and cut out paper dolls with her, the one who took her for walks and ice cream, the one she now and then tricked into going to a movie that was too violent, just because she herself wanted to see it. Elizabeth was the one who *tsk-tsked* when blood began to spill on-screen, but then later forgave her, telling her with a smile that she must never, ever trick her like that again. In this gentle way, Carrie learned about at least one facet of love. Elizabeth was the one who, after having been ill throughout one winter, was ashamed of her arms, which had grown extraordinarily thin. She had taught Carrie how to sew by hand, and together they had sewn additional lengths of material onto the short-sleeved dresses that were the only styles carried in the local stores for spring. Afterward they had made hot chocolate and eaten the last of the batch of molasses cookies her grandmother had baked days before, the two of them sitting across from each other at the small white kitchen table. Carrie remembered a warm spring day when they had sat there feeding crumbs to a bird that settled on the windowsill as a soft breeze wafted the sheer white curtains. A good memory, the kind she had only from the times with her grandmother, seldom from the times at home.

Leaning over, she held Elizabeth's hand, noting the lightness of the translucent skin.

"Grandmother...it's me, Carrie. How are you feeling?"

She had expected no response, and none came. But she knew the routine. Talk—just talk. About anything and everything. So Carrie told Elizabeth about the past several months, about being on the bestseller list, and how she still lived in San Francisco and had been to the opera that year.

Elizabeth, she knew, had always loved opera. She had come from a background of culture and gentility. She had been taught "proper decorum" at an early age, and never once could Carrie remember her saying a four-letter word, or for that matter, even raising her voice. Carrie wondered if her grandmother had even heard harsh words when they were spoken around her. Elizabeth Holder had a way of pretending she didn't notice when people were behaving in uncouth ways. She did, in fact, seem to float above and apart from them, in her own soft and much more pleasant world.

Carrie had admired that trait growing up, and in time she even learned to mimic it. When the painful memories of abuse would threaten to overtake her, she would hold her head high, as she'd seen her grandmother do, and pretend they had nothing to do with her. They had happened to someone else, some other little girl.

Now, holding the cold, unresponsive hand, Carrie

wondered how different things might have been. What if Elizabeth had been the kind of grandmother one could talk to about foul deeds—never mind foul words? What if Carrie had been able to tell her about Breen?

Instead she had learned not only from Elizabeth, but from her mother, not to talk about personal troubles. Though Carrie's father, Jack, had been an alcoholic for years, her mother had done everything in her power to hide that fact from his parents. Elizabeth and Carrie's grandfather, Sam, were never to know that their son was a drunk. They would never be able to take it, Alice Holder had said.

Carrie sighed. For long moments the two women sat quietly together, each in her own separate world.

Where were the words, Carrie agonized, that spilled out from her grandmother now and then, as Nan had said? And were they a sign that Elizabeth heard and was trying to connect? Or only an automatic nerve response, as Dr. Esmond believed? Something akin to the sounds that tumbled willy-nilly from the mouth without conscious thought, as with victims of Tourette's syndrome?

She wondered what would happen if she spoke the name "Breen." Would her grandmother respond? Would she even remember him? It was so long ago. Twenty-eight years, now, since it had begun, and twenty-two since it had ended. Her grandmother wouldn't have had the same reasons to remember Breen, not the horror or the loathing that had followed her granddaughter down the years.

It will follow you, Carrie had read last year in a book about child abuse, *until you resolve it. One day you will have to bring it into the open—shine light upon it.*

"Grandmother..." she said tentatively, "do you remember Christopher Breen?"

There was no response. Not even a sign Elizabeth had heard.

"He was an assistant teacher at Sunday school when I was little," Carrie continued in a conversational tone.

Still nothing.

Carrie began to turn away. But something brought her back, a flicker in her grandmother's eyes. Not much, but a light that could have been recognition.

Driven by hope, she decided to push, though Nan had told her not to. "Don't you remember, he played the organ when Daddy was—" She couldn't say "drunk," though that was the truth. "When Daddy wasn't there on Sunday. And he helped the teachers in the Sunday school. He was sort of a youth leader. Remember, he played the guitar and sang for the kids?"

Her grandmother turned her head slightly, till her eyes faced the sea. The late afternoon sun tinted their pale blue color to rose. Carrie saw moisture in them.

"We lived in Minnesota," she startled Carrie by saying.

And then she was gone. Not her body, which still breathed, but her mind, which held, like a treasured gem in a breachless vault, any tidbit of understanding Carrie had hoped to access and use.

In Nan's office, which she had decorated as a living room with comfortable chairs and a couch, Carrie found the Pines' owner making a pot of tea. A light, flowery scent drifted from the pot. Though Nan was much younger than Esther Gordon, the San Francisco therapist, she somehow reminded Carrie of Esther. She always had something nurturing at the ready, whether it was tea, cookies, warm banana-nut bread or just plain conversation.

"It's jasmine today," Nan said. "Very relaxing. Here, I've got cookies, too. Low sugar and fat."

Carrie sat on Nan's comfortable sofa, on one side of a glass coffee table. Nan set the teapot and cookies next to delicate cups and saucers. She took a seat in an opposite chair.

"You look like you need some fast energy," Nan noted. "A rough time today?"

"Not really. It's just that for a moment, I thought she heard me. I thought we connected. But then what she said was about something else entirely."

"What did she say?"

Nan poured, and Carrie took the cup she held out. "Only 'We lived in Minnesota.' She must have been talking about the year that she and my grandfather lived there. She really hated it, and I remember her telling me once that when they lived in Minnesota she never could get warm. She slept under three down comforters, and..." Carrie hesitated.

"And what?" Nan asked.

"I don't know. I remembered something, but then it was gone." She gave Nan a look. "Oh, dear God. Don't tell me it's catching."

Nan laughed, wiping a crumb of cookie from her lips. "If it is, I'm sunk. I've been here too many years."

Carrie shook her head, smiling, and sipped the hot tea.

"So Elizabeth and your grandfather lived in Minnesota?" Nan said. "That's a ways from here."

"My grandfather got a job at a college there. I think it must have paid more, or something. I'm not sure. No one seemed to really talk about it. My mother said Elizabeth hated every moment in Minnesota, and she and Sam nearly broke up over it. It wasn't long—months, really—before they moved back here.''

''How old were you at the time?''

''I must have been around eight or ten. Why?''

Nan shrugged. ''I just wondered if her speaking about Minnesota had anything to do with you.''

''I don't see how it could have.''

''What was the relationship between your grandmother and grandfather? Do you know?''

''Only as much as a kid can know. They seemed happy enough. In fact, I remember…'' Carrie hesitated again, a slow blush rising in her face.

''You remember what?'' Nan prodded, lifting a brow.

''Oh, just one of those silly childhood things. I walked in on my grandmother and grandfather once. They were…you know.''

Nan burst out laughing. ''Making love? And you thought grandparents never did that sort of thing, right?''

Carrie blushed even more deeply. ''Something like that.''

Nan smiled. ''You'd be surprised what goes on, even around here.''

''You're kidding!''

''My dear Carrie, our patients are old, they're not dead.''

''Well, I know, but I mean…what do you do about it?''

''It depends. If the two people are aware, healthy and in their right minds, so to speak, we tend to look the other way. They think they're pulling something over on us, and that seems to add more spice to the whole thing—the idea that they're doing something forbidden." She gave Carrie a bemused look. "You seem surprised."

"Well, not really. I agree with you that they should be able to lead as normal a life as possible here...."

"But?"

Carrie squirmed uncomfortably. "My, uh...grandmother?"

"Pure as the driven snow," Nan said, her smile widening. "At least so far as the staff can tell. Would you be upset if that weren't the case?"

"I don't know. I don't think so, but—"

"But she's still your grandmother, and you still can't shake the shock of having seen her in bed with a man? Even if he was your grandfather?"

Carrie laughed. "I guess that's it."

Nan propped her chin on her hands and said, "Pardon me if this seems blunt. But we've known each other awhile. Do you like sex, Carrie?"

Carrie stared. Did she like sex? How could she answer that? It was something she'd been asking herself her entire adult life. "Well," she said, "I guess I enjoy the act well enough. But the only man I slept with for any length of time called me 'too detached.'" She paused. "On the other hand, he wasn't much of a lover, so who could tell?"

Nan laughed. "There are no frigid women, only bad lovers?"

Carrie sent her a mock frown. "There are times when you sound irritatingly like a psychologist."

"Didn't I tell you that was my minor?" Nan looked at her watch and slowly rose. "Not that I'm always that good at it. I'm still trying to figure out why one of our patients feels she absolutely must march into the dining room stark naked every day. Speaking of which, I need to check on her. Gotta run.''

Carrie stood, wiping crumbs from her lap. Reaching into her purse, she pulled out a business card. ''I've written my number here in Holly Beach on the back. Thanks for everything, Nan. You'll call me if there's any change?''

''Sure.'' They walked to the door together. ''But you'll be here through Sunday for the festival, right? You'll be coming back to see Elizabeth?''

''I'm not sure about my plans right now. I'll try.''

Nan gave her that thoughtful look again. ''It may not be my place to say this, Carrie...but I will. Elizabeth seems to be in a transitional stage right now. My guess is she could come out of this. I think it might help her if you were to stay awhile.''

This seems a nice enough place, Elizabeth thought. She sat where Carrie had left her, looking out to sea. And though she could not always remember how she had gotten here, or when, she was grateful that she could see water and the sky, the clouds and setting sun. Grateful, too, for the warmth of the sun on her bones, which felt old and frail, and in fact, she noted with surprise, showed through her skin.

She stared at her bare arms. When did they get this way? Didn't she remember, if only in brief, shadowy glimpses, a young woman's skin, sweetly scented with a touch of...what was it now, White Shoulders? Estée Lauder? And didn't someone, a man, once say that he loved the way she smelled of fresh flowers, loved the way she laughed and could tell a good story, loved the way she walked, her hips swinging slightly from side to side? Nothing exaggerated, of course, nor too seductive. Just that slight swing, something she was unable to restrain completely when wearing high heels, no matter how many times her mother reprimanded and complained.

Elizabeth's fingers found the bright coral-colored shawl around her shoulders, drawing it more tightly against her breasts. If there was such a man, she could not remember his face. She did, now and then, still feel someone's touch. A shiver traveled along the old skin. A smile curved the dry, cracked lips. That beautiful male hand, its long, slender fingers trailing along her thigh, spreading her legs, stroking the tender flesh, heat rising....

Elizabeth, in her chair, began to tremble. The heat began between her legs, then rose to her throat, her face. She gasped. There were few things she could remember now. But this—perhaps this was all one needed. The fire from which all life began, and from which all life was sustained.

Who had said that? her mind interrupted, stopping the flow of fire. Some poet or other, she supposed. *Oh, go away, mind. Let me feel.*

Her thoughts drifted. Beyond the sea's horizon, she imagined, lay a country lane. On either side grew wild-flowers, acres and acres of blue cornflowers, wild pink roses and dandelions of such brilliant gold they brought tears to her eyes.

Beyond the wildflowers rose a forest, tall and dark. From inside the forest stepped a man. Elizabeth's heart leaped with joy. She had hoped he would be there, waiting. She began to run, one hand holding the big straw sunbonnet to her head. The man ran toward her, and suddenly they were in each other's arms. His mouth was on hers, then on her neck, her shoulders, her breasts. The bonnet fell to the ground as his hand parted the white lace of her blouse, his fingers slipping inside to expose her breasts and then finding a nipple, which had hardened at first sight of him, as they always did.

There was a time when she might have been embarrassed and behaved with more restraint. God knew what her mother might say if she could see her now. But that was only a fleeting thought, the kind that flew by like an annoying bird, then disappeared on the rush of a hot, blossoming wind.

Elizabeth felt him press himself against her, and as he did she curled herself to fit into every space. Her heart beat so fast she thought she might die, or at least faint and fall to the ground. But his strong arms held her fast, and she did not fall but rather was carried to the ground, to lie beneath him once more, his beautiful narrow fingers under her skirt, prodding and demanding. Her body arched, her legs wrapped around him, and then everything opened to him, in a way it had to no other.

For long moments Elizabeth sat unmoving in her chair by the window, her eyes closed, a smile curving her lips. There was a time, she knew, when her hand would have been at her breasts, keeping the dream alive. Making it last. But there was no use to that now. Her breasts were thin and withered. They no longer responded to her touch but simply lay there, like a pair of worn-out toys from which the stuffing had fallen.

She sighed, and the rattling sound of an old woman shocked her. Just as quickly the dream evaporated, leaving an empty husk where moments before the old frail bones had seemed so warm and supple.

No! she cried out silently. *Don't go!*

But it was gone, all gone. And she still hadn't seen his face. Oh, dear God…why could she never see his face? Why could she not see *anyone's* face, and put a name to it now?

There was only one consolation, she supposed. In forgetfulness might lay her one salvation.

7

Carrie made her way back to the Crest Inn moments before dark, on the heels of a driving summer rain. Thunder and lightning struck as she left the Pines, lighting up the sea and horizon and whipping the waves into a frenzy that sent them pounding in to shore. She recalled that a hurricane had struck the Carolinas the day before, and the tail-end rain had been predicted to graze the South Jersey shores. She welcomed the storm, the physical challenge of slogging through wet sand. It helped to push the depression away.

Powerless. That was the way she felt, leaving her grandmother at the Pines. Powerless to do anything for Elizabeth. And at the same time, so damned alone.

She didn't know what to do, from here on out. And she no longer knew what she felt. Memories washed through her, as if carried in on the tide that whipped at her ankles. With them came anger like none she'd ever known. One moment she wanted to kill Breen. To find a gun somewhere and walk right up to him, let him see her face, watch him remember who she was and what he had done—and then blow his brains away. The next moment she knew how insane that was. She could not remember ever having this kind of rage before. Not to the point of being willing to kill. It frightened her out of her wits.

There had to be an alternative. Go to the newspapers? Expose him that way, even if she weren't able to do so legally? Certainly there had been enough stories in the news about women claiming their bodies, and careers, had been abused by powerful men. Some lied, she knew, hoping only to cash in. Often they had powerful organizations and money behind them to fight their cause. Others told the truth, but had no one to stand behind them. They had the least chance of being believed.

And there she would be, one lone woman against someone as powerful, and as adored, as Christopher Breen.

The old helplessness swept over her, the impotence, the inability to change the way things were. *Except that was then and this is now. I am not helpless like...like my grandmother. I am not someone who cannot speak or make my thoughts known. And I do have the power to change things now. I do.*

Outside the Crest Inn Carrie reached into the pocket of her white shorts for her room key. The pocket was empty.

Damn. Somewhere along the way she'd lost that key. How stupid could she be? She would have to ask for another. There were voices and laughter coming from the kitchen of the D'Amico house. It sounded as if the whole family were home.

Carrie drew herself together and tapped firmly on the kitchen door of the main house. When it opened she was assaulted by warmth and the scent of onions, celery, tomatoes. A teenage girl—Sally, she guessed—stood at the stove, stirring and tasting what appeared to be a homemade soup.

Nicky D'Amico and two older men sat at a large round table, engrossed in what appeared to be amiable disagreement. One was perhaps seventy, frail, with thick white hair. The other man was short and stocky, dark haired. Nicky's father, she guessed.

Helen D'Amico's eyes widened as she saw Carrie, wet hair streaming, tank top glued to her shivering frame. Her canvas shoes were covered with wet sand.

Carrie wiped rain from her cheek with the back of a hand. "I'm afraid I've lost my key. Do you have a spare?"

"Of course." Helen reached for one on the pegboard by the door. "But good heavens, you're soaked clear through! Come down and have some hot soup with us after you've dried off."

Carrie didn't want soup. In fact, she wished she were anywhere but here. Nicky D'Amico stared at her now, not saying a word. She felt that he was assessing her, like a doctor, or a social worker, or...she didn't know.

"Thank you," she said, "but I can't. I, uh...have some work to do tonight."

Helen D'Amico nodded and pressed the key into Carrie's palm. She gave her a searching look. "Are you all right?"

Carrie smiled. "I'm fine. Really. I'm sorry to bother you with this."

"It's no bother," Helen answered. Her smile was gentle. "This happens all the time."

"Really," said the young girl at the stove. She had big brown eyes and dark shiny hair that danced in lively curls all over her head. "Most of our tenants forget where their *rooms* are. What's a little old key?"

"Sally Anne!" Helen said reprovingly.

"Oh, Mom! Just because I call them broccoloids doesn't mean I don't like them, you know."

The girl threw Carrie a grin, and Carrie knew she

was expected to smile, to say something amusing and appropriate about the mostly over-seventy populace of the inn. But she was weary, and her mind had gone blank.

Nicky D'Amico still stared at her. "Hi," he said. "You sure everything's okay?"

"Fine." She gave a bright smile to everyone as she murmured, "Thank you," and turned back into the rain. At the foot of the outside steps she ran for her room and the safety of what she knew best, right now, how to handle.

Being alone.

8

At nine-thirty that same night Carrie stood across the street from Anglesea, the conference center where the festival would be held this weekend. At the middle of the now imposing complex stood the church that her grandfather had helped to build more than fifty years before, not just with donations of money, but with hard physical labor. He and many of the parishioners of that time had carted bricks in wheelbarrows and then laid them, creating this house of God from the sweat of their brows and the gift of their hands. The end result was an imposing presence of brick and stained glass at the far north end of the island, a block up from the beach, only a few blocks from Carrie's old home.

She thought about how much this church had changed. She knew from the festival brochure that there were no longer services here. Attendance had gradually dropped off in recent years, and the church and surrounding acreage had been turned into a conference center. A great deal of money had obviously been put into the new complex. The old church still stood on a corner, but set back from the street were wings on either side. Light poured through windows of the left-hand wing, and decorative lampposts lined several walks. Carrie could see that scattered around the grounds were gardens dotted with small cottages. For guest speakers, she supposed. A low, naturally weathered rail fence, more artistic than protective, stretched all the way to the beach. On a stylish yet unobtrusive sign at the front had been carved one word, *Anglesea*.

Christopher Breen was inside that center somewhere. Carrie had called ahead and been told by a receptionist that he was rehearsing a show for the festival this weekend. Could she take a message? the receptionist wanted to know. He wouldn't be out of the rehearsal till almost ten.

"No, thank you," Carrie had answered abruptly, hanging up.

She didn't even know, now, why she'd called. It seemed almost as if she were being swept back into those dark days by a force beyond her will. Was it that she wanted to see his face? And what could she tell by that, anyway? He had learned years ago to fool people. He must be a master at it by now.

God, she hated that man.

The rain had stopped, a brief summer squall. Over as quickly as it began. Carrie stood in the shelter of a maple tree. She was shaky, more exhausted than ever. Though Holly Beach was said to be seven miles long, it seemed, now, more like twenty. Driven by anger and, yes, she had to admit it, fear, she had walked that evening from the middle of the island to one end, and now here, to the other. Her legs ached, and she was drained from lack of sleep. Even more difficult to deal with were her changing moods. One minute she wanted to burst in there, drag out Christopher Breen and hang him before the whole town. The next minute she felt too weary to lift a finger against a gnat.

She knew, from being with Esther Gordon last year, that an adult abused as a child might change moods rapidly, from anger at the person who'd abused her, to anger at herself and thinking she was to blame.

Until now, Carrie's own anger had surfaced only in the articles and books she wrote about women, injustice and men. She had been outspoken and harsh in her early years of writing, more tempered recently, with time. She had seen that as part of growing up—putting the anger away. That was the main reason she had left Esther, in fact. There came a point when she could go no further in dredging up her past. She had to put it away.

It occurred to her, not for the first time, that she had been going under and around honest anger all her adult life, much the same way she had gone under and around the ocean's waves as a child. Timing the swells of others' reactions, watching for signs of displeasure. That was how, in life, she had "won."

Once beyond life's breakers, however, she had to admit that all she did was float. Instead of taking full charge of her life, she had allowed herself to be carried off by every passing tide.

The previous spring there had been an attack as she left a book-signing at U.C. Berkeley. She had been knocked down, her purse taken, and it left her with nightmares over what might have been. So far that year, there had been seven rapes on the Berkeley campus, and numerous assaults. She had been lucky to lose only a purse.

Jake Sharley, a veteran security officer at Berkeley, had said as much afterward. "We're number one in campus crime these days, I'm sorry to say, Ms. Holt. Some day we'll get more lights up here, but right now, most of the students walk with friends. The place is like the goddamned countryside, you know? All these

trees and bridges. But it's bad news on the streets anywhere these days. And if you're gonna be doing anymore of these talks at night…''

Tough and outspoken, Jake was retiring that year.
He had worked at Berkeley through the turbulent six-
ties and seventies and had seen what happens when
crowds get out of hand. Carrie had returned a few days
later to interview Sharley for an article on campus
crime. They'd had coffee, become friends and met
again several times over coffee, just to talk. One of
those times, Jake had leaned forward confidentially and
said, ''Look, I saw firsthand what happens when chaos
takes over. It doesn't much matter what side you're on,
things get crazy. Ms. Holt, you gotta learn to protect
yourself.''

''I'm more careful now,'' she had said. ''I don't park
in dark areas, I carry my keys in my hand—''

He had cut her off. ''Nah, that's old stuff. Times are
changing, it's really bad out there. Look, what you
need is a gun.''

Carrie had stared, her coffee cup pausing at her lips.
''That isn't exactly legal in this state. To carry one, I
mean. At least not without a permit. And what good
would it do me on a shelf somewhere?''

Jake had leaned forward. ''Forget legal. What you
do is you carry it in your purse. Or under a coat on the
car seat, next to you.''

Carrie had smiled, shaking her head. ''And if I happen to be stopped for a traffic ticket? What do I tell
the nice officer? 'Oops, sorry about the gun. It fell out
of the sky'?''

Jake had grinned. ''He's not gonna see the gun.''

''Oh?'' Carrie could see an article arising from this.
''And what if he searches the car?''

Jake had sighed patiently. "He can't, not without a warrant. That's the law. Now, if you're stopped for some reason, like going through a red light, and the nice officer asks, 'Do you have any weapons in the car?,' then you know what you say?"

She laughed. "I say, 'Yes, sir, I do,' so he won't shoot me down when he finds out I lied."

Another sigh. Jake hefted his weight in the chair. "No, see, you got it wrong. He *can't* find out, because like I said, he can't make a search without a warrant, or at least due cause. So what you do is, you smile and you say, 'No, Officer, I surely don't have any weapons in my car.'"

"Jake, that's—" Carrie was about to say crazy, but Jake interrupted.

"It's smart, Ms. Holt. People do it all the time these days—decent, honest citizens like you. And you know why? Because the cops can't be everywhere. And that's where the bad guys are. *Everywhere.* They're on street corners waiting to stick a knife in your face. They're at the ATMs. They're in your driveway when you get home. And you never know when they're gonna be standin' over you at night when you're alone in your bed."

In a friendly way, they had argued the matter off and on for a couple of weeks, always over coffee at the bakery on Telegraph Avenue. Little by little, drop by persuasive drop, Jake had worn her down. Carrie finally agreed to go practice shooting with him, knowing Jake genuinely liked her and was only concerned for her safety. He began to pick her up on Saturday mornings, and they'd drive out to the police academy firing range.

At first, Carrie was intimidated at the thought of

even holding a gun. Especially when the hot shells from the Glock semiautomatic flew back at her and down her blouse. She had jumped and swung around to Jake, still holding the loaded gun, an automatic reflex. Never in her life had she seen someone go so pale. It had left her weak-kneed herself to think of the frightening power she had held in her hands, a power that with only the slightest tightening of a finger could kill.

But Jake had been a good teacher, reminding her calmly that one should always lay the gun down before turning away from the target—something she knew but had forgotten in that instant when the burning shells hit her chest. With his help she gradually overcame her timidity, and it gave her a certain confidence, knowing she didn't have to be afraid of guns anymore. That she could hold one, and it was only a piece of metal, deadly only in the wrong hands.

She was surprised, too, by her ability. Not that she'd ever qualify as a sharpshooter, but she wasn't bad. Jake was proud. He'd insisted she take her paper targets home with her and hang them on the wall. The black silhouettes on white paper, bullet holes around the heart or head, seemed a bit too gruesome for that. She'd shoved them into a drawer.

The day came when Jake declared her ready to graduate. He would take her shopping for a gun, he said.

At that point, something welled up in Carrie that she couldn't explain. It was something old, she guessed, perhaps linked to some memory in her past, though she couldn't pull it forth. She only knew that learning to shoot at a paper target had been one thing. Being willing to shoot at a living, breathing human being was another.

"You told me yourself, Jake," she argued, "that if

I wasn't sure I could shoot someone, I shouldn't have a gun around."

He argued that she'd had enough training, she could do it if she had to. Carrie reasoned, "Maybe—but I don't know if I could ever live with myself afterward."

She never did go with Jake that day. And she had never regretted that decision.

Until this morning, in Philadelphia.

Lifting one foot and then the other, Carrie stretched her sore legs. Her teeth chattered, though the night was warm. She had worn dark blue sweatpants with a matching top and white running shoes. The temperature was warm, yet her hands felt cold and numb. Now and then someone passed by, but people seemed strange and distant, as if they, or she, lived on another plane. Leaves rustled above her head, while inside her mind the battle raged on.

Pressing a button on her watch, Carrie illuminated the dial. Five minutes to ten. *This is crazy. I'm going back to the inn.*

A breeze rattled the leaves again, sending droplets of warm water against her face. Behind her a foot scraped against stone. A voice spoke.

"Hello, Carrie."

Every muscle in her body jumped. Carrie whirled around, her heart pumping blood at an alarming rate through her veins. Her breath caught and stopped, then began again, shallow and quick.

Nicky D'Amico. What was he doing here? And how long had he been watching her? Confusion left her dumb.

"You're a ways from home," he said. "Out walking?" Nicky's voice was easy, his hands shoved into the pockets of his jeans. He wore a green-and-white baseball-type T-shirt. His broad shoulders strained against the thin fabric, and when he smiled, his teeth gleamed white in the darkness. She thought momentarily of a wolf or a fox—something on the track of game.

It took every ounce of strength, every practiced ability to pretend, to steady her voice. And still it came out unconvincing and thin.

"I thought I'd check out the center," she was able to say at last. "Pick up some brochures. See if I have any messages."

"Good idea. Aren't they about to close, though?"

She didn't answer.

"Funny, our running into each other like this," he said mildly.

"Yes."

"You've been getting around today."

She remembered the way he had looked at her earlier in the kitchen. As if he knew something she didn't...and should.

"What about you?" she tried to say lightly. "Do you always go out walking this late at night?"

"Not always. I'm on a case, and I had some legwork to do."

"A case?" She shook her head, confused.

"I'm a cop," he said, watching her steadily. "A detective, on the Holly Beach PD. You didn't know?"

Her fingers, shoved into the pockets of her sweatpants, turned to ice. "No. How could I?"

Nicky shrugged. "I thought my mom might have mentioned it. She's not the type to bore people with family stuff, but you never know."

"We...we haven't talked much."

Carrie was shaking now. What was it Jake Sharley

had told her about cops? They have an instinct for people who have something to hide. You gotta be good to hide things from a cop.

But I don't have anything to hide. Not really.

A car approached from the far end of the street, its headlights picking out a row of maples along the way. It stopped at the curb near the new wing, long and dark, its engine a mere whisper. A door opened midway along the wing and Christopher Breen stepped out, his face and form illuminated by an overhead lamp. A driver slid out of the car and opened a back door for him. Breen came down the walk and stepped in.

Carrie tried not to appear to be watching. Her mouth went dry as the car pulled away. Beside her, Nicky D'Amico let out a soft breath.

"Wonder where he's going at this hour."

Carrie pretended ignorance. "Who?"

He nodded toward the departing car. "The beloved Christopher Breen. But I forgot. You don't know him, do you?"

She didn't answer.

They were silent for several moments.

"Are you from around here, Carrie?" he asked.

"I...yes," she said, deciding not to lie. If Nicky D'Amico was a cop he could find out anything. It was better to pretend it didn't matter that he knew.

"I lived here when I was little," she said casually. Then, yawning, "You know, it is getting late. I think I'll go back to the inn now."

He nodded. "Okay."

"Are you coming?"

"No. I'll be along in a while."

Carrie lifted her chin and smiled, then swung around lightly. "See you later, then."

Her back straight, she headed down the street. At the corner, under the streetlight, she turned and waved.

Nicky, feeling troubled, watched her leave.

It had been a shock coming upon Carrie Holt here—seeing her standing so still, her expression one of pain in the dim light. He had wanted to help her, but was afraid, more than anything, of frightening her away. The balance had been precarious for several moments, he knew. Then, in the blink of an eye, she had changed—as at Neal's—from a woman who was seemingly on the edge to one who was poised and calm. She walked away briskly, like a woman who is self-assured, who knows what she's about.

At the same time, there was a rigid set to her shoulders that told Nicky she knew he watched, and that she would hold this pose—God, yes, that was it, a pose—until she was out of sight.

The woman is an actress. She's learned to "act as if." Where had he heard of this?

In that instant, he knew.

Something bad had happened to Carrie Holt. Something so bad she had learned to pretend that it no longer had the power to hurt.

His gaze moved to the center across the street and the church from which it had sprung. A place where people were supposed to find salvation and support. Was Carrie Holt looking for that here?

Well, she'd never find it. Nicky knew too much now to believe that anyone could find salvation here.

Grabbing a low-lying branch of the maple over his head, Nicky twisted it until splinters dug into his palm. His eyes were dark and furious as they followed the path the limousine and its passenger had traveled moments before.

"I'll get you yet, you son-of-a-bitch," he murmured. "I swear to God I will."

9

An hour later, Nicky stood at the door to the sunroom at the Crest Inn and watched his mother quietly. He held a cup of coffee with both hands, sipping at it now and then, content to wait.

Helen turned to see him standing there and smiled. "Good evening, Nicky. I'll be with you in a moment. A minor adjustment here..."

He watched the light strokes of her brush, feeling awe as he always did that this unique woman was his mom. The urge was deep to cross the room and plant a kiss on her cheek, massage the narrow shoulders that had carried, this last year, so heavy a burden.

Not that his father hadn't suffered, too. But Mario handled things differently. He shut the pain out, losing himself in repairs to the inn and worrying long nights over account books.

Maybe that was the better way, Nicky thought, watching his mother now. Sally's trouble had taken its toll.

"There," Helen said suddenly, "I'm all yours. Is there something special, Nicky?"

He shrugged. "I just felt like talking."

She met his eyes. "About Carrie Holt?"

He showed surprise. "How did you know?"

"I'm a witch," she said. "I know things." She smiled and gave a sigh. "Sometimes."

"There's something odd about our latest guest," he said.

"I know. It was obvious earlier when she came in for the key. It's a wonder she wasn't swept away on the beach in that storm. And have you noticed how frail she is? Not in her body, which seems strong enough. But those hollows under her eyes...she didn't look much more than eight years old, Nicky."

He stretched his long muscles, then settled into his favorite wicker chair. Despite the coffee, he was incredibly tired. There were deep circles under his eyes and tired lines that hadn't been there two days before.

"She went out again," he said. "Has she come in?"

"A little while ago. I didn't see her, but I heard her go up the stairs."

Helen rubbed her temple with a finger, saw that the finger was covered with paint and wiped it on her jeans. "Nico," she said gently, using his childhood name, "whatever it is, please don't become involved."

He frowned impatiently, and his mother sighed again.

"I know. You'll do what you feel you must." She capped a tube of paint.

"I wish I knew why she was really here."

"I thought...for the festival, right?"

"I suppose."

"I didn't tell you. I saw her on *Today in Philadelphia* this morning. I was making coffee and listening with half an ear. She's a writer, Nicky."

"I know. There was a piece in this morning's paper about her speaking at the festival. Something about an inspirational talk to the kids, telling them they can succeed against all odds. I wonder what kind of odds Carrie has succeeded against."

"You might ask her."

He was silent for several moments, the frown lines above his eyes growing deeper. "I almost did, tonight."

"You saw her tonight?"

He nodded. "At Anglesea."

Helen raised a brow. "Nico, what were you doing there, and so late?"

"It's my job, Mom. You know that. With all those celebrities pouring in, I've got to keep an eye on things there."

"I do know that. I also know the festival doesn't start for four more days. What were you doing there this late at night?"

Nicky rose and crossed to the windows. Pushing the long hanging tendril of a plant aside, he stared out at the fifty-year-old maple in the middle of the lawn. It was spotlighted, and the automatic sprinklers had come on. At least three sprinkler heads were out of commission, though. Somewhere in the back of his mind he made a note to fix them after work the next day.

"More to the point," he said, turning back, "what was Carrie Holt doing there?"

"Well, signing in, don't you think? Don't the speakers have to do that early?"

But she wasn't signing in, Nicky thought. She was standing there staring at the place as if she dreaded ever having to step inside it.

The question was, why?

Nicky hadn't a clue. He only knew that whatever it was, the timing couldn't be worse.

"Nico, what is it? What's wrong?"

At the worried note in his mother's voice, Nicky's

face cleared. The last thing he wanted was to bring more trouble into this house.

"I can't talk about it. I'm sorry, I didn't mean to upset you, Mom."

Helen began to rinse out her brushes. "You didn't." But her brow had deep furrows now.

Damn. He crossed over to her and began to massage the taut muscles along her shoulder blades. For the first time, he looked directly at the portrait she had been working on. A tremor of shock ran through him. *Carrie Holt.*

Nicky's hands stilled as a premonition shook him.

There were dark, hovering shadows around Carrie, an aura of danger, of something terrible about to unfold. She looked frightened. In pain.

It wouldn't be the first time, he thought, that his mother had predicted something on canvas, something she couldn't possibly have known would take place.

After Nicky left, Helen worked long into the night, something she often did when troubled. She had heard Carrie Holt pacing in her room above the studio earlier, before she'd gone out. Helen resisted the temptation to go up and ask if there was something wrong. She seldom interfered in other people's troubles these days, becoming selfish, she supposed, with age—though she preferred the term "self-caring." All too often, women cared for others far more than themselves. And how would they ever command respect that way? Only in Uncle Mike's dog-eared, fifty-year-old *Lives of the Saints* were martyrlike women spoken of in glowing terms—and then only after they had come to violent ends.

Helen was fifty-seven. The vast majority of her years

had been given over to family, and she had never regretted a moment of it. She loved her husband and children with a passion that sometimes startled her. A few years ago, however, she had begun to realize that there was meant to be more. One could not go around living other people's lives, either for them or through them. It was necessary to experience something of value within oneself.

Programmed for practicality by early childhood training, she'd had to wait for relative security before daring to put serious energy into painting—purposely ignoring the way it nagged and called to her over the years. "Not yet, not yet, but soon," she would promise. "After the children are grown, after there's money in the bank...later, when no one needs me anymore."

Then, a few years ago, she had woken one night with the feeling she was smothering, her pulse hammering erratically. For several long minutes she had believed she was dying.

"Anxiety attacks," the doctor had determined. Helen was shocked. She, with the good husband, wonderful children, a nice home, and finally, finally, a modicum of financial security, was having anxiety attacks?

They had been diagnosed, but aside from medication that made her feel worse, no one seemed to know what to do. She came to feel that there was something missing in her, a gaping hole that had never been filled. Not something wrong in her life, but an absence of something right.

It was Mario, who said so little but knew so much, who had given her the easel, canvasses and paint on her birthday three years ago.

"I don't have time for this," Helen had protested cautiously, not wanting to hurt her husband's feelings.

"Dinnertime," he had said in his brusque way. "From now on. You paint while we get dinner—me, Nicky, Sally. You think we can't cook, or what?"

Helen had turned to thank him, tears in her eyes, but he was already gone. Moments later there were pots clattering in the kitchen, and by the time the familiar, sweet aroma of fennel and tomatoes was drifting through the sunporch door, Helen's first adult stab at serious painting was well under way.

Painting had revealed for her a quiet, purposeful joy. It was something she did not have to do as mother, wife or friend, but as Helen, alone and quiet, uncovering surprising layers of herself along the way. In time there were no more gaping holes, no empty spaces to be filled, no pounding heart and midnight terrors. Here before these canvasses she was total, complete. Even when the work was not what she had hoped for, it added to her understanding both of herself and the world.

She added another brushstroke now to this canvas and sat back to gain perspective.

There was something wrong with the portrait of Carrie Holt. Of course, Helen was working without benefit of its subject before her, trying to recall in oil the pain she had seen earlier that night. She recognized the pain, and in spite of herself she wished that she might understand and heal it, even as she captured on canvas its frightening force.

At times work would appear on the canvas before Helen in ways not expected. Violent, monstrous pieces like the one she had painted that unimaginable night last June. That piece was in the Arberson Gallery now, in New York. She had been offered a healthy sum for it, and it wasn't that she couldn't use the money. But the painting was a reflection of the state of her soul during those terrible weeks. As such, it had value beyond the realm of coin.

Helen shuddered now at the way it had come into being, all in a rush, that dark, desolate night. She had dragged herself to the sunporch on limbs that ached from one more long walk on the beach that didn't help, because afterward, the agony she felt was still there. Standing before her easel, her hair tangled from the dampness and wind, her lips bleeding from biting down to keep from crying aloud, she had raised her brush with stabbing motions and begun. The painting came from some appalling pit of despair inside the peaceful person she had always assumed herself to be. All those black-on-white pieces of arms, despairing eyes, a mutilation of flesh on canvas, reflecting accurately and shockingly the hatred that was going on in her soul at that moment for the man who had hurt Sally—her little girl.

And the guilt. She would always feel guilt.

First, for not knowing, not seeing what was happening to the child she had rocked and prayed for and sung to, wanting only, all those years ago, for her to grow up gentle and wise and kind. *"Pat-a-cake, pat-a-cake, sugar and spice…everything, everything, everything nice."*

Never telling the full truth. Neglecting to warn her beautiful Sally Anne of the dangers awaiting the pure. Foolishly hoping that ignorance would keep her innocent and unafraid.

Helen's own mother had never faltered in the matter of warnings. "You get home right after school!" she would order, imbuing the words with all the portent, fury and language of the old country. Wiping her hands, silky with pasta flour, on her apron. Cuffing the young Helen on the cheek—not enough to injure, but firmly, knowing there was only one thing Helen feared more than all the evils that lurked in the city streets: displeasure in her mother's eyes.

"Shooshing" Helen and her sisters and brothers out the door, watching from the window until they were way down the street. "Ten minutes after the school bell rings, you be home! Or you don't go out for a month!"

And even though the small house was often cramped and steamy, filled with visiting aunts and uncles and her brothers and sisters—and even though there was never a time or place to be alone—Helen would do as she was told.

She had so much wanted a different life for Sally. Privacy. A room of her own. And space to grow.

Helen believed that people were little different, in respect to growth, from other living organisms. Like Mario's beautiful angelfish in the den, for instance, growing only as little or as large as the tank they were in.

Thus Helen had meant, in all innocence, to give Sally room to grow—while neglecting to warn her of the dangers awaiting angelfish and angels when the organisms surrounding them burst out of control.

Even now, despite all the family therapy, Helen didn't know how much at fault she had been in what happened to Sal.

Why had she neglected to see the signs?

It was her nightly torment. *There must have been signs.*

10

Carrie tossed and turned. It was impossible to sleep.

Damn Nicky D'Amico, she thought. What was he doing outside Anglesea tonight? And damn myself, for taking this room.

But she couldn't have known he'd live at home—and not only that, turn out to be a cop. *Damn, damn, damn.*

She felt—irrationally, she knew—exposed. Since childhood, she had always assumed that people could see through her, know her every thought. For this reason she had learned to be wary, alert to possible attack from any side. And until she knew what she wanted to do about Breen, if anything at all, she didn't need Nicky D'Amico popping up out of the blue, trying to figure her out.

At the same time, she couldn't help wondering about him. He seemed, at the very least, not to like Breen. What was that he'd called him, in a less than friendly tone? "The *beloved* Christopher Breen"?

But why?

Put it together, Carrie. You're a writer, you're used to working things out. Nicky's a cop. Nicky doesn't like Breen. Therefore...

He has something on Breen?

Could that be it?

Calm down. If he does have something on Breen, it

might only be that he's filching Anglesea funds. According to that newspaper article, he's been connected to the center since the beginning. Might he somehow illegally have a finger in the pie?

Or does Nicky know something else? Something about Breen's penchant, say, for little girls?

And if so, could she trust him? Talk to him? Tell him about herself?

No. There was no way she could tell Nicky D'Amico what had been done to her. Just imagining the look on his face as she poured out her ugly little tale made her stomach turn.

After leaving him, she had walked back to the inn via the sidewalks, passing lighted homes along the way. Once she had glanced into a window and seen a woman sitting on a sofa, nursing a baby. One of those Hallmark moments, the mother lifting the baby to her shoulder, patting it on the back, waiting for the soft little burping sound that told her all was well.

But all was not necessarily well, Carrie thought. What if that child was a girl? What if, in six years or less, she innocently became involved with that great and famous man down the street, and he molested her? What if she grew up powerless, the way Carrie herself did?

Powerless. The very word brought to mind again her grandmother, sitting in that chair by the window, so alone, nothing to look forward to and no one to share it with even if there were.

It hadn't always been that way. Her grandparents had loved being together, Carrie remembered, taking walks on the boardwalk, watching foreign movies, holding their little salons on Sunday afternoons. Holly Beach was a small, introverted town in the winter, when the summer people left to go home to the cities. Her grandmother and grandfather had gathered their own little social group around them on Sunday afternoons after church. They would have tea and homemade cookies in the parlor, and friends would come. Carrie remembered classical music and someone with long, shiny brown hair sitting cross-legged on the floor, sketching. Someone else might sit at the grand piano, with a group gathered around singing. She remembered the sun streaming in, on good days, through the multipaned windows that looked out over the sea. On not so nice days, rain drummed against the panes, a big fire crackled in the fireplace and the scent of pine blended with that of strong, spicy tea and freshly brewed coffee.

Carrie was sometimes allowed to attend these salons after church, as long as she was quiet and polite. She had loved pouring tea for people, afterward finding a quiet corner where she could nibble on gingerbread cookies and listen to the animated conversation that swirled around her like a kaleidoscope, layer upon layer, hue upon hue. Life here with her grandparents was the direct opposite of that in her own home on Ocean Avenue.

That must be what kept me sane, she thought now. Having that other life. Knowing something else was possible.

Did my grandmother give me that on purpose? Did she guess about her son's drinking, about how difficult life was for us at home—despite Alice's attempts to cover it up over the years?

Carrie couldn't believe she'd ever had even a glimmer. Elizabeth wouldn't have let it go on.

Would she? No. She might have wanted to look the other way, but surely she would never have done so.

Carrie thought back to her conversation with Nan that afternoon. Though it was never spoken of, she had always known that her grandmother and grandfather had a good sexual relationship. She remembered the day she had told Nan about, when she had walked in on her grandmother and grandfather. She'd been, she thought, about eight. The door to her grandparents' big, high-ceilinged room had been left unlocked. Carrie wanted only to ask if she could help herself to a dish of ice cream. It was spring, and an ocean breeze played with the sheer, white curtains at the long windows. Sunshine slanted in on her grandmother's porcelain skin...which her grandfather, whose back was to Carrie, slowly, tenderly, stroked. Carrie watched, awed, as a smile of pleasure played on her grandmother's lips. She saw this woman suddenly as not a grandmother, nor anyone connected to her at all, but a player in a movie that spun itself out before Carrie's eyes. She saw the woman wrap her long, slender legs around this man, and she saw him press himself so hard against her there was no room left between them at all. She saw them move as one, up and down, up and down, to a rhythm of sighs that fell over and over from her grandmother's softly curved lips.

Stunned, yet awed, Carrie had backed away, moving silently down the stairs. She hadn't thought it could be this way. Up to this time she had known only that when men and women were together...or men and little girls...it was painful. Something to cry about, not smile.

Now, as an adult, she could thank her grandmother, silently, for having shown her this other side. *So many gifts.* And though Carrie hadn't fully realized at the time that they were gifts, she had always felt profound gratitude toward the giver. So much so that even when she was grown and living in California, she continued to come back each year to visit her grandmother. When she wasn't here, she phoned every week. And when it became clear that Elizabeth could no longer care for herself, Carrie had done what she could.

Had she not?

The question tormented her, as it always did. Carrie continued to toss and turn. When she slept at last, her dreams were anguished things she could not remember clearly when she woke.

11

Only one thing was clear when Carrie woke: she could no longer sit around feeling afraid. It was as if, sometime in the night, there had been a sea change. A voice had spoken somewhere deep inside her, leaving its message on the lip of dawn. *Go back. Challenge the demons. Either root them out…or let them be.*

It was, she knew now, what she had gone to Anglesea to do the night before. Some small part of her had been clinging to the hope that she would see something, perhaps even learn something that would tell her the evil she remembered was in the past, something she had exaggerated, even, and did not, all these many years later, have to do anything about.

But last night had been a wash. She would have to go back.

Lifting the phone, she called the center. The receptionist told her Breen was out, and might be till noon. Glancing at her watch, she saw that she might have an hour or two by the time she arrived there. It was more than she could have hoped for. And more than she would probably need to wrestle up a demon or two.

Carrie showered and dressed carefully, noting that her fingers shook. Pulling on the skirt to the green suit, she smoothed it and slipped into low-heeled sandals. She had made her face up carefully, but subtly. *I've got to look good, in case the unthinkable happens and*

I run into him there. I must look like an adult, not the trembling child I feel inside.

But he won't be there, she told herself. *Let him be gone. Let him be gone the entire day.*

Her teeth chattered. Sounds of a lawnmower drifted up from below. When it stopped she could hear doors slamming on the other side of the wall between her room and the D'Amico house. There was laughter, too, and she knew nothing was wrong, that the doors weren't slammed in anger. Still, just the sound of it sent a jolt of fear through her, as it always had. Her father had slammed doors like that when he was drunk. The crack of hardwood on wood had never been a good omen.

Driving to the north end of the island, Carrie felt her mind racing. She remembered a side door leading into the church from the courtyard. It was this side door Breen had used so many times on Sunday mornings, so that none of the parishioners would see him come down the steps to the basement kitchen where Carrie, who had been told to be there waiting, had waited.

If that entrance was still there, she would use it today.

Pulling up alongside the Anglesea sign, she saw several cars in the main parking lot. Center staff, she thought, preparing for the coming festival. Or there might be classes and other events, ongoing. Rounding the building to the left, she came upon the driveway into the courtyard. Nothing on this side of the old church had changed. And the courtyard itself was empty.

Her hands were wet with perspiration when she took them from the steering wheel. Her stomach was tight and she was chilled. Sliding out of the rental car, she stumbled a bit, feeling disoriented. She was not, she knew, in her "right mind," as some might say, and hadn't been, fully, for more than twenty-four hours. Her body walked, talked and made all the appropriate motions, but something had happened to her mind. She felt split down the middle—one side as it had been before, the other alien, not the Carrie she had so deftly created over the years.

Crossing the paved courtyard, she walked up the three low stairs to the heavy double doors. Pressing down on the cold metal handle, she had a moment when she thought it was locked. But as she pressed harder, it gave, and she saw that it had only rusted over the years. Pulling on the door, she saw, in her mind's eye, Christopher Breen on the other side of it—lurking there, like a ghost of Beelzebub fixed in time, waiting to grab her. Her fingers slipped on the knob.

But only silence met her, and time itself…the worst devil of them all.

It had been twenty-two years since she was last in this church. Carrie had been twelve. She stood at the back of the nave now, enveloped in the past. There was a scent of polish and wax around her, of musty hymnals and women's perfume, of men's old shaving lotion and long-dead flowers.

Only in churches, she thought, did time stand still. Here were the same oak pews with racks for the hymnals, the round holders for tiny communion glasses. She remembered grape juice in "shot" glasses, that only the older people, the baptized, could have, along with cubes of bread. She remembered how hungry she had once been during the adult services after Sunday school; recalled wondering why her grandmother, who had insisted Carrie stay for the service with her, wouldn't share.

At seven, eight, she never could understand why God would think her sinful for eating a cube of bread or drinking grape juice just because she hadn't been "'tized." In this church, children were dedicated, like cornerstones, at birth. They weren't baptized till they were twelve.

Carrie couldn't wait till she was twelve. One day she had "helped" the Women's Auxiliary fix the silver communion trays in the church kitchen, and when they weren't looking, she had sneaked a cube of bread and a glass of the grape juice, too. Always afterward, she wondered if she had brought upon herself the hurtful things that were done to her; if her sin, the sacrilege, had been so terrible that God was teaching her a lesson, telling her, "This is what happens when children are bad."

The church, surprisingly, was as large as she remembered, the ceiling of the nave high and arched, a monument to all the people who had helped to build this house of God in the twenties. Because her grandfather had given large amounts of money, as well as helping to lay the bricks, the round stained-glass window over the baptismal pool was dedicated to him. You couldn't see the plaque from here; it was brass and quite small.

"We didn't donate for the recognition," Elizabeth had whispered when Carrie asked. All the other plaques in the church were big. Her grandmother's lips had drawn into a tight, prim line of disapproval, and Carrie knew that it upset her to talk about money because it was either sinful or tasteless, and probably both. "People who take their reward on earth seldom find it in heaven," Elizabeth had told her.

It was a law that Carrie understood now to be metaphysical, and when she added it to the yogalike exercises her grandmother had done every night at bedtime, she was faced with a complex memory that was one she could only call endearing. On the one hand her grandmother, probably because of her upbringing, was a born-again Puritan. On the other, her spirit seemed to have reached out for so much more.

At the end of the aisle was the stage that held the pulpit, with rows of seats for the choir, and behind that the baptismal pool, with velvet curtains that were closed. Above the baptismal pool were the pipes for the organ, stretching from one side of the massive nave to the other. To the left of the stage was a grand piano, and to the right, the huge oak pipe organ.

For the first time, Carrie had an adult realization of how much money had been put into this church. In an age when so many religious services were conducted in school gymnasiums and cafeterias, Christopher Breen had latched on to the strong, successful image of Anglesea as his home base, his field of operations. And now—based on his "wonderful work with children," as the newspaper had described it—he was preparing to move that field of operations to the national front. Were she to even breathe a word against him, he would be a powerful foe.

Steps led up from behind the organ to the old church office. Seven steps. Carrie had counted them in her head years ago. She walked quietly down the carpeted aisle, then up the steps, listening outside the door, giving a timid knock. In the old days this office had been used only by Pastor Gillam. Now that he was gone, she hoped there would be no one here.

There was no answer, and Carrie opened the door.

She stood in the tiny office, flooded by memories, good and bad. There was old Pastor Gillam, who had seemed nice enough, doing baptisms—a black robe covering his best Sunday suit, starched white collar and cuffs, and shiny black shoes. He would go from this office through a door to the baptismal pool, then down the five or six steps directly into waist-deep water. He would stand in the middle of the eight-by-ten pool, and as each person came down the opposite steps he would hold them in turn, murmuring prayers as he dunked them backward, their hands folded around a palm frond. Baptisms were done only on Palm Sundays, she remembered.

After the ceremony he would walk back up the stairs from the pool to this office, dripping wet, the shiny black shoes squishing. From here he would run through a door at the opposite end of the office, down the brick outside steps to the sidewalk, and then to the parsonage, to change before giving the sermon.

Carrie remembered any number of Sunday mornings when her father had brought her here while he talked with Pastor Gillam after services. He would have played the organ for the services, persuaded somehow by Alice to stay "well," for at least that one day. Carrie recalled sitting quietly—children should be seen and not heard—while her father talked with the pastor about the next week's music. The office was small, with dark wood paneling, a mahogany desk, bookcases and stiff needlepoint chairs. People came here to sign marriage and baptismal certificates, and bridegrooms waited nervously for their brides to arrive, for their new and hopeful lives to begin.

The room had changed little. On one wall were two large, framed pictures of the type found in Bibles. One was of the child Joseph in his coat of many colors, being thrown into a pit by his envious brothers. The other continued the story: Joseph later, a powerful man in Egypt, with his guilt-ridden and fearful brothers standing before him, wondering if he would remember them and exact punishment for their early crime. There was a caption beneath the second picture: "And Reuben spake unto them, saying, 'Did I not tell you, do not sin against the child?'"

But the brothers had refused to listen to Reuben, who was also their brother. They had cast Joseph into the pit, then returned to sell him, before Reuben could intervene. And now, as a grown man and governor of all Egypt, Joseph had the authority to take their lives in return.

Carrie had never thought of herself as vengeful. It was a sin to be vengeful, Elizabeth had said. But her grandmother had explained to her that even Joseph, who was said to be fair and just, had exacted certain punishments before he had forgiven his brothers. Carrie had always wished she had Joseph's strength. His power.

Now she recalled that on one day, at least, in her own small way, she had found a modicum of strength. And it had happened right here. She had run to this room and hidden from Breen after services. Everyone else, including her grandparents, had gone home, and Carrie was supposed to go right home, too, but Breen had told her to go to the basement, where he would be waiting.

Instead, she had hidden here in the pastor's study, in the choir robe closet, for hours, it seemed, until she had dared to go home.

She was about seven then, she remembered, and

Christopher Breen had been molesting her for more than a year.

For a long, frightening moment now she became that child again, hiding in memory, surrounded by thick, black robes and darkness, the cloying scent of mothballs drawing that morning's breakfast up to her throat. She remembered huddling in that closet until her knees were stiff and her body cold, and she remembered hearing his footsteps in the church, the door to the office opening, how she had been so afraid that she had wet her pants and the hem of her good Sunday dress a little. She remembered her stomach knotting into cramps, and shivering, wanting to cry but afraid he would hear and find her, do those terrible things to her, make her do them to him. She remembered wishing that her grandmother had taken her out to the farm with them that day, wishing that she were there now, having chicken and dumplings and the tiny yellow eggs from the chicken, at the round oak table by the window, with the lilacs outside, and the birds....

Carrie came out of it suddenly, rigid, her breath coming in fast, harsh gasps. She spun around and fled from the office, yanking the door shut with a wet, trembling hand. It slammed, echoing through the huge empty nave. Her eyes stung as she retraced her steps across the front of the church, past the pulpit and through the doors to the dark hallway that led to the Sunday school rooms. Stopping there for a moment, she forced her breath to slow, composing herself. When the pounding of her heart was no more than a dull thud, she looked around.

This part of the church had been extended and seemed, now, to be part of the left-hand wing. She heard voices coming from farther down the hall, and she followed them unsteadily, searching for a rest room. Passing a large classroom with blackboards and several round tables with chairs, she glanced in and saw a young man and perhaps a dozen children. Something made her step back a pace and watch. The young man knelt to talk with one of the children, and Carrie noted that they were all dressed in long white gowns and angel wings, as if for a play.

A few of the children looked her way, and the young man turned and stood, smiling. "May I help you?"

"I...no." She shook her head and was about to move on when she spotted one particular child. She was thin, with soft blond hair in two braids. Her white gown was shorter than some, coming to midcalf. Her shoes were scuffed, and thin brown socks had slid down to her heels. There were bruises on the girl's legs that could have been from playing rough or bumping into things. Her expression was withdrawn. She scratched at her arm with a fingernail, digging into the skin, seemingly oblivious of the pain she must surely feel.

She was the child Carrie had seen on television in Philadelphia, resting her head against Christopher Breen's knee.

12

Carrie stepped into the room. "Hello," she said, swiftly bringing herself back to the present. Her eyes never left the little girl. "Looks like you're rehearsing a play."

"Right," the young man said. "For the festival this week. Are you one of the participants?"

"Yes," she said, everything changing in that instant. "I'm speaking on Saturday."

The young man smiled. "Hi, I'm Ron Devereaux." He held out his hand.

"Carrie Holt," she said, taking it.

"Carrie Holt… I read about you in the paper. You're a writer, aren't you?"

"Yes."

The smile widened. "I remembered because I'm here interning with Chris Breen for the summer, and part of my job is getting PR for the show. We sure could use somebody like you—a participant, that is—to write a special piece about it. Would you be interested in that?"

"I don't know. Why don't we see?"

A few minutes later she was sitting at one of the small tables. They were being pushed together so the children could sit side by side, with her in the middle. Carrie felt only a momentary twinge of guilt. She would probably never write that article. But running into Christopher Breen's assistant on a day when he himself wasn't here was too good an opportunity to pass up.

Ron Devereaux seemed the antithesis of Breen. Sweet and boyish, he had tight brown curls and a nose that Carrie found endearing for its crookedness, though the young man probably felt self-conscious about it, she thought, since he kept rubbing it with his finger as if to hide it. He was an inch or so shorter than Carrie, perhaps five-six, and if she hadn't known by his actions that he was in charge of the children, she might almost have thought he was one of them.

"Heads up, everyone," he said enthusiastically, putting the last chair in place. "Miss Holt is a famous writer, and she'll be speaking to you at the festival this weekend. She'd like to get to know us better, and then she may do a story about us for a magazine."

The children, who had been sliding curious glances toward Carrie since she'd walked into the room, smiled as Ron made introductions. "Carrie, this is Eleanor, Mary, Charlie, Donny, Lee...."

Carrie barely heard the names. She was waiting for the one he came to last. The one little girl who didn't smile back and say hi.

"And this is Tess," Ron said, giving Carrie a private look that seemed to say, *Please understand...this is one of the shy ones.*

"Hi, everybody. Hi, Tess." Carrie smiled at each child in turn, but as she came to Tess she patted the chair to the right of her, saying, "Here, Tess. Why don't you sit by me."

Tess hesitated a moment, then slid onto the chair. She sat on only half of it, letting her right leg dangle off one side and keeping a careful distance to the left between herself and Carrie. She didn't look at Carrie, nor anyone else.

"We were just getting ready for a break," Ron said, "weren't we, children?"

They nodded.

"Mrs. Lambert is fixing sandwiches in the kitchen. Why don't you get some craft materials from the shelves while you wait?"

The children, with the exception of Tess, ran to the bookshelves along the wall. Tess lagged behind. There was some good-natured arguing over who would get which clay, which crayons, which books or brightly colored pencils. Tess chose from what was left when the others were through.

The young assistant turned to Carrie. "Some of the children here are from the day care program that's run by the Anglesea Center. Some attend Sunday school here, too, but it's not required."

"Sunday school? I thought I heard that the church had closed."

"It did. Attendance dropped, and the regular pastor retired a few years ago. But a visiting minister comes each Sunday, and we try to make Sunday school classes available to all children in the community."

"I see. And how is the day care funded?" Carrie wondered aloud. "I'm assuming there's some help from the government?"

"None at all," Ron answered, shaking his head. "In fact, the entire Anglesea Center is backed by private donations. We have two or three 'angels,' so to speak—longtime church members. And, of course, Chris turns a lot of his personal income from the center right back into it. He's the one who originally set up the day care facility."

How convenient, Carrie thought. How damned convenient.

"That's one of the reasons I applied to intern here with Chris," Ron said, a note of pride creeping into his voice. "With so many government programs being cut or done away with entirely, I wanted to learn how they do it here. I think people taking care of people, hand-to-hand and heart-to-heart—" a faint blush rose in his face "—is going to be more and more important in the years ahead. Don't you?" He added this anxiously, as if afraid she might laugh.

"Yes, I agree entirely," Carrie said. She wondered what the young intern, whose aspirations were still so pure, might think if she were to tell him what she knew about Christopher Breen. She felt sympathy for this cute young kid who had come here in all innocence to study at the feet of a man in whom his faith was so misplaced.

One of the boys—Lee, she remembered—caused a ruckus at that moment, trying to remove his angel wings from the back rails of his chair. Lee had been horsing around with a friend, and the wings had become twisted so badly he couldn't get them free without running the risk of breaking them. Ron walked over, stooped down and worked with them quietly, reassuring the boy that he wasn't in any trouble. "You're an angel, after all," he said, grinning. "Who can yell at an angel?" The boy brushed his thick black hair off his forehead, looking relieved.

Carrie took the opportunity to turn to Tess, who was drawing a picture with crayons, seemingly oblivious to what went on around her.

"I like your picture," Carrie said, though in truth, this was only an opening gambit. Looking down at

Tess's drawing, she was appalled. "What is it about?" she asked.

For a long moment Tess sat silently, her crayon hovering over the paper. Carrie didn't think she would answer. At last, however, the child sighed, as if the burden of speaking were far too much to bear. "This is a mommy," she said in a small voice, "and this is a daddy. They live in this dark, spooky house."

"I see. Is this your mommy and daddy, Tess?"

The look the child gave her was totally devoid of energy or joy. "It's only a mommy and daddy."

"Oh." Carrie thought a moment. "Well, do they have a little girl?"

"No. They live all by themselves...except...well, they do got a dog." Tess drew in a three-legged stick dog.

"And do they like the dog?"

Tess shook her head firmly. Her fingers gripped the crayon and made stabbing motions at the paper, startling Carrie. "No, they hate it! They put it outside and don't feed it or anything."

"But that's terrible," Carrie said, her eyes widening.

Tess looked at her sideways. Her eyes were a pale, cautious blue. "You think so?"

"Yes, I do. Don't you?"

Tess shrugged. "I guess so."

"But why don't they like the dog?"

She didn't answer. Sliding from her chair, Tess crossed over to the bookshelves and began searching through the many colors of crayons. Carrie noticed that she limped slightly as she walked, and there were red sores on both heels where her socks had slid down and the skin was being rubbed by her shoes. Carrie winced, remembering that as a child she had never questioned the fact of blisters; they were something she always seemed to have, and she would put Band-Aids on them and try, as much as possible, to ignore the pain.

Her acceptance, both of the ill-fitting, hand-me-down shoes and of the constantly sore flesh, astounded her now.

The strong feelings of compassion that she had felt immediately for Tess surprised her, too. She had never really liked, or disliked, children. Rather, she had cultivated a deliberate disinterest, and it struck her suddenly that perhaps she had been afraid to get to know children, or to feel for them. Children were so powerless, so needy, and she—who had never been able to care for herself as a child—was terrified of the feelings of self-scorn they aroused.

When Tess came back to the table, she said, "Tess...why don't the mommy and daddy like the dog?"

"Oh, well..." With a new black crayon, Tess scribbled, with thick black slashes, a dark cloud in the picture's sky. "It makes trouble."

"I see." Carrie hesitated. "Do they, uh...hit the dog?"

Tess shrugged. "Sometimes. Sometimes they say, 'You are a bad, bad dog. You cause trouble. Everybody knows about you all over the neighborhood.'"

Carrie winced. She pointed to another figure, down low in a corner. "Who is this?"

Tess said, "Just a girl."

"Oh. Whose little girl is she?"

Tess didn't answer. She scribbled black lines over the image.

"Does the little girl have friends?" Carrie pushed, though she sensed she was going too far, too fast.

"No," the child said.

One more try. "That's too bad. Why not?"

"Because she's ugly. She's very, very bad."

Carrie turned away, her throat full. She couldn't go on.

It was Ron who saved her, coming up at that moment with milk and a sandwich for Tess. Carrie noticed for the first time that the other children were already having their snacks.

"Tess, it would be nice if you'd sit with Mary for a while," Ron suggested gently.

"Mary is Tess's partner angel," he said to Carrie. "They stand together at the foot of Lucy's bed at night, watching over and protecting her." He had explained earlier that the children were portraying guardian angels of the main character in the skit, an older girl named Lucy, who wasn't here today.

When Tess didn't move or even seem to hear, Ron touched her shoulder lightly and said, "Mary's sitting alone, Tess. Wouldn't you like to keep her company?"

Tess picked up her glass of milk and her sandwich, moving down the tables to sit by Mary. She didn't talk to the other girl, but simply sat there, picking at her food.

Ron shook his head. "Poor kid. But it looked like you two were getting along. I didn't want to interrupt."

"I don't know about getting along. I didn't feel as if I was really getting through to her."

"I know what you mean. I try to spend extra time with her, but I never know if it's really helping."

"Is she always like this?" Carrie asked as she followed him to a larger teacher's desk at the opposite side of the room. Sitting on a chair beside it, she took a slice of orange that Ron offered from a plate on the desk. Her mouth was so dry, however, and her concern about Tess so great, it tasted like dust.

"She's been drawing pictures like that ever since her sister died," Ron said. "I guess it doesn't take much of a psychologist to figure out that she's troubled."

"She had a sister?"

He looked at Tess, then back to Carrie, hesitating. "I don't know if I should be talking about this. Chris says I shouldn't talk about the children's private lives with outsiders."

Oh, does he really? she thought. "Any particular reason?"

"Well, because of them being here at the day care center. There are certain rules, you know, about confidentiality."

"Of course." *There would be.*

"I guess...if you promised to keep this off-the-record..."

It was all she could do to sit quietly waiting, while the young assistant wrestled with his conscience.

"And it's not like it's a secret," he said at last. "The publicity has nearly all died down, but..."

"Publicity?"

"You promise you won't write about this?"

"Of course, I won't, if you say I shouldn't."

Ron lowered his voice. "Tess's sister, Debra, died last month. Not too long after I came here, as a matter of fact. I didn't know her well, but it's had a terrible effect on Tess."

"My God. I can imagine. What happened to the sister?"

"Debra committed suicide."

Carrie felt her pulse leap. "Suicide? How old was she?"

"Fourteen."

Her voice caught in her throat. "Oh…oh, poor Tess. No wonder…"

He nodded. "The police were here asking questions, wanting to know who her friends were."

"But if it was suicide…"

He shrugged. "I suppose they have to look into these things. You know, to make sure there isn't any foul play. Debra was a lot like Tess, though. She didn't seem to have many friends. I guess the police reached a dead end."

Carrie looked over at Tess, who was still silently picking at her food. It might only be grief, of course, over the death of her sister. But if ever a child looked as if she might be abused, or at the least carried a heavy secret…

"The sister," Carrie said to Ron. "Debra. She came to church here, too?"

"Yes, but not regularly. You never knew when she would show and when she wouldn't. The family lives on the west side of the island, and a friend from school brought Tess here. After a while, Tess talked Debra into coming, too. There are always children like that, whose parents aren't members of a church, but who are looking for something. A sense of community, some kind of glue to hold their lives together."

They go from one to the next, she could hear Esther saying. *When one grows up or moves on, they find another.*

Carrie knew this was true, from all she'd read and heard over the years about child abuse. And it didn't just happen in families. There were any number of cases on record where as many as thirty, forty, fifty victims of teachers, priests, doctors and other men in power had turned up to testify, once a child molester had been revealed and charged. There were cases of boys being abused, as well as girls, of course. Two out of four boys by the time they reached eighteen, she had heard. And three out of four girls. Now and then the abuser turned out to be a woman. In most cases, however, they were men.

So, had Breen begun with Debra, then moved on to Tess once Debra was gone?

Ron swiveled his chair to the side, reaching for a paper cup on top of the water dispenser next to his desk. He motioned to Carrie, and she nodded. "Please." Pouring two cups, he swiveled back and set one in front of her, downing his own water in one gulp as Carrie sipped.

"Boy, that tasted good." He shook his head. "It's tougher work than I thought it'd be, putting on these skits. I can't imagine how Chris does it every single week of the year, especially without help. He really is some kind of superman."

And you are so naive, she thought.

Or maybe he hadn't been here long enough to see what was going on. If anything truly was going on.

What if she were to tell him her suspicions about Breen, based on her own past experience? Would he believe her?

Not likely. Not with those stars in his eyes.

"You say the police were here?"

"Frequently," he answered, "up to about a month ago. A Nicky D'Amico, one of the detectives on the police force here, was in charge of the investigation. He's pretty good, I hear. If there had been foul play, he'd probably still be asking questions."

If Carrie felt surprise at hearing Nicky's name, she

didn't show it. She was remembering, however, his presence across the street from the church the night before, and that he had claimed to be working on a case.

"What about the parents?" she asked.

"Not the best, I'm afraid. The father apparently drinks, and the mother seems ineffectual. That's why *The Christopher Show* is so important. It's been several years since there was a youth ministry here, and a lot of the teenagers have drifted away. *The Christopher Show* is taking up the slack in some of these kids' lives."

In as casual a voice as possible, she said, "Christopher Breen. He's especially good with the troubled children, I suppose?"

Ron smiled. "Absolutely wonderful. With Tess, for instance, he's taken great pains to give her special attention."

Carrie's mouth went dry. "I see. He...he sees her alone? I mean, aside from in the group? He sees children one-on-one?"

Ron sent her a curious look. "When children are having problems and there's little support at home, yes. That's Chris's mission, after all, to reach the kids who need special attention. I mean, he doesn't just do it through TV and *The Christopher Show*. He tries to reach out in a variety of ways."

Anger bloomed, and Carrie felt herself grow faint. She was angry first at herself. If she had told anyone when he was giving her all that "special attention," she wouldn't be here now, pretending to be something she was not. She was angry, too, at the system, angry that the police—that Nicky D'Amico, in particular— had come so close to finding out the truth, or what she was fast beginning to believe was the truth, then apparently backed away. *No longer asking questions,* Ron had said, *the case seemingly closed.*

So that Breen—who had begun, possibly, with Debra, Tess's sister—was free now to do whatever he wanted with Tess.

And God help her, Carrie was angry at Tess, too. She wanted suddenly to shake the blank look off that pale little face, jolt her out of the easy obedience, the failure to assert her rights, to even see that she *had* rights. The child was too willing a victim, going here and there, wherever adults told her to go, accepting what adults thought was best, withdrawing into a shell that set her too far apart from people who could help her. Trusting when it was dangerous to do so. Not trusting when she should.

Carrie wanted to rattle the child, shake some sense into her, bring her alive and into the world.

At the same time she wanted to hug her, to hold on and on and on and keep her safe from harm.

It was as though, that last hour, she had been looking into a mirror—a fright mirror that had taken her back in time and shown her herself, Carrie Holder, the child.

"Are you all right, Ms. Holt?"

Ron Devereaux was kneeling beside her chair. She focused on him, noting that he looked immensely relieved.

"I'm fine," Carrie said. *What happened? What did I do?* She couldn't remember. Everything had gone black, and then...

"Geez, for a minute there, I thought you were going to faint. You had me worried. Here, have some more water."

He held out her cup, and she took it, drinking deeply. "I just haven't eaten today. That piece of orange must have gone to my head."

"Look, just sit here and rest a minute. I'm taking the kids downstairs so Mrs. Lambert can work on their costumes, and while I'm down there I'll rustle you up a sandwich, okay?"

She waved a hand, rising. "No, please don't bother. I'll be all right."

Standing, he pressed her down with a hand on her shoulder. "I am absolutely not letting you out of here without some food. Now sit." He grinned. "And *stay.*"

She smiled back and relented. As he herded the children out the door, she saw him take special care with Tess, tugging lightly on one of her braids and apparently making a joke. Tess, unbelievably, laughed. *Thank God,* Carrie thought, *for the good ones.*

Closing her eyes, she rested her head in her hands, propping her elbows on the desk. *I wish this would all go away. I wish I were back in my apartment in San Francisco with sun shining through the miniblinds, or fog barreling through the Golden Gate. I almost wish I'd never begun that tour, never been on* Today in Philadelphia, *never seen* The Christopher Show, *never come back here....*

What was that her mother had always said? *If wishes were horses, missy, we'd all take a ride.*

"Here, this should fix you up," a woman said, startling her out of her reverie. "Hi, I'm Rosemary Lambert. Ron's with the kids. He said you needed some food."

Carrie returned the woman's smile, noting that she looked a young forty, with short reddish hair and a complexion free of makeup, revealing a fine dusting of freckles.

"Will this help?" she asked, handing Carrie a plate piled high with what looked like a turkey sandwich with lettuce, tomatoes and some kind of white cheese. Beside the sandwich were mounds of potato chips and slices of fruit.

"I...it's wonderful. Thank you."

Carrie took the plate and held it on her lap. She picked up half the sandwich with a shaky hand, taking a bite.

Rosemary Lambert gave her a concerned look. "You're sure you're all right?"

Carrie nodded, taking another huge bite of the sandwich. "I was starved," she said, swallowing. "Looks like you're as much an angel as those kids."

"If that's a thank-you—" Rosemary grinned "—you're welcome. And not to worry, it wasn't any trouble. I had all this stuff left over from the children's lunch."

"Well, it is a thank-you. This is great." Carrie sat back in her chair and rested for a moment, letting the food soothe her nerves. "What exactly do you do here?" she asked.

The woman sat in Ron's chair. "I'm sort of the kids' den mother. My two are both grown, and I like putting together costumes for the skits here."

"You've been doing this a long time?"

"No, just lately. I'm an architect, and business is slow. I just happened to have some time on my hands."

Carrie wiped her mouth with the paper napkin provided. "An architect. That's impressive."

"I suppose so. Somehow it feels more impressive, though, working with these kids." She smiled.

"They're lucky to have you," Carrie said. "Ron, too. I mean, he's lucky to have you to help."

"Well, kids need more attention these days, I think. There are too many negatives out there now."

"I know. I wish you..." Carrie hesitated, then fell silent.

"What?"

She shook her head. "I was going to say I wish someone like you had been here when I was a kid."

"Here? You mean at Holly Beach or Anglesea?"

"Both, I guess. I came to church here. And Sunday school. Back when it was only a church, not a center."

"Really. Was Chris here then?"

Carrie looked down at her plate and picked up the sandwich. "I don't remember," she lied.

"Hmm. I wonder...which years would that have been?"

Carrie shook her head, busying herself with the sandwich. "I guess I don't remember much about all that."

The woman made a few more attempts at conversation, but Carrie was noncommittal, and when she thanked her again for the food, Rosemary Lambert wished her luck with the festival and left. Carrie heaved a sigh of relief and leaned back in her chair, closing her eyes.

"Why don't I take that plate for you," Ron said, smiling.

Carrie's eyes flew open. She saw that some chips had fallen from the plate in her lap to the floor. She bent over to pick them up. "Sorry. I guess I almost fell asleep."

Ron set the plate on the corner of the desk. "Here, let me get those for you." He stooped down. "You've been on a book tour, I seem to remember from the paper. That must be exhausting.''

"It is. I'm still catching up. Thanks for sending up that food.''

"No problem. Rosemary wanted to meet you, anyway. She read your book, *Winter's End*, and loved it.''

"Really? She didn't say anything about that.''

"I don't think she wanted to bother you—you know, fall all over you and things like that.''

Carrie smiled. "I wouldn't have minded. Writing's a lonely business, and sometimes the only real pleasure I get out of it is meeting my readers, hearing them validate what I spent months—or in this case, years— working on.''

"It is great to have work that touches people, isn't it?''

He sat in the chair behind the desk again, and she studied him. "What about you, Ron? What are your plans? After your internship here, I mean.''

"Well, I'll be graduating next year, and I'm hoping Chris will take me on full-time then. I haven't really asked him yet, but I think if I do a good job this summer, he might be open to it. You know…'' He looked embarrassed, but went on. "This might sound silly to you, but I actually got down on my knees every night last winter and prayed to be accepted by Chris as his intern. This was really an answer to a prayer.''

Carrie didn't know what to say. But Ron continued excitedly.

"I'm getting a degree in communications, and someday I'd like to have something of my own like *The Christopher Show*.'' He said it proudly, yet with a touch of humility, as if even thinking such a thing was more than he should be hoping for. "I'm from Baltimore, see, and there are a lot of kids in the cities who need this kind of show, something to support them, to teach them values.''

"And you…'' she said carefully. "You think Christopher Breen does a good job at that?''

He gave her a searching look. "Yes, of course. Everyone loves Chris and the job he does. You're not saying you have doubts?''

"I…no, I wasn't implying…'' She reached for the right words, ending lamely, "I guess I've never really seen his show. Except for a few minutes of it in Philadelphia yesterday, that is.''

"You're kidding.''

"Well, with my writing, I haven't much time for television.''

"Oh, gee, you've got to see it, then! The kids *love* Chris. So do the parents. Heck, the parents knock themselves out to get their kids on *The Christopher Show*.''

"I didn't know that.''

"Sure. It's not just entertainment, that's the thing. He teaches them all those things kids need to know, like how to be discerning when choosing their friends, how to be careful about the decisions they make—''

"How to be cautious around strangers?'' she couldn't help saying. The words just slipped out. Ron remained oblivious.

"Sure, that, too. But it's more. He teaches them real values. That's what so many of the parents like. It's what I want to do, too. And once Chris takes the job with Washington, he'll be needing somebody to take over some of the shows.''

Carrie blinked. "Washington?''

"Oh, you probably don't know about that. They don't want word to get out till the announcement is made. But Chris has been recommended as national spokesman for a new program called Millennium Child. This is a special program the President asked for, and the President himself is going to announce Chris's appointment on television, at the end of the festival on Sunday. We're all really excited. Chris'll be able to reach so many more kids this way.''

Carrie was silent, aghast.

But Ron smiled, pushing a wayward lock of hair from his eyes. "You really never saw the show?"

"No," she managed, taking a sip of water.

"Shoot, you've got to see it. Here—you're in for a treat."

He stood and crossed to a large-screen television in the schoolroom corner, flicking it on. Pulling a chair close to the set, he motioned for Carrie to sit.

It was the last thing she wanted to do. And glancing at a large clock on the wall, she saw that her time was growing short here. Breen was due back soon.

"I don't think I have time right now," she said. "I have a lot to do this morning."

"But if you're going to do an article about us," he said persuasively, "you should know what you're writing about. Isn't that true?"

"I..."

"C'mon, give it a chance. It won't take long."

She couldn't see a graceful way out of it. Reluctantly, she took the chair he offered. She would watch a couple of minutes and then get the hell out of there.

Ron took a tape from the top of a neatly stacked pile, all of which were labeled by date in large black letters and numbers.

"This is a show from last month. We taped it at the

center here, to help get the word out about the conference.'' He smiled.

''Where do you usually tape?'' she wondered as he slid the cassette into a VCR.

''Sometimes at a studio in New York City. Sometimes here, though there's not enough equipment here yet to do the job right. Chris is working on that, though. He wants to have his own studio right here at the conference center. Says he doesn't like working in the city, and besides, it's too expensive. Here he can have a huge complex with lots of sets, and he can do a really great job. Chris says the better the show, the more kids he can reach with it.''

I'll just bet Chris says that. ''How will he finance all that?'' Carrie asked.

''Oh, he's already got that part taken care of,'' Ron said. ''There're a lot of people behind Chris, you know. Senators, congressmen... He even gave a show at the White House a couple of years ago. It's like I told you, people love Chris.''

The opening was much the same as on the show she'd seen in Philadelphia. In this program, however, she recognized the stage of the Anglesea Church, with the giant organ pipes in the background. As *The Christopher Show* title flashed on the screen, Christopher Breen appeared behind the graphics, surrounded by a group of children. Two were children she had just met in their angel costumes—a boy, Lee and a girl, Mary. Some of the others she hadn't seen before.

But Tess was there. She stood right smack next to Breen. His hand was on her head, as well as on that of Lee's, who stood on his other side. Choral music rose in the background, music slanted to an audience of children, yet as full and vibrant as the Mormon Tabernacle Choir. Organ music accompanied the singing, rising to a crescendo. Carrie shivered. In the next moment, she found herself unwillingly mesmerized.

The children arranged themselves around Breen on the floor. Dressed in jeans and a casual sweater, he sat cross-legged in their midst. Carrie couldn't help thinking that he looked for all the world like a Pied Piper, drawing the children to him, gathering them in with his fluted charm. Spanning the stage behind them was a colorful backdrop similar to that on many children's shows: trees with silver leaves that shimmered, oversize cardboard flowers with both sad and happy faces, and a cloth-covered bear that held its huge belly and giggled at Breen's humorous asides. To get his message across he used a variety of large puppetlike creatures, in a manner similar to that of *Sesame Street* or the *Muppets*.

Breen's messages, however, were not as general as those of *Sesame Street* or the *Muppets*. Openly religious, they went further than a simple stressing of values, into the realm of "why we were created, and by whom...a loving God." The children sat in rapt attention as the puppets spoke to them of turning to God for strength in difficult times, of being kind to each other for the sake of Jesus, who died for their sins, of obeying their parents and teachers...and of always being honest and truthful.

Carrie wondered how Breen equated obedience with honesty. What, for instance, would he do if Tess or any other child who'd "obeyed" him to the extent that she, Carrie, had obeyed him, were to suddenly decide to tell the truth about him? Wasn't he taking a hell of a risk in handing out such advice?

But Tess, in this show, at least, seemed as thrilled as all the others. And as adoring. While Breen related with the Muppetlike creatures, getting them to talk and play with the children, leaning over them to give them hugs and big silly kisses, Tess smiled and was, for all appearances, totally trusting.

For a moment Carrie wondered if she'd been wrong. Had she made this whole thing up about Tess and Breen, projecting her own troubled background onto a child who was perfectly happy and safe?

Then she remembered that even she, in the very beginning, had looked up to Breen. It was difficult to recall the exact beginning, though over the years she had somehow linked it with her sixth birthday. Before that, if memory served, there had been a brief period when he had taken her in, pretending to be her friend before making his true intentions known.

Was he doing that with Tess now? Carrie almost hoped that was true. Because if so, there was one bright side to all this: she was in time.

While her mind worked, part of her attention stayed on the screen, noting the video clips of movie, television and music entertainers imparting their own special wisdom. They were inserted into the show like a collage, and a well-known star of children's movies appeared in person, interacting with a group of teens in a song-and-dance skit that revealed real talent on the part of the children. Someone, Carrie thought, had worked very hard with them.

Overall there was an impression of glitz and glamour, of bold, modern lighting and music, of fast-paced excitement. This was, indeed, unlike any other children's television show she'd seen. No wonder even the parents loved it. Not only did they derive pleasure at seeing their children perform on television, many of the parents must be from the same era as the stars who appeared—stars who were still young enough, and lively enough, to catch the children's minds and hearts. This must, Carrie thought, create a subtle yet positive bridge between parents and kids.

And between them and Christopher Breen—who, though older than the parents of these children must be, somehow managed to present an illusion of himself as an ageless peer to all.

Thankfully, Ron ejected the tape before it was over. She couldn't have sat through much more. Turning back to her and tugging nervously at his lower lip, he said, "So...what did you think?"

Carrie knew it meant a lot to him to have her voice a good opinion. She was, after all, supposed to be writing an article about Breen's work, and the young intern clearly cared about good publicity for *The Christopher Show*. From the first he had been struggling to put his best foot forward. Or rather, his idol's best foot forward.

"It's...very interesting," Carrie managed to say, *interesting* being a word friends used when critiquing a piece of her writing they really didn't like. Most writers came to despise the word, and Carrie felt bad, using it on Ron. Apparently, however, it satisfied. The young intern was so caught up in his own enthusiasm, he didn't notice that hers was not quite equal to it.

She wondered if Christopher Breen was the only person he'd had to look up to over the years. "Ron, where do you live when you're not here in Holly Beach?"

"Still in Baltimore."

"And your parents?"

He shrugged. "My dad died a few years ago. My mom...we don't see each other much."

"Oh. I'm sorry."

"Well, it's not all that bad. She remarried and her new husband doesn't like me much. We get together on holidays. But it's awkward. You know?"

"Yes, I do." Carrie remembered how awkward things had been between her and Alice after she'd left home for Berkeley. She had begun to look at her mother with different eyes, to see the flaws in personality and wonder why Alice had made certain decisions—like staying with an alcoholic husband for fourteen years. Why didn't she break away sooner?

Carrie had always wondered if Alice knew what was happening to her daughter. Had she guessed finally why Carrie had begged and pleaded to be allowed to stay home on Sunday mornings? Why she had cried when forced to go to church? And was that why Alice had abruptly moved the two of them to Philly when Carrie was twelve?

There never seemed to be a good time to ask. Then, all too unbelievably soon, Alice had died. Too late to ask questions. Too late to learn the truth about so many things. *I thought she would last forever. And Elizabeth, too. But now...*

Carrie forced her attention back to Ron, who was straightening up the craft materials the children had left scattered on their desks, putting them back on the shelves. Her empathy for the young man grew at the thought that there might not be anyone in his life he truly cared about other than Christopher Breen. That alone could account for his blind spot when it came to Breen's true character.

"Do you have a girlfriend, Ron?"

He shot her a smile and blushed. "Not really."

"And what does that mean—not really?" she teased.

"I don't know," he said, staring at the colored pencils in his hand. "There are girls I like sometimes, but I never seem to be able to ask them out. I guess I don't do real well with women."

"Oh, I can't believe that."

"Well, it's true. I feel awkward around women. I never know what to say or do. I end up spilling things. Tripping over my own feet."

Carrie smiled. "You'll get over that."

He looked at her hopefully. "You think so?"

"Sure," she said. "In a few more years..."

He groaned. "A few more years? I'll be so old..."

"So *old?* You'll be what, twenty-five in five years?"

He frowned. "How did you guess?"

She shook her head, laughing. "You told me you were in your third year of college. I figured you must be about twenty, twenty-one."

"Oh." His expression was crestfallen. "Well, see? I told you. Always out of the loop."

She took pity on him. "Ron, I'm sorry I teased you. I just think you have plenty of time to figure out women. Meanwhile, you'll be getting all kinds of experience, in work, in life...."

"How to stumble over my own feet gracefully, how to make a stupid comment sound like I really knew better and it was all in fun...."

She laughed again. "How to be an even sweeter guy than you already are." Sobering, she added, "Ron, may I give you a word of advice?"

He shrugged. "Why not? Obviously, I can use all I can get."

"You might try taking some of your own advice," she said gently.

"In what way?"

"Well…you talk about how important it is to teach children to be discerning about the people they spend time with. Do you believe that?"

He looked surprised. "Of course, I do. Otherwise, I wouldn't say it."

"Do you also teach them to do as you say—not as you do?"

"I don't understand." His brow furrowed.

She took a breath. Was she going too far?

"Christopher Breen," she went on. "How well do you really know him?"

"Chris? Shoot, I've been watching him on TV since I was a kid. Like I told you, Chris is an institution. Like *Sesame Street, Captain Kangaroo, Mister Rogers*—"

"Institutions—not those, but some—have been known to have feet of clay," Carrie interjected.

His frown deepened. "I don't get it. You don't like Chris?"

"It's not a question of liking or not liking. It's just…"

"Just what?" His tone held an edge of defensiveness now.

"I just think we give people in public life too much trust sometimes," Carrie said.

Ron narrowed his eyes. "You *don't* like him, do you? And this was the first time you ever even saw his show! I don't get it."

"It's not about his work," Carrie said, forcing herself to speak calmly. She really liked this kid. She didn't want to turn him away from her, didn't want to see him falling for Breen's lies.

And in the back of her mind, she admitted, still lurked a small glimmer of hope that he might prove to be of help to her. If she decided to go to the police about Breen, she would need people behind her in this town. Reputable people. And someone like Ron, someone who'd idolized Breen since childhood and even worked with him...once he knew the truth, wouldn't he be shocked and disgusted enough to make the perfect ally?

"I just don't like the idea," Carrie said easily, "of children giving over their trust to public figures, just because they are public figures. I didn't mean to attack Christopher Breen, or his show, in particular. Let's just forget about it, okay?"

Ron hesitated, and seemed about to say more. But then he sent her a quick, sunny smile. "Sure. Okay."

Carrie stifled a sigh. *Youth. So full of passion. So impulsive. And, all too often, so unwise.*

She glanced at her watch again. *Time's growing short. Too short.* She picked up her purse and stood. "Ron, thanks for your time. I'll be in touch, okay?"

"Sure. We'll probably see each other this weekend, right? At the festival?"

"Right, I'll probably see you there."

Then, as if it were an afterthought, she said, "You know, I've got an idea. Tess, the little girl I was sitting with? You said she needed extra attention. I'd like to spend some time with her, maybe take her to the boardwalk or out for some ice cream. I might decide to make her the focal point of my article. Do you think her parents would mind?"

He smiled. "I don't see why. It's not like you're a

stranger. Not to me, anyway. Would you like me to talk to them for you?''

''That would be great,'' she said. Taking out a card, she wrote the phone number of the Crest Inn on the back of it. ''I won't have a lot of free time once the weekend starts. Could you call them today? And let me know as soon as you find out?''

''Sure. If I can reach them, I'll call you tonight.''

''Thanks.''

She turned, then, to the door. *Almost home safe,* she thought *A few more steps, across the courtyard to the car, and I'll be out of here.*

But those few steps proved to be a mile. The sound of loud voices came through from the hall. Male voices, clipped and businesslike. Stepping back, Carrie watched as two men dressed in suits, looking far too hot and formal for a beach town, entered the room. A third man followed them, taking a position off to the side.

From the newspapers and the festival brochure, she recognized one of the first two men as Senator Alan Weiss, who was to have been the keynote speaker before he'd been replaced by Breen. The man beside him seemed older, with white hair and a deeply lined face, the kind of face that seemed carved from granite. Carrie didn't know him, though he looked familiar. She thought she might have seen him in the news.

The third man crossed his arms and took an almost military stance. His face was big and rough, his muscles showing clearly through the stretched material of his suit. His eyes scanned the room from side to side, touching on her once, pausing for several seconds, then moving on.

A bodyguard, Carrie thought. Over the years, she had

interviewed celebrities, CEOs and politicians for magazine articles. Often they would bring someone like this along. He reminded her a bit of Jake Sharley, the retired cop at Berkeley. Even when they'd gone out for coffee, Jake was always on the alert for trouble. An old habit, he'd told her, one he couldn't shake.

But who was this bodyguard with? Senator Weiss? If so, what dangerous felon had he expected to come upon here in this ordinary schoolroom—a seven-year-old terrorist wearing angel wings?

The first two men turned and smiled as a fourth man entered the room. Carrie's heart raced. She could have been safely back at the Crest Inn. Five minutes ago, she might have been gone.

"Sorry, everyone," Christopher Breen said. "I got caught up talking to someone out there. Now, let's see. Where to begin? Ron? Where are the children?"

Too late now. Too goddamned late.

13

The shock of seeing Breen again in person was worse than she had ever imagined it would be. Momentarily, the room went black. Carrie raised a hand to her eyes. Her throat closed as her legs went stiff, her feet reaching like rods through the earth, holding her in place when she might have run. Old prayers came back, prayers she hadn't thought of in years. *Yea, though I walk through the valley of the shadow of death... Thou art with me.*

But was He? Was He with her?

God, are you there...anywhere?

Carrie's vision suddenly cleared, and she found that her foot had come unstuck, that she had involuntarily stepped back into the shadow of a large, freestanding blackboard. Her entire body shook, and she felt completely without poise, without an ounce of adult polish or substance. She realized now that she had hoped he would be smaller than she remembered, like any adult revisited when a child is grown.

But Breen was not small. He was nearly six feet—taller than God, she had thought as a child—and still much more powerful. Else why would he look so smooth and successful, while she, Carrie, had been spending these last days in grief for a lost childhood that could never be retrieved?

She inched back farther, hoping to remain out of

Breen's line of sight. At the same time, Alan Weiss, who was renowned for his power in the Senate, seemed to defer to Breen, stepping aside to let him pass. Something in the bodyguard's attention seemed to shift.

"Gentlemen," Breen said, beaming at Weiss and the other man, "as I said earlier, this is only one of our classrooms. The children meet here for Sunday school and day care. They've also been rehearsing a skit—"

He broke off, flicking a questioning glance at Ron. "I thought I asked you to have the children here," he said with an obvious edge in his voice. "I would like them to perform for our guests."

"They were here," Ron said quickly, "but I took them downstairs so Mrs. Lambert could work on their costumes. I'll call down and have her bring them up."

"Do that. And next time..." Breen didn't finish the sentence. Neither did he smile, until turning to the other two men. "Alan, Lloyd, let me show you around."

Carrie wondered if she were invisible, standing here in the shadows no less than fifteen feet away. She did feel herself straining to become invisible, all her muscles tensing as she tried to squeeze herself into a tiny ball, the way she had as a child.

At the same time, she acknowledged that she would not run now, even if she could. In spite of herself, she felt magnetized to the spot by the high energy that emanated from Breen as he proudly showed the men about the room, pointing out the large-screen television and the VCR, the books, the craft supplies, the state-of-the-art music equipment.

"We've done all of this so far with private donations," he said at one point, "but you can see why federal backing would help. We'd like to expand without losing quality."

As he gave his pitch, Carrie studied him. He might look somewhat different—he might have reinvented himself in many ways—but he was, she thought, the same monster she had known as a child. Yes, the hair was different, a stylishly casual blond, lightened professionally, she guessed. And it was longer, neatly clipped but reaching to his collar, like that of a cleaned-up rock star. In addition, he had gotten rid of the thick, steel-rimmed glasses she remembered from childhood. He must, she thought, wear contacts now.

The mouth, though—the mouth was the same. A thin, ascetic line, and she could still almost see traces of sugar on his lips, from the times he had taken her to the bakery on Pacific and plied her with sweets. He would take small bites of a glazed doughnut, the sugar gleaming on those lips as she watched it melt, unable to look away. He would see her watching and smile, as if he knew a secret about her. No, worse—as if they shared a secret between them. As, indeed, they did. She remembered casting her eyes down, so as not to feel the power coming from his, even then knowing there was something beyond human in those eyes, something malevolent and alive. Knowing, as well, that it was that malevolent, irresistible thing, not the yeasty chocolate doughnut he'd bought her, that would make her return to the church with him when they'd finished. That fear of something bigger and more powerful than herself, a something that would make her unable to say no.

The sound of light, running footsteps reached her ears, and the children tumbled in, holding their angel costumes high so as not to trip on the long white skirts. When they saw Breen they ran to him, hugging him about the knees and waist. "Chris! Wait'll you see what we can do!"

Breen smiled widely, hugging each in turn. Carrie could hardly bear to watch, especially when he lifted Tess in his arms and held her a moment, giving her an extra hug. But then Ron hurried over to them, checking out their costumes and telling them they all looked great. He took a few reluctant hands and tugged at them, pulling the children away from Breen. "C'mon, let's get started."

Breen gave him a look that she couldn't discern. For a moment Carrie thought it might be jealousy. But, no. Something else?

What, then?

There was a piano in one corner, and as Rosemary gathered the children together and lined them up, Ron began to play an old song Carrie remembered from a Hansel and Gretel play. The children's voices rose, clear as a bell: "When at night I go to sleep…fourteen angels watch do keep." In the play, she recalled, the lost children sang this to themselves while lying in bed, afraid.

How incredibly strange, she thought, to hear these children sing this particular song. Her gaze went to Breen, who was smiling and nodding as if this were the proudest day of his life. The children smiled back, obviously just as proud of themselves. One angel scratched his nose, and another straightened her halo. Senator Weiss smiled and whispered something to the other man.

As the children finished, everyone applauded and gave them lavish words of praise. They beamed. Rosemary Lambert gathered them together and said, "We still have a bit of work to do on the costumes, Chris. Okay if I take them back down now?"

"Of course. And, Rosemary…thank you. You've done a wonderful job with them."

He crossed over to the children, giving them each a final hug. Ron smiled at Breen anxiously, seeming to wait for his own verbal pat on the back.

Breen said only, "Thank you, Ron." The young man's face fell.

Poor guy, Carrie thought. I wonder if he's closer to the truth than he let on. Breen wouldn't want anyone around who's on to his little secrets. Not for long. Maybe I should talk to him, after all.

It was almost as if Breen had heard her thoughts.

He turned her way, and Carrie realized that the shadows that had once sheltered her were gone. The sun had moved, leaving her now in blinding light.

"Hello…" Breen said. "And who have we here?"

He glanced at Ron, then back to Carrie, the lines around his eyes tightening, though the smile never left his lips.

Carrie could not help trembling. Fast on the heels of her own fear, however, came the thought, *What is he afraid of?* For there was definitely fear, or at least apprehension, in his eyes. She would swear it.

"This is Carrie Holt," Ron said quickly. "She's speaking this weekend at the festival, and she may do an article about us for a national magazine."

He said it as if proud to tell Breen he had scored a small coup. His smile faltered, however, when Breen didn't respond immediately, but seemed thoughtful.

"Carrie Holt," he said finally. "Holder, wasn't it? You were in Sunday school here, years ago. Yes, I remember you." Breen smiled widely and closed the distance between them, holding out his hand. "It's good to see you again, Carrie!"

She could not have been more shocked. Nor could she move. *He's pretending that nothing ever happened. Or...no. Was it possible? He couldn't have forgotten!*

"Senator Weiss, Congressman Tanner," Breen said, withdrawing his hand casually when she didn't take it, "this is an alumni of our Sunday school, from years back. Her grandparents, Sam and Elizabeth Holder, were one of our founding families. They had much to do with building this church, and then seeing to it that it continued to operate in the black."

His smile drifted between Carrie and the men, seemingly genuine. "So you're back here for the festival, Carrie? That's wonderful. It's been quite some time, hasn't it? Ten, fifteen years since you left Holly Beach?"

"I..." Carrie, still confused, felt all eyes on her. Ron, she knew, was looking at her with bewilderment, wondering, no doubt, why she hadn't told him she'd attended Sunday school here. Senator Weiss and the others waited for her response.

There was only one way she could respond. Only one way, given that she had learned her lessons when young, at the feet of a master of deceit. "Twenty-two years," she said, forcing a smile. Despising herself for the pretense that nothing was wrong.

"That long! My goodness! I hear you're a famous author now, Carrie. The festival is honored to have you here."

She couldn't meet his eyes. "Thank you," she said.

Senator Weiss and the congressman smiled at her, murmuring, "Pleased to meet you," and other appropriate niceties. An uneasy silence filled the room. The bodyguard's puzzled expression moved from Carrie to Breen and back again.

Weiss eased the awkward moment. "We must be going, Chris. Walk us out, will you?"

"Of course. I'll be right along."

Tanner gave a perfunctory nod to the bodyguard. "Vincent." The two men walked into the hall with Vincent following.

Breen said in a clipped voice to Ron, "I'll be in the old pastor's study. When you're finished here, I'd like to talk with you."

"Right…" Ron said, but his expression was worried. "There's nothing wrong, is there, Chris?"

Breen, still tight-lipped, turned away.

In the hallway he spoke to the other men, his words carrying back into the room, but fading as they walked down the hall. "As you can see, we have a great set-up here, Alan. Once the announcement is made, it shouldn't be hard to wangle the funding…and it's just the right platform.…"

A door opened and closed. Carrie could hear no more.

"Are you all right?" Ron murmured, touching her arm. "You really don't look well, Ms. Holt."

With some effort she brought her focus back to him. "I'm fine."

"You're sure?"

She nodded, moving toward the door.

"I'll phone you," Ron called after her, "at the number you gave me earlier, to let you know about Tess."

But Carrie was barely listening. The sight of Breen standing there in person, the shock that he'd remembered her, yet pretended nothing had ever happened…

After all those hours of pacing the floor, of fearing a meeting, of wondering what to say and how to say it, what to do and how to do it…

She leaned against a wall outside the classroom, sick, wanting to throw up, yet hoping she wouldn't embarrass herself by doing just that. Nausea rose in ever-stronger waves, and she tried to stop it, to pretend she was somewhere else entirely, the way she had as a child. But her ability to pretend crumbled suddenly. The memories would not be stuffed down. They rose in her throat, and Carrie ran in the direction of a sign, Women, down the hall.

It was the memories, it seemed, that she vomited, kneeling in a stall in the new women's rest room, surrounded by chrome and blinding white porcelain, the cubicle threatening to close in, the flushing of the toilet willing her to go with it, to drown.

Mother, she cried silently, tears streaming from her eyes. *Mother, where are you? Oh, God, I need help. Someone help me, please.*

She didn't know how long she knelt there, numb and unable to move. Her arms rested on the toilet seat, her face hidden in her hands. It was the lingering smell of vomit that brought her back, finally, making her gag.

Carrie lifted her head and looked around, seeing clearly for the first time the degrading position she was in, feeling for the first time the cold floor beneath her knees. Someone had written in lipstick on a white-tiled wall: "If Jesus could see you now." The scrawl was that of a teenager, the message meant to be funny. But Carrie grabbed at the graffiti as at a straw.

I can see me now, she told herself angrily. *I* can see me now.

Flushing the toilet, she stumbled from the cubicle and wiped her wet mouth with a wad of rough paper towel. In the mirror over the washbasins she saw the pale face, the makeup smeared, an expression like that of a broken bird. Her anger grew. *I will not let him do this to me. Not again.*

Ripping open her purse, she drew out her makeup. Carefully, with cold, precise strokes, she renewed it, paying attention to every line. Her eyes were red and swollen, and the result would not fool anyone, she knew. But there were times when applying makeup had calmed her, even given her strength. Times when she had wondered if this was why ancient warrior women, going into battle, wore paint.

Finished, she stood back, surveying herself. Her chin rose. *I am a grown woman now. I am no longer the child who had to wash the hated taste of him out of her mouth at a water fountain. I could even... God, I could kill him now. If I wanted to I could kill him, instead of just wishing him dead.*

He would be in the old pastor's study, he had said. The one she had been in earlier. Carrie let her feet take her there, while her mind raced and her anger grew. By the time she reached the door to the study and flung it open, her fury was full-blown.

14

Breen was alone. He sat at a large polished desk beneath diamond-paned windows. Heavy drapes were half-pulled, shutting out most of the late morning light. A green-shaded lamp cast murky shadows about the room.

Slamming the door behind her, Carrie raged, "Who the hell do you think you are? You're not getting away with this, damn you! Not any of it!"

"Carrie?" He stood slowly, a puzzled expression on his face. "Good heavens, what's wrong? What is this?"

Her fists clenched. "Stop that. Stop pretending you don't remember. *I* remember. I remember every sick, filthy thing you did to me."

He shook his head slowly. "I don't know what you're talking about. Carrie, please sit down. You're obviously upset."

His tone was one of concern, a tack she supposed others might see as genuine. He gestured to a chair, but she ignored it. His eyes closed briefly as he rubbed a hand across them, and his voice became a degree cooler.

"Carrie, if I had known you were coming today, I could have given you more time." He glanced at his watch. "As it is, I have a show to rehearse for the weekend, and a script to write. I'm sure you know how that is.'' He flashed her a smile. ''I can talk to you briefly about *The Christopher Show* another time, if you wish. You told Ron you wanted to write an article?''

''Shut up, dammit. Just shut up. Don't try to cover this up as if it never happened.''

''As if *what* never happened? Carrie, I have no idea what you're talking about.''

''Don't lie! You molested me, you monster. And you're still at it. If it's the last thing I do, I swear to God I'll make you pay.''

Breen's expression went from bewilderment to anger. ''Good God, this is preposterous. You think something like that happened? Carrie, I can't even imagine where you got an idea like that. You must be—you must be sick. You really should leave now.''

Carrie stood rooted to the floor in shock. What kind of game was this? Did he honestly not remember? She had thought, if she faced him with it—

Then, suddenly, she remembered that it had always been this way. As if the things he had done to her never happened at all.

But they did. They had.

She even remembered, now, how it had begun.

He had come to the house—a visit, like Pastor Gillam always made, except that it was him this time. He came to see her mother, he said. ''Pastor Gillam sent me. He's been wondering why your mother doesn't come to church anymore. Is it all right if I come in?''

Alice wasn't home. She had told Carrie not to let anyone in. But Chris was the teaching assistant in Sunday school. She saw him every week, and he had always been friendly to her. Even her teacher liked him. She couldn't say no.

She stood back from the door and let him in.

"This is a nice house, Carrie," he said, shoving his hands in his jeans pockets. She had noticed that they shook, and wondered why. "Mind if I look around?"

There are just so many ways of seducing, Carrie had learned with disgust over the next years. Holding the child on your lap, fingering her breasts while your crotch gets tight. Slipping up behind her, pulling her close, rubbing her nipples while your leg pushes hers apart from behind…unbuttoning the blouse, inching the waistband of the skirt down…

Clichés. Men who molested weren't men at all. They were stupid, criminal juveniles performing clichés. Clichés that took childhoods away. And Carrie had read about, or experienced, them all. But not before that day.

He had taken her onto his lap. To read Bible verses to her, he'd said, while they waited for Alice to come home. He had brought his own Bible with him, the one he usually had in Sunday school, and he had read from the Song of Solomon. The words had confused her, about kisses and breasts and "opening to my beloved." She didn't half know what they meant. But his voice shook as his free hand began to stroke her leg, first at the knee, then sliding along to the soft inner flesh of her thigh. Carrie had wiggled uncomfortably, wanting to get down. By then his breath was against her ear, his voice husky. When his fingers slid inside the loose cuff of her shorts, she pulled back as if burned, but his other arm held her head, pulling her mouth toward him. "Be a good girl, Carrie," he had whispered. "See? It feels nice."

It didn't feel nice. It felt ugly and wrong. Carrie held her breath while he did it. She didn't dare say no. His hand had gone inside her shorts, rubbing her skin there, while his tongue moved inside her mouth, so wet and ugly and awful she nearly threw up. And before he was done she was cold and shaking, her stomach sick, frightened of what he might do next...she was...shaking...she was cold and shaking...she was...

She was here in this room, with him now.

Carrie opened her eyes, which had closed as if to curtain off the past. She realized that her hand had gone to the back of one of the needlepoint chairs for support, and that her knees were weak. Words seemed to stick to the roof of her mouth. The rage that filled her was shattering. "Don't you *remember?* Don't you feel guilty at *all?*"

Breen was behind his desk, still standing, his fingertips spread on its leather top.

"I remember you, Carrie," he said gently. "Of course, I do. But none of the things you think happened are true. I swear it. You were a lonely little girl, and I tried to help you. Remember how you came to me all the time to fix things for you? You even brought me your doll once. Remember?"

"Oh, I remember, all right. I remember the price you made me pay before you'd give it back."

She had dropped her doll in the courtyard. Christy was dirty, and one of the other girls had pulled Christy's arm off, jealous of the new toy. Carrie had gone inside, down to the basement kitchen, to wash Christy off. She was at the sink, barely reaching it, rubbing water on the soft vinyl arm, splashing it on her Sunday dress...and then he was there. He had taken Christy and fixed her arm, and then...and then... "I did something nice for you," he had murmured, "now you do something nice for me."

That was how it had been, that first time at the

church. After he had been to her house. Carrie clutched at her sides now, in pain. She moaned. "You are a monster," she said, her voice low in her throat. "I should kill you for what you did to me."

There was a long moment when something unreadable crossed Breen's eyes. Then he sat, and the deep sorrow in his next words confused her.

"I tell you I did nothing at all, Carrie. I was always your friend. Nothing more. My God, how could you have twisted all that in your mind?"

Her head moved back and forth, her mouth open in disbelief. Of all the things she might have expected from a confrontation, this was the last.

It was too much. The anger she had been harboring for years, the rage her memories had invoked, blossomed with a force that threatened to splinter what little control remained. But she could not destroy herself over this sick, disgusting creature. He wasn't worth it; she saw that now. Wasn't worth killing. There were worse punishments, and she would see that they were exacted in full measure for every single child he had ever abused. She would not only see that they were exacted, she would be there to applaud.

Her voice was thick with fury. "I am going to expose you for every evil deed you have ever done. I know I can't have been the only child you molested over the years. I know there have been more. And I'll find every one. I'll bring charges, and they will, too. You'll be lucky if you aren't lynched before you ever get to court."

Breen stood, reaching a hand out to her, as if to touch her. Carrie jerked away. He shook his head sadly.

"Carrie, people will never believe this terrible story you've concocted. It's simply not true. And everyone will know it's not true. This is a small town. People will remember the kind of family you came from. Your mother let you run wild. And your father..."

He fell silent, his eyes lowering to the desk.

Carrie heard the words through a thick red haze. "What about my father? You mean because he drank? This is a new age, Breen. The sins of the father are no longer visited on the child. And I'm a new person. I'm grown and I'm respected, both as a person and an author. People will believe me now."

He picked up a leather-bound Bible from the side of the desk, and seemed to be choosing his next words. As he did so, he rubbed the spine of the Bible with his fingertips. Back and forth, back and forth. Carrie remembered those same thin fingers stroking her flesh...back and forth, in that same slow way. She was hearing him say, "It feels good...so good..."

"Stop that!" she cried. Lunging over the desk, she wrenched the Bible from his grasp and slammed it down. "You are filth. You are the worst sort of pervert."

He stood and rounded the desk quickly then, his hand raised in a gesture of silence. His pale eyes were like stones. "It's time you left. I don't need this kind of trouble from you, young lady."

Carrie took a step toward him. "Young lady? Oh, you'd like it if we all stayed sweet, obedient young ladies, wouldn't you? You could continue to control us that way. But I'm willing to bet there are women out there who remember you the way I do, and who are strong. I intend to find them, and when I do, we'll either see you in jail—or dead."

"This meeting is ended," he replied coldly.

"Not by a long shot."

He picked up the phone. "If you don't leave now, I will call the police."

"Fine. Why don't you do just that. We'll all sit down and have a nice little chat."

"Hush, Carrie. Lower your voice."

"In fact," she said, raising it even more, "let's start out our chat by telling them about you and Debra Stanley."

He frowned and shook his head, as if not understanding.

"Debra Stanley," she said again. "Tess's dead sister? I'd be willing to bet you remember her."

Breen lowered the phone. "I haven't the faintest idea what you are talking about."

"Too bad. Well, maybe the police will."

"Carrie, I have worked extremely hard for many years to build a spotless reputation in this town. I'm a respected leader of the community here now, and people will believe what I say. If you pursue this, they will think you are insane. Which, sad to say, you clearly are."

Carrie raised her hand to strike him, then stopped midway. She couldn't touch him, couldn't come that close. His proximity made her flesh crawl, and she backed away.

"Count the days," she said softly. "They're almost over for you." She turned, reaching out to open the study door.

"Wait!" She heard him move behind her. And there was something in his voice, a hint of resignation. "Carrie, wait."

She should have ignored him, she thought later. In fact, her hand was on the brass knob of the door. But there was that odd tone in his voice. Carrie heard him settle into his chair and then breathe a loud sigh. Slowly she turned. Breen's shoulders were slumped. He looked beaten.

Despite every instinct to the contrary, she stood silent, waiting. What now? she wondered bitterly. What kind of act is this?

But when Breen lifted his head, his face was pale and strained. "Carrie," he said softly, "I never dreamed you would turn on me like this. Why do you think you are here?"

She felt confused. "Here?"

"Yes, for the festival. How do you think you came to be here?"

"I don't think, I *know*. I was invited by the board of directors."

"But not by happenstance. Carrie, I am the president of the board of directors. Do you think I would have allowed them to invite you if I'd known you harbored these terrible thoughts about me?"

She couldn't think what to say.

"It's simple," he said. "We—the board—set up a selection committee for the festival every year. This year we were looking for local and formerly local authors, and I approved of their inviting you because I had fond memories of the child you were. I saw you as a local hero, someone who had made good in spite of so many family obstacles. Carrie, do you honestly think I'd have allowed you to come here if those things you said about me were true?"

She laughed, but uneasily. "You're lying. You knew I was coming? And you approved it?"

"Of course. Carrie, I thought you would enjoy returning to your hometown as a success and passing your wisdom along. That's all we're trying to do here, you know. We try to help children by example. We like them to see and hear from others who have gone through difficult childhoods and come out of them with flying colors. You're someone who's done that, Carrie. But if I'd even dreamed that you would accuse me of such terrible things..."

His expression seemed genuinely anguished. "Are you telling me you honestly don't remember what really happened to you as a child?"

"What *really* happened? I know damn well what *really* happened. You molested me. And I don't believe a word you're saying about wanting me here. There's something else..."

There was something else, some other reason. She knew it. What was he up to? Why was he doing this?

"No, Carrie," he said gently. "It did not happen the way you've remembered it. Not at all. Somehow, over the years, your memories have become twisted. Carrie...I'm sorry to have to say this, but you've mixed us up."

Her mind whirled. "Mixed up? Who? What the hell are you talking about?"

"Carrie, when children are abused, they often have memories, as adults, that are skewed. They may think it was one person who abused them when it was another. They may even have what they think is a true memory of being abused. Then, later, it turns out that the memory is false."

"I know all about the false-memory syndrome," she said angrily. "I assure you, my memory is crystal clear."

Breen sighed deeply. "Not if you think I abused you, Carrie. Because it definitely was not me. My dear child...you have mixed me up with your father."

15

When her senses returned, Carrie's first clear thought was that she was indeed sick, just as Breen had said. Then her strength came back, and along with it rage.

"Just how far will you go?" she said in a low, icy voice. "And how dare you say such things about my father? No, never mind, I know. You'll say anything now to stop me, to make me doubt myself—and to save yourself. You are more of a monster than I ever dreamed."

"Think, Carrie. Don't you remember? Think back."

"I have thought back! It's all I've done for days now. I thought I'd put your rotten soul behind me, but I don't know now if I ever will. I remember *you* in the church basement. I remember how *you* taunted me with my doll, not giving her to me till I..." Her mouth went dry. Words failed her.

"Carrie, please. I can help you with this. We can sort it out."

He pulled out the chair in front of his desk, urging her to sit. She ignored it, sliding instead onto the needlepoint chair along the wall, as her legs had gone weak.

Returning to his own chair, Breen folded his arms on the desk and leaned toward her. "Go way back, Carrie. Try to remember. Who else could it be?"

She didn't want to listen, didn't want to do as he

said. But a memory swept by, suddenly, blurred like an old photograph that had faded with time. She rubbed her eyes, as if to clear them of whatever had caused the blurring. All she felt there were tears.

"I don't want to do this," she heard herself say. But the voice came from childhood, tiny and insignificant. She was like an infant again, or a teenage girl in a doctor's waiting room, waiting for her first internal exam. Afraid. Exposed.

"I know, Carrie," Breen said gently. "I know. But trust me. If you get it out, it can only help. Remember how you came to me when it was happening to you? You told me I was the only one you could talk to. I swear to you, it was your father, Carrie. Not me."

"Liar," she whimpered, still in that childlike voice, still wiping at tears. "Liar."

"Think back, Carrie. Remember how he drank? Remember how your mother hid that? She hid other things, too."

Carrie came back to life. Without conscious thought she jumped to her feet, crossing the short distance to his desk in three angry strides, reaching over the desk to strike him. "Don't you dare talk about my mother that way! She was a good mother, she did everything she could, she tried to protect—"

But instead of striking him, her hand paused midway and flew to her mouth.

A memory. Her father drinking.

All right, he drank. But he never—

"Remember the plane?" Breen prompted. "Remember the red model plane? You came to me, crying about it, Carrie. Remember what happened?"

Like a rogue wave, the memory overtook her. *The red model plane.*

Clear and sharp suddenly was a Christmas morning when Jimmy Gresimer, a boy who lived down the street, had given her a model airplane that he'd built. She had gotten up early, and when Jimmy's soft knock came at the door she was sitting cross-legged by the Christmas tree in her pajamas and robe, playing with the Lionel train her mother put together every year on Christmas Eve. The morning air was icy, and there were dimestore candies on the coffee table, their artificial chocolate scent blending with that of pine. Carrie had asked for a skating doll, and her mother had fixed up an old doll with a skating costume and tiny white figure skates, since the "real" skating dolls at the store were too expensive. She had somehow managed to buy white figure skates for Carrie, too. "So that the next time the ponds freeze over, honey, you won't have to wear those awful old hockey skates I got at the rummage sale."

Alice had nearly always seen to it that her daughter got the things she asked for.

She had tried.

But the other thing Carrie remembered was that the reason she got up quietly and alone on Christmas mornings was that her father would have been out drinking. And if he woke before he was ready, there would be hell to pay.

When Jimmy Gresimer knocked at her door that Christmas morning, scarcely concealing behind his back her present, a red model plane, Carrie was both overjoyed and embarrassed. She had coveted that plane for months. Its wing span was nearly three feet, and Jimmy had covered the fragile sticks of balsa wood in bright crimson tissue. The plane was a work of art, and Carrie didn't know what to say when he gifted her with it. Excited, but nervous at the unexpected show of friendship, she'd offered Jimmy some cookies. Then, getting out a bottle of milk, she'd dropped it. There was a loud, resounding crash as the heavy bottle hit the bottom of the fridge on its way to the floor. Her father came stumbling from the bedroom, his hungover face contorted with rage.

"What the hell?"

Alice rushed out after him, her hair in curlers, her expression one of fear. "It's nothing, Jack! I'll clean it up. Go back to bed."

She ran for a mop, shooing Carrie and Jimmy into the living room, out of the way. Carrie's father continued to shout, but then went back to bed. It seemed that all was well.

Later that day, however, after the turkey dinner Alice had cooked, Carrie watched in horror as her father stood in the living room, swaying drunkenly, the red airplane in his right hand, pretending to make it fly— up and down, up and down, the delicate wings bending, cracking—

"No! Daddy, don't! Please don't, it'll break! Stop, Daddy, please!"

A laugh. The words slurring. "Won't break, watch!"

The plane soared in the drunken hand, faster and faster, too much for its fragile structure, a wing tearing and falling, then another.

Carrie had run to her room, crying.

"No big deal," her father had taunted, laughing. "Don't be such a crybaby. Stupid little plane."

He had stumbled off into the night, not returning for three days.

At least, that was the way Carrie had remembered the incident over the years. Now, in this small church office, she was horrified to recall that the night had not, in fact, ended that way. Rather, her father had come to her room late that night and apologized for breaking her plane.

"I'm sorry, Carrie. I didn't mean it." He had stroked her cheek, wiping her tears away, and she had snuggled up against him, grateful for this small and unusual show of comfort. But her father's hand had moved down to her bottom, rubbing, then up to her breast. His mouth had followed, tugging at her flat, childish nipple. "It's okay, honey, don't stiffen up like that. Relax. Let me make you feel better."

Remembering, Carrie stood before Christopher Breen and felt her entire world revolve, then explode before her.

She began to cry in deep, gulping sobs. Breen came around his desk and put a hand on her shoulder. He patted it stiffly, awkwardly. "I'm so sorry, Carrie. I didn't realize... I honestly thought you remembered."

Carrie jerked away, wiping at her eyes. "Damn you for bringing me here! Damn you for—"

But she no longer knew what to damn him for. All those memories, all those years...

She felt them gather force inside her, the old pictures evolving into something different, something more terrible than all the rest as other memories rushed back. Her father coming to her room, her father with her on the beach alone at night, her father...

Shattered, Carrie turned on her heel and ran.

When Carrie had gone, Breen sat for a long time, fingers laced together, staring at the picture of Joseph with the brothers who had betrayed him, throwing him into a pit for his coat of many colors.

He thought of Carrie's parents, remembering with distaste the father, playing the pipe organ in church on Sundays, pretending to be righteous and good. Except for the Sundays he "wasn't well" and stayed home nursing a hangover.

No one at church knew the truth, of course, because the mother covered up the drinking. He, Breen, had only known the entire story because Carrie had told him. Breen had sat in for Carrie's father on Sundays, at the organ, when he had been on a weekend binge. He remembered hating to touch the keys, as if they were tainted from Jack Holder's having been at them— the same way he was always at Carrie.

The mother, Alice, wasn't much better. Too afraid of her husband to raise a hand, too afraid to protect her little girl. No wonder Carrie had run to him, looking for a friend.

He remembered how it had begun, Carrie turning to him for solace the first time. A child had fallen from the second story of Carrie's home, a summer visitor whose parents had rented out the Holders' upstairs apartment. Carrie and a friend, both of them around six at the time, had been sitting in the shade beneath the stairs when they heard a terrible thudding sound. Shock set in as they turned and saw the two-year-old lying still and pale on the gravel. Carrie had held her fear in all week, then broken down in Sunday school. Chris had been assisting the Sunday school teacher, playing his guitar, the children singing along, and he had stopped to hold Carrie on his knee, comforting her until her shaking had stopped. The Sunday school teacher brought Carrie a glass of juice, but she hadn't been able to drink it. She was still seeing the little girl, the crumpled body.

The child had lived, but would never be the same. The parents, in their grief, had "cursed" Carrie's entire family, rather than shoulder the blame for the accident themselves. Carrie had asked him that Sunday about curses, and if that meant God would make her and her parents suffer from that day on, as her father had said. Alice, she added, had laughed at the curse.

Chris had looked at the frightened child, her lips trembling and the green eyes full of unshed tears. He realized the other children were watching, waiting for his answer. He tried to reassure Carrie. But given the way his own life had gone thus far, he couldn't reassure anyone that God was a God of love, not vengeance.

He had felt such compassion for that child. Still did, for that matter. The child she used to be, and the adult she'd become. And now...to have her come back here and accuse him...

The clock on the mantel, a Baby Ben, sounded the hour with mournful tones.

If people hear about this, he thought, they might believe her. All the supporters, the voters, the believers. She could ruin everything now.

Somehow, she had to be stopped.

16

Warm rain came down in torrents. Carrie wiped at tears that flowed constantly, obscuring her vision. Still, she could barely see through the rain-streaked windshield. She rubbed at fog inside the window with a fist, cussing and crying. *Where is that damned house?*

On previous visits to Holly Beach she had studiously avoided looking for her old home, and was shocked now by how much the area had changed. Where there had once been open lots with only holly, bayberry and pine, there were tattered motels and restaurants that had been built quickly to take advantage of the burgeoning tourist trade in the eighties. Many were falling into disrepair.

Tell me it's not gone, she cried silently. It's got to be here. If I can find my house, I'll know.

Turning down one street and then another, she swerved and braked, avoiding fools on bicycles out in the storm. Once she blew her horn loudly and long, startling a cyclist so much that he ran up onto a sidewalk. She swore at him, too, though he couldn't have heard.

Poor man. He's no more a fool than I. A damned fool. All this time.

Pulling over to the curb, she let the car idle, willing her hands to stop shaking.

She tried to sort out the truth, tried to tell herself Breen had been lying and that even that memory of the red plane had been wrong. But now when she thought of Breen touching her, her father's face was superimposed over his. Even that incident in the old pastor's study, when she'd hidden among the choir robes...now it was her father outside, her father's footsteps coming closer and closer while her heart raced and her bowels twisted, her blood turning to ice. And now the memory went further than it ever had, as she saw the doorknob twisting, the door opening, her father's face...

Tears came in torrents, greater than the rain, and it no longer mattered that she could barely see. She stabbed a foot on the accelerator and pulled out into the street. She had to find it, had to know. The house would tell her—the house she had lived in for the first twelve years of her life and could not raise a pure fond memory of, no matter how hard she tried.

The key word, of course, was *pure*. Every now and then over the past twenty years, someone—a shrink, a curious friend—had tried to raise a happy memory of Carrie's life in the house on Ocean Avenue. But in wiping out the pain, Carrie realized now, she had wiped out the good that must have happened, too. Any gentle, loving thing. She had preferred to build a new history to replace the old. New memories to wipe the much-too-painful ones away.

Now, however, Breen's revelation had opened a secret vault, one that had been closed up tight for far too long, so that the poisonous memories had bloated and expanded and could not help bursting forth. One ugly scene poured out over another as she remembered the things her father had done.

He had beaten her mother, time after time. Carrie

hadn't forgotten this, but she'd hidden it in that secret vault and left it there. He had taken away her mother's health—and hers, too. Carrie remembered now how she had developed a jerking in all her muscles—stomach, arms, legs and jaw—when she was eight years old. "Nerves," the doctor had said.

Her mother had laughed. "Children that age don't have nerves."

Minor tics, largely unnoticeable, came back even now when Carrie was under stress, as did the nightmares she'd been plagued with all her life.

And there was always the depression that would surface, seemingly for no reason at all.

Turning a corner, she saw the house suddenly. It was over a block away and a half block up from the beach. The streets were crowded with parked cars. Jerking the wheel, Carrie pulled into the first vacant space she came to. Standing outside the car on the sidewalk, she began to shake again. Parts of the sidewalk lay crumbled by high tides and storms, and bayberry grew wild in the cracks. Still in her dressy summer sandals, Carrie stumbled over jagged stones and sticky brambles, scraping her toes. A fiddler crab scuttled close to one foot, then rushed sideways into a sandy hole alongside the paving.

With the old, sweet scent of wild bayberry in her nostrils raising even more devils, Carrie pushed on.

She didn't know what she'd expected to find. Or how she would get inside. She only knew she would, somehow. Feverishly, she had come up with schemes while driving. She might tell the owner she'd grown up here, and ask if she could see her old room. People did that sometimes. **Fai**ling that, she might introduce herself as a well-known author whose first stirrings of talent had begun here. With any luck, the owner would be impressed—or at least feel safe enough to welcome her inside.

None of the plans that rose from her tortured mind proved necessary, however. It was almost as if the house had entered into a pact with her long ago: it would wait. The small beach cottage, once surrounded by block after block of vacant scrub, now crouched defensively between a motel and a deli, its white paint flaking. A peeling For Sale sign had been staked into the tiny patch of front yard.

Glancing around, Carrie noted that the few other remaining cottages on this side of the street had For Sale signs in front of them, as well. A new hotel moving in? she wondered. Or was the neighborhood being abandoned?

She stood on the sidewalk watching for indications of life inside the house and found none. Carrie shivered. Her bare skin felt taut against the thickening air, her nerves rigid with renewed fear. She went up the three steps to the porch and knocked. No one answered. She hesitated, then crossed to the living room window. The pane was encrusted with salt and dirt, and she scratched a round opening to see through, half expecting someone to peer back at her—perhaps an apparition of herself, an ugly, too tall, too skinny ten-year-old girl. Carrie swallowed, wrapping her arms around herself in unconscious self-protection.

But the house was vacant. There was no furniture, and the floors were strewn with the kind of litter left behind when people moved.

She went back and tried the door. It was locked. Carrie left the porch and walked around to the driveway, where someone had put down crushed white shell. Tall sea grass grew through the shell, and dandelions. She heard breakers from the ocean and smelled a sharp tang of fish on the sticky, storm-laden air. Over all lay a heavy, brooding aura of depression.

Walking cautiously behind the house, expecting at every step to be stopped by a neighbor or Realtor, Carrie paused next to stairs leading up to what once had been an apartment her parents leased to summer visitors. An old memory flitted by, giving her a chill. It was gone before she was able to catch it.

Moving on, she stood before the old garage. It had been converted into a small apartment, and it, too, seemed vacant. No one challenged Carrie's right to be there—no one from the deli to the left or the motel to the right. Perhaps, she thought, the real estate company often sent people to look around on their own.

Or perhaps no one in this now seedy neighborhood cared.

She followed a path to the shallow back steps, leading to a pantry door. It hung half-open on a broken hinge, and she remembered that it always had. She stepped up, pushing the door open. A loud screech accompanied her entry into the pantry, and she flinched, hearing angry words in her head. *"Carrie, can't you be more quiet? You wake your father up and you'll be sorry, young lady!"*

Carrie had used a curtain rod or a bucket to prop open the door, as a child.

She stood motionless, hardly daring to breathe, then took a step forward into the kitchen. With shock, she saw that the floor, though worn, was as it had always been—black-and-white-checked linoleum, the white squares yellow from a buildup of wax. Her throat tightened. She had strong second thoughts about intruding here. Too little had changed. She was frightened, without knowing why.

Tiptoeing into the living room, Carrie was shocked to see how much smaller the house was than she'd remembered. How could so much have happened within these narrow rooms? So much unhappiness, squeezed into so little space.

This was where she had played on the floor Christmas mornings. Plaster was cracked, and the fireplace, its outer bricks black with soot, held papers and rusting cans. An odor of mildew permeated the entire house. That, and dampness and rot. A yellowed window shade hung crookedly, soiled fingerprints along its bottom edge.

Carrie remembered Patsy, her dog, jumping for the strings on those shades, or ones much like them, when they blew in the wind.

She remembered Patsy and felt weak, sinking cross-legged to the floor.

It was her birthday, and she had been told to sit in the living room, just like this, and close her eyes. Then suddenly there was a warm bundle of fur skidding over the wooden floor, hurtling into her arms. Patsy.

The dog—half collie, half malamute—was to be her best friend for two years, from the time Carrie was nine.

They had played hide-and-seek in the vacant lots. Carrie would tell her, "Wait here, Patsy," and the dog would stay. Then Carrie would run off, sometimes blocks away, and once hidden in the scrub and low trees, she would give a whistle. Patsy would come running and find her, no matter how far she had gone.

There were nights when she had cried into Patsy's

fur, and days when she saved the dog from being beaten with a paper for dragging dead fish home from the beach and proudly dropping them on the beds.

They were always saving each other, she and Patsy. Like the time she had fallen, roller-skating on the uneven sidewalks, and torn open her knee. Patsy had licked the wound as if trying to heal it, then had gone for help. "Go get Mom," Carrie had ordered, and Patsy took off—a black-and-brown streak of longhaired mix, more loyal than Lassie, more brave than Rin-Tin-Tin.

True to her mission, Patsy came back with Alice, who had driven them both home in the car.

Then one night, after Carrie had been in bed for a while but was not yet asleep, she heard her father on the phone. He had been drinking, and her mother was out. She heard him say, "I have a dog I want put to sleep. Wondered when you could do it. No, nothing's wrong with her, we just can't have her around anymore. This weekend? Fine."

There was nothing to compare with the terror that flooded through Carrie at those words.

She lay rigid and frightened, out of her mind. Not Patsy—he can't be talking about Patsy, she told herself over and over, her entire body shaking. But as she listened to her father make the arrangements, she knew that he was. The pain, the incredible, unbelievable hurt, rammed into her gut and went on and on.

Early in the morning, drained from crying, from doing it quietly so that Daddy wouldn't know she had heard, she held Patsy in her arms and murmured plans. They would run away. They would live together in the woods or find a home somewhere in the country where they were both loved and could stay. For if Carrie needed final proof that her parents didn't want her, didn't love her, she had it in the fact that they were taking her best friend away.

She knew she had done something wrong—something so terrible, so unforgivable, they had to teach her a lesson that she wouldn't forget.

Like the time Alice gave her toys to Judy Reinhardt, down the street.

Carrie had spilled water on her friend's play stove, shorting the wires, and Alice, faced with an angry parent, had given the child all of Carrie's favorite toys.

"You should've been more careful," Alice said, tears streaming from her own eyes as she put the treasured items into brown paper bags: Carrie's toy sewing machine, her games, her marbles...and Christy, the doll she told her troubles to. "You have to learn," her mother said, tossing Christy into the bag.

Carrie couldn't think what she might have done that was worse than that, bad enough to make them take Patsy away. And it was only at this moment, standing here years later, that she saw how totally without power she had come to feel.

Because the way it actually happened was that she'd carried out none of the noble, Lassie-like deeds she had planned for saving her dog. Instead, she went to her grandparents' farm that Friday as arranged, and afterward, she couldn't remember the weekend at all.

Did she feel anger those two days, knowing they were killing her dog? Remorse or pain? Or had she blocked out the entire thing? Even now, she didn't know.

She did remember her father picking her up in the car Sunday night and driving her home.

"I have bad news," he'd said. "Patsy ran away."

Carrie had scrunched into the far corner by the car door, her throat filling with tears. She didn't challenge her father. She never told either parent that she knew. But the way she would always see her father after that was as someone who performed cruel acts, then lied.

Carrie had run to her room and huddled under the covers. She had cried for so long and so hard that her mother had finally come in and pleaded, "You've got to stop crying, Carrie. You're scaring me now."

Carrie wanted to frighten her mother. She wanted to frighten them all, to teach them that they couldn't do things like this to her again.

She had, eventually, stopped crying. And Patsy was never mentioned again until Carrie was older, in her teens, and she and Alice were living in Philly.

"He was jealous of the dog," her mother told her then. "It was better to let her be put to sleep. Once I caught him burning her. He was supposed to be burning off ticks—you know, the way we did it, with a match? But he was holding a lighted cigarette against her skin and she was crying. He had hold of her fur and wouldn't let go."

Thunder crashed, and Carrie came back to the present. She was surprised to find that there were tears on her face. She wiped them away. A shade flapped behind her in the room that used to be hers. She got to her feet and followed the sound. In the now empty room, she stared at the ceiling.

Remembering.

"Don't! Please, Jack, don't!" Her mother, crying *softly in the next room at night, her words muffled with pain.*

Carrie, at nine, was in some ways naive, yet horribly lacking in innocence. She didn't know much about sex between a man and woman. She knew what was being done to her—that it was terrible and ugly and wrong. But she didn't know what married men and women did in their beds, except for what some of the boys in the schoolyard whispered about, the *F* word. The other girls telling her what it meant. "Putting it in." Into that awfully little place…a place she couldn't even see.

She had tried to imagine the act her friends described and knew it would have to hurt. She was glad that no one had done that, at least, to her yet.

She was frightened the night she heard her mother crying, "No, you're hurting me, Jack!" But she couldn't go into her parents' room and see what was happening. Her father would hit her, she knew.

Later, on a weekend home from college, her mother had told her about that, too. They were having coffee one Saturday morning at the little breakfast bar in their Philadelphia kitchen. In a rare moment of confiding, of ruminating over the past, Alice had tugged at a curl of her graying red hair and said, "He used to come home late at night drunk, and he'd beat me. He'd force me to…you know…and it was like he didn't even know I was there."

Even then, at twenty, Carrie had begun to shake as her mother talked.

"Why did you let him?" she remembered saying, her throat so tight, her whole body so frightened it hurt.

A shrug. A quick draw at the ever-present cigarette, lipstick bleeding into weary lines around Alice's mouth. "I thought I had to."

Now, with all the locks torn open, all the memories flooding back, Carrie stared at the ceiling of her old room and remembered how she had lain in bed in this room, memorizing every swirl of plaster.

There had been that night the summer she was ten. Her mother was out and Daddy had come to her room. He had lain down beside her, just holding her awhile, the way she knew her friends' fathers sometimes did. She had snuggled up against him, as she had when she was younger and had run into her parents' room after a bad dream. It felt good with Daddy, safe and secure. Until his hand slipped inside her cotton pajama top, feeling her. Rubbing her chest, squeezing at her nipple, the way...

The way she had thought she remembered Christopher Breen doing. But now again her father's face was superimposed on his, and it was her father's hands invading, not Breen's. As if there were something special about it, that nub of skin, something she didn't understand but knew was wrong.

She remembered now, staring at the ceiling, frozen, pretending it wasn't happening, pretending he wasn't there. His lips, his beery breath on her mouth, his hand sliding down to the waistband of her pajama bottom. Her hand stopping him. "No!" A plaintive no, a pleading. This is *wrong. It's wrong.*

His fingers tugging. "Come on, honey. Just take these off, okay?"

Whimpering. "I don't want to."

"It's all right. I just want to see you, honey."

Crying.

"Please, Carrie?" His hand between her legs now, stroking, even though she held them together hard. Held her whole body stiff and unyielding, and her breath the same way. Standing it as long as she could. Then, pushing at him, pushing away. Running.

Running to the bathroom. Slamming the door. Turning the old-fashioned skeleton key. Backing up, sitting on the edge of the claw-foot tub, doubled over, hugging herself with her arms.

And cold.

So cold. So scared.

Daddy knocking at the door.

"Carrie? Come on out, honey."

Silence.

A few minutes later, his tone anxious. "Carrie? Your mom will be home soon. Come on out. I won't hurt you."

Covering her ears with her hands. The knocking louder, then Afraid he'd do something awful, like the time he was hitting her mother and she tried to call the police. He had yanked his hunting rifle from the linen closet and jammed it against her mother's throat.

"You put that phone down right now, little girl! You want me to shoot?"

Remembering the rifle, afraid he would break down the door and get it again…make her come out…make her do those things with him. The memories like an assault, a fresh new attack.

Sliding down onto the bathroom floor. Squeezing into the tight space between the toilet and wall. So afraid.

Then suddenly, strangely, feeling nothing so much as numb.

He's gone away.

But staying there, hunched, not moving until she heard her mother's voice. Hardly aware that time had passed.

"Carrie? Are you in there?"

Opening her eyes.

"Carrie?"

Looking around and seeing where she was. Slowly

pulling herself up. Flushing the toilet, running water in the sink. Pretending to wash her face. "Yes."

"You okay?"

"Yes."

Coming out, but not looking at her mother. Ashamed, embarrassed. Afraid her mother would guess. Crawling into bed in the dark. Crying herself to sleep. Not looking at her daddy at breakfast, ignoring his teasing about her angry silence. "Miss Priss is in a bad mood this morning. You get up on the wrong side of the bed, Miss Priss?"

As if it were silly, as if she were silly. As if she had no right to feel that what he had done to her was wrong.

And then at school, wondering if everyone could tell. Feeling numb all day. And after that, for years.

Numb for years, and different. Different and ugly... alone.

17

Carrie had no idea how she got back to the Crest Inn. One minute she was running to her car, shoving the key in the ignition, a terrible pain crushing her chest. The next thing she knew she was lying on the bed in her room at the Crest, shivering, covers pulled to her chin despite the late afternoon heat. Physical pain slipped into something else, something worse that went on and on. Her mind raced in twenty directions at once.

Is it possible? Did those things really happen with my father?

They must have. They were far too real to deny.

But if they did happen—how had she survived? Hadn't there been too much? Too much for one small child?

I survived by forgetting.

As swiftly as the thought came, she knew it to be true.

The mind is a complex organ. It saved me, without my ever knowing how or why.

Then what about Breen? What about the things she *still* thought he had done, could still see him doing whenever she closed her eyes, no matter what he said?

Dear God. Somebody help me. Somebody help me, please.

She had never been close to her father. Because of his drinking she had been afraid of him. Yet there were moments when she had tried, tried to be close, the way other kids were close to their parents. *Children will forgive their parents anything,* Esther Gordon had said. *They come out of the womb loving and needing to be loved. It can take a parent years of abuse to destroy that love. And even then...*

Yet it had been Breen she remembered. Always, and at all times, it had been Breen. No one else.

He had called them false memories. Carrie tried to remember what she had learned in recent years about that. There were women, she knew, who had been accused of having false memories of abuse. Many times, it seemed the memories actually were false. In a number of cases, however, they had proved to be true. Evidence had backed them up.

So what about the false ones? Where did they come from? It seemed no one really knew. Hypnotists were blamed, and dishonest therapists. "Using the patient to further their own agenda," some said. There were other theories, as well, most of them having to do with the invalidation of women. "She imagined it. She wanted revenge. She's sick."

Things haven't changed much, Carrie thought, since the days of Freud. Men still fear women so much they continue to devise ways to put us down.

Exhausted, she noted the bitterness in her thoughts and could no longer contain them. Turning onto her stomach, she shoved her head under the pillow and drifted into an uneasy sleep.

Her last thoughts were of Christopher Breen, not her father. It was he who held a red model plane above her head, the plane swooping and diving, then crashing with a thudding finality into her heart.

* * *

Carrie stood several feet above the floor in a large room. At the far end was a piano, and she floated toward it, overwhelmed with joy. She sat at the piano to play, though she had never been able to play by ear. Now she was certain that she would strike just the right chords, and though the song she played might not be known, it would be her song—a triumphant, harmonic melody that would please.

Placing her hands over the keyboard, she brought them down. She played chords with both hands, then a melody with the right—crashing, pounding sounds that made her feel empowered and happy, that made her feel strong.

Then, suddenly, the piano was mute. No key would play, and she understood that she had broken the soundboard. She had ruined everything, as she always did. She felt deep sadness and a sense of loss.

As she watched with growing horror, the keys began to move by themselves, like a player piano with no scroll. Ugly, discordant noises issued from the keyboard, frightening sounds like that of devils howling, and she knew that something else had taken over, was in this room with her, threatening her life, even her soul. Unseen hands pushed at her back, then clutched her throat, twisting and bending her into painful contractions and shapes, mouthing evil words into her ears, laughing with hot breath against her mouth, pinching with hard, sharp fingers at her breasts, moving downward, downward, parting her thighs....

Carrie ran from the room, terrified. She staggered through double doors onto a porch. The night was dark and freezing; the chill air hit her fevered skin like a blow. The hateful music grew louder. It gushed from the windows of the house like pus from a broken boil.

She felt it pour against the back of her neck and gagged at its foul smell. She had no coat, no shoes, she was barefoot, but she ran without looking back, faster and faster, her breath short and painful, her heart pounding.

The music followed. It poured from every opening of the house, then every opening of herself, louder and louder, chasing, then becoming part of her. Carrie screamed in her throat, "Someone help me, help me get away!" She began to fly in the manner of someone swimming through heavy water, with panicky breast-strokes, lifting herself higher and higher, getting nowhere, then gaining, losing—her life's energy, in the struggle, draining away. At last she was above the other houses, above the town, and she knew that soon everything would be all right. She was going to her mother, to the one person who would make her safe.

She walked into a hospital, a child in an adult body, crying, and approached a nurse. "I have to see my mother, she's expecting me." The nurse rolled her eyes as if Carrie were always bothering her mother—a busy doctor, everyone knew.

Then her mother came out into the hallway toward her, not red-haired Alice, but someone short of stature, plump, in a black dress, with black hair. She held out her arms and Carrie flew into them, sobbing, hanging on tight and feeling her mother's arms come around her, reassuring and close. "I'm so scared," she cried. "Mother, I've seen him, I've seen him!"

Her mother's arms tightened even more. Her mother knew. She understood. Other people were standing around, people who were skeptical. Carrie knew they didn't believe her. But her mother did. Thank God!

Carrie awoke.

Lying rigid, hardly daring to breathe, she saw every moment of the dream before her, as if it had truly occurred. She knew that her mother in the dream was not Alice, but the therapist, Esther Gordon, and she knew she should think about that, about what it meant. But it gradually came to her that the cries that issued from her lips in the dream were real, and they were coming not from her, but from somewhere on the other side of her wall, in the D'Amico house. They grew stronger, piercing.

"Mommy! *Mommy!*"

Before she realized what she was doing, Carrie flew from the bed. Grabbing the terry cloth robe, she flung it over herself as she raced to the door. Her hand grabbed the knob, slipped, grabbed again. Jerking the door open, she followed the sound of the cries, running along the landing to the door Helen had pointed out the first day, the one leading to Sally's room. Carrie's bare feet slapped against the wooden floor. She felt a splinter dig into her right foot, but didn't stop. If she hadn't been brought up short, she would, without thinking, have flung open Sally's door. But the curtains over the French doors were open, and the sight in the young girl's room stopped Carrie cold.

At first glance, the room looked like that of a typical teenager. There were posters of rock stars, stuffed animals, a guitar hanging on one wall and a traffic light that blinked red and green in a corner. On a dressing table were powder and perfumes, lipsticks and makeup brushes.

But there was nothing typical about Sally now. She sat in her bed, huddled against a white wicker headboard, her arms wrapped around herself tightly. Nicky was in the room with Sally, and she was crying, "Stop it, Nicky! Leave me alone!"

Carrie stood stock-still. What was he doing? What was wrong? *And where was the mother?*

Even as she thought it, Helen ran into the room, knelt beside Sally on the bed and put her arms around her. Carrie couldn't hear the words she murmured to Nicky. But he turned angrily on his heel. For a brief moment his eyes met Carrie's through the door. Then he turned the opposite way and strode across the room, slamming the inside door behind him.

Helen D'Amico crooned, "Shh. It's all right, honey, I'm here. It's all right. Oh, baby, baby, my sweet little Sal."

"Mommy, I hate Nicky! I hate him!"

"Shh, baby, shh. It's all right. It's all right."

Carrie slowly backed away. Returning to her room, she stumbled over the threshold, fighting for balance. Her hand gripped the door frame, then the knob. She half fell through the doorway. Closing it, she leaned against it, shaking. There were tears in her eyes and her mouth trembled. She tasted blood inside her cheek from biting down so hard to keep from crying aloud.

"What is it?" she whispered. "What the *hell* is going on?"

Her hand went out, as if she might in some way comfort Sally through the walls. But her knees buckled and she sank onto the bed, her arms wrapping around her legs in a fetal position. She stayed that way for a long time, and when, hours later, a knock came at her door, her eyes were closed, though none of the ghosts had gone.

"Carrie? Carrie, are you awake?"

Helen D'Amico's voice carried to her, through a fog.

"Carrie? I'm so sorry to bother you, but there's a phone call. A Nan Martin. About your grandmother, she said."

Carrie opened swollen eyes and squinted at the small travel clock next to her bed. Ten after five in the morning. Shaking her head to free it of cobwebs, she ran to the door, tightening the belt of the robe she still wore.

"My grandmother?" Anxiety pushed its way through her tired mind.

"It sounds urgent," Helen said. "Otherwise, I wouldn't have woken you. I can transfer it up here, if you like."

"Yes, yes, that'd be good. Thank you."

There were dark circles under Helen D'Amico's eyes and lines that hadn't been as visible the day before. As Carrie waited for Helen to transfer the call, she wondered what had transpired in Sally's room that night. She wondered, too, at her own reaction to it.

Wouldn't it have been more normal to have tapped on Sally's door and asked if everything was all right? Wasn't that what most people would have done? Why had that scene in Sally's room so paralyzed her that she'd been unable to do anything but sleep?

A small red light on the telephone began to flash, and Carrie quickly grabbed up the receiver.

"Nan? What's wrong?"

"Hi, Carrie. Sorry to call at this hour. I don't want to alarm you unnecessarily, but your grandmother has been, shall we say, agitated. She claims she woke up and saw someone trying to break in through her window. Security checked the grounds and the building thoroughly, and there was no one here who shouldn't have been here, only a doctor and a couple of people visiting other patients who were restless—''

"Wait a minute. I don't understand. My grandmother told you she saw this person? She's speaking?"

"That's the good news. Loud and clear. For a few minutes, at least. She woke everyone, yelling. I'd asked the nurses to keep me apprised of Elizabeth's condition and to call me right away if it changed. Your grandmother's been gradually calming down ever since, and she's sleeping now. She still seems restless, though. As if there were a million demons waging some battle in her head. I thought you'd want to know."

"Absolutely. I'm glad you called, Nan. I'll get dressed and come right over."

"I don't know if that's really necessary. But you always did have a calming effect on her. In fact, I'm surprised this is going on now, when you're here."

"She's never done this before?"

"Never."

"Nan, I'll be there in a few minutes. I just have to dress. Will you stay with her till I get there?"

"Absolutely."

She found Nan at her grandmother's side. Elizabeth was sleeping, and Carrie murmured her thanks.

"No problem." Nan stood and yawned. "I need to catch a few winks before the day begins, though. I'll talk to you later, if that's all right?"

"Sure."

Carrie sat in the chair left vacant by Nan. Elizabeth's eyes were still closed, her chest rising slowly and evenly beneath the embroidered silk nightgown Carrie had brought her on her last visit. The long sleeves had become pushed up, and Carrie's heart broke at sight of the thin arms, the tendons and veins standing out in sharp relief, the "age" spots on Elizabeth's hands. Carrie was sure that in her more lucid moments, her grandmother would be horrified to see her most despised flaws exposed like this. Gently, she reached out to pull the sleeves of the nightgown down, settling them as well as she could over the spotted flesh.

Though as a child she hadn't seen it as such, Carrie knew that Elizabeth had been proud to the point of vanity. For years she had rubbed lemons on those spots, fading them as best she could. There were even vacations that Elizabeth had returned from looking so "rested" Carrie had wondered if she'd gone somewhere for a nip and tuck. Her grandmother had seemed to be fighting a constant battle with age.

But that was many years ago. Elizabeth had been, perhaps, in her early fifties. The fact that her grandmother's vanity stood out in Carrie's mind was largely because she remembered when Elizabeth had stopped caring—or at least fighting. There had come a time when she seemed to go inside herself more, reading books at night and writing in her journal every morning before rising. It was a time when she seemed to take less delight in the Sunday socials, becoming less vivacious and more thoughtful.

Elizabeth stirred.

Carrie jerked to attention. "Grandmother? It's Carrie. I'm here." She took her hand, squeezing it softly.

"Carrie?"

Elizabeth's voice quavered, then strengthened as she tried to sit. "I have to tell you…"

Her hand slipped away as she threw off the covers. Her entire body trembled.

"Grandmother, just rest. Please. It's all right, we can

talk later.'' With much difficulty, Carrie eased her back down.

''But—''

''Shh. We'll have plenty of time.''

''But he came to get me. He tried—''

''Grandmother, it's okay,'' Carrie said soothingly. ''No one's here. The guards checked, and they didn't find anyone. It must have been a shadow. The trees...see how they reflect on the glass?''

Elizabeth shook her head. Tears fell from her eyes. ''He was here. You don't know...''

Carrie stroked her brow. It might be better, she thought, to let her grandmother talk. She seemed to need that. ''Who was here, Grandmother? Who did you see?''

Elizabeth's eyes met hers for several long seconds. She didn't speak, and Carrie thought she might have changed her mind. But then Elizabeth covered her eyes with her hands and began to cry.

''I thought it was over,'' she sobbed. ''I thought he was gone.''

After that, Elizabeth slipped back into that other world, disappearing as surely as if a veil had fallen between them. Carrie sat by her side stroking her hand, feeling that she had lost her yet again. That was the heartbreaking thing about these visits. It was one thing to lose someone once, in death. Yet another to lose them over and over, to have them come back and then leave, come back and leave. Even worse was never knowing when it would happen. Would she ''be here'' today? Or would she be gone? And if she were gone, would she ever again return?

This man her grandmother claimed to have seen at

her window. A nightmare? A delusion? What had she meant when she said, "He came to get me"?

As far as Carrie knew, Elizabeth had never made an enemy in her life. This had to have been a nightmare. Perhaps she had dreamed of her husband, Carrie's grandfather. Perhaps she'd seen Sam Holder in a dream and thought she was about to die, that he had come to take her with him. That might also account for her saying that she thought he was gone. In her confusion, she might have thought, contrarily, that Sam had come back to life.

Carrie released her grandmother's hand and leaned back in the chair. She sighed, so weary she didn't know how she'd make it to the car to drive back to the Crest. "Oh, Grandmother," she said softly, thinking aloud, "if you only knew. Would you help? And what could you possibly do? Hold my hand? Say that little night-time prayer you taught me when I was three? 'Sleep tight, wake up bright to do what's right with all your might...sleep tight.'" She sighed. "I've tried to do what's right, Grandmother. I've tried to live a good life. I may not be the most well-rounded person in the world...or even the most psychologically sound..." At that, a low laugh escaped her lips. "But I've done my best. I put it behind me...I thought. All that business with Breen. I thought he had—well, you don't have to know what I thought he did to me. It was too horrid, too unspeakable. And now I don't even know if I was right about him, or if..."

She realized her voice had risen, and her eyes flew open. *Had Elizabeth heard?*

But her grandmother's eyes were still closed, and the little shudders that had followed her outburst of tears had stopped. Her breathing was once more slow and barely discernible. It was so slow, in fact, her chest seemed not to be moving at all. It was as if—

Please, no! Panicked, Carried jumped to her feet and leaned over her grandmother, putting her ear to the older woman's mouth to listen. For a long moment she heard nothing. Searching for a pulse in Elizabeth's neck, she thought there was none. Carrie felt the world reel beneath her feet, then thunder away.

But then—yes, there it was. A quiet, life-affirming throb beneath her fingers. A soft sigh from the dry, cracked lips.

Oh, thank God. Thank you, God. Carrie fell back into the chair, her legs so weak they would no longer support her. *I will never again complain when she drifts away. Just keep her with me, God. I swear I won't ask for more. Just don't leave me here alone.*

18

At six o'clock that same morning, Ron Devereaux stood in the parking lot outside the exclusive Bahia Hotel, feeling bewildered and nervous. Alan Weiss, the senator, had asked him to come here to this biggest and glitziest hotel on the island. At the far south end, and set apart on several acres, it was one of the few that managed to stay open all year and do well, Ron had heard. He had also heard that there was mob money in the Bahia, and that more illegal deals were made here in one week than in a year in Atlantic City.

But why Senator Alan Weiss would want to talk to him, and at this hour of the morning, was anyone's guess. He had never even met Weiss before he'd come with Chris and the other man to the Sunday school room. Ron had wanted to talk to Chris about this meeting, check it out with him, but Weiss had asked him not to tell anyone. Ron didn't feel comfortable with this, not at all. He just hadn't known how to say no.

Ron tucked his white shirt into the clean jeans, the only thing he'd found in his closet. *I've got to remember to do laundry tomorrow. Darn. I should have dressed better, should have found something, somewhere....*

Swallowing the lump in his throat, he followed a long, winding walk with small signs pointing to the lobby. On either side were gardens with flame-colored tropical flowers. White, decorative fire pits were studded about the garden, between wrought-iron benches. A handful of early birds sat on the benches watching the rising sun, or possibly resting after a run. Ron guessed that they appreciated the heat from those fire pits. He shivered. It could be pretty cool here this early, especially with the tail end of that hurricane still dropping rain and wind on south Jersey every other day. It might not be raining now, but the wind had picked up.

Even so, Ron knew that the cold rushing through and over him wasn't from the wind. He steeled himself against a strong urge to stay right here, not take another step, to park himself on one of those benches under a tree and…well, hide. The last thing he wanted to do was meet with Alan Weiss. What could a senator want with him? And why did he have this shimmery feeling in the pit of his stomach, the one he got only when he knew something was real wrong?

Shrugging off the feeling as best he could, he allowed curiosity to get the better of fear. Rounding a bend to the ocean side of the hotel, he came upon a well-groomed beach. Closer in, a strip of velvety grass and palm trees fronted a lobby that was straight out of an old Arabian Nights movie: stark white turrets, arched windows and doors, striped canopies waving in the morning breeze. Hammocks were slung between some of the palm trees. Rows of white, molded chaise longues, with holes in the arms for cocktail glasses, faced out to sea.

He took that back, about the movie. This was so surreal it seemed more like a Las Vegas casino. Ron imagined the rooms with gold bathroom fixtures, spa tubs and crystal chandeliers. For sure, a room here would cost more than he'd ever be able to afford as an assistant to Chris—provided Chris decided to hire him next year. Still, Ron didn't plan to be an assistant forever. He thought that if he worked hard, did all it took, he could one day—with a tad of luck thrown in, as well—be as good as Chris Breen. Ron loved interning with his childhood idol. But he had grown up poor. He wanted the chance to make good money. Even more, he wanted people to look up to him the way they did to Chris.

Not that they'd ever "look up" to him the same way—physically, that is. Ron had always been short, for a man: five-six. And yes, he knew that wasn't as short as some. Still, when it became apparent Ron had stopped growing, his father had told him that he would have to compensate, make people like him in other ways and for other reasons. "Tall men run the world," his dad had said, shaking his head sadly as he scanned the teenage Ron from head to toe. "Look around you, Ronny. The short guys, they go into movies and TV. People can't tell so much on screen how short they are. Like Dudley Moore, you know, and Dustin Hoffman. They made the most of their wits and talent, and look where it got them. Nobody ever thinks of them as short, not even the women." His father had given him one of those "man-to-man" winks, like when he'd told him about condoms. "It's always been like that, son. Look at Alan Ladd, in the old days."

Ron knew his dad was right. At fifteen, he'd already begun striking out with girls. One day in eighth grade he had screwed up his courage to ask Julie Matthews to the graduation dance. Julie sat in front of him in some of his classes, and she had long, shiny blond hair that he longed to stroke. He just knew it would feel as soft as the fuzz on a peach. Sometimes he'd think so long and hard about touching Julie's hair, he'd get an embarrassing warm feeling in his groin, right there in the middle of class.

Ron was pretty sure she liked him, too. They passed notes back and forth to each other in class—nothing heavy, just funny little things about the teacher, or jokes, which Julie passed on to the kid in front of her. One day, after thinking about it for a good two months, he had written—the pen and his hand both shaking— "I like you." Then he'd waited what seemed a thousand years, just staring at that gorgeous hair, till Julie opened the note and read it. She had turned slightly, giving him a quick, shy glance, her face the color of a beet, her beautiful pouty lips turned up into a smile. So he knew she liked him, too.

But when he asked her to the dance, Julie had laughed and tossed that golden mane of hair, the hair he had longed to stroke. "Ronny, you're a whole head shorter than me!" she said. "We'd look silly!" After the dance he heard from some friends that while he was at home staring at the ceiling over his bed, Julie had been dancing with Lyle Peterson, some kid who worked on the school paper, and who was, Ron knew, several inches taller than him.

Later, when Ron had gotten over the hurt, he'd met a nice, quiet girl who was no more than five-two. They'd dated throughout high school, off and on. Just the formal things that you needed a date for, like the junior and senior proms. Tracy, to be polite, was somewhat empty-headed. She giggled nonstop. And Ron had learned, somewhere along the way, that a girl being a whole head shorter than him wasn't necessarily a good reason to date.

One day, frustrated at this state of affairs, or to be

more accurate, nonaffairs, Ron knelt on the floor of his room, picking up pieces of broken glass. He'd thrown something, he couldn't remember what, across the room. In doing so he'd knocked over and broken his favorite framed photograph of Christopher Breen, the star of a TV show he'd loved when he was little. After he cleaned up the glass, he sat cross-legged on the floor for a long time, looking at himself in the mirror on the sliding closet doors.

So, he had thought finally. *I'll never be tall. Or for that matter, handsome. Not with this nose. But I can be somebody people like. And maybe I can figure a way to be rich.*

It seemed like fate had answered his call when, last winter, Ron had applied for—and gotten—this internship with his childhood idol, Christopher Breen. Chris wasn't classically handsome. More what women called "cute," even at his age, which must, Ron thought, be at least fifty. And he wasn't even excessively tall, not like a basketball star, though at almost six feet, he towered over Ron. One thing, though, Chris had learned was how to make the most of his charm and wit. And he'd certainly become rich.

It was here, only weeks ago, that Ron had finally found his path: he would follow in the footsteps of Christopher Breen.

"So, Ron," Alan Weiss said. "You've been working with Chris for how long now?"

"Since the beginning of summer," Ron said, clearing his throat.

He glanced quickly around the fancy hotel suite, then at the white-haired congressman who had been with Chris and Senator Weiss at the classroom the day

before. Both the congressman and Weiss sat across
from him at a glass conference table. Each had a tumbler of water before him, but neither glass had been
touched. Ron longed to reach for his own water, to
down it in one huge gulp and ease the fire in his dry
throat. But he didn't want to seem nervous. Instead, he
tried to meet the eyes of each man in turn, as if, for
some reason, he was supposed to convince them he had
nothing to hide. They had seemed friendly when they
were with Chris at Anglesea. Now they were stony
faced. He felt like he was before some tribunal. The
Inquisition, or something. But that was a different re-
ligion, wasn't it? He wasn't even Catholic. Shit.

"And what do you think of Chris, now that you've
been with him awhile?" Weiss asked.

Ron shifted uncomfortably. A tic began in his eyelid,
and he imagined everyone could see it. It wasn't as if
he had anything bad to say about Chris. He just didn't
know what they wanted to hear.

"Do you, uh, mind if I ask why you're asking, sir?"

Weiss smiled. "That seems fair enough. I hope
you're not feeling uncomfortable about this, Ron?"

"No…no, sir. I just don't know why I'm here."

The senator nodded, the smile still in place. "I know
Chris has told you that he's been chosen to be national
spokesman for a program called Millennium Child.
This is a new program set up by a special task force,
in answer to a plea by the President. The President
wants to reach children and teens by appealing to what
he believes is their inborn sense of morality."

Weiss paused for a moment, then went on, as if reading from a political pamphlet. "In other words, it is no
longer enough, the President believes, to tell children
to 'just say no.' The children of this new millennium

are independent thinkers, more so than any generation this earth has known. Because of that, their souls, as well as their minds, must be appealed to. They must have a firm foundation grounded in ethics and honor…morality, if you will.''

Ron nodded. "Yes, sir. I do know about that. And I understand the President himself is going to announce Chris's appointment on TV, at the end of the festival on Sunday. Chris is very excited about it.''

"Indeed.'' A brief look passed between the senator and congressman. "Ron, this is a pet project of the President's. And the position as national spokesman is a very responsible, very important one, with high-level visibility.''

"Yes, I understand that, sir.''

"And did you know that Congressman Tanner here is a member of the task force that recommended Chris for that position?''

"Yes, I, uh, Chris told me that last night.''

"Well, Ron, naturally, we must be certain, before sending in our final recommendation, that we have the right man.''

"Well, sure. But I thought that had already been decided. I don't see how you could find anyone better than Chris.''

"Tell us why you say that,'' Weiss suggested. "What do you see as Chris's special qualifications for this position? We realize you haven't been with him long, of course, but in three months you must have formed an opinion.''

Ron shifted uneasily. "Well, yeah, I mean I know I haven't been here long, but I've been a fan of Chris's for years. He's great with kids, and even the parents love him, you know. And there're the movie stars and all the other entertainers. They're on a list to be on his show. I mean, Chris doesn't have to ask them," he said proudly. "*They* ask *him* if they can be on. And he doesn't just put on a show, he spends time with the kids, talking to them and listening to their problems. They aren't all different kids each time, you know, like on some shows. Most of the kids on the shows that are taped in Holly Beach grew up around Chris, and he's always tried to be a role model for them. And when he heads up the Millennium Child program, he'll be bringing in lots of inner-city kids, like street kids who don't have anyone to be a role model...."

Ron stopped short. He was babbling, he knew.

"Yes, we are aware of all that," Weiss said a trifle irritably. "Ron, how do you see Christopher Breen as a person?"

"A person?"

"A man. His private life. What is that like?"

Ron went blank. A few moments passed, and finally he said, "I guess I, uh, don't really know. I mean, Chris is so busy with the show, he doesn't have time for much else."

He looked over at the congressman, who had shifted in his seat and sighed. Ron had begun to think the guy was dead. His hair sure looked like it. Thick and white, it was so stiff and shiny from some spray, or something, it reflected the tiny teardrops in the chandelier above the table.

"Can we get on with this?" the congressman said in a weary voice. "He obviously doesn't know anything—"

Weiss cut him off. "What my friend the congressman means, Ron, is that you apparently haven't spent much time with Chris alone this summer."

"Well, no, not much...I'm usually rehearsing the children, or working backstage, while Chris is on."

If he hadn't liked the feel of this earlier, he liked it even less now. It was almost as if these men—who were supposed to be friends of Chris, he thought—were looking for something on him. Something wrong.

Ron sat straight in his chair and rested his palms on the table. Noting that his hands shook, he made every effort to firm his voice. In spite of himself, it rose. "Sir, I don't mean to offend anyone. But I don't think I know whatever it is you want to know. And I don't like it that you got me down here at this hour of the morning to give me some third-degree about Chris. May I go now?"

There was a moment of heavy silence as Ron felt sweat form on the glass table beneath his hands.

"I apologize," Alan Weiss said at last. "We meant no harm. This is all simply routine. I do hope you understand."

Ron stood and rubbed his hands on his jeans to dry them. "I guess." He turned to go, but Weiss's voice stopped him.

"One thing, Ron."

Geez. He looked back. "Yes?"

"We would appreciate it if you didn't say anything to, uh...to Chris about this." He smiled. "We wouldn't want him to feel uncomfortable, especially with the festival at hand. I'm sure he has quite a bit to do, preparing for it."

Ron hesitated. His first instinct was to drive like heck back to the center and tell Chris *all* about it. But then he figured they were right. Chris had all he could handle right now, with the festival.

"Okay," he said reluctantly. "I won't mention it. At least, not now."

"Not at *all*," Alan Weiss emphasized. "All right, Ron? It's best to be discreet about these things."

Ron didn't answer. *These things.* For the second time that day he swore, though only to himself. What the hell *things?*

Before he left the hotel he made a side trip to the men's rest room, where he washed his face with cold water, then stared at his pale complexion in the mirror. *What's going on? What in the name of God is going on?*

After Ron left, the two men sat looking at each other. The white-haired congressman from Nebraska was the first to break the silence.

Taking a cigar from his inside pocket and lighting up, he said, "Now do you understand why we wanted you in on this, Alan? It looks like he's got everyone hornswoggled, even his own assistant."

Weiss rubbed his eyes and heaved a sigh. "But we still can't be sure. You think the kid will tell Breen we talked to him?"

"Hard to tell," Lloyd Tanner said. "It was a risk."

"I know. But he might have told us something useful. Damn it all! The kid can't see beyond those stars in his eyes."

"And if he talks—and this all turns out to be untrue—we'll be on Breen's shit list for all time. Meantime, Breen? He'll be sitting on the President's knee." The already considerable lines in the old man's face deepened into worried grooves.

"Of course," Weiss said, "it could depend on how

he puts it to Breen. If he tells him what I said, that it was only routine…''

"The kid might have bought that. *Might* have. That's iffy. And if Breen hears about it, he certainly never will."

They were silent for long moments, each lost in his own thoughts. Weiss's stomach growled.

"Hungry?" Tanner asked, tamping his cigar out. "We could order up some eggs."

Weiss shook his head. "Not for me. I can't eat before noon anymore." He patted his stomach. "Indigestion, you know."

The congressman sighed. "The downside of politics. Wait till you're my age."

Weiss stretched and stood, drawing back a curtain to let in the morning light. From the window he could see a length of emerald green grass, the beach and the sun rising over the Atlantic. It rippled like pink silver across the waves, bringing back an image of himself in third grade, singing at the top of his lungs *"From sea to shining sea!"* He remembered the proud swell of his chest at being an American, and it was there in third grade, he thought, though he didn't fully realize it then, that his future took shape.

That, of course, was long before he knew how it all worked. The days when he too had stars in his eyes.

"Look," he said, turning back, "we had to try with the assistant, Lloyd. Chris Breen has been my friend for years. I recommended him to you because I'd have sworn he was pure as the driven snow, the perfect person to head up the President's program. Now, if your constituent is telling the truth…"

"Well, I, for one, tend to believe her," the congressman said firmly. "She's from a good family. They moved away from Holly Beach because of him, she says, and over the years she tried to put it all in the past. But when she heard from a friend on the task force about Breen's pending appointment, she was outraged. She thinks it's a sacrilege that he's still working with little kids.''

''Maybe so. Maybe so. But, Lloyd, you know how much shit comes out of the woodwork when a man is up for a high-profile position like this. Especially a man with star quality like Breen. Women have been known, for whatever reason, to lie about these things.''

''I've considered that, Alan. But let's say it's true. So far, this show of his is big with kids and their parents, and yes, it does pull in the stars. But how many adults really watch these kiddie shows? On a regular basis, I mean. How many really care who's on morning TV? Not many—yet. But when Breen's name becomes a national byword because of the Millennium Child program—and believe me, it will, not only in the schools but in the big corporations when he's out there asking for money—God only knows how many other women might feel as outraged as my constituent. Enough to come forth with their own stories to tell.''

''Again, Lloyd—if it's true. And we have no proof.''

Tanner sighed. ''Must I point out that we've got that tape now? We know there was more than one victim. *May* have been more than one victim,'' he corrected.

''I'll admit the tape was disturbing.''

They had been up all night, playing it over and over, listening for some false note in it, some sign that Breen had been lying to the woman, Carrie Holt, when he swore he hadn't abused her.

''How long have you had him bugged?'' Weiss said.

''Since my constituent first came to me, a week ago.

Naturally, I had to at least consider that she might be out to get Breen for some other reason. As you yourself pointed out, that happens.''

Weiss groaned. ''What a goddamned mess. Lloyd, maybe you should have gone directly to the President with this. If he makes the announcement on national television Sunday about Breen's appointment, and it comes out later that Breen really did molest these women—''

''May I remind you, my dear old friend, that despite our differing political beliefs, we were the ones who recommended Breen to the President in the first place. On our recommendation, the President invited him to give a performance at the White House. They even brought kids in from the inner city to be on the show with him. And now Breen's the President's boy. His kids love him, the first lady loves him, the first grandmothers love him....''

Weiss waved an impatient hand. ''I know, I know. Either way, the President will have our heads. He'll make sure we're tarred with the same brush as Christopher Breen—leaving himself, as much as possible, lily-white. And I say again, what a goddamned mess.''

''Which is why I called you in on this.''

Weiss stood and began to pace. ''Well, I wish you'd done it sooner. With only four days left before the announcement, I don't see what I can do.''

Tanner laced his hands over his ample stomach and leaned back in his chair. ''You could talk to Breen. You're the one who's known him for ten or more years. You're the one whose favorite causes he contributes heavily to.''

''All the more reason,'' Weiss said dryly, ''why I

can't just walk up to him and say, 'By the way, old pal, you don't happen to be a child molester, do you?'"

"Oh, please, Alan. In the thirty years you and I have known each other, you've proven yourself to be quite a diplomat. You might tell Breen, for instance, that certain rumors have arisen, and it might be in his best interest to back out before the announcement Sunday. That way, he wouldn't have to admit to anything. He could simply tell the President he suddenly realized he has too full a plate and wouldn't be able to do justice to such a demanding position."

Weiss shook his head. "Rumors or no, I don't think he'd do that. Just from the little I've seen of him while I've been here, he's flying high on this whole thing. Can't wait to get the program going and make it work."

He gave the congressman a pointed look. "Besides, if he did back out, that could be interpreted as an admission of guilt."

Tanner sighed again. "You're probably right. The only way is to clear him—or get proof and face him with it. But how?"

There was a tap at the door, and their security agent stepped inside.

"Vincent," Weiss said. "Anything?"

Vincent Petrelli shook his head. "Nothing. Breen is clean as a whistle."

"You checked everything? His room at the center? Every conceivable place in the church?"

"I tell you, there's nothing there. No photographs, no kiddie porn. I even checked his computer. Nothing under favorite web sites, no 'cookies' to anything even hinting at an improper interest in little kids."

"But if this thing is real…"

Petrelli nodded. "There should be something. I agree. I just haven't been able to lay my fingers on it. I'll keep at it."

"What if we talk to the woman?" Weiss said. "The one on the tape."

"The writer? Shit, she's a wild card. I followed her for a while. Since Breen threw that at her about her father, she looks like she doesn't know one end from the other. My guess is he did it deliberately to confuse her. And distract her."

"Still—"

"No, Lloyd," Weiss interjected. "It's a bad idea. She's staying at that inn the cop's family owns. And you told me he's already too close to this. If the two of them put their heads together, and he convinces her she was right about Breen all along…"

"All hell could break loose," Tanner agreed reluctantly. "If even a hint of this gets out to the media before we have time to cover our own tails…"

Weiss sat heavily in a chair. "Everything we've worked for will go right down the drain. And we—not only us, Lloyd, but the whole damned task force— might as well resign."

Tanner stood. "Well, I for one do not intend to let that happen."

"Meaning?"

"The woman. Carrie Holt." He lowered his voice. "She can be silenced. So can the cop."

A cold sweat broke out on Weiss's forehead. "Silenced? What are you talking about, Lloyd?"

"I think you know."

Bloodred color rose in the senator's face. "I can't believe you're saying this. I won't—I *can't*—condone that sort of thing!"

"Alan, I have worked too hard and too long to get where I am. I will not be smeared—or forced to resign."

"Listen, Lloyd," Weiss said persuasively, his tone just short of panic. "Even if I agreed with you, it's too late for that sort of thing. What about the woman in Nebraska?"

"She's a constituent. She trusts me. I can handle her, too."

19

Stepping from her car at the Crest Inn, Carrie marveled at the group of elderly people on a side lawn, playing croquet. Where do they get so much energy at this hour of the morning? she wondered. It was not quite nine o'clock, and she felt exhausted, her nerves frayed. She had left her grandmother sleeping peacefully, but couldn't remember the last time she herself had slept through an entire night.

She noted, too, that one of the men she had seen in the kitchen the other night, the one she had taken to be Nicky's father, was mowing the front lawn. It occurred to her now that she had seen him out here other times, weeding flower beds and sweeping the walks. He must be at least thirty years older than me, she thought. Where do people that age get their energy, when I so often feel I've lived a thousand years and can't go another step?

Two of the women playing croquet looked up at her, smiled and waved. Carrie waved back, but headed to her room with her eyes down, hoping she wouldn't have to talk to anyone.

A sound make her glance up. Nicky D'Amico stood outside the D'Amico kitchen door, and it was obvious from his expression that he was waiting for her.

Aside from the fact that she was tired and irritated, the scene the night before in Sally's room was still

fresh in her mind. The last thing she needed right now
was a conversation with Nicky D'Amico. Carrie picked
up her pace, heading for the stairs.

"Carrie, wait."

She pretended not to hear, but he caught up, moving
to stand in front of her. His tone was all-business, coplike. "We need to talk."

She shook her head. "Sorry. I don't have time."

"I heard about the incident at the Pines. How's your
grandmother?"

"My..." She frowned. "How did you know about
that?"

"The nursing home called it in. They have to report
incidents like that, Carrie. The department's sending an
officer over to take a report."

"Well, he's a bit late, don't you think?" she
snapped. "Besides, there was no one there. My grandmother imagined it. Now, will you move out of my
way, please? I need to sleep."

He didn't budge. "How can you be sure there was
no one there?"

She had started to go around him, but his question
caught her up short. "She said she saw someone at her
window. Security checked the grounds and they didn't
find anyone. Besides, who would want to hurt my
grandmother?"

"Do you really want an answer to that?"

A chill swept through her. "What do you mean?"

"Well, let's start with Christopher Breen, why don't
we? Carrie, I need you to tell me all you know about
Breen."

The chill turned to ice. *What does he mean? Even
more—what does he know?*

She couldn't face it, whatever it was. Spinning

around on the gravel, she decided to go back to her car.

He grabbed her arm. "If you don't want to talk to me here—"

"Let go of me!"

Again, the image of Sally raced through her mind. *Stop it, Nicky. Leave me alone.* And Sally crying out to her mother, "I hate Nicky! I hate him!"

At the same time Carrie saw herself crying, "Stop it!" to her father, "let go of me," him grabbing her arm when she tried to break away, pulling her back, back to—

Deeply afraid, Carrie freed herself and half ran to the closest shelter she could find, the open door to an empty room with glass on every side. Twisting around to slam the door behind her, she tripped against an easel. As she did, the cloth covering the painting on the easel fell to the floor. Facing the portrait, Carrie faltered. Her hands went to her mouth.

"That's *me*," she cried softly, stepping closer. "Oh, God, that's me."

She recognized herself immediately in the painting by the clothes she had worn on the beach the night she'd walked back from the Pines in the storm. Other than that, she was not Carrie. She was someone incredibly small—a child. Her eyes were hollows, no more than dark holes, her face a thin membrane stretched over bone, her hair more white than blond, blowing wildly about her in snarls.

Remembering that Helen was a painter, she whirled back, finding Nicky just behind her. "Your mother, she did this? *Why?*"

To her horror, she began to cry. The past two days had been too much. Too little sleep, not enough food,

Breen, the old house, the memories of her father, her grandmother... She felt as if the Carrie she had constructed so carefully over the years, yet hardly knew, was disintegrating, bit by bit.

"Look," Nicky said, turning her lightly to face the portrait. "All my mother saw was the pain. The evil isn't coming from you, but from around you, Carrie."

She looked again. It was a terrible, frightening image, yet what Nicky had said was true. The evil that emanated from the painting seemed not to come from her, but from forces that moved about her.

She felt her knees buckle.

Nicky grabbed her just in time. She wanted to shake him off but was too exhausted to do so. She let him lead her to a wicker chair, sinking into it gratefully and leaning her head against its high back. Nicky took one of Helen's clean paint rags and dabbed awkwardly at the tears that still clung to her cheeks. Carrie grabbed the rag from him. Nicky sighed and sat back on his heels.

"Carrie, I might as well just come right out with it. I heard you had a talk yesterday with Breen."

She stiffened. "How could you possibly have heard that? Who told you?"

"That doesn't matter. Just tell me how you're involved with him."

She didn't answer.

"Look, when you came back from that you looked like hell. Sorry. I just happened to be at the kitchen window, and I couldn't help noticing. Carrie, I'm thinking maybe you knew Breen from when you lived here before. Is that right? And did you have some trouble with him?"

Outraged at the invasion of her privacy, she could

barely speak. "How did you...how did you know I lived here before? I didn't tell you that."

"It was in the newspaper," he said mildly. "The one about the festival."

When she didn't respond, he said, "Look, I know you don't think it's any of my business. But you've got to stay away from Breen. You don't know what you might be stirring up."

"A nest of vipers would be my guess," Carrie said, reviving slightly. She wiped her face with the paint rag, then sat gripping it in her hands.

Nicky's eyes narrowed. "You may not know how close that is to the truth."

"Don't bet on it. I saw him yesterday with a couple of politicians. They were thick as thieves. Look, I don't see what my business with Breen—if I had any—has to do with you."

Nicky rose and stood before Helen's painting. "My mother sees things. She puts them on canvas—like this. Carrie, she sees you in trouble."

Carrie gave a nervous laugh. "What kind of cop are you? Is that your evidence? And what kind of trouble is it evidence of?"

"It's not just my mother," he said, turning back to her. "How much do you know about Breen?"

Carrie shrugged, unwilling to take him into her confidence. "I know he's got some children's show on TV, and that he's involved somehow with Anglesea."

"He's head of the board of the center," Nicky said pointedly. "And he runs the place. What's more important is that he's being appointed by the President to be national spokesman for a program called Millennium Child. It's a position of trust that will have him working with, and advising, kids all over the U.S.

Maybe even the world. It's supposed to be some 'bold new plan' to energize the minds of our youth by bringing the focus back to old-fashioned virtues.''

"I know. I heard."

But that no longer mattered, did it? Things had changed. With the advent of her father as the real molester, hadn't Breen cleared himself of her suspicions, turning her in another direction entirely?

Carrie rubbed her hands together, trying to warm them. *And didn't he do an excellent job of it, too.*

Tears rose in her eyes and she blinked them back. She would not let Nicky D'Amico see them.

"Carrie," he said, "I suspect that you, as well as I, know that Christopher Breen is not the man to hold that position."

She was silent.

He drew a piece of paper from his T-shirt pocket. "This message came while you were gone."

As he watched, Carrie unfolded the lined yellow paper and read the message. It was from Ron, at the center. *Tess's mother said you could pick her up at noon today, if that's okay. Let me know, if not.*

She had completely forgotten that she'd asked him to arrange for her to take Tess on an outing.

Her eyes met Nicky's. "So?"

"So he's talking about Tess Stanley, right? Why have you taken an interest in Tess Stanley? Did you know her before you came here a couple of days ago?"

"No. I just met her yesterday at the center. Why?"

"Why? That's my question. Why are you getting close to her?"

"God!" She got up and moved to the windows, looking out at the lawn. Nicky's father was still busy mowing, and Helen was on her way across the grass with a tumbler of something cold to drink. From here Carrie could see the ice in the glass, but she couldn't hear the words Helen called out to her husband. The buzz of the mower carried to the window, along with the scent of freshly cut grass. It sent a pang to her heart, remembering that scent on her grandmother's farm so many years ago and how she had loved it.

What must it be like to have a family like the D'Amicos? she wondered. Everyone still here, still together? People to lean on, to count on....

When she turned back to Nicky her voice was cautious, composed. "I am not 'getting close' to Tess Stanley, as you put it. I sat in on the children's break after their rehearsal yesterday, so I could write an article about them and *The Christopher Show*. Ron—Breen's intern—said Tess needed extra attention, and I have some time before Friday, so I thought I'd see what I could do for her. Is there something wrong with that?"

"There's a lot wrong with it," Nicky said. "I need you to stay away from Tess Stanley."

"Oh, really? You need that, do you? Well, I'm sorry, but I don't intend to stay away from her."

Momentary anger showed in Nicky's eyes, then faded. "Let me put it this way, Carrie. If you don't agree to stay away from Tess, at least for the next few days, I'll take you in."

"Take me..." She laughed, though her tone was harsh. "You mean, arrest me? On what grounds?"

"Hampering an investigation. How's that for a start?"

"You're impossible! Hampering what investigation?"

"I can't tell you that."

She folded her arms. "Well, then I can't *not* see Tess Stanley."

He ran an impatient hand through his hair. "Dammit, what is it with you and this girl?"

"She's a child in need of a friend. And I care about her."

"You think I don't? Christ! I've been working on this thing for months, I barely sleep—"

"What *thing?* What have you been working on? Tell me that. If you don't, I'm leaving." She glanced at her watch. "I've just got time to shower and dress before I pick up Tess."

"I told you, I can't—"

She headed for the door.

"All right, all right!" He swore, catching up with her midway. "I'll tell you."

She paused, turning back.

"You absolutely must not tell anyone about this," Nicky said. "Have I got your word?"

"I don't know." She folded her arms. "We'll see."

"Dammit, Carrie!"

"I said we'll see."

He blew out a loud breath. "Sometimes I wonder what perverse fate brought us together in that bar."

"I seem to remember telling you to leave me alone," she reminded him sharply.

"And I remember thinking even at the time that I was making the worst mistake I'd made since fifth grade. Look, let's not do this. I'll tell you what I'm working on. I just hope to God you'll have the sense to keep what I tell you to yourself."

She tapped a foot and waited.

"I've been investigating Christopher Breen," Nicky said quietly. "For child abuse. And rape."

Carrie's arms fell to her sides. She sucked in a breath. "You..." *Dear God.* "What has this to do with Tess?" she asked, dreading the answer.

"I think Breen molested, and possibly even raped, Tess's sister, Debra. I also think Tess could be Breen's next target. Meanwhile, I'm raw from worry that he's going to do something, and worry that he won't. He has to make a move before I can get anything on him that's worth taking into court."

In that moment, it was as if the world shifted back again, righting itself to where it had been before the confrontation with Breen. Before he had almost succeeded in making Carrie doubt her instincts, her memories, her very life.

It was him, too, then, she thought. It must have been. Not just my father. And he's still doing it. Oh, dear God, I could kill him. I could wrap my hands around his throat—

"What do you need to take to court?" she said, her voice tight. "You must have *something.*"

"Only suspicions, so far. His name, given to me by a friend of Debra Stanley, Tess's sister. She says Debra was 'involved' somehow with Breen. And Debra, we know from the coroner's report, was pregnant."

"Pregnant! And you think Breen was the father?"

"I'm almost certain of it. But our very inept Holly Beach coroner destroyed the fetus, and I wasn't able to run DNA tests. The only thing I can do now is watch Breen. I've been tracking him ever since Debra committed suicide, but I haven't seen him do anything he shouldn't be doing. Maybe he's lying low, since Debra died. Maybe he's waiting for things to calm down."

"But the girl—the friend. She could testify to the fact that Debra was involved with him, right?"

"Unfortunately, no. Her story is hearsay, not admissible. I have to have proof, and it has to be current proof. Till I do, I need you to trust me. Carrie, you've got to stay away from Tess."

"Wait a minute. Current proof? What the hell does that mean?"

For a moment he looked away, but then he faced her squarely. "It means that I have to catch him in the act of molesting a child, Carrie. Or have physical evidence that he just did molest a child."

Her eyes widened in horror. "You mean medical evidence, don't you? And just what are you doing to get this proof?"

"I can't tell you that."

"Oh, right. But I'm supposed to trust you. Well, maybe you can tell me this, Mr. Ace Detective. What about Tess? Is he molesting her now?"

"I...no. I don't think so."

Carrie stared. "You don't think so! Meaning that even after weeks of investigating, you still don't know?" Color rushed to her cheeks. "You don't have someone following him—or at least her? You aren't protecting her in some way?"

The level of fear that rose up inside her made her reel. "I am not going to let him hurt that little girl! I don't give a damn what you do, I won't let him hurt that child while I'm around!"

"Yeah, well, if you get in the middle of this," Nicky countered just as angrily, "you're using Tess as surely as Breen. You're seducing that kid."

She paled. "That's a horrible thing to say."

"It's true. Moving into her life, asking questions? Leave that to me, Carrie, it's my job."

"A job that you're obviously not doing very well. Breen has to be stopped!"

"Don't worry. I'll stop him."

"How?"

"I have a plan."

"For God's sake, what plan?"

"Just trust me, okay?"

"Like hell I will!"

"Look," Nicky said, "I'm a cop, I know about these things. Just give me a little time."

"You've had a little time, dammit!"

"More," he said doggedly, grabbing her shoulders. "I need more. Trust me, Carrie. I won't let you down."

"Take your hands off me," she said in a voice that frightened even her.

Nicky dropped his hands.

"Don't ever touch me like that again."

He stepped back, holding his palms up. "I'm sorry. I really am sorry. But, Carrie, I won't have you ruining this. I forbid you to go anywhere near Tess Stanley."

Her eyes widened. "You *what?* I'm not sure I heard that correctly. You *forbid* me?"

"I'm running an investigation, and that gives me the right to tell you to keep the hell out of it."

"You can take your damned investigation and—" She headed for the door. "I don't intend to sit on my ass the way the police have. That man is a monster, and he has to be stopped."

"Carrie, let it be. Please. Let it be. It has to be a righteous bust, or it's no good at all. He'll end up getting off."

"Not if I stop him."

"And how do you plan to stop him?"

When she had no answer, he said, "That's what I

thought. You haven't even got a plan. Carrie, you've got to work within the system.''

"The *system?* You've just convinced me how hopeless that is.''

"Then work with yourself. Deal with your anger. And, for God's sake, leave Christopher Breen to me.''

He reached out, as if to touch her again. Carrie gave a violent thrust and shoved him away.

"Get off me! You can't manhandle me the way you do your sister. Is that why she told you last night to leave her alone?''

Nicky went still. Every ounce of anger drained from his face in an instant. "Carrie, I'm sorry. I had no right to touch you that way.''

"Sorry doesn't cut it. And as far as I know, this is still a free country. I can go anywhere I want and do anything I want, and if you try to 'take me in,' as you say, you'll be using the law against the innocent.'' Her eyes narrowed shrewdly. "You wouldn't do that. I'd bet my life on it.''

"On the other hand,'' Nicky said, matching her tone, "there's always protective custody. It could be for your own good.''

Carrie gave an icy laugh and thrust both arms straight out. "Sure it would. So cuff me, D'Amico. I dare you. When we get to the station I'll tell the nearest reporter I can find all about Christopher Breen and his penchant for little girls. It'll be on all the wire services within minutes.''

"You wouldn't do that. Not if it would ruin any chance of my getting the goods on Breen and putting him away.''

"Oh, but I would. I'd trust the media to ferret out the truth and get Breen, before I'd trust you.''

It was a wild, impulsive bluff, and for a long moment she wasn't sure if it had worked. She could almost feel the cold steel of handcuffs clamping around both wrists.

"You know," Nicky said finally, throwing up his hands and turning on his heel, "you're so far out on the edge, it scares the hell out of me."

He left her staring after him as he strode across the lawn, joining Helen and Mario. Mario had turned off the lawnmower and taken a white handkerchief from his pocket. He started to mop his brow, but Helen reached for the handkerchief and did it for him. Then she hugged him lightly, and he hugged back.

Carrie heard Nicky say gruffly, "I'll take over, Pop." He pulled the lawnmower to the other end of the yard, then knelt down and yanked angrily at the rope. The engine caught after several tries. Nicky, muscles flexing with what Carrie thought must be rage rather than exertion, began to mow. He pushed so hard, the blades of the lawnmower caught in the grass and growled to a halt.

Nicky's father called to him, smiling. "Easy, Nico. It's only grass, not a robber."

Nicky seemed not to hear. But he released his grip and gave his father a smile. "Sorry." When he grabbed the lawnmower again, it was with a softer touch.

Carrie turned to the portrait Helen had painted of her.

What did Nicky's mother, with her perfect, loving, supportive family, know about someone like her? What could any one of the D'Amicos know about the hell she'd lived through? Least of all Nicky.

Self-righteous ass. But she'd won her bluff. He'd backed off.

Her victory lost some of its sweetness the longer she gazed at the portrait. Helen couldn't really have seen danger around her, could she? While it was true that creative people often had "second sight," it was just as true they had vivid imaginations.

So that was all it was. Imagination. Right?

Still, Carrie couldn't shake off a sense of deep foreboding as she climbed the stairs to her room.

20

Shortly after noon, on the west side of the island—the back bay, which had always been "the other side of the tracks"—Carrie stepped from the rental car. There were no ocean breezes here, and a blast of hot, humid air hit her face. A heavy, oily smell of fish drifted along a street lined with largely older cars and dying trees.

Carrie remembered that scent from childhood, when her grandfather Sam had brought her here to go crabbing with him. She could still see him in his old khaki pants with the legs rolled up to the knee, pulling the baskets, full to the brim with that night's dinner, out of the water.

As if it had happened yesterday, she remembered, too, sitting on the edge of a dock with him, silently, for hours. She didn't mind the silence. It gave her time to draw word pictures in her mind, pictures that she would go home and write down in a spiral-bound notebook.

Her grandfather was a man of few words. Still, he wasn't unkind. If anything, he had become something of a shadow in her mind now. Carrie had instinctively felt, back then, that there might not be enough fight in her grandfather. She had asked Sam Holder one day, "Grandpa Sam, why do you look so sad?"

He had answered, "Sometimes a man knows when

he's beat, Carrie-girl. He knows when it's time to give up and go home."

Carrie had assumed that he meant it was time to go home because the catch wasn't good that day. Now, from her adult perspective, she realized that he must have meant something else. Something much deeper. But what?

She stood beside the rental car and stared at Tess Stanley's house. At peeling green paint and a front porch cluttered with odds and ends of junk: an old refrigerator, a torn sofa, piles of yellowed newspapers. In stark contrast, boxes of bright red and pink geraniums hung from the porch railing, like brave little flags in the midst of a battlefield.

Following a short path to the porch, she approached a rickety screen door and opened it, knocking tentatively on the inside door. A television blared, and when there was no answer, Carrie knocked again. When she raised her hand a third time she heard rustlings inside. The knob turned; the door cracked. A male voice said irritably, "Yeah?"

"Mr. Stanley? I'm Carrie Holt. Ron Devereaux, from the church, called? He said it was all right with Tess's mother if I took Tess to the boardwalk today...."

Carrie's voice trailed off as the man she assumed to be Tess's father peered at her suspiciously. When he finally opened the door, she resisted the temptation to shove a foot into the opening, like a vacuum cleaner salesman. This man looked annoyed enough to chop it off.

He was tall and thin, with what might at one time have been a good physique. But a belly puffed out above the waistband of his jeans, stretching tight over a Redskins T-shirt. His eyes were a watery blue, with deep circles beneath them. They traveled the length of Carrie's trim body and back up to her face.

"Who is it, Ray?" a tired female voice called out.

"That lady from the church. She's here to get Tess."

He didn't move aside or invite Carrie in. As he cracked the door open a bit farther, however, she caught the scent of alcohol on his breath. A woman stood at an ironing board, clothes hanging from the frame of a door leading into a kitchen. The air drifting from the room was fresh, like Niagara starch. The woman's hair, dark blond at the front, was pulled back in a ponytail, and there were piles of unironed clothes on the small dining table beside her. A baseball game blared on a color TV.

"Hi," Carrie called out to the woman. "It's Carrie Holt. From the church? Ron said I could take Tess out today. He, uh, he said he talked to you, and you said it was all right?"

Tess's mother nodded and crossed the room to turn the television down. Ray, however, interrupted as his wife drew closer and opened her mouth to speak.

"Sorry. Tess is grounded today," he said.

Carrie looked at him and then again at Tess's mother, who seemed to fade into the background, deferring to her husband.

"But I thought—"

"Not today." He started to close the door.

"Could I just say hello?" Carrie asked quickly, feeling uneasy and wanting more than anything to see Tess and make sure that she was all right.

"She's asleep—" Tess's mother began.

She was interrupted once more by her husband, who said, "You one of them ministers?"

Carrie shook her head, and Stanley added, "Well, I don't know what you want with Tess, but we've had enough trouble here. I think you'd better just be getting along. Tend to your own business."

He started to close the door, and Carrie fought back her anger. Thinking fast, she said, "I'm a writer, Mr. Stanley. I'm writing an article about *The Christopher Show,* and I wanted to feature Tess in the article. There might be some money in it."

Stanley hesitated. "We don't want Tess talking to strangers about family stuff," he said finally. "We don't want any more trouble."

"Of course not," Carrie said. "I understand completely. But this isn't about the children's personal lives at all, just *The Christopher Show.*"

He gave her a shrewd look. "What's that you said about money? You paying people for this article?"

Gotcha, Carrie thought.

"Absolutely," she said.

"How much?"

"I'm not sure yet. I have to talk with my editor, but it'll be a substantial amount." She thought of her shrinking bank account and wondered how much she would have to offer to ransom Tess for the day. What was the going rate on seven-year-old daughters these days?

Shrugging, she turned slightly away. "I just thought I'd take Tess to the boardwalk and we could talk at the same time, but if she can't go out—"

"Wait a minute."

Stifling a sigh of relief, she faced him again. "Yes?"

"We don't want you writing about her sister. If that's why you want—"

"No, absolutely not, Mr. Stanley. I just want to ask

Tess about *The Christopher Show,* and her part in the play this weekend. I'll be talking to the other children, too.''

"Well, if that's all..." He appeared thoughtful. "Who gets this money? Do you make a check out to me, her father, or what?"

"I can do it any way you like," she said, trying to hide the outrage that burned in her gut, yet ashamed at the same time that she was standing here, seeming to participate willingly in the selling of Tess Stanley.

Tess's mother had left the room as they were talking, and now she came up behind her husband, Tess in hand. She stood with her palms on Tess's shoulders, her fingers red and rough against the small child's white flesh.

"I'm Mary Stanley," she said. "And this is my husband, Ray." She darted a nervous glance at her husband. "We don't mean to be rude. It's just that ever since...well, for the past few weeks..."

It startled Carrie to see moisture fill Ray Stanley's eyes. He looked away, blinking. "You don't have to tell her anything," he mumbled. "It's none of her business."

Tess's mother gave Carrie a weary smile. "Tess can go with you. Just please bring her home before dark."

Tess's eyes were swollen and red. Carrie, looking at her, knew that no matter how low her funds were getting, she would spend them all to get Tess out of this house today.

"Would you like to go to the boardwalk with me?" she asked her.

Tess glanced at her father as if expecting him to forbid it. He wiped at one eye with the back of a hand and sighed. "All right, go on." Then he added in a tone of warning, "Just remember what I told you, young lady, about family business."

Tess nodded.

Carrie took her hand, and she didn't think it was her imagination that Tess hung on tight. As they walked down the steps to her car, she caught Tess's fear. Shuddering, Carrie looked back only once, to say, "Don't worry, I'll have her back before dark." Her words fell into dead space. The door had already closed.

It wasn't until they were blocks from the house that Carrie felt as if a cloud had lifted from her. She put the car radio on, tuning it to some lively jazz.

"Well," she said with false heartiness, "let's have a good time today, okay?"

Tess gave her a look that was beyond her years, a look that said, *I'll try if you will,* and Carrie wanted to cry.

They sat in a booth at Animal Ice, an ice cream shop on the boardwalk. It was new since Carrie had lived here, but Tess had told her all about it on the way, in the car. "They make animal shapes out of the ice cream, and you can put on any kind of topping you want."

Apparently it was a popular place with kids, and Carrie had decided to bring Tess here in the hope it would put her at ease.

Tess ordered a white polar bear, covering it with coconut and sticking licorice bits on for the eyes. Carrie did the same, watching with fascination as Tess ate hers delicately, taking tiny spoonfuls and making them last. She remembered that her grandmother used to do that, in the days when Elizabeth would take her to Corson's Drugstore for a "small scoop of vanilla," as she would put it.

"This is nice, isn't it?" Carrie said. "I mean, going for ice cream on a summer afternoon."

"I guess." Tess licked the back of her spoon and studied Carrie. "Did you live here when you were little?"

"Yes," Carrie answered, "I did."

"Did you go to church here?"

"Yes. I went to Anglesea, same as you. It wasn't a center then, though. Just a church."

"Have you been to Animal Ice before?"

"No, this is my first time. Have you?"

Tess nodded.

"A lot?"

The child shrugged. "Sometimes."

"I don't suppose your mother lets you come alone, though," she ventured.

"Sometimes...sometimes I come here with somebody."

It was her tone, more than anything, that put Carrie on the alert. "Really? Who?"

Tess shrugged again. "Nobody special."

"I see." Carrie tried to sound casual. "A secret?"

Tess wiggled and kicked with her toes at the metal support holding up the table. "Sort of. I'm not supposed to tell."

Her throat going dry, Carrie searched for words. "Well, uh, sure. I can understand that." She hesitated, then went on. "Of course, I wouldn't say anything if you told me. That's the thing I'm best at, keeping secrets. It's sort of a special talent I have."

"It is?"

"Uh-huh."

"Well…sometimes," Tess said cautiously, "Chris brings me here."

Carrie stared. *This is too easy.* As much as she'd hoped to get something out of Tess, she had never dreamed it would come this easily.

When she could speak again, she hoped her voice sounded normal. "Chris? You mean Christopher Breen?"

"Uh-huh."

"I see. And is that fun?"

The question would have been ludicrous in the best of circumstances. There was nothing in this child that spoke of fun. The thing that had been chilling Carrie since the first time she laid eyes on her was that she seemed so devoid of joy.

Tess shrugged. "I don't know. He brought me here after my sister died."

Dear God…oh, dear God. Where do I go from here? What can I say that won't scare her away?

"Did Chris bring your sister here?" she managed to ask lightly. "Is that why he, uh, brought you here, too?"

Tess didn't answer.

"I mean—" she forced a smile "—well, if he's your friend, maybe he was your sister's friend, too."

Tess leaned forward and said in a confidential tone, "That's what he said. That we'd be friends just like…just like…"

Terrible pictures rose in Carrie's mind. Laying down her spoon, she sat heavily against the back of the booth, unable to go on.

Tess looked at her, the blue eyes becoming shadowed. "Are you okay?"

Carrie tried to recover. "Yes. Yes, I'm fine."

"Can we go now?" Tess asked.

"Of course," Carrie said, picking up a paper napkin to dab at her mouth. "Of course we can."

But she couldn't just let her go. Not now, not knowing...

As they slid from the booth, Carrie held out her hand and smiled. "How about if we go on some rides? Would you like that? I haven't done that in years."

Any other child might have jumped up and down. Instead, Tess took Carrie's hand and, like an obedient puppy, followed her outside to the boardwalk. Nicky's words rang in Carrie's head: *You're using Tess as surely as Breen.*

Was he right? And if so, was she wrong to do it, if it might lead to Breen's arrest and conviction? If it got him out of Tess's life, and the lives of all other innocent children who might cross his path?

She wasn't certain how to answer that. In the next instant, however, she decided to at least give Tess this day. She would not ask any more questions. Instead—and in spite of everything—Tess would have fun. And that's all it would be. A good day, a day to remember, a day to help chase the shadows away.

They went on the carousel, the roller coaster, the big and little Ferris wheels, the Super Scooters.

After a while, Carrie abandoned the fiction that she was doing this just to give Tess a good time. In a way, she was reliving her own childhood. Good memories came back, surprising her. Memories of evenings on the boardwalk with her mother or grandmother, walking its length up one side and down the other, eating caramel corn, taking in all the sights and sounds. There had been sightseeing boats in the water, the murmur of waves, the musky-mellow aroma of tropical fruit juice stands, the smokiness of grilled hot dogs. She remembered monkeys driving race cars, a midget dressed as a cop in the arcade, the house of mirrors, and baby pigs in cages, till someone threw a ball at the right target and turned them loose. She could still hear the piglets squealing as they came careening down the slides.

There were no longer pigs in the arcade, or monkeys. She supposed animal welfare advocates had put a stop to that. Otherwise, however, the boardwalk was much the same. There were frozen bananas, hot, thick pretzels and many of the same old rides. Carrie and Tess sat on a bench facing the sea, with the new water park below them on the beach. It was a monumental enterprise, with slides and chutes, a couple of pools. A hundred brightly colored inner tubes.

Carrie stretched her legs in front of her and slumped back against the bench, feeling tired but good. ''I don't know about you, Tess, but I've had a good time. Thanks for doing this with me.''

Her words were sincere. She had enjoyed the small girl's company more than she had ever thought possible.

''It costs an awful lot of money,'' Tess said solemnly.

''That's true. I remember rides being a quarter. You could go on them all day if you wanted to. Do you come down here very much?''

Tess shook her head. ''Not anymore. Debra, my sister, she used to bring me here.''

''Oh.'' Carrie looked at her. There was a smudge of mustard and salt on her cheek from the pretzel she was eating, and Carrie took the napkin she'd shoved into her pocket at the ice cream parlor and dabbed at it.

"I'm sorry about your sister, Tess. It must have been a terrible time for you."

Tess shrugged. She swung her legs and nibbled at the pretzel, staring as two teenagers went down a water slide in tandem, screaming and shouting. They landed in the pool with a loud smack and surfaced with giggles. Tess sighed.

"I used to have a slide."

"You did? A big slide?"

She shook her head. "No, just a little plastic one. With my wading pool. It broke."

"That's too bad."

"I got it for my birthday. My daddy broke it a couple weeks ago."

"Oh?" Carrie kept her voice carefully even.

Tess said in a monotone, "Ever since Debra died, he's sort of been mad a lot. Like kicking things, you know? He broke a lot of stuff that day."

"The day your sister died, you mean?"

Tess nodded. "He kicked things and broke them, and he never even said he was sorry."

Carrie bit her lips. "I'm sure he was," she said gently. "He probably just didn't know how to say it."

The child frowned. "I don't care. He didn't have to do that."

"You're right, Tess. He didn't have to. But you know, adults sometimes do things that hurt children, because they're hurting, too. That doesn't make it right, of course."

She decided suddenly to share her own experience with Tess. "I remember a Christmas...." She told Tess about the red model plane.

"I'm sorry," Tess said solemnly when she was

through. "I didn't think anything like that could happen to somebody like you."

Carrie was touched beyond words by the child's sympathy. She stared out to sea.

"It can happen to anyone," she said at last. "My father is dead now, but when he was alive he drank a lot."

Tess nodded. "Ever since Debra died, my dad drinks all the time. Why do they do that?"

Carrie shrugged. "I don't think I really know."

She had never understood much about her father at all, had never really wanted to. But now she reached into the past, for Tess. "My father had a lot of frustrations, I guess. He played the piano beautifully, and he had a scholarship to the Boston Conservatory of Music when he was young. For some reason, he didn't take it. He ended up being a printer, instead." She looked at Tess. "I don't know if it was that. It's hard to put things together after people die."

Tess nodded. "Like Debra," she said, her voice low. "I don't know why...why she did what she did. But I think...I think it was my daddy. What he did. Like locking Debra in her room."

Carrie felt her scalp prickle. She tried to keep her expression bland and her voice natural as she said, "Your father, he locked your sister in her room?"

Tess nodded. "He didn't like her going out at night, but she'd sneak out anyway. So Daddy...sometimes he'd lock her door from the outside, to keep her in her room. And sometimes he'd forget to let her out in the morning, and that's why...why, when she didn't come downstairs that morning, I thought she was just locked in, so I went up to let her out, and I saw..." Tess's voice had begun to shake as she talked, and now it grew hoarse and faded away.

Carrie said with shock, "You found your sister? The day she died? You were the one who found her?"

Tess nodded, staring at her shoes. "In the closet. She was h-hanging there, from the l-light in the ceiling...."

Carrie couldn't restrain herself. She put her arms around the child. "Oh, Tess," she said, tears filling her throat, "I'm so sorry that happened to you."

The child was like a board in her arms, and Carrie let her go, saying carefully, "What about you, Tess? Does...does anybody do anything, you know, bad to you?"

Tess didn't answer, and Carrie thought for a moment she had gone too far. Damn! She hadn't meant for the day to turn out this way. She wanted to see Tess smile again, hear her light, childish laughter as it had been an hour before on the rides. But they had gone way beyond that. What should she do?

Tess kicked at the metal rail in front of them. Carrie had bought them both a pair of thick white socks when they got to the boardwalk. "It'll make walking around a lot easier," she had said, being careful not to show that she'd noticed the child's ill-fitting sandals or blisters. Her grandmother had bought her a new pair of shoes once for that very same reason—embarrassing Alice and making her angry.

"You think I can't buy shoes for my own child?" Alice had stormed.

"Apparently not," Elizabeth had said calmly. "The child can hardly walk. Look at her feet!"

When Carrie was growing up, her grandmother had been, above all else, a friend. Someone who'd cared about her when she needed that more than anything in the world.

Could she, Carrie, be that for Tess?

"Would you like to tell me about Chris?" she said quietly. "You said he was Debra's friend. And now he's yours?"

She waited while the child obviously considered her next words.

"Chris *says* he was Debra's friend. But she used to cry all the time when she came back from seeing him. She thought I didn't know, but I did." Tess kicked at the rail again. "My mom and dad said she was lucky that somebody that important was interested in her. They said she shouldn't tell anybody, because some people might get jealous. Then when Debra got…when she got sick, they were real mad. They said she was a—a bad girl, and that people would find out, and she'd better not tell anybody. But Chris already knew."

Carrie forced herself to speak calmly. "He did?"

"Sure. I heard them talking about it. He gave Debra some money." Tess's lower lip began to quiver, and tears filled her eyes.

Carrie sighed, feeling a great weight lift from her shoulders. Debra Stanley was pregnant, just as Nicky had said. And Breen was the father. He gave her money to get rid of the baby, and Debra killed herself, instead.

So this is it. We've got him. Nicky and his "we need more evidence" be damned—we've got him.

She touched Tess gently on the arm. "You don't have to talk about this anymore right now." She used an edge of the napkin to dry the child's tears.

But the weight of Tess's story hung heavy about them. Finally, Carrie said, "Will your parents be mad if they find out you've told me about all this?"

"I don't know."

"Because I don't want you to get into trouble, Tess. But I don't want to ask you to keep it a secret, either. I think it's really wrong when adults ask children to keep secrets. They should be able to talk about things any time they want."

"You think so?" Tess looked at Carrie, her moist eyes round and trusting.

Carrie smiled. "I *know* so. And I'm glad you talked to me. Any time you want to, it's okay. And any time you need me—if you're scared, or worried—here's my number. I want you to call me."

She took from her purse a business card and, just as she had for Nan Martin and Ron, wrote the Crest Inn number on the back of it. "This is where I'm staying for a while. I'd like to see you again, Tess. I'd like us to be friends, and I want you to call me any time at all. Okay?"

Tess took the card, slipping it into the pocket of her yellow shorts. "But you don't live here, do you? I mean, you'll be leaving soon."

Carrie knew what she was asking. Tess had just lost her sister. She would be cautious now about making friends with someone who might go off and leave her again.

"No, I don't live here," Carrie said gently. "But if you want me for a friend, I'll never be gone for long. I'll be here when you need me. That's a promise."

It was the most passionate commitment she had ever made to another person in her life. And almost immediately, Carrie half regretted it. She was torn with confusion. How could she possibly keep a promise like that, when she hardly knew what her own life would bring?

Yet, how could she not?

She drove Tess home and reluctantly let her go, not knowing what else to do. Tess's needs were being neglected, that much seemed clear. But was there actual abuse going on, as well? And where did one draw the line between neglect and abuse? When did the father's drinking—his anger, grief and probable guilt over the death of his older child—cross the line into serious abuse?

Was there even a line? Or did one melt into the other, like cubes of butter on a hot day, impossible to tell where one ended and the other began?

Instinctively, Carrie had wanted to grab Tess up and run.

But you couldn't do that to a child. In the first place, it would be kidnapping. And it might hurt Tess even more than leaving her where she was, at least temporarily.

Carrie had to handle this somehow. But she had to do it right.

Child Welfare? There must be an office nearby. She could tell them...

Tell them what? That the father drank? That he broke things in anger? That he had locked his teenage daughter in her room, to keep her in at night?

No. That he had taken hush money from a monster, upon learning that his daughter was pregnant with the monster's child.

That should be enough. Still, Carrie didn't need Nicky, or his precious *system*, to tell her that it most likely wasn't. She had no proof that these things had been done—only the word of a tiny child, who might or might not be believed. And even if she were believed, half the well-meaning parents of teenagers in America probably did some or all of those things, at one time or another. At the most, Child Welfare might go to the house, investigate, question Tess and her parents. They might even come away with Tess. They might put her in a foster home while they investigated the "allegations." Tess would be taken from the only family she knew.

And she would learn that Carrie had betrayed her trust.

Back at the Crest Inn, Carrie paced the small confines of her room, torn between wanting to act and being afraid to. Before she could destroy what Tess had, she would need something better to offer her.

Meanwhile, there was the matter of Christopher Breen. And Debra Stanley—pregnant with his child. Dead, now, at the age of fourteen.

Carrie tossed and turned all night, feeling more and more helpless as the hours wore on. She understood more than ever now about childhood rage—footstomping, fist-clenching, face-growing-red rage. It was the impotence inside coming out, feeling ground under a huge, heavy boot, unable to move in any chosen direction, being forced to submit to *theirs*.

It was the kind of anger that had overcome her in Philadelphia, when she first saw Christopher Breen on television. When she'd wanted to smash him and smash—

By the time the sun rose, turning the sheer white curtains pink, then hot yellow, smothering the cool night air, Carrie knew only one thing—that she would have to pull herself together. A child was at risk. She could not simply stand by.

Her muscles ached as she dragged herself from the

bed. She felt like an old person, crippled and bent with emotional pain. Trembling, she stood beneath the shower and let it run, let it beat on her back, her shoulders, her breasts. She pictured it washing all her past sins away, leaving her pure. Righteous. Strong.

Afterward she stood before the bathroom mirror. Her wet hair lay on her shoulders. Water from her cotton nightshirt dripped onto the tile floor. She had somehow neglected to remove it before stepping into the shower.

That wasn't important now. What was important— no, vital—was to erase the image of horror that suddenly faced her in the mirror. She rubbed with her fingers. The apparition remained. She scrubbed at it with a towel, faster and faster, her movements becoming frantic. The specter only grew more clear. It frightened her deeply, though some small, sane part of her knew it couldn't be real.

Superimposed on her own adult body was Tess. Little Tess—her blond hair wild over Carrie's, her face a mask of terror and pain. From her eyes, in place of tears, blood flowed in great torrents, running over her breasts, then over Carrie's breasts, her stomach, her thighs…their life's blood, together, seeping away.

21

An hour later, Carrie sat on the beach in a small, secluded cove she had found. True swimmers tended to stake their claims to the north. Here at the south end, waves began to flatten out as sea melded into bay. The sun, so hot when she woke, had turned dim behind clouds hovering over the sea.

Talk to Nicky, a small voice said. *Tell him everything you know. Tell him now.* It was the only thing she could think to do, the only action that made any sense. She just hadn't been able to bring herself to go in search of him.

She sat with her knees pulled up to her chin, thinking, her arms wrapped tightly around her legs. Her thoughts were a mish-mash, ranging from the specter in her mirror earlier to the meeting with Breen, the memories in her old house, her time with Tess...and the argument with Nicky yesterday.

Who am I? she asked herself. Am I someone who can't accept help? Am I someone who is so afraid of consequences I can't act? And is writing the only way I can make a difference? Am I too afraid to become involved in any other way?

Worse—have I struggled so long and so hard to put my past aside that I've become a person twice removed? *Am* I using Tess as a vehicle for my own anger, even my own revenge?

One of her great weaknesses, Carrie believed, was that she'd always felt like an observer of life rather than a participant. The only things she knew about "life"—other than her own, which had been too difficult to delve into—were make-believe images from the multitude of movies, books and television dramas she'd escaped into over the years. Her knowledge of life as others presumably lived it was largely drawn from celluloid, or from between the covers of books. She herself had never strolled along a sidewalk in New York, as Judy Garland did in *Easter Parade.* She'd never had a *White Christmas,* like the Bing Crosby character in the movie of that name. Nor had she been to Beirut or Bosnia, though she'd written, from secondhand knowledge, about the troubles there. And not once had she battled a Moby Dick, or driven a wagon west.

Still, she had assumed over the years that others did these things, or at least something akin to them. That was "life," was it not?

Or did these images, implanted in her mind over the years by screenwriters and authors, never really happen to *anyone?* Were they mere fantasies from the first— perpetuated over the centuries, from the time man learned to put pen to paper, or chisel to rock?

Which left out a ton of nonfiction, she admitted. Though even that was often largely imagination, an author's reinventing of his or her past.

And how much of her own past had been reinvented—shoved away, hidden away, driven away, to make room in her mind for these other more fascinating, more compelling lives?

Still, wasn't it better, when one's own life images were too painful, to lose oneself that way? To spend nights, weekends and vacations in pure escape? After all, in movies, books and television, things usually worked out in the end. Boy met girl, boy got girl and the villain got thrown in jail.

Carrie closed her eyes and, as if in answer, saw Esther Gordon in her combination apartment-office in San Francisco. Carrie had crossed to a far window overlooking the city she had tried to make her home since college, and yet was never completely at home in. At times, when she was walking, the buildings seemed too tall. She would stumble, become dizzy, afraid she might fall.

On this day that she remembered, she had just told Esther that she couldn't continue to visit. "I have too much to do. Another book to start, a tour coming up for *Winter's End....*" Esther had quietly poured tea as Carrie continued with her mental list of prepared excuses.

When she had finished, Esther said, "There may come a time when the cracks in the walls you have only begun to break through will open up. A time when you see the entire picture all at once and can no longer deny how badly hurt you were as a child. If you aren't ready for that, Carrie—" a worried look crossed the therapist's face "—I fear for what might happen. Not only to you, but to those around you."

Carrie shivered now, though the sun had begun to break through and warm the sand beneath her. *Esther was right. I'm beginning to see the entire picture, and it isn't good. Those memories yesterday. They weren't fiction. They were true. The gun in my father's hand, pointed at my mother—not once, I know now, but several times. There was a rifle, a hunting rifle, and then a revolver he bought from some buddy in a bar....*

I blotted it all out. Abandoned myself, really. Not only my grown self, but that little girl in the church basement, the one in that bedroom at the old house, the one who hid in the bathroom.

I abandoned them all.

She stared out to sea, where a gull, with a skill and precision born of experience and instinct, circled and swooped, coming up with a fish half its size.

Breen was like that gull, circling around innocent children, then swooping in for the kill. But she could fight him, couldn't she? And maybe even win? So what if he was larger than life? Stronger, faster, more clever? So what if she had stood on the sidelines all too often? She had still come through a lot. It had taken strength to get through college and to build a successful career. It had taken enormous amounts of strength, for that matter, just to survive. She could, if she chose, walk out of the pages or screens of all those fictive lives and straight into a world that was real, if frightening beyond all measure.

"You're looking thoughtful," a voice said, interrupting her thoughts.

Carrie jumped. Looking up, she saw Helen beside her, dressed in khaki shorts and a T-shirt spattered with paint. She carried sandals, and her feet were bare. Her brown curls, barely touched with gray, were scattered, as if she'd been up all night and hadn't thought to comb them. Her arms and legs were deeply tanned.

"I came down for my morning walk," she said. "May I join you?"

Carrie nodded. "Of course."

Helen hesitated. "You're sure I wouldn't be intruding?"

"No, no, it's all right."

Helen tossed her shoes down and sank to the sand beside Carrie. Stretching, she let out a long, satisfied sound and said, "It looks like it's going to be a gorgeous day. First we've had all week."

"Yes," Carrie agreed. "It seems the tail of the hurricane has passed."

"Still, it feels like there's another storm on the way," Helen said, looking at her.

Something in her tone warned Carrie that this was not to be a simple, by-the-way sort of chat. She met Helen's gaze.

"Are you talking about a real storm—or something else?" Recalling the portrait Helen had painted of her, she thought she already knew the answer.

"I'm not sure," Helen answered, not unkindly. "You tell me."

Carrie was silent. She began to draw vague lines in the sand.

"Okay, I'll start," Helen said. "I'm worried about Nicky. I think he's becoming too involved with you."

Carrie was stunned at her bluntness. Though her tone, again, had not been unkind, her eyes were dead serious.

"There's nothing going on between Nicky and me," Carrie blurted out with a short, nervous laugh. "We've only had a couple of conversations. In fact, if anything, we haven't gotten along at all."

"That's what I'm worried about," Helen said wryly.

Carrie shook her head, confused. "I don't understand."

"For someone who hardly knows you, and doesn't even get along with you, Nicky's spending an unusual amount of time worrying about you, Carrie."

"Helen, look—I'm sorry, but you're wrong. It's not

me your son is worried about. It's the case he's working on."

"Which," Helen said pointedly, "you happen to be
involved in."

Carrie stared. What did she know?

"Oh, he's shared only the barest of details with
me," Helen said. "Nicky doesn't tell me too much
about his cases. He knows it only worries me."

She stretched out her legs, digging her toes into the
sand. "It's not easy, having a police officer as a son.
One tends to lie awake nights imagining the worst...as,
I suppose, the wife of a policeman must."

She gave Carrie the full impact of her worried brown
eyes. "Can you imagine that, Carrie? Being the wife
of a police officer?"

Again, Carrie shook her head. "No, not at all. I
mean, I never even thought about it. Helen, I swear to
you, there's nothing between your son and me. This
case he's working on has him climbing the walls, and
I...I just happen to know about it. I'm concerned about
someone involved."

Which wasn't the entire truth, but if Nicky D'Amico
preferred not to have his mother know too much, it
might suffice.

Helen squinted out to sea, then scanned the beach to
the south, a hand over her eyes to shield them from the
sun.

"Nicky hasn't been this angry in almost a year. The
other night, with Sally...you saw that, didn't you?"

Carrie thought of lying, but knew that Helen must
have seen her outside on the landing. "Yes. I did."

"Well, Sally went through a difficult time last year.
And Nicky, who had never in his life been a violent
person, nearly killed someone because of it. Sally's

nightmares are all about that, Carrie—not about what she did, or what happened to her. That she can deal with. Her fears are about Nicky. That he'll 'lose it,' as she says, again. And that someone will be badly hurt.''

''I see.'' Carrie studied the other woman, unable to dislike her. With her smooth, tanned face devoid of makeup, her small though strong-looking limbs and her intelligent mind, Helen was someone to be reckoned with. A woman of both outer and inner strength, Carrie guessed. A woman she could be as blunt with as Helen had been with her.

''Do you honestly think,'' Carrie said, ''that having me around is what's making Nicky angry? That isn't giving him much credit. Shouldn't he be able to take responsibility for his own actions?''

''Absolutely,'' Helen agreed. ''Unfortunately, Nicky's problem is that he's so busy being responsible for everyone else, he doesn't think about himself.''

''Well, there's a word for that, Helen.''

Nicky's mother laughed softly. ''I know. Codependent. But, Carrie, there's another way of looking at that. When I was a kid, looking after people used to be called love.''

Carrie's return laughter was a bit short. ''Right. And isn't that what got us into trouble in the first place? Calling dysfunctional relationships love?''

Helen sighed. ''Oh, Carrie…I don't know. Is it dysfunctional, then, to be our brother's—or sister's—keeper? Somehow I don't think so. At this point in my life I believe there really is only one moving force in this world. Only one way to win—or, if you prefer, to conquer. Through love.''

She reached over and took Carrie's hand, gently brushing the sand from her fingers. Carrie's first instinct, as usual, was to pull away from the touch of someone she barely knew. Instead, she met Helen's eyes. "I guess, right now, I trust anger more than love," she said.

Helen nodded, touching two of her own fingers to her lips, then making a cross on the back of Carrie's hand. "My dear, sweet child, that is why I am so afraid. Not just for you, but for Nicky."

After Helen left, Carrie sat for a long time, staring at the lines she had drawn in the sand. In them she could now make out a stick figure, much like the one Tess had drawn the first time Carrie had met her. Above it were jagged clouds, lending an ominous look to the figure.

She reached down and swept a hand over the clouds, removing them. The stick figure became only that—a few lines in the sand. When the tide came in it would be even less. It would be wiped away.

Sighing, she stood and stretched her cramped muscles. Until her talk with Helen, she had just about made up her mind to go back to the Crest, find Nicky and tell him all she'd learned from Tess. She would then see what the two of them, together, might do to help the child.

Now she had to think, first, about Helen's concerns for her son. She knew Nicky's mother meant well. And perhaps she was right to be worried. From what she herself had seen, Nicky D'Amico was walking a thin line.

But Helen's instincts were just that, weren't they? Helen's? If Carrie had learned anything, it was to listen to, and trust, her own.

She glanced at her watch and saw that it was nearly

noon. Yesterday she had promised her grandmother that she would have lunch with her today. Elizabeth might never know if she didn't show up—but a promise was a promise.

Walking down to where the sand was hard, Carrie headed south toward the Pines. On the way she would think about how much, or how little, to tell Nicky D'Amico.

It was almost as if she had conjured him up. One moment she had been walking along the shore thinking, and the next he was there, a hundred or so feet in front of her. He stood motionless, as if waiting for her. His thumbs, as usual, were hooked into the waistband of his jeans, his feet planted firmly apart—in what, she thought, he must have decided was a nicely assertive pose for a cop. *Betcha he worked for years perfecting that.*

"I saw you talking to my mom," he said as she reached him. "Is everything all right?"

Her eyes were level with his T-shirt, which had Holly Beach Little League printed on it in dark green letters. She looked up into his face, which shielded her from the sun. The light gray eyes, such a contrast beneath the dark brows and hair, were clearly worried—if not about her, then about something else.

How she ever got saddled with this guy, when all she'd ever wanted was to be left alone, was beyond her.

Swallowing an urge to tell him to mind his own business, Carrie said, "I suppose that depends on what you mean by 'all right.' Your mother is concerned about you."

"Oh? She said something to you?"

"She thinks I'm to blame for your being...edgy, shall we say?"

"My mom worries too much."

Carrie started to walk again, and he strolled along beside her, hands in his pockets.

"So how come you're still living at home?" she said. "Why don't you move out and give the poor woman some peace?"

He grinned. "As a matter of fact, I'm building my own place. I was about to go up and check on it."

He pointed in the direction they were walking, to a house under construction at the edge of the sand. It was several hundred feet up from the shoreline, but Carrie recalled seeing it when she walked here before, on her way to the Pines the first time.

"That's yours?"

"That and twenty years of payments." He smiled. "You're right about one thing. A man my age, especially a cop, shouldn't live with family. It's worse for a mom, or anyone in the family, for that matter, to know what's going on. If I'm out of the house, they won't think about it so much."

She paused and squinted at him. "Oh, yeah? Don't bet on it. That's one special mom you have."

"And don't think I don't know it. I guess I've been telling myself I could help them around the place more if I lived there. Lately, though, I've been looking forward to my own space."

"I don't imagine your sister will mind."

It was out before she could call it back. And she wouldn't have blamed him a bit if he'd thrown her own words of yesterday back at her and told her to mind her own business.

Instead, he said, "It's been a hard year for Sal. For all of us, in fact. We're in counseling together."

That surprised her. "Do you want to tell me about it?"

"No." His already firm jaw lifted a trifle higher in the air.

"Fine. Fine, then." So much for that.

Still, the fact that he was difficult didn't sway her from what she knew in her heart, now, she had to do.

"Nicky, I've been thinking. I need your help."

His astonishment was obvious. "And when did all this come about?"

"After I talked to Tess yesterday."

"You talked—" His voice rose with anger.

"And don't try to tell me you didn't know that," she interrupted. "You were having me followed."

"As a matter of fact, I was not."

"Then who—"

"Who was following you? That's anybody's guess at this point. Dammit, I warned you—"

"Will you stop it? I've heard all that. And I must have been wrong. I thought there was someone in a car behind me, once, that's all. I must have been mistaken."

"Uh-huh. Right. I'm sure that's it."

"Will you stop being so damned all-knowing? Geez! This town doesn't need a God, it's got you!" She began to walk away from him. "Never mind. I thought you might help. I guess I was wrong about that, too."

He caught up with her. "No, you weren't. Here." He motioned to a low shelf, formed in the sand by the tide. "Sit down, talk to me."

"Only if you stop giving me orders like sit down, talk to me, do this, don't do that...."

His mouth tightened. "I don't have much time right now for the niceties."

"Then skip niceties. How about common courtesy?"

He sighed and threw up his hands. "You're right. I'm sorry."

"Golly. An apology. Pardon me while I catch flies with my mouth, which is dropping open at an alarming rate."

His tone turned to exasperation. "You know, I didn't realize you had such a smart mouth."

"Yeah, well, I get that way when I'm angry."

"Angry?"

"When I decide to get even."

"Ah... Well, then. I can't wait to hear about that." He sat with a sigh and a groan. "I swear to God, I get stiffer and older every time you appear on the scene. Ms. Holt, will you please do me the honor and the kindness of having a seat beside me here on these oh-so-charming grains of sand?"

She sat, stifling a smile—her first that day.

"And now, how may I be of help to you, Ms. Holt?"

"Oh, shut up. As I was saying, I've talked to Tess. The chances of her talking to you—the police, that is—are almost nil. Her mother and father have warned her not to speak to anyone about Debra. I doubt she would tell you anything about herself, either. She's too afraid."

"But you got her to talk to you? That's something."

"It was monumental. But not enough. I've come around to thinking the way you do. Scary, isn't it?"

"But satisfying, I must say. So what did you learn?"

"I can't tell you everything. I promised her I wouldn't."

He frowned. "Well, that was a damn fool promise.

How am I supposed to help her if you don't tell me what you know?"

"Listen, D'Amico, you threatened to put me in jail if I even went near her. Now you want me to tell you what I, alone, managed to find out?"

He fell silent. But not for long.

"Carrie, do you honestly think I don't know what I'm doing? If you do, you're wrong. Over the last year I've made it my business to know more about sexual abuse than I ever did in ten years on the force. I know exactly what the odds are against women and young girls in court. The laws are archaic. Sexual abuse is taken so lightly it would make your skin crawl. There's always the implication that the girl, or woman, either lied about it or must have somehow asked for it. They have to defend themselves against that on the stand. And even when the case is proven, offenders are sentenced lightly and released too early."

"I know all that," she said irritably. "I watch the news."

"You may know intellectually how it works. But until you've lived in this town..."

"Good point. What the hell is it about this town? It seems every time I turn over a rock I find something else dirty beneath it."

"I'll admit things look bad. But the truth is, Holly Beach isn't all that different from a thousand other small towns with financial difficulties. Oh, sure, everything looks bright around here in the summer. Tourists piling in, everybody having fun. But in the winter this is the damnedest, darkest, loneliest place in the world. You know how many women I've seen battered here? How many parents I've suspected of abuse? People are out of work, there's not enough money, they start drinking or doing drugs. Usually, it's both. They get violent. They take it out on the women and kids. And we don't have the right programs in place to handle it.''

"Well, for God's sake, why don't you do something about that?"

His voice rose. "And why don't you stop complaining when you don't know what the hell you're talking about? It just so happens I'm already backing up the beat cops all summer long, besides doing my own job. I'm behind in every investigation I've got going.''

"Can't the police department hire more help?''

"Not when there's no money coming into the town nine months out of the year." He glanced at her. "You might think of staying here. You'd be the perfect person to set up something for battered wives and children.''

Her eyes widened. "Me? I don't know anything about programs like that.''

"You could learn.''

"What makes you think—''

"Are you saying you have no experience with child abuse?''

It was a direct hit. *He knows. I don't know how, but he knows. About me, about Breen. And God knows how much more.*

"Let's get back to Tess," she said roughly.

"Sure. We don't have to talk about you. Not if you really don't want to.''

"I really don't want to," she snapped. "What I want is to make sure Tess is safe. There's something about those parents. They may just still be in grief over losing Debra....''

"Well, it hasn't been that long.''

"And for a moment, yesterday, the father had tears in his eyes. But hell, Nicky, to get Tess out of that house for even a couple of hours, I had to promise to pay him."

Nicky frowned. "Pay him?"

"Never mind. The thing is, I know for a fact they aren't protecting her from Breen."

"How do you know that?"

"I can't tell you. I promised Tess I wouldn't."

"Oh, for Christ's sake!"

"Look, I didn't decide to tell you this so you could swear at me!"

"All right, all right. Sorry. But you're tying my hands. What is it you want me to do?"

"I'm not sure. But is there any way we could somehow get Tess out of that house for a while? Some way she'd be safe, not only from whatever's going on there, but from Breen? At least until we can get enough evidence for you to charge him?"

"The only way would be to turn the parents in for either abuse or neglect. You could do that with a simple phone call to Child Welfare. They'd investigate, and if they decided the charges had merit, they could arrest the parents."

Carrie shook her head. "That might harm Tess more than it would help her. They'd probably put her in a foster home, right?"

"Most likely. And if they proved their case against the parents, Tess could wind up in a foster home for good."

"That's what I thought. I don't want that to happen to her, Nicky. I don't even know for sure if her parents are all that bad, or just misguided. The father, for instance. Is it just grief, or is he one of those people who was a jerk even before tragedy came along? Until I know more, there's got to be another way.''

She watched as an elderly couple walked hand in hand along the beach, stopping to pick up a shell now and then. How simple life seemed for them, how easy, she thought.

"One thing," Nicky said. "You may not have to worry about this much longer."

She turned to him. "Meaning?"

"That I'm just about ready to move on Breen. Carrie, if you tell me what you learned from Tess—if we put our heads together—this could all be over in days. Maybe even hours."

"And Tess would be safe?"

"I...well, I can almost guarantee it."

She frowned. "Almost isn't enough, Nicky."

He made an impatient gesture. "All right, all right! I do guarantee it."

Carrie was silent, thinking. She had decided earlier to tell him what she knew, hoping it might help. Nothing had changed since then. Had it?

At last she said, "I need your promise that this won't go any further than you. If Tess found out I'd betrayed her trust, there's no telling what it might do to her. She needs someone she can talk to, Nicky. You can't blow that for her."

"It's a promise. Trust me," he said.

So she sat there on the warm sand beneath a normal-seeming sky, with normal-seeming people walking along the shoreline of a normal-seeming sea, and told him about deeds so dark they hardly seemed possible within the realms of anything commonplace at all. She told him how Debra's father had locked her up to keep her in at night. About Debra's meetings with Breen, his "taking her under his wing," and the parents warning her not to tell anyone. Especially when Debra got "sick."

"She was pregnant, just as you said," Carrie told him.

He nodded. "Four months. We didn't know Breen was giving her money. It helps that you found that out."

"The scary thing is, he's moving in on Tess now. With Debra gone, he's been after her."

Nicky made a sound of disgust. "She told you that? Specifically?"

"She said he'd taken her to the boardwalk for ice cream. He told her he wanted to be her friend—just like he was Debra's friend."

"Holy shit."

"So you see why something has to be done, and fast. I know you said you were about ready to move on Breen, Nicky, but you've got to do it *now*. There's really no time to waste."

He was silent.

"Meanwhile," Carrie said, "I intend to stay as close to Tess as I possibly can."

He shook his head. "Absolutely not. Look, you've done a great job with her. But let me take care of it now."

Carrie gave him a sharp look, her eyes narrowing. "There's no way—Nicky, what are you planning to do?"

"I can't tell you."

"You can't tell me?" The green eyes went dark with anger. "After I've broken my promise to Tess, you say you can't tell me what you plan to do about her?"

"That's what I'm saying, and for the same reasons

I gave you yesterday. I think you're too closely involved.''

She jumped to her feet, looking down at him. ''What the hell does that mean?''

''It means that until you tell me the real reason, *aside* from Tess, that you're after Breen, I can't trust what you might do.''

''My reason doesn't matter! It should be enough that I want to bring him down.''

''Well, it isn't. Tell me this—how much do you want to bring him down? What would you do to bring him down? How far would you go? Those are the questions, as a cop, that I have to ask myself in deciding how much to let you in on. Let's say Breen abused you, for instance.''

She paled and tried not to let him see it. The words, however, spoken aloud in his voice, hammered through her heart.

''Let's say he abused you the same way he abused Debra,'' Nicky continued, watching her closely, ''and the way he's getting ready to abuse Tess. I can see where that would make you pretty angry, Carrie. Maybe even a little bit crazy. In which case, you might go off half-cocked and blow the whole thing.''

''Blow the whole thing!'' Her voice shook, and her hands formed fists. She jammed them into her pockets. ''Blow the whole thing? You think I would do that? You think I'm some sort of deranged female—''

''Carrie. Listen to me. I did not say that.''

''But you think it.''

''I do not. It's just that I have to follow procedure.''

''Well, fuck your procedure!''

She flinched as the words left her mouth. They reminded her all too much of her father and the way he had shouted when drinking.

More quietly, she said, "I'm sorry. Of course, you have to follow procedure. I understand that."

Nicky looked relieved. "I'm glad, Carrie. I need your cooperation. I'm honestly not trying to shut you out. Do you believe that?"

She didn't answer.

"Will you go along with me on this?" he insisted. "Will you stay away from Tess, for now?"

She hedged. "What if something happens and she needs me? I won't abandon that child."

"You won't have to. I think I can wrap this up in twenty-four hours. Will you give me that much? Think, Carrie. It could all be over in twenty-four hours."

All be over. Was it possible? Breen in jail, Tess safe? Everyone safe, at last?

"Twenty-four hours," she finally agreed, though nothing about it felt right. "No more."

"It's a promise," Nicky said.

He stood and faced her, holding out his hand. "Truce?"

She hesitated, then took the proffered hand. "Truce."

Looking to the south, she added, "That's it, then. I'd better get going."

He smiled. "Why don't you come up and look at my house first?"

She shook her head. "I have to get to the Pines. I'm worried about my grandmother."

"I was at the Pines a little while ago. Your grandmother is fine."

"You saw her?"

"I looked in on her, just to make sure. It's my job. After the other night, you know."

"Right. After the other night."

Despite the talk they'd just had, she didn't know what to make of him. Was he concerned about her grandmother as a person? Or had he another agenda? Where did the cop end—and the human being begin?

"It's almost finished," he said persuasively.

"Finished?"

"My house." He grinned. "Come on."

Why does he even bother with me? she wondered. Or I, him? Why don't we just leave each other alone?

Sighing, she followed him up through the sand.

It was a beautiful house. Carrie could see that, even though the walls were still open between the framing, and the final flooring had not yet been laid. The living and dining rooms were large, with windows facing the ocean in front, the bayside on the other. He would have the morning sun from the east and the setting sun in the west.

The kitchen was huge, as well, with room for both a small dining table and a breakfast nook. The beams had been left exposed, and the walls were being done in a light, natural wood, farmhouse style. A fireplace had already been built into one wall. Into another a large greenhouse window had been framed. She could almost see African violets on shelves there, catching the gentle morning light.

"It's great," she said, feeling an odd pang. "Your wife, if you plan to bring one here, that is, will love it."

He gave her a curious look, and when he didn't end it, she turned away, blushing. She hadn't meant to be forward. Had he taken what she said the wrong way? "I just meant—"

"I know what you meant," he said easily. "It's a great house. Any woman would love it."

"Well, let's not be humble here," she said tartly.

He laughed. "I just had a really great architect. She's an old friend, and she knew what I'd like—even though I didn't, quite."

"That's nice. It must be good to have a friend who knows you that well."

Carrie walked to the greenhouse window, looking out at wild sea grass. "Will you leave the outside this way?"

"Absolutely. Everything natural, all the way around."

"That's good, too."

There was a small silence.

"Do you live in a house, Carrie?"

"No, an apartment." That was the reason for the almost envious pang, she was sure. She had always dreamed of having a house of her own. She just didn't know if she'd ever be able to afford one.

"I guess I'd better be going," she said, glancing at her watch. "I did promise my grandmother I'd be there for lunch, and it's getting late. Thanks for showing me your house, though. I'll bet you bring everyone you know here to see it. Not that I blame you. You have every right to be proud."

"Well, I am proud. But I don't bring everyone here. Mom, Dad, Uncle Mike, Sally. And now you."

She met his eyes. "I feel especially honored, then."

He grinned. "Thank God."

She raised a brow.

"I mean, it's better than you wanting to hit me in the head with a two-by-four."

She smiled, and they looked at each other, an awkward silence growing between them. Nicky ran his fingers through his hair. A nervous gesture, she knew by now. She cleared her throat.

"Well..."

He smiled and shrugged. "Well."

"I guess I'll see you later."

"Right."

"You'll, uh—you'll tell me what's going on? About Breen, that is? You'll let me know the minute anything happens?"

"The minute I've got anything, I'll tell you."

Neither of them moved. Grinning, Nicky blew out a deep breath and took her arm. "C'mon, I'll walk you out."

"We're already out," she said, as a gull flew past the open walls. But she smiled. And she didn't pull away this time.

Elizabeth wasn't in her room. Carrie checked her watch. Far too late for lunch now, she thought. Maybe they've taken her to the recreation room. They often did that in the afternoon, she recalled.

When Elizabeth wasn't there, either, Carrie sought out Nan in her office.

"One of the aides took her outside," Nan said with a smile. "After all the rain we've had, most of the patients can use some sunshine and fresh air."

From the searching look Nan gave her, Carrie knew immediately there was something she wanted to talk about. Taking her usual place on the sofa, she said anxiously, "Is something wrong?"

"You know, I'm not really sure. Certainly, there's something different."

"In what way?"

"I've been trying to put a finger on it. And I think it's that I feel I don't know Elizabeth as well, lately. In the past few months, she's changed, and that change seems even more pronounced since you came back this time."

"Well, I've been talking to her, the way you suggested. But I always do that. Do you think she's coming back? I mean, all the way? You said the other day that you thought she was deliberately trying to forget."

"I didn't say that precisely, only that it was a possibility. Right now I'm wondering if she's actually going in and out. Sometimes with us, sometimes not. And when she is with us—or when I believe she is—she doesn't always let on."

"Why do you think she would do that?"

"Possibly because she doesn't want to be dragged all the way back? I don't know, I'm just guessing. Maybe there are things she doesn't want to come back to. Things she doesn't want to remember."

Carrie shook her head. "I can't think of anything in my grandmother's past that would make her feel that way, Nan. She always lived such a normal, ordinary sort of life."

Or did she? Carrie wondered. With her grandmother's distaste for talking about personal matters, how could anyone know?

"Carrie, Elizabeth was a very bright, aware woman when she first came in here with that broken hip a year ago. It was only when her recovery took so much longer than expected that she became depressed and eventually withdrew."

"But we don't know for sure it was the depression that made her withdraw."

"No, only that there seemed to be no physical cause. According to all the tests that were taken, she has none of the classic markers of either Alzheimer's or senility."

"Still, the medication she was taking for depression didn't seem to help."

"Well, that may not be entirely true. The fact that she's responding to physical therapy, and even walking again, may be because the medication brought her back enough to at least try."

Nan motioned to the ever-present plate of cookies, and Carrie shook her head. Nan took one and bit into it. "Ugh. It's stale." She put it back down and brushed crumbs from her hands. "I have a theory," she said, "that I'd like to fly by you."

"Okay."

"What if your grandmother had something else going on in her life—something that brought her so much sadness, or grief, she would have withdrawn eventually, anyway? What if the broken hip, and what might have been a normal, postsurgical depression afterward, were simply the final straws?"

Carrie thought back. "It's true that she changed after my grandfather died. But isn't it normal to go through a period of grieving? Especially when you've been married so long and your partner dies?"

"Absolutely normal. But, Carrie, that was five years ago. How was she, say, two years ago, when one might expect she'd be recovering from that grief?"

"I'm ashamed to say I don't really know. My grandmother never liked talking about herself, so the few times I came home to visit, there really wasn't any way to tell.'' Carrie gave an apologetic shrug. ''The truth is, I didn't come home all that much, until my grandmother broke her hip and I brought her here. My mother used to keep in touch with her on a regular basis, before she died. As for me, I was so busy living my own life, I was pretty much oblivious to what was going on with either of them.''

''Well, don't beat yourself up for that. Children seldom think about their parents' or grandparents' mortality. We like to think they'll be here forever.''

''But you know,'' Carrie said, ''I have been thinking that my grandmother seemed more subdued in recent years. More than I remembered her being, that is, when I was a child. There was a time when she was so energetic, full of excitement and life. She used to hold what she called her Sunday salons, and she was beautiful, really vibrant with all those people around her. It seemed she loved everyone, and they loved her.''

''No kidding? That's an image of Elizabeth I never would have come up with. When did her personality start to change? Can you remember?''

''Well, the Sunday salons ended years ago. It seemed they reached a high point before she and my grandfather moved to Minnesota. Then, when they came home a year later, everything ended abruptly. My grandmother began to change after that. Some might say she 'settled down.' And when she grew even quieter over the years, I guess I attributed it to her getting older.''

''But people don't lose their zest for life just because they're getting older, Carrie. Usually there's a reason, like bad health, or some emotional trauma. Something makes them so tired of life, they simply disengage.''

Carrie sighed. ''I guess I never thought of that. And

I should have. You know something, Nan? I've been disengaging from life all my life.''

"I gathered that.''

Carrie raised a brow. "Have you been psychoanalyzing me, my friend?''

"Only at odd moments.'' Nan smiled. "But I'll let you off the hook for now. Tell me more about Elizabeth.''

"I don't know if I can. The only thing that comes to mind that might be troubling her now is that she might be afraid of dying. After the other night, when she thought she saw someone at her window, she was quite upset. She said, 'I thought he was gone. But he came back.' Or something like that. I don't remember the exact words. But she said he 'came to get me.'''

"And you translated that to mean…?''

"That she must have had a nightmare, and in that nightmare she saw my grandfather coming for her.'' Carrie smiled and shrugged. "Like Death, you know.''

"I see. Well, it's certainly possible. It could account for Elizabeth's extreme reaction. Fear of dying, fear of being 'whisked away in the night,' so to speak, to some netherworld.''

"I'm just not sure, after thinking about it, if that fits. My grandmother's always had a strong spiritual side. As far back as I can remember, she prayed in the morning, and then again at night. She never seemed the kind of person to be afraid of meeting her Maker.'' Carrie sighed. "But then…what do I know?''

Nan seemed thoughtful. She folded her hands, perhaps unconsciously, in a church and steeple position, leaning her chin on her upraised index fingers.

"There's one thing about religious beliefs, Carrie. They often go hand in hand with guilt.''

"You think some sort of guilt is what's making her withdraw?"

"I just think that even when Elizabeth does have her more alert moments, she doesn't seem very happy."

Carrie shook her head. "I really can't think of anything, Nan. But are you sure there isn't a simpler explanation for what's going on with my grandmother right now? One thing I do know is that when people are seemingly 'out of their heads,' it doesn't pay to overlook the obvious. Are you certain there was no one here who shouldn't have been here? No one who might have disturbed her in some way? I understand the police were called. Did they come up with anything?"

"I'm afraid not. I told them everything I knew, and they took a report. Security found no one on the grounds, and only the usual people in the building—a doctor who'd been called in to see a patient who's critical, the usual staff and a few visitors who are well known to us and trusted. A minister, a rabbi...people like that."

Carrie stood. "Well, let me go and sit with her now. Maybe I can get her to talk to me today. You say she's in the garden?"

Nan gave a nod. "An aide took her out there a little while ago. See what you can do, Carrie. It may be time to press a bit more. Give her a jolt—gently, of course. Something from your own past, perhaps?" She gave Carrie a steady look.

"Why do I get the feeling you've got me all figured out?" Carrie said.

Nan stood and touched her arm. "I would just like so much for both of you to be well."

Carrie didn't find Elizabeth right away. She was seated in a wheelchair, far out beyond the main garden and oddly out of the line of sight of any of the nurses or aides who were looking after patients there. She faced the ocean, on an isolated spit of sand surrounded by hedges and sea grass.

Why on earth did they put her all the way out here? Carrie wondered with more than a touch of irritation. Was there a new aide on the job who didn't know any better? Nan should be told about this. If Elizabeth needed something, or if anything happened to her, no one would ever know.

Carrie's irritation, however, was tempered by the fact that her grandmother did in fact seem more alert today. As Carrie drew near, Elizabeth's eyes turned her way.

"Hi! You look so much better," Carrie said, smiling and kneeling beside her. "I'm sorry I'm late, Grandmother. I meant to be here for lunch, but I ran into someone and started talking. Are you okay?"

Her grandmother smiled.

Next to Elizabeth were a heavy round table, badly weathered, and two wooden lawn chairs in similar condition. Carrie pulled one chair close and reached for her grandmother's hand. She noticed then that beneath her grandmother's folded hands was a flowered book.

"What is this you're reading?" she asked out of curiosity.

With a quickness that startled Carrie, Elizabeth slipped the book into the space between her hip and the chair. She gave Carrie a defiant look.

How odd. She's trying to hide it.

But that's good, isn't it? It means she's responding to me, at least.

"I wasn't going to take your book," Carrie said

soothingly. "I was just curious. I'm glad you're reading again."

There was a glass of water on the table at Elizabeth's side. It was full, as if untouched. Carrie leaned over and picked it up, then held it out to her grandmother, thinking her lips looked dry.

Elizabeth shook her head vehemently, locking her lips and turning her head away.

"It's getting warm out here," Carrie said. "Please, Grandmother. You don't want to get dehydrated."

Elizabeth's mouth remained a tight, firm line. Like a little kid who won't eat her creamed spinach, Carrie thought with a touch of amusement. She sighed and set the glass back down.

"I've decided to stay on a while longer, Grandmother. I wanted you to know that I'll be coming every day. I'm not leaving when the festival is over."

Elizabeth's eyes met hers, but there was no joy there. Carrie had hoped for a hint of pleasure. If anything, however, there might have been a trace of fear in the faded blue eyes. Startled, she wondered why.

"Grandmother, do you remember the other night, when you thought there was someone outside your window? Can you remember anything more about that now?"

Elizabeth's gaze swung away.

"Was it Grandfather?" Carrie pressed. "Did you dream about him? Or was it something else? Did anyone try to hurt you?"

The thin hands clenched.

There is something, then. What is it?

The thought had crossed her mind, while talking with Nan, that there might be someone here who was harming her grandmother in some way. It seemed that every time Carrie opened a newspaper or turned on the evening news there were stories, now, about patient abuse by aides and nurses in convalescent homes. Carrie knew that anything could happen, from thefts to threats to outright physical abuse.

The Pines, she had felt, was the one place where things like that would never happen. She had trusted Nan implicitly, not only to run a tight ship, but to personally keep a close eye out for any kind of maltreatment.

Still, Nan couldn't be everywhere at once. No one could be, in spite of the best intentions. And sometimes the wrong kinds of employees slipped through even the tightest of security nets.

"I would never let anyone hurt you," Carrie said to her grandmother, taking her hand. "You just have to tell me. Please, if there's anything at all…"

Elizabeth closed her eyes, and Carrie continued to stroke the back of her hand.

Give her a jolt, Nan had said. She knew what Nan meant, even if Nan herself didn't know, specifically, but had only guessed. *Talk about the family secrets, whatever they are.*

But how to say the words? How to speak about such terrible things? She hadn't been able to do it as a child, and it seemed no more possible a feat now. Instead, Carrie said simply, "Grandmother, tell me about my father."

She hadn't expected an answer. But her grandmother's eyes opened and slowly drifted her way.

"What do you remember about him?" Carrie asked, encouraged. "My father," Carrie repeated softly. "Remember? Jack? He used to play the piano, the old songs you liked. 'Bye Bye Blackbird'... 'As Time Goes By'..."

She stopped, nearly choking on a brief, unbidden memory herself. Her father sitting on the piano bench with her in his lap, playing one-handed, the other hand...

Carrie shook her head, as if doing so could shake the memory away, back into some black hole of the mind where it might, if she were lucky, be swept into a void.

"Remember, Grandmother?" she continued unsteadily. "He..."

But the old woman's eyes had come to life.

"Bye...bye...blackbird," she whispered softly.

"Yes," Carrie said, sitting forward eagerly. "Grandmother, you remember?"

Elizabeth squeezed her hand—a soft, feathery squeeze that Carrie barely felt. But it was there.

"Grandmother, what do you remember? About him and my mother...and me? Did you know about...about things he did? How much did you know?"

It was like taking a lid from a box filled to the brim, so that even the slightest crack let pieces of the past fall out. Carrie could no more hold back those pieces than the moon.

"I have memories, Grandmother. Terrible memories. I don't really believe you knew. Or my mother. Did Alice know?" She laughed shakily. "I don't even know why I'm asking you this, and I don't want to hurt you, honestly I don't. It's just the most important thing to me now, that you never knew."

For a long moment Elizabeth didn't respond. Her hand lay lifeless in Carrie's. *She doesn't even hear me. She's gone again, that quickly.*

Then, abruptly, Elizabeth came to life. Straightening her spine, she lifted her chin and said in a firm, icy voice, "The man was a devil! I sent him away."

Carrie couldn't have been more shocked. She rocked back in her chair, trying to gather her wits. "You did what? You sent him away?"

"I most certainly did."

Oh, my God. "Grandmother, tell me why. Why did you send my father away? And when?" She couldn't remember a time when he'd been gone.

Elizabeth's shoulders drooped. "So long ago," she said softly. "I loved him. I did love him. But it wasn't right, what he did." Her eyes met Carrie's and didn't waver. "It wasn't right—was it, Alice?"

A cold chill went through Carrie. At first, she couldn't speak. Then, "Grandmother? It isn't Alice. It's Carrie. Can you hear me? Do you know me at all?"

"Of course I do! What do you think, that I'm deaf, dumb and blind besides?"

Carrie almost laughed with relief. This was the grandmother she remembered. Elizabeth sat before her as she had once been—spirited, full of life, her eyes flashing.

"I'm so glad—" Carrie began, taking her hand.

Then, in a twinkling, it was over. With her free hand, Elizabeth waved like a child.

"Bye, bye, blackbird," she said in a high, piping voice. "Bye, bye."

Turning away, she fixed her gaze once more on the view.

The sun blazed overhead as Carrie sat beside her grandmother, thinking of their brief conversation. And the way it had ended. Just when she'd thought... *Oh, God, I am so tired.*

Elizabeth's eyes were closed. She seemed to be sleeping.

She never drank her water, Carrie thought. She never even touched it. And it's warm now.

It was the only glass on the table, and the usual blue plastic pitcher was nowhere in sight. *I'll take her back to the main garden and ask a nurse to bring her a fresh glass. She should have water that's fresh and cool on a day like this.*

She herself was thirsty, however, and warm or not, Carrie lifted the glass and drank, wetting her parched tongue.

The tide was coming in now, faster than she'd realized, almost up to Elizabeth's chair. Making sure that her grandmother was comfortable in the wheelchair, with her feet on the footpads, Carrie turned the chair in the sand and headed up toward the hedges that separated this spit of sand from the main gardens. She thought she remembered coming down a paved path through the hedges, one that led directly from the sand to the main garden. Once into the mazelike thicket, however, she couldn't remember the way out. She was surrounded by shrubbery too high to see over, and there seemed several directions she might take.

Her limbs began to feel oddly heavy. Then amazingly light. With only the slightest effort, she felt as if she might float. Bright sunlight blazed down, blinding her. Carrie's scalp felt tight. She began to push the wheelchair down a different path, but the chair grew heavy, as if the brake were on. Checking it, she saw that it wasn't.

I wonder if the wheel is in a rut. I wonder what

would happen if I just pushed harder. I should just push harder.

She tried, but the chair moved even more slowly, as if through molasses.

Or under water.

She saw then that she and her grandmother were both moving underwater. *How strange. Everything is blurry, too.*

From the water in my eyes, she thought. Odd, though, that I can still breathe. People can't breathe underwater.

With that, her breathing became more labored. *Why is it so damned hard to push this chair? Has Grandmother gained weight?*

Carrie smiled. Of course not. Her grandmother never gained weight. It wouldn't be nice.

Leaning over to look at Elizabeth, Carrie found that she did look big, though. She was huge now.

No, small. Smaller than ever.

Huge *and* small.

My skin feels so hot. I'm freezing. And my skin is burning.

She pulled the shawl around her grandmother's shoulders to keep her warm. *I can't let her freeze out here in the snow.*

Snow. Snow fell all around now, pink snow, like cotton candy. Carrie lifted her face and stuck out her tongue, catching flakes on it. Throwing her arms out, she twirled in a circle as she had in childhood, then threw herself on the ground, making angel wings.

"Look, Grandmother! Look at my angel wings!" Her grandmother smiled at her and clapped. "You do it, too, Grandmother!" Carrie cried.

Her grandmother stood and dropped to the ground beside her, flapping her arms in the snow.

"That's right! Isn't this fun?" Carrie began to laugh. And laugh.

She couldn't stop laughing. She was laughing and laughing and laughing—

She laughed so hard, in fact, she could no longer catch her breath. A fullness rose in her chest and throat, blocking any passage of air. Her heart pumped so hard, it broke through her chest. And as its beating stopped, the sun that had blazed so hard only moments ago went out.

22

Congressman Tanner stood looking out the window of his room at the Bahia. From here he could see a long way up the shore to the north. He couldn't see the Anglesea Center, because the shoreline curved long before that. He saw it in his mind's eye, however, beyond the boardwalk and the pier, saw Breen holding court over "his" children, the children he held so much power over and could do anything with.

Tanner shook off feelings of guilt that threatened to overwhelm him. He'd been up most of the night, bile rising in his throat from heartburn, the pains in his stomach radiating into his chest. The deeds he'd ordered done had brought with them a high price. Much more than the thirty pieces of silver that damned bodyguard, Vincent Petrelli had demanded.

It was my responsibility to take action, he reminded himself. Weiss never would have. My responsibility to see those kids are safe from now on—without bringing the whole damned mess to light and destroying everyone involved. The task force, Weiss, me...

There was a knock at the door. He crossed the large living room of the deluxe suite and opened it. "Vincent." He sighed. "Come in."

The bodyguard stepped into the room.

"How did it go?" Tanner asked, half dreading the answer.

"Without a hitch," Petrelli said. "I slipped something into her water."

"You managed to find a sedative? You put enough in to..." Tanner fell silent.

Petrelli shook his head. "There were too many nurses and other staff around. I couldn't risk it. It was hard enough just getting her away from everybody. Besides, a sedative strong enough to kill her would have shown up in an autopsy, and there would have been an investigation. What I gave her won't leave a trace after the first hour or two."

The man looked worried, Tanner thought. "I don't understand. What exactly did you give her?"

"I, uh...bought something off the streets."

"Off the *streets?*" Tanner's voice rose in alarm.

"It's not that hard, sir. Not in a beach town. Don't worry, the guy I got it from won't remember." Petrelli laughed. "Shit, he can't even remember his own name."

"That's not what I'm worried about! For God's sake, man, what the hell did you give the woman?"

"A...uh, a couple of spinners."

"Spinners." Tanner's tone was icy. "What the hell are spinners?"

"They're sort of a, uh, hallucinogen."

Tanner paled. "A hallucinogen! Christ Almighty, man! I wanted her dead, not jumping off buildings!"

"It's not like that, sir. This is something new. Don't worry. It'll have her cruising like crazy, then it'll knock her out."

"May I remind you," Tanner said angrily, "that the whole idea was to remove the woman permanently? I can't have her talking about what Breen did to her granddaughter, now that she's starting to recover. *Any-*

one who can talk about Breen's past must be removed. That was the whole point, for God's sake.''

"I told you, sir, don't worry.''

"Don't worry? If, as you say, this hallucinogen doesn't kill her—''

"That's the beauty of it, sir. We're gonna let the tide do that. It's just about due in, and where she is, she'll be swimming with the fishes before she ever comes to.''

Tanner shook his head. "This is too damned risky. If someone finds her first, while she's still under the influence…''

"They'll think she's a confused old lady. No harm, no foul. We'll just try again.''

"Dammit, man! There may not be time for that!'' Tanner began to pace. "I am not happy with this, Vincent.''

The man was a loose cannon. Why hadn't he seen that? Anything could happen now. Anything at all.

23

"Carrie! Carrie, can you hear me?"

It was Nicky's voice, somewhere close to her ear.

Carrie opened her eyes and saw Nicky kneeling beside her. "You're all right," he said. "You're in Nan Martin's office at the Pines."

She realized she was lying on Nan's sofa. She tried to sit.

"Don't get up," another voice said. A man she had seen somewhere before stood behind Nicky. *Dr. Esmond, my grandmother's doctor. Why is he here?*

"What's wrong with me? What's going on?" Her mouth felt fuzzy, and her head ached. It was difficult to focus. "Nicky? What are you doing here?"

Nan came into view beside Nicky. Sitting at the foot of the sofa, she said worriedly, "You apparently blacked out, Carrie, way beyond the hedges. I thought it best to call Dr. Esmond. It also seemed prudent, after that incident here the other night with your grandmother, to call the police."

"I'd just gotten to the station," Nicky added, "and I took the call. Carrie, can you tell us what happened? What were you doing all the way out there?"

"I..." She searched back, trying to remember. "I found my grandmother there, and then..." She struggled to a sitting position, fighting off Nicky's hands when he would have restrained her. "My grandmother! Where is she? Is she all right?"

"She's in her room, resting," Nan said gently. "Lie back, Carrie. Your grandmother is fine. She actually managed to get out of her chair and find a nurse when you blacked out."

"She did that? Alone?"

"She sure did." Nan smiled. "It took her awhile. She was confused and didn't precisely know where she was going, apparently, so I'm guessing sheer instinct drove her on. Carrie, what happened?"

She eased back, grateful for the sofa beneath her. Her mind, if not her body, was spinning.

"I don't know. I sat with her awhile. But it was getting hot, and she wouldn't drink any water. I was afraid she'd become dehydrated, so I started to bring her back up here. I had my hands on her wheelchair and we were coming up through the hedges, and then...then everything went odd."

Something nagged at the back of her mind, something important. What was it?

Her gaze swung to Nan. "Somebody put her there, Nan. They left my grandmother alone out there."

Nan's eyes widened. "I can't believe that. Are you sure?"

"Of course I'm sure!" she said irritably. "Sorry. My head hurts. But that's where I found her, after I talked to you."

She looked at Dr. Esmond, who had reached past Nicky to take her pulse.

"What's wrong with me? Do you know?

"Well," he said, dropping her wrist and shining a thin, bright light into her eyes, "one cannot be certain of a diagnosis in these circumstances. We would have to do a thorough workup to rule out any number of possibilities. Without having done that, one can only guess.''

"Then take a crack at it, dammit!" Carrie said testily. She never had liked this man.

Dr. Esmond's mouth tightened. "My guess, young lady, would be that you had an episode of arrhythmia. Your heartbeat is still irregular and much too fast."

Carrie focused on his white hair, then the gray eyes. "Arrhythmia?"

"Rapid and/or irregular heartbeats. Do you have a history of heart trouble, Miss Holt?"

"No. I've never had anything wrong with my heart at all."

"Of course, it is an unusually hot day. You may well have been suffering from heat exhaustion, with an attendant loss of sodium and potassium. This may have caused your heart to stop briefly, bringing on temporary unconsciousness. You're a very lucky young woman, Miss Holt. People have been known to die in the midst of an arrhythmia. If your grandmother hadn't gone for help—"

But it was coming back now. *The snow. The angels.*

She interrupted, glancing down at her arm. "Excuse me. Did you take any blood before I came to?"

Dr. Esmond lifted a white brow in surprise. "Blood?"

"For testing. You said you couldn't be certain what was wrong with me, without a thorough workup."

"I did say that, yes, but in this case I don't see that a full workup is necessary, Miss Holt. A simple case of heat exhaustion—"

Carrie looked at Nicky. "Make him take some blood. You can do that, can't you?"

"I...yes, I can do that," Nicky said carefully, his gaze swinging from her to the doctor and back again. "What's up, Carrie?"

"I was drugged. That's what's up. And I want proof."

All eyes swung her way.

"Drugged?" Nan said with horror. "Carrie, are you sure?"

"I didn't spend six years at Berkeley for nothing, Nan! Of course I'm sure!"

Again she felt as if she should apologize for her irritation. It was just that her nerves were jangling, and everything, suddenly, was moving far too slowly. Why couldn't people move faster; why was all this taking so damned long?

"Miss Holt, I'm sure you must be wrong," Dr. Esmond said. "There is absolutely no reason to think—"

She interrupted him, looking at Nicky again. "There was something in my grandmother's water. There was one glass on the table, just one, and she wouldn't touch it. When I tried to get her to drink some, she refused. She wouldn't even open her mouth. She knew there was something in it, Nicky. I'm sure of it. She just couldn't tell me."

Nicky turned to Nan. "Who took Elizabeth out there in the first place?"

Nan shook her head. "I have no idea. I saw one of our aides with Elizabeth on the lawn, just before Carrie arrived. I can get her in here. But the aides here are exceptionally well trained. They never would have left Elizabeth, or any patient, all the way out there. Especially not alone."

"Call her in, would you please?"

Nan gave a nod and picked up the phone.

"Meantime," Nicky said, "about those tests. Dr. Esmond, I'd like you to take some blood now, and I also want you to schedule Carrie for a thorough physical exam."

Carrie touched his arm. "On second thought... The police department, Nicky. You have a lab there?"

His eyes met hers with a question. "We've got someone who can draw blood. We send it to an outside lab for testing."

"Why don't we have Dr. Esmond draw the blood and you take it and send it out for testing through the police department? Can we do that?"

Nicky flicked a glance at Dr. Esmond, then back at her. "Of course, if that's what you want. Dr. Esmond?"

The doctor stiffened, clearly angry, but took the necessary equipment from his bag.

Carrie held out her arm. Esmond tightened a rubber tourniquet around it, tamped the inside of her elbow with his fingers, swabbed the spot with alcohol, then drew the required sample. He handed Carrie a clean cotton swab to hold over the needle spot, and gave the tube of blood to Nicky. Standing, he removed his gloves. Putting his stethoscope and a digital thermometer into his bag, he closed it with a loud snap.

"If that's all..."

"Thank you, Doctor," Nicky said.

Esmond's gray eyes assessed Carrie coolly. "You're looking much better, Miss Holt. If I may, I would suggest you stay out of the sun and drink an abundance of fluids over the next twenty-four hours."

At the door, he turned back. "Oh, and by the way. Get some rest. It might do your temper a world of good."

As the door closed, everyone fell silent. Finally, Carrie let out an almost shamefaced laugh. "My estimation of the good Dr. Esmond just went up a few points. I have been pretty bad, haven't I? I'm sorry, Nan."

"Even so," Nan said, "I never did like that man. Personally, that is. If your grandmother hadn't insisted on him as her physician, I'd have found someone else."

"I think he may be the only person in the world who knows her deepest secrets," Carrie mused. "My grandmother comes from a time when women thought their doctors were God. They told them everything."

The voice of a police dispatch officer came from a hand-held radio on the coffee table. Nicky picked it up and crossed the room, talking into it quietly. At the same time, another man, blond and broad-shouldered, in a T-shirt and jeans, entered the room. Nicky motioned to him. They spoke a few moments, and the man shook his head. They both crossed over to Carrie.

"Where exactly were you when you drank from that glass?" Nicky said.

"I was with my grandmother, out on some spit of sand beyond the hedges. I'm not sure exactly where that was. I just came upon her all of a sudden. There's a white wooden table and a couple of lounge chairs there, and it's not too far back from the ocean."

"I know which one she means," Nan said. "It's really just a place for the staff to sit during their breaks, out of sight of the patients. That way they get a few moments of undisturbed relaxation."

Nicky looked at the other man. "Hal?"

"If it's the place I'm thinking of, and it sounds like it, I checked that out, too. There wasn't anything there, just the table and chairs, like she said. No drinking glass of any kind. But you should know—the tide's way up there by now.''

"The glass wouldn't have been there, anyway," Carrie said, remembering. "I had it in my hand when I started to push my grandmother's wheelchair. I was going to give it to an aide and ask her to bring my grandmother a clean glass and some fresh water. Then things got weird, and the next I knew I was making angels in the snow.''

Nicky and Nan looked at her as if she were crazy.

Carrie shook her head and shrugged.

To the other cop, Nicky said, "Try searching the grounds again in the same area where they found her. If you don't come up with anything the first time, keep looking, will you? I want that glass.''

The cop nodded and left.

"My partner, Hal," Nicky explained when he'd left. "If there's anything there, he'll find it.''

"Won't it be enough if they find the drug in my blood?" Carrie asked.

"Not if it's something that's already out of your system. Traces of it on a glass, though, along with your fingerprints, can go a long way.''

"Not to mention the fingerprints of whoever put that drug in the glass.''

"I don't think we can count on that," Nicky said. "It was probably wiped clean before you even got there.''

Carrie frowned. "You're right. Nicky, there's something that troubles me. That drug wasn't lethal. I'm still here, I didn't die. So what was the point of giving it to my grandmother? Even at her age, how much harm could that do?''

"Quite a bit," he said, "if you hadn't found her

there before the tide came in, cutting her off. Or if she'd wandered into the ocean on her own."

"He's right," Nan interjected. "High tide easily reaches the very spot where Elizabeth was sitting. You can see the waterline on the table and chairs each morning. That's why we put only the older, wooden ones out there. They get pretty beat-up, but they're heavy enough to withstand the pull of the tide."

Nan shook herself, as if warding off a chill. "If Elizabeth had become confused from the drug, and gotten out of her chair and fallen…"

Carrie, too, shivered. "I didn't think of that."

"And," Nicky said, "no one would have been the wiser. It might have seemed like a classic case of accidental death."

"Not only that, but you know what occurs to me, Nicky?" Carrie continued. "Who would have been called to sign the death certificate? Dear old Dr. Esmond."

Nicky narrowed his eyes. "What are you thinking?"

"I don't know," she replied. "I just don't trust the man. Never have, really."

"Any particular reason?"

"No, I—" She broke off, searching her memory for something she had heard about Dr. Esmond in the past. But her mind was a blank.

"Carrie, you did, just now, say your grandmother might have had secrets. Secrets only the good doctor might know."

"That's true. I just don't remember anything specific. Nan—I still don't understand how my grandmother ended up so far away from the main grounds."

"Neither do I. But—" she looked up as a young

aide entered the office "—we may be about to find out."

Carrie recognized the girl immediately as Sharon Cook, a high school student who had volunteered her time at the Pines during Christmas vacation. She had seen Sharon with her grandmother any number of times then, and had always liked and trusted her.

Nan took a seat behind her desk and motioned to Sharon. The girl stepped into the room.

"Hi, Nicky," she said, smiling shyly.

Nicky returned her smile. "Hi, Sharon. How's it going?"

"Pretty good." The girl smoothed her long brown hair.

"You know each other?" Nan asked her.

"Well, uh—"

Nicky interrupted. "Sharon's in one of the youth programs at the Anglesea Center. We met a few weeks ago."

"I didn't realize that," Nan said, her gaze moving from Sharon to Nicky and back again. "Sharon, sit down, won't you? We'd like to ask you about Elizabeth Holder."

The young woman took a seat beside Nan's desk, looking back at Nicky as if for reassurance. He nodded.

What the hell's going on? Carrie wondered. More than a simple, *Yes, we met a few weeks ago.*

"Sharon," Nan said, "I saw you awhile ago in the garden with Mrs. Holder. You were taking her somewhere in a wheelchair. Can you tell me where?"

"I just took her over to that place by the fountain," Sharon answered. "She likes sitting there and listening to the water. I've been encouraging her to take her journal and write in it. I think she just reads it a little, though.''

''And did you leave her there, Sharon? Alone, I mean?''

Sharon bit her lip. ''I thought it was okay. I usually do leave her there for a while alone. You said we have to give the patients some respect that way, and not treat them like they're being watched all the time.''

''You're absolutely right, Sharon. And it wasn't wrong to leave her there. But somehow Mrs. Holder ended up way out beyond the hedges, at the employees' rest area. She was left all alone there. Do you know how she got there?''

The girl's eyes widened. ''No! I swear to you, Ms. Martin, I never took her there. I never would have. Not and leave her alone, especially.''

''I believe you, Sharon. But do you have any idea how she got there? Did you see anyone around who shouldn't have been here?''

The girl shook her head, clearly still appalled. ''I don't think so. Just the usual staff and visitors. And I think I saw Rabbi Silverstein. Oh, and Chris.'' She smiled.

''Chris Breen?''

The girl nodded. ''I saw him talking to her.''

Carrie flew to her feet. ''Christopher Breen? He was here? With my grandmother? What in the name of God—''

Nicky touched her shoulder. ''Why don't we let Sharon talk,'' he said quietly.

''No! I don't understand. An outsider like Breen can just walk in here and get that close to my grandmother, and no one thinks anything of it? Nan, why didn't you tell me this before?''

Nan, looking from one to the other, seemed thoroughly confused. "Carrie, Chris's being here isn't all that unusual. He makes visits to the patients on a regular basis. He's been doing that for years."

Carrie ran a hand through her hair. "Good God! Why? What business has he being here?"

"He makes sick calls to members of the parish, Carrie, the way Pastor Gillam used to before he retired. He's actually taking up the slack until Anglesea gets a new minister and they get the church going again. We've been very grateful to him. Carrie, what's wrong?"

"What's wrong is that I don't want Christopher Breen anywhere near my grandmother," she said angrily. "You've got to keep him away from her, Nan."

"Well, all right, of course, if that's the way you feel. I'm sorry, Carrie. If I'd known there was a problem..."

Carrie looked at Nicky, a plea in her eyes.

"Nan, I have to say I don't understand this, either," he said. "When that incident occurred with Carrie's grandmother the other night, we sent an officer out to take a report. I even came and talked to you myself, and I thought you had told me everything. Why is this the first I've heard about Breen?"

"Nicky, what I told the officer, and you, was that only known visitors were here, ones that visit the patients on a regular basis. I assumed you knew Chris was one of them. His name was on the list I gave the other officer."

Carrie looked at Nicky again, and he shook his head, saying, "I never saw that list."

Nan turned to the young aide. "Sharon, when you've been here, have you ever seen Chris harm Mrs. Holder in any way?"

"Not at all, Ms. Martin. He always seems friendly to everyone." The girl's forehead wrinkled. "Well, there was that one time..."

All eyes turned her way. "Yes, go on," Nan said.

"I guess it was about a week ago. I saw him in Mrs. Holder's room, and she was crying afterward. I didn't think anything of it, because sometimes the patients get depressed and cry. They miss their families, and things like that, and they tell us in training not to be upset by that kind of thing. So I tried to just forget it. I'm sorry. I guess I should have told someone."

"It's all right, Sharon," Nan said gently. "You didn't do anything wrong."

The young girl twisted in her seat to look back at Carrie, who stood rigidly by the sofa. "I wouldn't let anyone hurt your grandmother, I swear. Not for anything in the world."

Carrie barely managed to speak. "Thank you, Sharon," she said, her voice hoarse. "I'm sure you wouldn't."

"May I go now, Ms. Martin? I was in the middle of bathing Mrs. Cartwright when the nurse sent me here."

"What do you say, Nicky? Can she go now?"

Nicky gave Sharon a long look. "Sure," he said finally. "Take it easy, Sharon. And thanks for your help."

The young aide gave Nicky another shy glance and left the room.

For a long moment, no one spoke. Finally, Nicky stood before Nan, hands on his hips. His voice was hard and angry. "Okay, spill it."

Nan rocked back in her chair. Her brow furrowed. "Spill it? Spill what? What are you talking about?"

"The real reason Chris Breen has such easy access to this place, dammit!"

A deep flush rose in Nan's face. "Don't you swear at me, Nicky D'Amico. I told you, he visits the patients the same way a minister makes sick calls. It's part of his mission to look after the sick. Everyone knows that."

"Bull!"

"Bull nothing! I demand an explanation, Nicky. Just what are you accusing me of?"

"Of choosing your companions from the bottom of a barrel—at the very least."

"The bottom..." She gasped. "I can't believe you said that! You've known me for years, Nicky. We've gone to the same schools, the same church. You think I've got something going with Chris Breen? Something wrong? For God's sake, just what are you implying? Not only about me, but about him?"

Carrie broke in. "Take it easy, Nicky. Nan isn't part of this, whatever the hell it is. She can't be."

I've trusted her. I've handed over my grandmother's life to her. I can't be that wrong about people—can I?

"I don't know what either of you are talking about," Nan said coldly. "What is it I'm supposed to be—or not be—a part of?"

Nicky studied her. Finally he settled down. His voice grew soft. "You don't really know, do you? You don't have a clue."

"Dammit, Nicky! What are you talking about?"

"About Christopher Breen being a child molester!" Carrie blurted out.

Nicky swung her way, shaking his head, but it was too late.

Nan stared at them both, an expression of shock on

her face. "I can't...I can't believe that. I *don't* believe
it! What proof do you have?"

"We have a child..." Carrie began.

Again Nicky sent her a warning look. *Don't blow
this,* it said. *Don't mention Tess. We're too close.*

Carrie opened her mouth to finish the sentence. But
Nicky was right. She couldn't tell anyone about Tess.
It might ruin everything.

"We have me," she said wearily. "Nan, we have
me."

They sat on the sofa across from Nan. She had heard
the entire story, all Nicky and Carrie, between them,
had to tell. As Carrie told about her own experience
with Breen, she had begun to cry once, and Nicky had
taken her hand. He was still holding it firmly.

She had thought he would detest her when he heard.
See her as dirty. Ugly. He didn't, and she wanted to
cry again, but this time with relief.

"So you see, Nan," she said finally, her voice still
shaky, "you've got to keep Breen away from my
grandmother. Now that I've confronted him, he may
be trying to get to me through her. I mean, it has to be
him. I don't know who else it could be."

Nan looked up from her clasped hands. There was
moisture in her eyes. "I understand completely. I'm so
sorry that happened to you, Carrie. And I can't believe
I've been so blind. Tell me what I can do."

Carrie leaned back with a sigh and looked at Nicky.

"I think we have to go on the assumption," he said,
"that it was Breen who wheeled Elizabeth out beyond
the gardens, and Breen who left her there with a hallucinogen that could have put her in extreme danger.
It may be that he's trying to browbeat Carrie into si-

lence, like she said, by showing her how easy it is to get to her grandmother.''

He turned to Carrie, letting her hand go, but gently. ''One thing doesn't fit, though. He hasn't outright threatened you, has he? Ordinarily, a threat to remain silent would come first, then retaliatory action when you didn't.''

Carrie shrugged. ''He threatened that no one would believe me. That they'd believe him first. He never said a word about my grandmother, though. I didn't think he even remembered her.''

Nicky turned to Nan. ''Nan, I want to believe you're innocent in all this—''

''For God's sake!'' She threw up her hands.

''All right, I do believe you. Sorry. But, Nan, you've got to tell me what you know about Breen. Starting with why he has such easy access here, and why you feel so comfortable with that. Somehow, it doesn't add up. There's something more. Isn't there?''

Nan hesitated. ''Nicky, I'm not supposed to ever tell anyone. It's, uh…part of the agreement.''

''What agreement?'' Carrie said sharply.

''I—oh, what the hell. Chris Breen is our anonymous benefactor. His donations over the years are the only reason we've been able to do as good a job as we have for our patients.'' She looked pointedly at Carrie. ''They're the reason your costs, and Elizabeth's, have been so low. A third of the cost of her care comes directly from Chris Breen—just as it does for the other patients here.''

Carrie, shocked, looked at Nicky, who seemed just as stunned.

''Blood money!'' Carrie cried, turning back to Nan. ''It's blood money, Nan! To ease his conscience.''

Nan's tone hardened. "I couldn't have known that, Carrie. For God's sake, from what you say, the man has apparently fooled any number of people over the years. Cut me some slack!"

Carrie studied her a moment. "You're right. I'm sorry."

Nan rested her head in her hands, then looked up. "No, Carrie, I'm sorry. It's just that all of a sudden it feels like my world's coming apart. With medical costs skyrocketing, and more and more people in this area running out of money for good health care, Breen's contributions have been not only a blessing, but a necessity. If we lose that now, we might have to close down."

"Realistically, Nan," Nicky said, "you might want to start looking around for another endowment. This guy is going up for good by the time I get done with him."

She groaned.

Nicky stood, clipping his police radio onto his belt. "Nan, I need your help. I want to put an undercover officer in here to watch over Elizabeth for the next couple of days. I'm thinking she could pretend to be an outside consultant of some sort, looking into patient care for your certification. Is that all right with you?"

"Of course. But why not just put a guard outside Elizabeth's room?"

"Because that would put Breen on the alert, and I don't want him knowing we suspect anything. Meanwhile, I need you to tell all the staff that except for Carrie, Elizabeth isn't to have any visitors for a while. Make sure you tell them that includes Breen. Don't make a big thing of it, just say she's been upset by what happened to her granddaughter, and needs absolute rest. No visitors, absolutely no exceptions, other than Carrie, of course. Can you do that?''

"Yes. But, Nicky, what about the other patients? If they're in danger, too—''

"I feel reasonably certain they're not. But the person I put in here will be on the alert for any trouble at all.''

Nicky motioned to Carrie. "I have to go and set things up for this. Do you want to come with me? I can drop you off at the house so you don't have to walk back.''

"Thanks. I'd like to stay here, though, and sit with my grandmother awhile.''

He looked worried. "I'd feel better if you were with me.''

She smiled. "I'll be fine.''

Nicky sighed. "Promise me one thing, then? Call me to pick you up? Or if you can't reach me, take a cab home? I don't want you walking home on the beach at night.''

She gave him a mock salute. "Right you are, Captain. Lieutenant. Whatever.''

He rolled his eyes and left the room.

When they were alone, Nan said, "It's nice that he's looking after you like that.''

"I guess so. He sure can be bossy, though.''

Nan laughed. "That's Nicky's way of saying he cares.''

Carrie shrugged.

"*Really* cares," Nan said, making a point of it.

"Shut *up!*" Carrie said.

"Don't tell me you're surprised.''

"We've only known each other a few days, for heaven's sake.''

"Carrie, fate has a way of bringing the right people

together in odd ways and at odd times. If I were you,
I wouldn't fight it. You and Nicky are lucky to have
found each other.''

"And you are one crazy lady. There is absolutely
nothing between Nicky D'Amico and me.''

"Sure, right.'' Nan grinned. "Even so...I wish you
much happiness and many children.''

Carrie sat beside her sleeping grandmother, thinking.
Even if what Nan had said about Nicky's feelings for
her were true, this was no time to be getting into a
relationship, not with anyone. She had too many things
to work through now, too much to remember...and to
try to forget.

Besides, she didn't feel that way about Nicky. As
she had told Nan, she found him irritating and bossy.
Not that she didn't appreciate the way he'd stood by
her while she was telling the story of Breen's abuse to
Nan. But in truth, she barely knew him. And there were
still the questions about Sally, his sister, and why she
had cried that night for him to leave her alone, then
told her mother that she hated him. *He nearly killed
someone last year,* Helen had said. *Sally's afraid he
might do that again.*

There was, it seemed, much more to Nicky D'Amico
than met the eye. And even if she were attracted to
him—which she definitely was not—she had to be
careful now. Throughout her adult years, since college,
it seemed she'd deliberately become involved with men
who were either unavailable or completely wrong for
her in some other way. Friends would warn her about
this one or that, and she would throw herself, unheed-
ing, down dark uncertain paths that had ended in one
emotional abyss after another. It wasn't until she'd be-

gun to talk with Esther Gordon last year that she'd been able to see that she had sabotaged herself from the beginning, picking the wrong man and then chasing after him, in an attempt to prove to herself that all men were jerks, or that she was incapable of a relationship with anyone at all.

Either way, the process had been painful. And the one thing she knew now was that she had no intention of repeating it, ever again. She would die a lonely old woman first, with only a couple of cats for company.

Wondering if her grandmother needed more spending money, or if she still had the twenty-dollar bill Carrie had left in her nightstand earlier, she opened the drawer and looked in. Yes, it was there, under the notepad and gold pen. Carrie almost wished it were gone. That, at least, would indicate Elizabeth had shown some sign of wanting something. Anything. God, what she wouldn't give to see her grandmother come back to her old, vibrant self again. When she woke, would she be like that, after this afternoon? Or would she have withdrawn again? Carrie rubbed her forehead tiredly. *Bring her back, please. Bring her back.*

Elizabeth continued to sleep soundly. The attending nurse had assured her that her grandmother was none the worse for wear from her ''adventure'' that afternoon. Carrie, looking at her tiny grandmother, could not believe the physical effort she'd put forth. Not to mention the mental clarity it had taken to go for help that way.

On top of the nightstand beside Elizabeth's bed was the book she had tried to hide from Carrie when she'd first come upon her in the garden. Carrie wondered why. It was only a journal, she saw now, one Elizabeth had brought with her to the Pines months ago. What secrets could her grandmother possibly still have, after all these years? No one who might have been involved in them was left alive now. The entire family was gone.

The flowered book was grass-stained and torn, most likely from having fallen on the ground when Elizabeth rose from her wheelchair to go for help. I should take it back to the Crest with me and fix it, Carrie thought. Maybe I can borrow some tape from Helen. Elizabeth probably wouldn't mind. She knew her granddaughter wasn't the type to snoop.

In the back of Carrie's mind, however, she was honest enough to admit that she was curious. Could there possibly be something in her grandmother's journal that might help to shed light on why Breen—or some other person—had tried to drug and perhaps even kill her? Was there more going on than either she or Nicky had guessed at?

Not likely, Carrie thought, sighing. Her grandmother's life, no pun intended, had always been an open book. Would that her own had been so uncomplicated, so virtuous and pure.

Taking the journal, she slipped it into the side pocket of the small beach bag she'd carried with her from the Crest Inn so many hours earlier. The clock on Elizabeth's small table showed the time to be nearly four in the afternoon. Carrie yawned and stretched. She felt torn about what to do next. Stay with Elizabeth till she woke? Or go home, take a nap and come back after dinner, when her grandmother would surely be awake again?

If she went back to the Crest, she might run into Nicky. And he might have the results from the tests on the blood Dr. Esmond had drawn. In addition, she felt she needed to call Molly Blair and let her know that she was definitely staying for the festival.

The festival. It was starting tomorrow. And on Sunday, Breen would be announced by the President of the United States as the director of his new pet project, *Millennium Child.* He would have widespread contact with—and access to—children around the world.

Something had to be done. And quickly. But could she trust Nicky to do it, as he'd promised?

Carrie reached for the small local phone book on the bottom shelf of Elizabeth's table. She looked up a number and punched it into the phone.

"Yellow Cab?" she said after a moment. "I need a cab from the Pines Convalescent Home to the Crest Inn." She listened. "Yes, that's fine. I'll wait out front. Thank you."

Carrie leaned over her grandmother, kissing her lightly on the forehead. "Don't worry, Grandmother," she said softly. "I let Breen hurt me when I was little. I didn't tell. And now, God help me, he's at it again, and I've got to stop him. But, Grandmother, I swear...I will never let him hurt you."

Before leaving, she spoke briefly with Nan, who told her that Nicky had called, saying the undercover police officer would be on her way shortly. Till she arrived, Nan assured Carrie that she herself would look after Elizabeth.

Even so, Carrie felt an odd prickle of fear as she stood outside waiting for the cab. Casting it off as nerves, she told herself not to worry. Her grandmother would be all right.

Elizabeth drifted...feeling, not thinking. Before her lay the woods, so dark and safe. She tiptoed in, traipsing lightly over moss and leaves, hoping to surprise him. There was nothing she loved more than surprising him. He seemed to take so much joy in it, like a little boy. He had always seemed a little boy, always ready to play. She loved to play.

Like the day he had taken her big straw hat with the wide brim and tossed it into the wind so it could fly. It took off high over the fields, its ribbons streaming behind. He had run over the fields, then, to fetch it back for her, laughing, but there had been a big old bull with other ideas. He had run like heck from that old bull, still laughing all the way.

The glory of that day was worth having to explain the loss of a dumb old hat when she got home.

He was there in the glade, now, waiting for her. Sneaking up behind him, she covered his eyes with her hands.

"Lizzie!" he cried, laughing. "You're getting better at games every day."

It had taken her awhile to learn. First there was her father and mother, telling her that the things she felt were wrong. Then Sam. Everything was wrong, all the good feelings, everything had to be clamped down on, dispelled, forgotten. Even with her husband, Sam.

Sam was the one who made her pray every night. Not that there was anything wrong with prayer; she had embraced it all her life. But Sam spent an hour or more on his knees next to the bed, praying, before he'd come and lie down beside her. She would wait, her body turning cold and rigid as she wondered if sex with her were something so bad that her husband had to seek redemption for it beforehand. Then, suddenly, Sam would say "Amen" loudly, as a signal to her he was ready. And he'd be pulling back the covers, letting in the cold night air before throwing himself all over her in some ninety-second fever she never did understand the purpose of. "C'mon, honey," he'd say. "Let's make love."

As if she enjoyed that—or could even do it—with the eye of God still looking down.

In the beginning, there were nights when tears she tried desperately to suppress slipped down her face, as she waited that way for Sam. Then suddenly, one night, something went *pop* in her heart. It was like that—a tiny pop that reverberated through her entire being. In that instant, sadness turned to indifference, hope to despair. From then on, when she heard that dreaded "Amen," Elizabeth feigned sleep.

Poor Sam. He never did understand. And she couldn't bring herself to tell him. Sex and her own needs were things she'd been taught never to speak about.

But the other one—he knew without her having to say a word. And he made her feel as she never had before. He made her laugh, and with him she felt like a woman. He could even bring out the child in her, making her play after all that had happened. After the dark, lonely winter in Minnesota, and just when she thought her life was over—that she was too old to be a child again—he'd taught her to feel joy once more. He was the one she had waited for all her life, the one she could trust with her hopes and dreams and give her heart to, at last.

Until that day, the darkest of days, when she found him—her dearest love—with *her*. At that moment, Elizabeth's whole world had come crashing down. The shock went on and on. She thought she would die, had even begged God to let her die. In the end she'd had to face him, had to straighten her spine and hold up her head, though her entire body quaked. It was the only way she knew.

"I saw you," she said, her voice choking in her throat. "I *saw* you."

He denied it, of course, But she had seen what she had seen. And she made him admit it, finally, on his knees. She made him grovel and promise never to do it again. He swore he wouldn't, on the name of Christ.

Even so, she had sent him away.

Then, one day, he came back. He came back swearing, on the same Christ, that he had changed, he wasn't the same person, not at all. She didn't trust him. Couldn't, after what had happened. She watched every move he made, and as she watched, her youth—or her pretense at it—slipped away. Her skin aged; her eyes lost their luster. She grew old overnight, as all the good and joyous moments became entombed in the past.

Were they ever real, those joyous times? she had wondered throughout the endless nights. Or had she been acting the fool all along? A foolish, middle-aged woman in love with a younger man, a man who was never, ever, as he seemed.

In time the wounds healed, and the doubt and the questioning passed, both of herself and of him. She had watched and seen nothing. She had come to trust, over the years, that oath he'd made.

Until now.

Elizabeth clenched her hands till the nails bit into the paper-thin skin, drawing blood. *Now, by all that was holy, she would stop him—once and for all.*

She knew she could do it. Her muscle strength was nearly back to normal, and she was stronger and more clearheaded than they thought. Oh, for a while she'd gone off somewhere. When her hip had broken and not mended right away, she had thought that would finally and thankfully be the end. What was there to live for, anyway? Only the pain—and the remembrance of past sins.

It was Carrie who'd brought her back, piece by piece, as if—poking through the veil—first an arm, then a leg came through. Carrie talked to her, reminding her of good times in the past, until at last her mind had followed the rest. She had even come to want to live again, if only to please her beautiful grandchild.

It was not so easy, however, coming back. Not as simple as it had been to leave. Elizabeth found herself slipping in and out. She knew the nurses thought she often feigned sleep. Sometimes she did. It was easier that way. No questions to answer, no hopes to fulfill.

She also learned things. People talked about matters they never would, otherwise, and sometimes the matters they talked about were terrible, unimaginable horrors, like something dredged up from the bowels of the earth. She had heard those kinds of horrors here recently—from Carrie. She had lain here in the night afterward, frightened out of her wits, not knowing what to do.

From the moment Elizabeth had seen Carrie drink that water, however, and fall to the ground unconscious, she had known she would have to return all the way. She couldn't let Carrie be harmed again. She would find the strength to do what she must.

Moreover, what strength she didn't have, she would pray for. Not with the kind of prayer Sam had tried to teach her, she thought scornfully. Not the kind of weak begging for mercy he espoused. No, her prayer would be to the God of vengeance. She would tell the God of vengeance what she knew, what she had known all these years, and He and His many angels would see her through.

As afternoon turned to dusk, Elizabeth lay quietly, forming a plan. At one point she heard loud noises coming from somewhere in the front of the building. She thought she heard people running, and breaking glass. The sounds alarmed her, and she longed to know what caused them. But her plans for the night were foremost in importance, and when the aide came with dinner as she always did, Elizabeth decided there must be nothing wrong outside her room, after all. She pretended to sleep, remaining in her head and tending her plan as one might a tiny plant that must, miraculously and within hours, become a giant stalk. When someone else entered the room moments later she assumed it was another aide, so she continued to feign sleep, lying on her side with her back to the door.

Darkness fell, and Elizabeth rose. Easing her thin legs to the floor, she felt a twinge of pain in her hip, from the arthritis that had plagued her for twenty years. Standing in her bare feet, she bunched pillows under the sheets, making her bed look as if she were sleeping there.

She couldn't risk a light. Feeling her way in the dark to her closet, she tripped over a pair of shoes that had somehow been left by the closet door. Reaching down, she felt for them, noting by their shape that they were the good walking shoes, the ones that were sturdy, yet soft and quiet. She picked them up, holding them against her chest with one hand as she reached into the dark closet for clothes.

Wait. Was that a sound? Was someone breathing?

Elizabeth went still, fear skittering down her back in icy waves. She thought she could feel a presence, a sharp displacement of air, the filling of what should have been a vacuum.

No, that was silly. She was imagining things. Determinedly, she felt for something suitable to wear and came up with slacks and a sweater. The sweater might be too much for this time of year, she thought, but she was suddenly cold. Again she heard what she thought might be breathing.

"Is someone there?" she demanded in the most autocratic tone she could recall from her past. Her voice trembled, but she didn't let that stop her. "Is someone there, I said! Show yourself!"

There was no further sound, and Elizabeth laughed softly at herself, taking the clothes and shutting the closet door firmly. "Blessed Lord, I'm losing it again. Just like the other night. Oh, please, show me the way."

She stood quietly for a long moment with the clothes and shoes held against her, praying to Michael the Archangel for strength, to the Blessed Spirit for enlightenment, and finally to the God of Vengeance—who she had once insisted did not exist, but who she conjured up now, in this desperate time of need.

After dressing as quickly as her frozen fingers allowed, Elizabeth crossed to the telephone beside her bed. Lifting the receiver, she searched her memory for the button that would redial the last number called. What was that button?

Of course. *REDIAL.* How stupid of her.

Elizabeth pushed the button she knew had that word on it. The phone at the other end rang, and she knew who would answer. She had heard Carrie make her own call, before she left.

"Yellow Cab," a man's voice said.

Bless you, Carrie. "Yes. I...I would like to have a taxi," Elizabeth said softly.

"What's that? I can't hear you."

"A taxicab," she said more firmly, cupping her hands around the mouthpiece to muffle the sound.

"What's your address?" the dispatcher asked.

"The Pines Convalescent Home," Elizabeth said as crisply as she could. She hoped she sounded like a nurse.

"And where are you going?"

Elizabeth told her. "I want you to pick me up on Greenhurst, however. On the corner of Pine."

"Right you are," the dispatcher said. "Fifteen minutes?"

"Thank you," Elizabeth said politely, laying the receiver down.

She sat on the edge of her bed for five minutes, praying, then rose and slipped quietly into the hall. It was after nine-thirty, and most of the patients were in bed by now. Whatever all that noise had been, it had stopped. A finger of dim light slid from below Ned Kelly's door across the hall. There was no sound, but Elizabeth knew his habits. An old newshound, he'd be up half the night listening to Art Bell on radio. Ned said CNN used to be the one news source that told the truth, but now it was more fluff than stuff. There were all kinds of terrible things going on that people didn't hear about, he said, but Art had guests who knew the real deal. Ned kept everyone entertained at lunch with stories of solar flares that were due to ravage the earth, killing millions—provided tornadoes, earthquakes and/ or governmental conspiracies didn't get them first. Some people called Ned crazy. Art Bell, too. Elizabeth had lived long enough to think both of them might be crazy, all right—crazy as a fox.

So Ned would be glued to his radio earphone at this hour. Never heard a thing that went on around here at night. The rest of the hallway was silent as well. Even the nurses were nodding at their stations, Elizabeth saw as she crooked her head carefully round the corner at the end of the hall. It was near the end of their three-to-eleven shifts, and the nurses here worked hard. Tonight they looked more tired than usual, one of them resting her head on her arms at the desk, another two talking quietly in a room lined with file cabinets, drinking coffee. They would be desperately trying to stay awake, she knew, with their brains half-asleep. Elizabeth had counted on that.

The nurses, of course, didn't think she noticed anything. Any more than old Ned did at night, or Gladys down the hall, who just lay in her bed and yelled "Help!" over and over, even though she was, from all Elizabeth had heard—or overheard—being treated pretty well. Or that other one, the one whose name she didn't know, who ran stark naked into the lunchroom day after day, with only a cross to hide her poor dried-up, shrunken body. The nurses said she used to be a nun. They didn't say that directly to Elizabeth, of course, because they thought she didn't hear. But she knew. When it came right down to it, she guessed she knew too infernal much for an old woman. But what was done was done, and all she could do was hope to right things as best she could.

Elizabeth's mouth tightened into a straight line. Her

chin lifted, the fine hairs visible in the hallway's overhead lights. She didn't think, as she had when she first
"came back," about plucking them. Or of the myriad
little details that had captivated her sense of vanity over
the years. All she thought about now was *him*.

The undercover policewoman Nicky had sent to the
Pines never made it there to see Elizabeth leave.
Though she left her home at five on the dot, there was
a major traffic accident on the long stretch of main road
between central Holly Beach and the Pines. Pat Bailey
was in that crash, her car totaled. She tried to call
Nicky on her cell phone, to let him know what had
happened, but the battery failed. She scrabbled through
the rubble of the crash for her police radio, but never
found it. And when the paramedics arrived, they insisted she let them take her to the hospital to be
checked out. Bailey protested, but when her vision
went double, she couldn't convince anyone that she
was all right and had a job to get to.

Nicky heard about the accident over his radio, and
was close on the heels of the paramedics, the fire trucks
and a dozen police cars. The accident was a major
event on the island, a twenty-two-car pileup. It stopped
traffic both ways for hours before the wreckage could
be removed. Nicky went too far into it in search of
Bailey, and became part of the trapped mass of vehi-
cles. Once he got news of Bailey, he stood, frustrated,
by his car and tried to rouse Nan on his cell phone.
She didn't answer her private line. He then had her
paged, only to find that there was a crisis at the Pines,
as well. It took Nan several minutes to get to a phone
in the lobby.

"All hell's broken loose here," she said, her voice

loud in his ear. "One of our patients tried to 'borrow' a staff car and drove right up onto the porch and through the front of the building. God, Nicky, these people will be the death of me—"

"Nan?" he interrupted, his voice tight. "What about Elizabeth?"

"Elizabeth? I don't know. I assumed your undercover officer was here by now, looking after her. You told me ages ago she was on the way."

"Dammit, Nan, you said you'd take care of Elizabeth till the officer got there!"

"Well, pardon me, but I've had my hands a bit full. There's broken glass all over the place, and dazed patients walking through it in bare feet before we can stop them. We've got them crying, some of them hysterical, thinking the end of the world has come. Ned Kelly's telling them it's some sort of magnetic anomaly, and one World War II vet is certain we're under German attack. You don't know what it's been like."

"Okay, okay. Look, I'm sorry. But there's a major accident on Ocean View Road. That's where I am now, and I can't get out of here. My undercover officer was in the accident, and she'll be on her way to the hospital as soon as the paramedics can make their way out of here. I'm trying to find someone else to send out to you. Meantime, I know you've got your hands full. But you've got to find someone to take care of Carrie's grandmother."

"Nicky, I told the staff that she's not to have company. No one at all except for Carrie. I emphasized that. The nurses and aides understand. They were keeping a special eye on her, anyway, after what happened earlier today. But all the nurses are busy with patients now, either that or the cleanup. This is an emergency situation here, Nicky.''

"Dammit, Nan—!''

"Oh, for God's sake! All right. Take it easy. I'll look in on Elizabeth. *And* I'll find someone. But, Nicky, relax. I'm sure she's all right.''

Nicky hung up, cussing loudly. He ran a hand through his hair and then banged on the top of his car. "Dammit, dammit, dammit!''

He looked around at the mess of tangled metal and the people who stood or sat in confusion, wondering what had happened and what to do next. There were volunteers moving among them with blankets and hot coffee, and several teens he recognized from the high school were comforting the children. Paramedics wound in and out with stretchers, and cops were busy talking to victims and taking notes for their reports.

There wasn't much he could do here except add to the chaos. On the other hand, he might be able to do something for Carrie by looking after her grandmother till he found a substitute for Bailey. It would be a while, with nearly the whole damned force tied up here.

Pulling his car off the road, out of the way of the tow trucks, he locked it up, clipped his police radio onto his belt and spoke briefly to one of the cops, letting him know where he could be found. Then he took off across fields of sand and sea grass, some of it marshy and thick with cattails.

It was growing dark, but with any luck, he thought, he could be at the Pines within the hour.

24

Elizabeth slipped out of the Pines without being seen, largely because she had kept her ears open over the past weeks, ever since security had been tightened. Not that she'd expected to go anywhere, but you never knew what information might come in handy, and when. She had overheard one of the nurses talking about there being only one way a patient could get out now without being seen: an old gate with a broken lock, in the hedges that spanned the side lawn. The lock was due to be repaired, but the maintenance men had gotten behind.

The gate was all but invisible, and Elizabeth had a devil of a time finding it in the dark, especially as she had to dodge the new security guards. But she made it out, and then to Greenhurst Street, breathing prayers all the way.

The taxi was late. Nearly ten minutes late, and as the headlights of other cars passed, she hid behind a tree, like some wretched villain in an old mystery movie, up to no good. There were moments when she felt afraid, thinking there was someone watching, someone who'd followed her from the nursing home. When no one approached her, she shrugged that off as nerves.

Twenty minutes later, after an even more nerve-racking ride along back roads—"An accident on the

main highway," the cabdriver said, "a godawful
mess"—she arrived at her destination. The whole episode, from dressing to arriving here, then making her
way through the now unfamiliar grounds and buildings,
had left her weak and shaky. To make things worse,
her mind was playing tricks on her. It kept wanting to
swing back to the way things were when she was
young. Elizabeth went through one wrong doorway,
then another, turned down one wrong, empty hallway,
then the next, becoming more and more exhausted. The
energy that had driven her out of bed and brought her
here was fast failing. But she would find him, if it took
all night. *Help me,* was her constant prayer. *Show me
the way.*

Whether it was prayer or pure dumb luck, Elizabeth
didn't know. But she came at last into the wing that
housed media rooms for conference participants. It was
after ten-thirty, and the hallway was almost pitch-black.
Only a finger of light stretched through a window at
the end of the hall. Elizabeth felt frightened, without
knowing why. Evil spirits seemed to lurk in the darkness here, waiting to pounce.

She knew her imagination was hard at work, and that
the only evil spirit was behind one of these doors. Still,
she hurried along the corridor, relieved yet not surprised that no one was about. In fact, she saw this as
due in part to her own clever planning in coming here
so late, and partly as an answer to the prayers that fell
silently and constantly from her half-parted lips.

As she hurried, her footsteps made light, muffled
sounds on the tiled floor. Elizabeth opened one door
after another, finding only empty rooms with large tables, telephones, audio-visual equipment and comput-
ers. She had begun to panic, thinking she had guessed

wrong, when suddenly her search was rewarded. A fourth door opened into another, similar room. And there he sat—lounging back in a swivel chair, making notes on a script as he watched a tape of *The Christopher Show* on a mammoth projection screen against one entire wall.

Her memory hadn't failed her in this. She had learned his habits from the long years of watching, and she had felt certain he would be in one of these rooms. He would be analyzing his previous performance as he geared up for the coming festival, the one Carrie had told her about during one of her latest visits, though Elizabeth had pretended not to be awake nor to hear. He would be deciding what to take out and what to leave in, what worked and what didn't. In the same cold, calculating manner that he did everything in life, he would dissect his own presentation, as well as that of others, spending nearly the entire night on it, before tomorrow's festival began.

He was so absorbed he didn't hear the door open, nor did he see Elizabeth as she leaned against it, trembling.

Reaching inside the pocket of her lightweight jacket, she felt to make sure she had brought what was needed. Her fingers tightened around something hard and metallic. Yes, this would do.

Breen's mind drifted as last week's show played out before him on the projection screen. Since the day Carrie Holder—Holt, now—had been here, he hadn't been able to get her out of his mind. And now Carrie was about to expose the secret only he and she had shared—that he had...that he had touched her as a child.

The words stuck in his mind, making his heart nearly stop. Until she had accused him of it the other day, he had been able to remember it as something less—immodest behavior, at the most. As she told it, however, the things he had done took on monstrous proportions.

He felt incredibly sad at this turn of events. His thoughts carried him back to a day when he was seven, when he was supposed to turn in his homework and didn't, as he hadn't for weeks. He had been called into the principal's office. It was an inner-city school, and the principal, seeing how afraid he was, had taken him under his wing. He had taught him how to talk to people without seeming to be intimidated or afraid. To "whistle in the dark."

Then the principal had taught him other things. Terrible things that no little boy should know. Chris had learned, though, how to get along, how to be loved and accepted. He had tried to pass this on, teaching it to children he came into contact with as a young man. Like Carrie, for instance. And the others. He had done his best—until Elizabeth had found out and taken it all wrong, casting an impure light on his actions. Just as Carrie was doing now.

To silence Elizabeth all those years ago, he'd had to leave. She'd demanded nothing less. And there were promises made. Promises he had struggled with all his might to keep, before daring to come back.

He had never married and was surprised sometimes to find himself still single. His decision not to marry was based on the fact that he preferred keeping things light, playing the role of eternal kid—always feeling, even looking, younger than his age. In addition, having responsibility for the entire world, as he often felt he did of late, was somehow easier than being responsible for any one particular soul.

Since returning to Holly Beach, he had done his best, he thought, to live a good life. He had worked hard to build the reputation and career he now enjoyed, and he had given most of the money he had made to good causes, both social and political. Here in Holly Beach he had favored Anglesea with large donations, for obvious reasons. It was his base of operations. He had also chosen to support the Pines Convalescent Home, largely because of the way his mother had suffered for years from ill health, then died when he was twelve. If she had had better health care from the beginning, he might not have been left alone to fend for himself. Things might have been far different.

As it was, his work had never been about money, but about being respected. One might even say…loved.

And it had worked—it had all worked—until Carrie showed up. The minute he had heard she was on the speakers' list, several months ago, he'd done his best to have her removed. He'd spoken directly to the selection committee and recommended someone "more well-known," while not seeming to talk Carrie down. That might have had them asking questions.

The selection committee, unfortunately, had come back with the response that while they might have made the change, the invitations had already gone out. They had been in the mail for two days.

Those two days had made all the difference in the world.

His world.

Elizabeth's anger grew as Breen failed to acknowledge her presence. *Always the same, these days, com-*

pletely self-absorbed. My, how he's changed from that
young man who taught me to laugh.

She made a deliberate sound in her throat. The shock
on Breen's face when he turned and saw her would
have satisfied any bean counter of sins on Judgment
Day, she thought with satisfaction.

"Lizzie! Good Lord! What are you doing here?"

"I'm here to see you, Chris." She drew closer, her
hand still in her pocket. "Well, that is not quite accurate. I am here to rid the earth of a piece of scum."

He rose slowly, his expression turning to one of concern. "I don't understand. How did you even get
here?"

"You mean, how did I manage to survive all the
emotional attacks you've made on me these past few
months? All those damned unholy times you told the
nurses you were making a sick call, when all the while
you were trying to get me to stop Carrie from coming
this week?"

"My God, Lizzie! I didn't even think you'd heard
me half the time. For heaven's sake, sit down. You
look terrible."

Her smile was bitter. "That isn't what you used to
say, Chris. 'Lizzie, you are the most beautiful woman
on earth. Lizzie, I can't take my eyes off you. Lizzie,
I love you....'"

As she reached him, her frail hand smacked him,
hard, on the face. Though the blow was muted by a
certain weakness, the shock of it sent him reeling. "Oh,
and by the way," she said, her eyes narrowing to angry
slits, "don't call me Lizzie."

Breen held a hand to his cheek, his eyes wide and
stunned. *The Christopher Show* continued to play on
the wall behind them, choir voices rising in a terrible

accompaniment, the organ sounds in Elizabeth's ears like a million devils laughing. She slammed a white, spotted hand down on the remote control device on the table in front of Breen. The sound muted, but the pictures continued to play, a bizarre backdrop, and there he was, larger than life—with his hand on a little girl's head.

"Lizzie—"

She reached out to slap him again. This time, however, he was ready for her, grabbing her wrist.

"What in the name of all that's holy are you doing? Have you gone completely mad?"

"No madder than I was when I let you come back here and build a name for yourself, you spawn of the devil! I should have told everyone about you then. I should have spoken out. How I could ever have believed you—"

He took her by both arms and shook her slightly. "I told you the truth, Elizabeth. You made me go away, and I kept my promise. I got treatment. I got better, and I made my amends. Elizabeth, I swear I've never touched another child since that day you caught me with...with her. I swear it."

Elizabeth made a scornful sound. "*Her?* You don't even remember her name, do you? Well, I do. It was Janey. Janey Pearce. And she was ten years old. She trusted you, and you touched her with your filthy hands."

She jerked away. "How many more, Chris? How many more did you do that to?"

She wanted to hear him say it. She wanted him to tell her what she didn't know then, but knew now—that, God help her, he had molested Carrie, too.

"Elizabeth, we've gone over all this before. And I

swear to you, I haven't touched another child since then. Don't you remember? You threatened to expose me if I did.''

Her eyes flashed. "Giving you a second chance was the biggest mistake of my life. I should have told everyone back then."

"Lizzie," he said softly, "don't you remember why you didn't? You kept quiet for Carrie's sake—not mine."

She remembered that soft voice, the way it had turned her fifty-year-old body to mush, making her think she was young, a girl again.

"Oh, how deft you are at twisting things," she said. "But then, you always were. Threatening to tell Sam about our affair if I exposed you. Reminding me that if it came out, became public knowledge, I'd lose Carrie—that she'd be ashamed of me and shamed *by* me. You knew I couldn't do that to her."

"Lizzie, I didn't threaten you. I just wanted you to do the right thing. And you did. You were the only person in her life she could turn to. Alice was no help. And her father—"

"Was a drunk. I know. Alice may have done her best to hide it, but did anyone think I really didn't know? And you were right. I was all Carrie had. I knew that then, and I know it now."

His voice fell to a murmur. "Oh, Lizzie…my Lizzie. Is that all you knew back then?"

Her eyes narrowed. "What are you talking about?"

He shook his head, not answering at first.

"What are you talking about, dammit?"

"I'm talking about your son, Jack…and what he did to Carrie."

Elizabeth went pale. "What evil lie are you making up now?"

"I swear it's true. Lizzie, Jack molested Carrie for years."

She fell back as if struck. "Liar," she breathed, her senses reeling. *"You're lying."*

But his eyes met hers, and she saw in them truth. Truth from years before, when he had made love to her and held her and told her he loved her. Truth she had come to know and recognize, even depend on, just as surely as she had come to recognize the lies, later.

He wasn't lying now. She, of all people, could tell. Moreover, his words brought to her mind an image, a memory. Like a hot poker it seared through her brain: Carrie sitting at her bedside saying, "Did you know what my father did? I can't believe you knew."

I thought—Dear God, I thought she meant the drinking.

"How could *you* know Jack did such a terrible thing?" she demanded of Breen, her eyes tearing up. "How is it you could know this?"

"Carrie herself told me, Lizzie. Years ago. She told me when it was happening."

Elizabeth stared at him, shocked. "When it was *happening?* And you never did anything to stop it?"

"I..." He fell silent, caught in a trap he hadn't foreseen.

"You didn't do anything because you were molesting her, too." Elizabeth's voice was low now, horrified. "And it would have upset the applecart for you."

"I never—"

"Don't you dare lie to me about that!" Sobbing, she beat on his chest with her fists. "Don't you dare! Carrie told me what you did to her. She didn't think I heard, but I did. I know you molested her back then, along with Janey Pearce. And damn you, Chris! She knows what you're doing now. She knows you're still doing it. *God damn you to hell!*''

He grabbed her fists, and for a long moment he held her, sobbing, against his chest. ''I'm so sorry, Lizzie. I never meant it to end the way it did. I swear I didn't. I loved you. I loved you more than anything on earth. But then I needed...I needed other things. And Carrie was so much like you.''

''Oh, my God.'' Elizabeth slid to the floor, burying her face in her hands. ''It's my fault. All of this is my fault.''

He knelt on one knee in front of her, taking her hands from her face and holding them. ''It was not your fault. It was *never* your fault. You couldn't see what Carrie didn't want you to see. She learned to hide it too well.''

''No. It must have been the baby,'' she continued softly, as if she hadn't heard. ''When I lost my baby...''

''My baby, too,'' he reminded her gently, wiping her tears away with a thumb.

''When I lost her in Minnesota, I thought I couldn't possibly ever be that lonely again. But then Sam found out the baby was yours, not his, and he turned on me—''

''And you came home. You came to me again. It was the only thing we could do back then, remember? We needed each other, Lizzie. Neither of us had anyone then. No one at all.''

She almost agreed. In spite of herself, she felt the closeness again...reveling, for one brief moment, in the feel of his hand stroking her cheek, then smoothing back her hair. For that one brief moment in time she wanted to lean forward and kiss the lips that had once been so beloved, and that were so near, now, after all these years. She wanted to feel the old joy.

Then her mind cleared. "Except that you *did* have someone, didn't you," she accused, drawing back. "You had Janey Pearce. And Carrie."

Pushing him away, she struggled to her feet, in full fury once more. "I almost let you make me forget that for a moment! You've been working me, haven't you? Just as you did all those years ago. Manipulating my emotions, making me think our affair was somehow right and good. And all the while you were performing your monstrous acts on those poor little girls. On my *grandchild!*"

Her hand reached into her pocket. "Oh—and one more thing. You didn't know, did you, how Sam died? You couldn't have, because Dr. Esmond covered it up, for my sake and Carrie's."

Breen shook his head, as if she weren't thinking clearly. "Your husband died of a heart attack, Lizzie. Everyone knows that."

"Everyone knows nothing! My husband killed himself, Chris. He took an overdose of pills when he could no longer live with the knowledge of my sins. It took him years, of course, working up to it. Years of dwelling on it, unable to wipe it out. Years of praying for the rescue of my soul, till his own just withered and died."

Breen was on his feet, his face a study in shock. But she didn't even stop for a breath.

"Well, it's over, Chris. It's over now. You will never hurt me or anyone I love again. And you will never touch another child again."

Her fingers closed around the metal object in her pocket. Stepping closer, she saw the flicker of fear cross his face. She felt good, seeing that. Righteous and just. She felt like the God of vengeance must feel on Judgment Day.

25

After leaving Elizabeth at the Pines, Carrie knocked on the kitchen door of the D'Amico house, in search of tape. She had expected to find the D'Amicos at dinner. Instead, Helen called out to her from the sunroom. "Is that you, Carrie? I'm in here."

Carrie walked back the few steps to the sunroom and stepped in. As her eyes adjusted to the slightly dimmer light in the room, she saw Helen, at her easel, cover a painting she'd apparently been working on. Carrie wondered what Nicky's visionary mother had conjured up this time.

"I thought I saw you pass by," Helen said, stretching and rubbing her lower back. "How is your grandmother?"

"I...she's all right now. Did Nicky tell you what happened?"

"Not a thing," Helen said. "In fact, I haven't seen him all day. What do you mean by 'she's all right now'? Did something happen?"

Carrie sighed. "It's a long story. Can I tell you about it another time?"

"Of course. You don't even have to tell me about it at all." Helen smiled to soften the words. "I really didn't mean to pry."

"No, I know you didn't. And I appreciate that you asked."

Carrie found she meant that. The more she saw of Helen D'Amico, the more she liked her.

"It's just that I'm so darned tired," she said. "And I want to fix my grandmother's journal for her, then get back to see her. I wondered if you had any tape?"

"Sure. In fact, I've got tons of craft materials in this drawer over here." Helen rose and crossed to a large buffet, its oak wood mellow from years of careful polishing. "A lot of this stuff is left over from when the kids were in school. I can't seem to throw things like that out. But I do have some new things. This might be useful."

She handed Carrie a tube of glue for repairing cloth, and then a roll of tape.

"Thanks. I...I'll be up in my room for a while, if Nicky comes in. I'd like to talk to him. Could you let him know?"

"Of course." Helen smiled, and Carrie thought she seemed anxious to get back to work. But she made no move to lift the covering from the canvas. "Is there anything else, Carrie? I've plenty of time if you want to talk."

"Thanks," Carrie said again. "Really. I just need to get this fixed. I'll see you later, okay?"

In her room, she washed up, then sat at the antique desk, opening her grandmother's journal to the first page, which was torn. As she worked, she nibbled on M&M's she'd found in her suitcase, an emergency stash from the airport in Philadelphia. She realized she was hungry, and knew she hadn't been eating right. Her mind felt shaky, along with her body.

Had it really been an entire day since she'd had that hot dog on the boardwalk with Tess? And what about Tess? What had she done today? Carrie had promised to call her. But then she had also promised Nicky she would stay away from Tess for twenty-four hours.

She shouldn't have done that. The child would be waiting for her call. Surely a simple phone call couldn't hurt.

But when she lifted her hand to pick up the phone, Carrie couldn't control its shaking. Her mind went funny, and she couldn't think how to find Tess's number. Where had she put it? Or did she ever have it? Ron Devereaux had told her simply to pick up Tess at her house, hadn't he?

I can't remember. And I stupidly forgotten to ask Tess for one.

Didn't I?

The missing number became of utmost importance suddenly. Why couldn't she remember it? she wondered, panicked. And why couldn't she get this damned piece of tape to work? It kept twisting around her finger before she could put it on the torn page.

Then she saw that the page she had been trying to repair was no longer torn. It had been fixed, miraculously. A miraculous page.

Carrie smiled. She liked miracles. Elizabeth had always told her life was full of miracles, if one only looked around. Carrie looked around—her eyes drifting down the page, picking up words. *To my dear granddaughter, Carrie. When I am gone, I want you to know the truth.*

Well, see? That was a miracle, if there ever was one. Someone telling the truth.

Carrie's eyes traveled down the page. And then the next. Though she would never in a million years snoop and read another person's journal, she remembered now that she had hoped to find some clue to whoever might have wanted to hurt her grandmother. That wasn't snooping, was it? It was…Carrie couldn't remember the word. But it was something else.

So absorbed did she become, reading line after line, she forgot about the weakness in her limbs and the trembling in her hands. Now and then she did shake her head to clear her vision. When that didn't seem to work, she held one eye shut and squinted with the other, which helped, though not much.

At one point she laughed with delight. Her grandmother had written a story. A story about a man and a woman and their love affair. The writing was so good, Carrie could actually see them in a field of tall grass and flowers, the man chasing after her windblown hat, while a bull chased him. She saw the man, long-legged and skinny, with a shock of blond hair that looked familiar. She saw him give up and come back to the woman, the two of them hugging, then kissing, and then…

Another vision came to Carrie. A vision of these same two people in a bed, making love, while she—Carrie—stood just outside the bedroom door. She had wanted to ask if it was okay to help herself to a dish of ice cream. For long moments, however, she couldn't move. A breeze blew gauzy white curtains; the woman's legs wrapped around the man's, whose back was to Carrie. At first she thought this was her grandmother and grandfather, and she knew she had thought this at some time before.

She had been wrong, though, hadn't she? This wasn't her grandmother and grandfather, it was…it was her grandmother and…and someone else.

Carrie's eyes widened. A hand went to her mouth. It was her grandmother and—and him. The man with the shock of blond hair, who had been with her in the fields.

Her grandmother had had a love affair—with someone other than Sam. How perfectly wonderful!

Avidly, Carrie skimmed the next pages for a name. It was always just "him." And she remembered how she, Carrie, had always called him that, too—"him"—rather than say his name. Because his name was a secret she had to keep, just as it must have been a secret her grandmother had had to keep.

She tried to recall that name, to bring it to the surface. She almost knew who he was, now, that man her grandmother had been in love with. She recognized the face she saw before her, as her grandmother's story unraveled. All she needed was a name.

Of course. Oh, of course. She knew the name now. It was...it was...

The room went dark as Carrie slipped, unconscious, to the floor.

She came to with Helen shaking her. "Carrie! Carrie, wake up! Oh, thank God. I knocked and knocked, and you didn't answer. I let myself in. You poor child, what happened?"

Carrie felt numb. Dazed. Struggling to sit, she fell, dizzy, against Helen. *I'm sick,* she thought. *I must be sick.* She hung on tight to Helen's arm, grateful for her support.

"Let me call a doctor for you," Helen said. She stood and moved toward the phone.

Carrie shook her head as the afternoon came back. The scene at the Pines, angels in the snow... "No, wait. Wait, Helen."

She laughed shakily as her head cleared and her

strength began to come back. "I must have had some sort of flashback. I think I'm all right now." She tested herself for body parts, needing, for some obscure reason, to make sure they were all there.

Helen frowned. "Flashback?"

"From a drug."

When Helen's frown deepened, she explained, "I accidentally took it earlier at the Pines. Nicky's having some tests run."

Helen clapped a hand to her forehead. "Nicky! I almost forgot. He's on the phone from the Pines. It's about your grandmother."

Carrie jumped to her feet, then held her head, which pounded. Helen picked up the phone and handed it to her. Carrie took it with a shaking hand.

"Nicky? What is it? Is something wrong?"

"Carrie, I am so very sorry, but there's no easy way to say this. There was an emergency here at the Pines, nothing to do with your grandmother, but in the confusion she managed somehow to slip out."

"Slip out? *Slip out?*" Carrie rubbed her eyes and tried to swallow the anger that welled up in her. "Where the hell was that undercover cop?"

"She was in an accident on Ocean View. They insisted she be checked out at the hospital, and by the time I got to the accident site and found out what was going on... Anyway, Carrie, I got here as soon as I could. It's just that, by then, your grandmother was gone. I am so very sorry."

Carrie felt tears rise in her eyes. "She's hurt? Or worse? My God, Nicky, tell me! She's not—"

"No, no, I didn't mean that. We don't know how Elizabeth is. In fact, no one knows *where* she is. I'm just sorry, that's all. I promised you she'd be all right."

His voice sounded heavy and extremely tired.

"What are you doing to find her?" she said, forcing herself to speak calmly.

"We've got people searching the neighborhood, including the beach. We've put out an APB, so every cop in town is looking for her. And we're checking all the cab companies. Carrie, could she have taken a cab somewhere? Did she have money?"

"I…" She frowned, trying to clear her mind. "Yes. There was twenty dollars in her nightstand. She could have used that."

"I'll check and see if it's still there. Anything else you can think of? Any place she might have gone?"

"Her house and the farm were both sold a year ago. Unless she was confused and didn't remember that, I don't think she'd go there."

But there was something. Something Carrie remembered from just before she'd passed out. What was it? If only her head didn't hurt so…

"Nicky, give me a few minutes. I'll call you back."

"Okay. Look, Carrie, don't worry. We'll find her."

She didn't answer.

"Are you all right?"

"Sure."

She laid the receiver down. Turning around, she saw that Helen was still there, sitting on the edge of the bed.

"I just wanted to make sure you were all right before I left," she said, standing. "Can I get you anything?"

"No. But thanks, Helen. I mean that. Thanks."

"I just don't want to see you hurt, Carrie, any more than you already have been."

"What do you mean?" she said sharply.

Helen smiled slightly, shaking her head. "I don't

know. Don't mind me. Just being silly, I guess.'' But her brow was furrowed, and there was a haunted look in her eyes.

"Helen…"

Carrie didn't know what to say. And she couldn't think about it, suddenly, because there were pictures screaming through her brain. Pictures of her grandmother. *A field. A bed.* And pictures of someone else. *A man.*

Carrie's heart plummeted as the picture cleared and she saw the man's face.

She grabbed her purse and took off running, leaving Helen at the door, that same haunted expression on her face.

Carrie knew all too well where her grandmother had gone. To Breen. To the man she had loved—unbelievably—all those years ago.

Unless…unless the story she thought she had read in her grandmother's journal had only been induced by that drug. Something she'd imagined reading, while under the influence of it.

No. Now that her head was clear, the words in the journal were coming back just as clearly. As was the image of Breen, lying beside her grandmother in Elizabeth and Sam's bed.

A cold, hard rage swept through Carrie. How had he done it? How had he tricked her grandmother into loving him? Worse, into being unfaithful to her husband? Didn't she know what he was?

No, Carrie realized. Because I never told her. Not back then. And she was lonely. She wrote that in the journal. She was lonely and turned to Breen. Blinded by love, she must never have seen him for what he was.

She knows now, though, Carrie thought as she drove recklessly to the north end of town. She knows now because I as much as told her, when I thought she was asleep.

That's why she's gone to him now. And God help her. God help her if she threatens to expose him. He'll never allow that, with all he's got to lose. He'll kill her first.

The shot rang out just as Carrie was stepping out of her car in the Anglesea parking lot. It was muffled slightly by the sound of waves and could well have been a car backfiring. Carrie, however, who had taken shooting lessons all those months ago in Berkeley, knew it for what it was.

She ran across the parking lot in the direction of a light in the low, right-hand wing of the center. It was the only light visible anywhere, and she had to trust it led to Elizabeth and Breen.

Throwing open a door, Carrie let it slam behind her. She was then in absolute darkness. Only a flicker of light came from beneath one of the doors along the hallway. Then, as if it were carried along on that light, she heard the sobbing of a woman.

Carrie flew in the direction of the sound. Yanking the door open, she found Elizabeth on the floor by Breen, who was white and unmoving. Elizabeth knelt over him, praying softly, a gun in her hands. In the background ran a film of *The Christopher Show* on a screen.

Carrie ran to Elizabeth. "Grandmother...my God, what happened?"

Elizabeth continued to clutch the gun, but she raised her stricken face to Carrie. "I killed him. I killed him, Carrie."

Carrie put an arm around her grandmother's shoulders, while with her free hand she gently pried the gun from her fingers. "Here, let me have that."

Elizabeth relinquished the weapon without protest. Carrie held it, the steel gleaming wickedly, even in the dim light. She could hardly bear to touch it, so she set it beside her on the floor. Then she looked at Breen, who lay in a pool of blood that seemed to seep from beneath him.

"What in the name of God happened?" she said hoarsely. "Tell me."

Elizabeth shook her head, tears rolling in torrents down her cheeks. "I don't know...I don't know. We were talking. I told him to write...to write...and then there was a terrible sound, and the next thing I knew he was lying here, just like this, and I had this gun...."

She covered her face. "Oh, dear God, Carrie, I killed him."

"Shh. Shh, it's okay." Carrie held her tight. "Grandmother, where did you get the gun?"

"I don't...I don't know."

"Did you bring it with you?"

"I c-can't remember," Elizabeth stuttered. Shaking her head, she began to sob again.

Breen moved then. He uttered a moan. Carrie, not fully aware of what she did, picked up the gun and shoved it into her purse. She bent over Breen.

"Lizzie?" he whispered. "Lizzie?"

Carrie felt for a pulse, which was weak and thready. She took him by the shoulders, lifting him to one side to see where he'd been wounded. The back of his shirt was entirely soaked with blood, and an enormous amount of the red, viscous fluid gushed from his back.

"Lie still," she said. "I'll call an ambulance." She started to rise.

But it was already too late for that. Breen's mouth worked once and then again, but the words he tried to speak never came. His eyes widened and stayed that way. A shuddering breath escaped the thin lips. Then he was gone.

Carrie laid him back down and took his head in her lap. She held the dead man and cradled him, seeing, in this moment, not the man who had robbed her of her childhood, but a soul taking its leave. It was the soul she cradled, while at the same time her grandmother lifted a blue-veined hand and gently closed Breen's eyes.

In this way the two women, together, ministered to the man they had despised for years. And in this moment, Carrie saw the tragedy of his life, and hers, play out before her eyes...an old tragedy, nothing to be afraid of anymore.

26

Homicide investigators had come, and Nicky was talking with them in the room where Breen had died. They had roped it off with their yellow crime scene ribbons, and the coroner had arrived.

Carrie sat with her grandmother on a pew in the old church. Nicky had vouched for them both, telling Carrie to wait there for him. Red lights from patrol cars flashed through stained-glass windows, and disembodied voices from police radios carried into the nave.

Carrie held Elizabeth, rubbing her back and stroking the soft white hair. The older woman looked up at her granddaughter through eyes red and swollen from tears. She had been talking almost nonstop for the past ten minutes, and when Carrie tried to stop her, she didn't seem to hear. It was as if a dam had broken.

"I didn't mean to hurt him, Carrie. I just wanted him to write the note. I wanted to take it to the police, because I knew that was the only way to stop him once and for all. But I didn't mean to kill him. I swear to you, Carrie, I didn't mean to do that."

"I know, Grandmother. It's all right." What else could she say? Her grandmother was confused. There had been no note.

"'Write it,' I told him. 'Just write it!' And he said, 'Please, Lizzie, no.' He begged me not to make him do it. I said, 'Don't call me Lizzie! Write the damned note!' And he said, 'I don't understand. Why are you doing this now? Why are you so sure I've been doing those things again?' 'We know,' I told him. 'Carrie knows.'"

Elizabeth grabbed Carrie's arm. "But, Carrie, he insisted he didn't do those things anymore." Her eyes fastened on her granddaughter's. "We both know better, don't we? You know better. You know he's been hurting another little girl."

"Yes, Grandmother. I know." Carrie gently kissed her forehead.

"I was so blind," Elizabeth said. "I suppose I wanted to be. But I never saw him do anything else. Just that one little girl, back then. I never saw anything that made me think he was molesting anyone else. Especially not you, Carrie. My God! Do you think I'd have kept quiet if I'd known?"

"No, I don't, Grandmother. I know how much you loved me."

Still, she could not help wondering. How could even Elizabeth herself be sure? The ability of the human mind to trick, when one loved a man or was dependent on that man, was nothing short of phenomenal.

And when the molester wasn't someone in the house? When he was someone of repute, someone trusted and powerful, whom everyone had come to love? Why would anyone want to believe such a thing?

"Carrie? Elizabeth?" Nicky spoke from behind. Coming around the pew, he squatted in front of them, speaking softly.

"I fixed it so you could both go home. You'll have to make a statement tomorrow, but for now you're okay. I told the others that I came into the building just as Breen was being shot, and that I saw someone running down the hall. That's not true, precisely, because I didn't get there till after it happened. But with no weapon in sight, that has to be the way it came down. Somebody came in from outside, shot him, then ran.''

He looked from Elizabeth to Carrie. ''I mean, if either of you had shot him, you'd have had to hide the gun before I got here. I can't see Elizabeth dashing around in the garden in the dark, stashing it under a bush somewhere. And if you'd found it...you'd have told me.'' He paused. ''You would have told me, right, Carrie?''

She couldn't answer. The weight of the gun in her purse became a burden of immense proportions.

''Carrie?''

''Leave her alone, young man,'' Elizabeth snapped, drawing herself upright. She raised her chin. ''You don't have to ask any more questions. *I* did it. I killed him.''

Nicky's startled gaze swung to her. ''Say again?''

''Pay attention, for heaven's sake.'' Her chin rose higher. ''I killed him and I'm glad of it.''

Nicky looked at Carrie, who shook her head.

''She's imagining it,'' Carrie said, laughing nervously. ''Grandmother, hush.''

''But the gun,'' Elizabeth said, tapping Carrie's arm. ''The gun...''

Carrie took her hand and squeezed it. Wetting her lips, she said again, ''Hush. You didn't have one, Grandmother. Remember? There wasn't any gun.''

''Wait a minute,'' Nicky said. ''Elizabeth—what are you saying?''

''Nicky,'' Carrie said irritably, ''she's wandering in and out. She's lucid one moment and not the next. She doesn't know what she's talking about.''

"And you do?"

"I do," she said, thinking fast. "I was there with her when someone shot from the hallway. You were right, Nicky. There was someone who ran down the hall."

He studied her. "I've vouched for you and your grandmother, Carrie. I told everyone you were okay. I know you wouldn't let me down."

She couldn't meet his eyes.

"Of course, she wouldn't let you down," Elizabeth said crossly. "I was merely saying that he *thought* I had a gun. I stuck my hand in my pocket, and I swear to goodness, he thought I was going to shoot him." Her lips tightened. "It was only this."

Reaching into her pocket, she pulled out a slender gold pen, holding it up in front of Carrie. From this angle, Carrie could see embossed lettering that hadn't been visible when the pen lay in her grandmother's drawer.

"'Christopher J. Breen,'" she read aloud. "What is this, Grandmother? Why have you got Breen's pen?"

"He left it behind in my room, on one of those ungodly visits. One of the aides stuck it in my drawer, and I remembered it tonight and brought it with me."

She smiled at Nicky, clearly pleased with her cleverness. "I wanted him to write the note with his own pen. It seemed like divine justice, somehow."

Nicky sent a questioning look to Carrie, who shrugged. "There wasn't a note. I think she must be imagining it."

Elizabeth glared at her, in a way that Carrie remembered from childhood when she'd spoken out of turn. "I am not imagining anything, child! For heaven's sake, what do you think I am, addled?"

From her pocket she drew out a sheet of lightly crumpled stationery, with the letterhead Anglesea Conference Center across the top. "Here." She shoved it at Nicky. "Here's the note."

Nicky took it and began reading aloud. "The following is my full confession regarding crimes committed by me against children. I, Christopher Jamison Breen, do hereby confess—" Nicky broke off, looking with amazement at Carrie, then Elizabeth. "He wrote this? This is his handwriting?"

"Of course it is, young man. His own handwriting, written with his own personal pen."

She tapped the paper with satisfaction. "What's more, it's signed. See? 'Christopher Jamison Breen.' And beneath that, 'Child Molester.'" She sighed. "It was mean of me, I suppose, to make him write that. But somehow it seemed a suitable touch."

Nicky looked at her with wonder. "I don't understand. Elizabeth, if you showed him that what you had in your pocket was not a gun, but a pen, how did you make him write this note?"

"Well, I threatened him, of course. I said I'd tell the entire story, or at least all I knew of it, going back to the beginning. That was his greatest fear, you know. That everything he'd worked so many years to build would one day come crashing down."

She squeezed Carrie's hand. "I dread to think how far he might have gone to destroy you, Carrie, if you'd so much as raised your voice against him. But he knew better than to take me on again. He'd have had to kill me this time to shut me up." A shadow crossed her face. "Whatever else Chris was, he wasn't a killer. In fact…he was, I believe, a bit of a coward."

"A coward?" Carrie asked.

Elizabeth sighed and patted her hand. "My dear grandchild, who else would use a position of power to molest a child? He couldn't have a real relationship with a woman, you know. Oh, Chris was charming and fun, and so easy to love...." Biting her lower lip, she frowned. "But it was all a facade. I think, when it came right down to it, Chris was afraid of women. In his heart, he was still an adolescent—and women were mothers, who would always let him down."

"Even so, Elizabeth," Nicky pointed out gently, "I don't see what Breen gained by writing this note. Why didn't he just let you tell the police, and then deny it?"

Elizabeth gave a small shrug. "I persuaded him that by confessing his sins openly, he might hope to throw himself on the mercy of his followers. Well, after all, look what a public confession did for Swaggart, for Jim Bakker...and then, of course, there have been all those politicians over the years. Where are they now? Selling their tell-all books on CNN and *Fox News,* for heaven's sake."

Nicky grinned. "Elizabeth Holder, you are an incredible woman. Do you know what you've done?"

Looking him square in the eye, she said, "I've rid the world of a piece of scum. That's what I came here to do, and I did it. Much too late, I'm afraid. But I did it."

Her face clouded over. "I didn't mean to kill him, though. I just wanted him put in jail, so he couldn't do those things ever again."

Nicky shook his head, the same wondering look on his face. Squatting down beside her, he met the brave eyes, touching with his fingertips the trembling chin. "Elizabeth, *did* you kill him? Are you sure?"

She shook her head. "I don't know, my dear. As God is my witness, I simply don't know."

27

The Children's Festival of the Arts at Anglesea was canceled. Participants who had already arrived were given the option to either return home or stay through the weekend in a hotel on the beach—a vacation, of sorts, the tab to be picked up by the Anglesea board of directors. The children who were to attend responded in a variety of ways. Some were shocked by the news of Christopher Breen's death. Others, young enough to not understand fully, were simply disappointed. All were promised that another festival would take place in six months' time. Anglesea quickly elected a new director for its board, and festival organizers—still so stunned they could barely move—started scurrying as best they could to put the new event together. Only new publicity, connected to a new festival, could wipe out the memory of these darkest of days. For they were the darkest of days. In Holly Beach, it seemed the entire world had come crashing down.

Parents, more than anyone, were devastated. Some, unwilling to face the fact that they'd put their trust where it did not belong, did not at first believe the news that came out about Breen. But then how could they not believe it, they whispered over back fences and before flickering television sets, when he had left a note in his own hand confessing to child molestation?

The most shocked of all was Breen's assistant, Ron

Devereaux. Carrie felt sorry for him, now that the truth about his idol had come out. He had agreed to stay on and help the center until college began in the fall. He had also been approached by the board to come back next year and in some way continue with Breen's work. Carrie hoped he would accept. Everyone agreed that in spite of everything, Christopher Breen had done much for the youth of the nation. Even the President spoke out—not in person, of course, but through a spokesman—evincing both sorrow and outrage at this terrible turn of events.

The fact that Breen had confessed in his note only to molesting children when he was in his teens and early twenties, and none at all since then, did not alter the shock and betrayal the parents and children felt. The story spread like wildfire across the nation, fast becoming hotter than any of the political or Hollywood scandals that had rocked the country in recent years. Television and print reporters filled the town. Tourists, overwhelmed by the sudden traffic and parking nightmares, fled the filled-to-capacity restaurants and overrun beaches. Within the first few hours, Holly Beach resembled an armed camp, with hundreds of photographers and newscasters jostling each other, each after the next photo, the next sound bite, the perfect fifteen or thirty seconds with which to open the evening news.

As word got out about Breen, women began calling the various media, even the Holly Beach police station, with stories of having been abused by him as a child. One woman was from Nebraska, two from California, another three from Illinois and Ohio. All had either lived or vacationed in Holly Beach as children. Though one of these women turned out to be a publicity seeker, not a true victim, the others proved to be sincere, wanting only to share their stories as part of their recovery. In this way they hoped to help other victims—those who might still be silent—to know they weren't alone.

It was curious, however, and Nicky agreed, that none of Breen's more recent victims had spoken up, either to the reporters or the police. They could only assume that these younger victims were still too close to what had happened to them, still hiding it from everyone they knew. Sadly, many would never tell, Carrie thought, and she couldn't say she blamed them. Why do so now, when Breen was dead and it seemed nothing could be helped by unveiling what, to them, must still be a terrible sense of shame? In time, perhaps they would find another way to heal.

Three days after the night Christopher Breen died, Carrie sat on the grass at the Crest Inn, doing her best to relax in the sunshine. It was Mario's birthday, and Helen had set up a picnic on the lawn. A light breeze blew off the sea, fluttering a gaily flowered cloth on a table holding huge bowls of homemade pasta and desserts. Another table held jugs of iced tea, red wine made by Nicky's uncle Mike and soft drinks. Helen had asked that this one day, at least, be apart from the turmoil still surrounding Breen's death. Nicky had agreed, and Carrie was just as willing.

In a few hours she would pick Tess up at her house and take her to the boardwalk again. Tess had sounded excited, as if she couldn't wait. Meanwhile, Elizabeth sat beside Carrie in a lawn chair, enjoying her first trip away from the Pines in over a year—if one didn't count her excursion to Anglesea three nights before. Elizabeth was sleeping, or so Carrie thought. She smiled. One could never be sure with her crafty grandmother, even now. But ever since the night Breen was murdered, she seemed to crave enormous amounts of sleep.

Better that than to answer questions? Carrie wondered. If so, she could relate. She thought about the gun, which was still in her purse, shoved into a drawer upstairs. Now that the moment for truth had passed, she didn't know what to do with it. She had thought of hiding the gun in a better place. But was there any spot in this house where Nicky couldn't—if it came to that—find it?

She was stupid to have taken it in the first place. An instinctive but foolish act to protect her grandmother. But why had she even assumed that the gun was Elizabeth's? Where on earth would she have gotten it from? And how could she have brought herself to use it—much less shoot a man in the back, which, according to the coroner, was the way Breen had died? The bullets, more than one, had entered through the back and hit a major artery, causing him to bleed to death within minutes after being shot.

No, her grandmother could not have done that. Furthermore, the fact that she had forced Breen to write the note of confession seemed to prove that she had meant for him to live, to pay for his crimes in jail.

Carrie realized she might never know the truth. Not unless the police came up with another killer—one, unimaginable as it seemed, who had slipped into the room and shot Breen before her grandmother's eyes, stunning her so far back into that other world that even now she could not remember what, in that moment, had occurred.

And if no one like that appeared and Elizabeth were charged? Carrie would tell Nicky about the gun. She would wipe off any trace of Elizabeth's fingerprints and make sure hers were on it. She would confess to the murder of Breen and go to prison willingly, if in doing so her grandmother might be spared.

Carrie was grateful that Nicky had vouched for them, and that they hadn't yet been called to the police station to give a statement. It had given her a few days with her grandmother, to prepare her for what might come. But she could tell from the strain on Nicky's face that the lie—that he'd arrived on the heels of the shooting and seen a man run through the hall—was taking its toll. He of all people, having espoused honesty and truth throughout his career as a cop, could not live long with a cover-up. She would soon have to relieve him of that.

For that matter, she could not live much longer herself with the lie between them. She knew, though Nicky had not said as much, that he wondered if it were she—not her grandmother—who had shot Breen. He didn't want to think this, she guessed. But he couldn't help it, and every time she looked at him, she saw the question in his eyes.

Carrie glanced over at Mario and Helen, who sat a few yards away on lawn chairs, holding hands. Mario, a short, stocky man with an olive complexion and eyes that were as relaxed as Nicky's were stressed and watchful, was obviously embarrassed to be overwhelmed with gifts. Sally kept insisting he open them, and her father finally gave in. Afterward, there was much good-natured teasing about encroaching old age. Mario took it patiently enough before reminding everyone that he was the baby of his parents' family of sixteen, strong as a bull, and just look at his brother, Mike, still strong at eighty-two.

What's more, he bragged, if it weren't for him, the

roof of the Crest would never get repaired, the screens never painted and the storm windows never hung. He had the strength of three men, and dared anyone to claim otherwise.

Nicky reminded him, with the same good-natured humor, "I didn't get these muscles chasing crooks around Holly Beach, Pop."

"True, you've always done more than your share," Mario agreed. "But I've been missing you, Nicky. This has not been an easy time for you, has it?"

Nicky knelt down next to his father's chair and gave his arm a warm squeeze, but he didn't answer the question. "Next week," he said. "I'll paint that part of the fence I left half-done, and we'll see about reseeding this lawn. Okay?"

"Forget the lawn. I'm worried about you."

"Don't be, Pop, I'm okay, I really am. And just to prove it—" he raised his voice "—I intend to pull a team together and wallop the daylights out of anybody who's fool enough to pit themselves against said team in five innings of softball."

Sally, whose mouth was full of thick, crusty bread dipped in olive oil and herbs, nevertheless squealed and grabbed Carrie's arm.

"C'mon, Carrie. You haven't lived until you've played a D'Amico softball game. We'll beat the hell out of 'em." She broke off and looked quickly at her father. "Sorry," she said, wiping her mouth with the back of her hand and grinning. "But we will, you know."

Helen crossed over to sit with Elizabeth, who'd woken up with all the noise, and Carrie let Sally lead her to a far corner of the lawn. There they collected bats, gloves and balls from a storage shed. Nicky called after them, "Wait'll you see your competition. You don't stand a prayer, not a prayer."

He tore off in the black Jeep Carrie had seen him leaving for work in each morning, and Sally groaned, "Oh, no."

"What's wrong?"

"Nicky. I know exactly what he's doing, that creep. He's going after the Obscene Machine!"

"Who?"

"His softball team. He coaches the PD Little League, and a meaner bunch of foul-mouthed little delinquents you've never seen. We'll have our work cut out for us." She piled Carrie's arms high with equipment. "Nicky's awful, you know—he can't stand to lose. It's his worst fault." But she smiled.

Carrie wondered at her obvious adoration of her brother, given the scene she'd witnessed the other night. Sally's moods, apparently, swung hot and cold regarding Nicky.

A half hour later, Nicky and his team were setting up a softball diamond at the far end of the green, with lifeboat cushions as bases. There was a lot of arguing and cussing in the name of team spirit, and Carrie swore to Sally that one of Nicky's kids, a tough type who kept spitting on the ground whenever Carrie walked by, had been in the original *Boys' Town* movie in the forties. They were in a time warp, and Sally was right; there was no hope for them now.

Carrie's job was organizing the girls' team, and she wasn't doing very well. So far, she had four neighborhood girls: a seven-year-old with glasses and a problem with coordination, a nine-year-old who could run fast but was too lightweight to hit very far, and two twelve-year-olds who were obviously there to flirt with Nicky, not to play ball.

"Maybe we should give your team a handicap," Nicky said. He shook his head sympathetically. He was dressed in jeans and the green-and-white T-shirt Carrie had seen him in before. Barely concealed amusement turned up the corners of his mouth.

Carrie stuck out her chin and said irritably, "Why?"

"Well, you know, all those…girls."

Carrie's eyebrows rose, and Nicky grinned. "I didn't mean that the way it sounded."

Carrie drew herself up, assuming a haughty pose she had learned at her grandmother's knee. She said, enunciating every word clearly, "We are going to demolish you, D'Amico. When this game is over, my team will have given a whole new meaning to the word *balls*." She crammed on the cap Sally had given her and sauntered to home plate. "Play ball!" she yelled, picking up a bat and taking a stance.

Nicky, on the pitcher's mound, stared. Then he grinned.

"Ball one," Sally called as his first pitch, a good one, sailed by.

"Strike!" Nicky yelled.

"Not in this game," Sally yelled back. "You know we never have strikes in family games unless the batter actually swings."

"Those rules were for little kids," Nicky argued. "No special favors today."

"Like hell," Sally told him. "You never said that. Play ball!"

Nicky frowned. "Someday," he muttered, "I'm gonna get to play with the big guys."

An hour later they were in the bottom of the fifth, the number of innings they had agreed to play. The score was 3-0 in favor of Nicky's team. But the seven-year-old with the glasses had actually gotten a hit off Nicky when he pitched her an easy one, and he had walked the lightweight because he felt sorry for her, too. Then one of the twelve-year-olds, Patty, had shocked him by hitting one into right field. He never would have believed it, but the bases were now loaded, and he was starting to sweat.

Still, he didn't have that much to worry about. Carrie was the only batter left, and he'd strike her out easy. Carrie talked tough, but she couldn't hit; he knew that by now. He almost felt sorry for her. She'd been real loyal to her team, and he had, in fact, agreed to the handicap—no strikes unless you swing—although his own kids had protested fiercely that this wasn't a soft-ball game, it was more like golf.

Well, hell, how could you take advantage of a team whose captain pitched like a schoolgirl—no power in her arms? Most women didn't have upper torso strength. It wasn't their fault, just nature.

Still, he wasn't about to take any chances. He wouldn't cut Carrie any slack. It was the bottom of the last. Anything could happen.

And Jesus, Mary, it did.

He pitched Carrie a fast one, well inside. She should have swung, but didn't. Nicky was mad. He stood with his hands on his hips, glowering, his eyes dark, his mouth and square jaw set in a look of displeasure.

"Ball three," Sally yelled.

"No way!" he yelled back. "She should have swung at that one!"

Carrie squinted at him from beneath her cap. "But

you agreed, Nicky. No strikes if we don't swing, just balls.''

"Only because—'' He broke off irritably. "Never mind. But you're taking advantage. And it's an unwritten rule you have to play fair. You have to swing at the good ones.'' *Dammit all, anyway. Girls!*

"Sorry,'' Carrie said softly.

Nicky swallowed his agitation. "Never mind, it's okay. But you're gonna have to swing next time, see, because you can't just stand there all afternoon while balls go by. You especially can't do that when the bases are loaded, see? It's not fair.''

Carrie's shoulders slumped. She was dusty and sweat-streaked and looked forlorn. Damn, he hadn't meant for her to feel bad; it was only a game, after all.

"Maybe somebody else should hit for me,'' Carrie said, her voice soft and dismayed.

Nicky sighed. "Just swing, Carrie, okay? Swing!''

He pitched her another fast one, his irritation giving it power.

Carrie swung. Her bat connected with a loud crack, and the ball went soaring over the cottages to the left and on into a neighbor's yard five doors away. Carrie's girls all began screaming at once, so excited they forgot to run for home. Sally jumped up and down, yelling, "Go, Dinah! Patty, run! C'mon, you idiots, *run!*'' She was so excited she threw her cap down and stomped on it, then tossed her mitt into the air so hard it landed halfway across the yard and barely missed the rum cake. Helen and Mario and the others jumped to their feet to watch, and even Elizabeth began to cheer.

Helen yelled, "Go, Carrie, go!'' Nicky's outfielder ran to retrieve the ball, but he had to climb two fences and round a twelve-foot hedge, so it was really all over.

He knew it, and he stopped halfway, turning, disgusted, to look at Nicky, whose stunned eyes were glued to the action on the diamond. Dinah, with the glasses, tumbled into home, followed by Jean, then Patty, the twelve-year-old. Carrie followed them, running as if Willie Mays himself were in the outfield and the ball on its way to home on her tail.

When she crossed the plate, she and her team tumbled into each other's arms, yelling and laughing and slapping each other on the back, while Nicky and his boys watched. The looks his team gave Nicky were sour, their comments snide.

Finally, Nicky motioned to them, and they all walked over to home plate. Nicky shook each of the girls' hands, gave them a winner's pat on the back, and said with a grin, "Great game. Really. A great game, all of you."

He turned and glared at Carrie, though, pulling her aside.

"You could hit all along, couldn't you? You were holding out until you needed it, playing me for a fool."

Carrie, who had played softball every spring and summer of her high school years in Philly, shrugged. She smiled proudly at her team. "Great young women, aren't they?" She gave Nicky a demure look from beneath thick blond lashes. "Real pros."

He shook his head with exasperation. "Which is more than I can say for their captain. You, of all people, using feminine wiles to win a game! What would your readers think?"

"Screw feminine wiles," Carrie said, smiling sweetly. She stuck her hands in her pockets and strutted away. "Street smarts," she called back. "You know about them, D'Amico?"

Nicky growled something unintelligible and stomped off the field.

After that, it seemed an excellent day. Carrie felt almost as she had before the night in Philadelphia, when she could still sweep all the memories under the rug and think, act, appear normal. Temporarily, she swept them there again.

While Elizabeth and Helen sat on lawn chairs and listened to old records, sipping iced tea, Sally kept busy at the food table. Nicky walked over to Carrie, who was sitting on the grass with a plate of fruit. His irritation seemed forgotten as he asked if he might join her.

"Sure. But can I ask you a question?"

He sighed, settling himself, cross-legged, on the grass beside her. "Go ahead."

"This is none of my business, so feel free not to answer."

"Don't worry. I will." He munched on a hot dog.

She didn't know how to put it nicely, so just laid it on the line. "I heard Sally the other night. When she said she hated you."

He nodded, frowning. "I was sure you did."

"She seems fine now. But the other night, she was pretty upset."

He wiped a trace of relish from the corner of his mouth with a thumb. "Well, sometimes she is...then she's not."

"Can you tell me what happened?"

Nicky sighed again. "Sally seems to have glommed on to you. She really likes you, you know, so I guess she wouldn't mind. A neighbor of ours, a woman Mom had known for years, died last summer. Mom started sending Sally over with food for the husband. Casseroles and soups, you know. We trusted him. We thought he was a great guy, and we just wanted to help him get over the loss of his wife." Nicky's eyes darkened. "He got over it, all right. He raped Sally."

Carrie's hand, which was midway to her mouth with a slice of apple, stilled. "*Raped* her?"

He shrugged. "Well, Sally thought she was in love with him. But the guy was thirty-five, and Sally was only fifteen. By law, that's considered rape."

"Are you telling me Sally had sex with this guy willingly?"

"That's right. That's what she said, anyway. But how can a kid that age make a decision like that for herself?"

Carrie looked across the lawn at Sally, who was laughing and talking with one of the boys from Nicky's softball team. She seemed mature for her age, assured and beautiful, with that mop of dark curls and big brown eyes. Nearly a woman.

Yet, for all that, still a girl.

"Nicky...what did you do?"

"I lost it. The night I found out, I beat him to a pulp. Then I put him in jail. I got him convicted of rape."

Carrie picked at the slice of apple in her hand. "And Sally," she said thoughtfully, "still thinks she loves the guy, right? So she blames you for taking him away from her."

"That's about it. At least, there are times when she feels that way. Other times, we're all right. Or as right as we can be. We're all in counseling—Mom, Dad, Sally and me. But not just because of what happened between Sally and the guy. It's mostly because of what I did that night."

"You mean because it frightened everyone," Carrie said, remembering Helen's words. "The violence."

He squinted at her.

"I've been there," she said. "Physical violence scares the hell out of me, too."

Nicky put his plate on the grass beside him. "Sorry. Of course it would. To tell you the truth, it scares me, too. That night was the worst night of my life. And the worst of my family's. I'd never done anything like that before, and that's what scared them the most. The shock of it, coming from me."

Carrie was silent, thinking back to nights of hiding under her covers, nights of hitting, screaming, threats and accusations.

But Nicky wasn't like that. He had been pushed beyond reason upon learning what had happened to Sally. He would never lift his hand to a woman. She was sure of it.

"You want to know what bothers me most?" he said. "I know it was wrong to beat him up. That's a given. In fact, I'm lucky I wasn't charged for it. There were a few weeks when that seemed a strong possibility."

He laced his fingers together, cracking the knuckles. "But the worst of it is not even knowing anymore if I was right to throw the guy in jail. Was it rape—or love? Can a fifteen-year-old girl love a thirty-five-year-old man, and vice versa? Sometimes I wonder."

"Well, there must have been a trial."

"There was."

"And a jury of his peers decided he was guilty of rape?"

"They did."

"Then it wasn't you who got him convicted, Nicky. The courts did that. The system."

His brief laugh was bitter. "And isn't that precisely what we were arguing about the other day? Whether or not the system works?"

She sighed. "Yes. And you argued that it did."

Carrie looked over at Helen. She thought about how terrible all that must have been for her.

"Your mom didn't know? She didn't have a clue?"

"Not till the day Sally told her. If Sally acted different—which, by the way, she did—we all passed it off as teenage hormones. And why not? Teenagers are experts at being closemouthed, even under the best of circumstances. And at lying. 'Sorry I'm late, Mom, but Tracy's car broke down and we had to wait for a tow truck. What do you mean, why didn't I phone? There aren't any phones out on that road, Mom, you know that! I called you as soon as I could.' And then, of course, the final lob. 'God! Why don't you ever trust me?'"

Carrie almost smiled. If Sally's dilemma hadn't been so serious, she would have, remembering how she had uttered the same kinds of challenges to Alice when she was in her teens. All, of course, in tones of righteous outrage.

Nicky's pager went off, and he checked the number on it, then glanced at his watch. "Sorry, I've got to answer this."

He went inside to make the call and returned only moments later, looking strained. Picking his plate off the ground, he said, "I hate to do this, but I have to go."

"Today?" Carrie asked, surprised. "You're working on your father's birthday?"

"It can't be helped," he said, his voice tight.

He stopped by to talk to his father, then his mother, kissing each on the forehead in turn, and putting his plate with the other dirty ones on the table.

Curious, Carrie watched him climb into the Jeep. What was that all about?

She would probably find out later. Meanwhile, she tried to relax, lying back on the grass. From the old-fashioned record player next to Helen and her grandmother came Nat King Cole's "A Blossom Fell." It reminded Carrie of Alice, singing along with that tune while back-combing her hair into a beehive on Saturday mornings, then drawing on eyebrows with Maybelline. Promising a grand life now that they were in Philly, with a big house, a pony, a swimming pool. Promises never to be fulfilled.

But life had been better there. Alice had knocked herself out to make it work, and, in many ways, it had. Without ever saying it, she had done her best to make up for those early years.

Carrie watched Mario set up a sandbox for several neighborhood kids on the lawn. It was obviously home-made, and the tin bottom of the box gleamed brightly in the sun. The children "helped," scooping sand into it with their tiny sand shovels, though more of it landed on the lawn than in the box. She thought how many times she had wished for a family just like the D'Amicos—large, and burgeoning with love. Yet at this moment, she loved her mother more deeply, and was more grateful for the life she had provided, than ever before.

Now that Breen was dead, and Tess was safe from him, Carrie wanted to do something to help her. Tess's mother seemed well-meaning, but the father...

Carrie didn't know why she cared so much about
this child. Suddenly, however, she felt tender toward
all children, thinking of their earnest, vulnerable lives,
their longing to learn, their right to grow and be free.

She wanted to save them all.

Drifting, Carrie let her mind wander back over the
past week, and was nearly asleep when Sally called out
from the kitchen.

"Carrie? Phone call. It's Tess, for you."

"Tess?" She sat up and wiped perspiration from her
face with the sleeve of her shirt. Glancing at her watch,
she wondered if she'd forgotten the time. No—there
was still an hour left before picking Tess up.

Was something wrong?

Brushing off her shorts, she hurried across the lawn.
She had given Tess this number to call for any reason,
she told herself, not just in an emergency. Maybe she
simply wanted to talk.

Somehow she couldn't see that quiet, sad child picking up the phone just to talk.

By the time Carrie reached the kitchen her heart was
beating wildly. "Tess?"

"Miss Holt?"

"Yes, it's Carrie. Tess, are you all right?"

"Uh-huh. But I can't go to the boardwalk with you.
You said to call if I couldn't."

"Oh." She had forgotten she'd said that, had just
assumed that Tess would be free to go. She began to
breathe normally, her hand gripping the phone less
tightly. "I'm sorry to hear that, Tess. Could you make
it if we went later, do you think?"

"I don't think so. I have to…I have to go somewhere."

"Oh. Tess, have your parents changed their minds? Don't they want you to go out with me?"

"No, it's not that, it's just…" Tess's words trailed off.

What on earth could be wrong? Something *was* wrong. Carrie could hear it in the child's voice.

"It's just I'm not supposed to tell," Tess said softly. "You know, Carrie. It's a secret, remember?"

Carrie shook her head, bewildered. "A secret?"

"Like I told you before."

"Before…you mean when we talked, on the boardwalk?"

"Uh-huh."

Carrie half smiled. "But, Tess, that's all over now."

"No, it's not, Carrie. I have to go see him."

"I don't understand. Him?"

"You know. *Him.*"

A chill raced up Carrie's spine. "Tess, Chris is dead. He died the other night. You do remember that, don't you?"

"Uh huh."

"Well, then, he can't have told you to come and see him."

"I know that, Carrie," the child said, as if explaining something for the fourth time to a two-year-old.

"But you said…"

"Not Chris, Carrie. *Him.* I have to go now. He wants to see me in his office."

What in the name of God—? Then, all at once, Carrie knew.

"Tess, wait!"

"No, I have to go."

"Tess!"

The line went dead.

Dropping the phone, Carrie flew from the room.

"Sally!"

She found the young girl just outside the kitchen door.

"Where's Nicky? I need him! I need him right now!"

Sally shook her head. "I don't know. Didn't he go to work?"

Of course. She'd forgotten. "The number, Sally. I need the number at the police station."

"Here—it's on the wall, next to the phone." Sally came inside and read the number aloud from a typed list. "Carrie, what's wrong?"

She didn't answer. Harried, she stabbed at the numbers on the phone as Sally gave them to her. When a male voice answered, she asked for Nicky.

"Nicky D'Amico? Sorry, he's off for the day."

"But he's—"

Where the hell is he?

It can't be helped, he'd said. *Where did he go?*

"Carrie? Are you all right?"

She turned at the sound of Helen's voice just behind her. "It was Tess," she said shakily, "canceling for tonight. We were supposed to go to the boardwalk—" Carrie swallowed, her voice cracking "—but she has something else to do."

"Oh. Well, I know you must be disappointed. But surely you can go another time?"

Carrie barely heard her. "I have to do something, Helen. Will you take care of my grandmother?"

"Of course I will, but—"

"*Please.* I have to go."

Running outside, she took the stairs to her room two at a time. Inside, she grabbed her purse and car keys.

Take care of her, she breathed. *Please, God, take care of that little girl.*

28

It was pure luck, Nicky thought, having Carrie stay at the Crest. In the several weeks since Debra Stanley had died, he hadn't come any closer to nailing Breen for his involvement than he had at the beginning.

Of course, the girl had committed suicide. But Nicky had wanted Breen for rape of a minor. It was all he could think of, after what had happened to Sally. There were too many damned men in this town who thought they had some right to do whatever they wanted with kids. And they all had some excuse for it. They were "helping" the kid, "being a friend," they "weren't thinking, got caught up in their emotions." There was an epidemic of child abuse everywhere these days, and Holly Beach was no exception.

The hell of it was, except for his partner, Hal, Nicky no longer knew who he could trust at the station. Breen had too much power in this town, and half the force depended on the extra cash Breen paid them for working security at Anglesea events. That meant he and Hal had to go it alone.

As Nicky saw it, the problem from the beginning had been twofold. First, with Debra Stanley dead, all he could do was try to catch Breen with someone else. Pull him in on that, and while he was at it, wring a confession out of him about the Stanley girl. Second, he had to keep Breen's next victim safe. Nicky was pretty sure there would be a next victim; that was the usual M.O. And if things ran true to course, Debra's sister, Tess, could very well be Breen's current prey. He had easy access to Tess, and would probably figure that if Debra hadn't talked, Tess wouldn't, either.

With that in mind, Nicky and Hal had alternately tailed Breen in their off-hours for weeks. In all that time, they had turned up nothing. The man, Nicky thought, was lying low. Nicky even started to question whether he'd been wrong about him all along.

Then one day Breen had started taking Tess to the boardwalk, that Animal Ice place. Nicky figured he was moving in on the kid, making an initial overture. He knew he had to do something more than just follow the guy, and fast. With a child at risk, there was no time to lose.

First, he'd put Rosemary Lambert in the center as a sort of mole, helping with the kids while secretly keeping an eye on Breen. Rosemary was an old friend and the woman who'd designed his house. She had time on her hands, and he trusted her. Then he'd solicited the help of Sharon Cook, a high school student who belonged to one of the Anglesea youth groups. She also happened to be an aide at the Pines, which Breen was known to frequent. Trying to keep it casual, he had asked her to let him know if anything untoward happened at either Anglesea or the Pines. Sharon was handicapped somewhat; though Nicky had known her since she was born and was pretty sure she was a good kid, he didn't feel he could mention Breen by name. All he'd wanted her to do was tell him if something "odd" happened, and hell, the kid couldn't have been expected to report back Breen's visits to Carrie's grandmother. Even he didn't know there was anything wrong with that, till Carrie arrived.

His latest move, last week, was to wangle an evidence permit from Judge Newton—Jerry Newton, who had been a few years ahead in school, but a friend. Nicky and Hal had then gained access to a storage room in the church basement and planted a tape. The way they got in wasn't exactly kosher, but the best thing about Hal as a partner was that little things like picking locks didn't bother him, provided the cause was pure. And if it came up in court? The door was open; they'd had legal access. That's what they would say.

They rigged the tape recorder in an old fruit cellar that looked like it hadn't been used in years. There were cobwebs and dust everywhere. With the hardware in place, they'd planted three mikes, one in the large Sunday school room, one in the basement kitchen and one in the small office next to the baptismal pool. If Breen was planning a move on Tess, Nicky reasoned, it would not be in the busy center, but in the more isolated areas of the old church. Certainly he wouldn't try anything in public; his face was too well-known in this town.

The bitch of it was, nothing had come over those mikes to implicate Breen. Nothing, that is, except Carrie, a couple days ago—confronting Breen about her past.

When he'd heard that, Nicky had been appalled, yet at the same time excited. If he could get Carrie to talk to him, tell him what Breen had done to her, he might be able to get her to testify in court. That could go a long way toward nailing the monster for what he'd done to Debra, and who knew how many more kids.

Well, Carrie had talked. And Nicky just had to make sure, then, that she stayed out of the way for another day or so. From what Hal had told him, things were heating up. Breen was seeing Tess more often, suddenly. And they both knew child molesters had a way of starting up, even after a long period of doing nothing, when they were under stress. Carrie's confrontation, apparently, had been all the stress Breen needed to push him over the top. The only thing was, Nicky didn't want Carrie getting caught in the middle of it, maybe even hurt.

Then, three nights ago, Breen had been murdered. He, Hal and Carrie, though stunned, had heaved a sigh of relief. Tess and any other of Breen's would-be victims were safe. That was all that mattered.

Until today.

When Breen was murdered, Nicky and Hal had stopped checking the tapes each day. It was all over; there was no need for them anymore. But then Hal had come in today to dismantle the equipment, and for no reason other than that he had some time on his hands, had sat down and listened to the last few minutes of the final tape.

Someone, he told Nicky excitedly over the phone moments later, had been in Breen's office by the baptismal pool. And that someone had set up a meeting there this afternoon—with Tess Stanley. Furthermore, he had not asked, but rather demanded that she come.

Hal didn't know who that someone was; he hadn't recognized the voice on the tape. But when Nicky heard the tape, he was pretty sure he knew.

He sat on the storage room floor now, his back against dusty boxes, monitoring a fresh, new tape through headphones. The tape recorder was sound-

activated, and had started running forty-five minutes
before, when a Bible class had begun in the large Sunday school room. If a sound occurred in either of the
other two rooms, a light would flash on the console,
telling them to turn up another mike. Hal stood by the
console, watching.

Nicky's ordinarily dark complexion was sunburned
through his tan, his nose tender. Hal had given him a
small tube of Noxzema to rub on it, and the white ridge
gave his high-cheekboned face a fierce look. He was
in jeans and a black T-shirt.

He yawned deliberately, relaxing his muscles in
preparation for whatever was to come.

"What time is this thing supposed to be over?" Hal
complained. "My apologies to King David, but I'm a
little weary of the Psalms."

Nicky glanced at his watch. "Another fifteen
minutes or so. Five minutes before Tess's meeting with
that asshole."

"Is she in that Bible class?"

"No, she's at home." Nicky closed his eyes again.

Hal began an agitated pacing in the small area, as
far as the cord of his own headphones would take him.
"How can you do that, man?" He ran a nervous hand
through his short blond hair. "You look like you're
stoned out at a concert, not waiting to make a bust."

Nicky said easily, "You've got to learn to relax
when you can. Store the energy up so it's there when
you need it."

Hal made a derisive sound. "You mean like not having sex before the big game?"

Nicky grinned. "Something like that."

"What about this Holt chick? You getting something
there, pal?"

Nicky's soft answer belied the rock-hard stillness in his gray eyes. "I'd rather you didn't talk about Carrie that way."

Hal shrugged. "Sorry." He began to pace again.

But Nicky wondered what he really felt for Carrie Holt. Compassion? That much he'd admit to. Carrie had been a victim—and he had this damned weak spot for victims.

But it was more than that. In his work he had seen a lot of women victims and felt for them. But he genuinely liked Carrie Holt.

He admired what she had done with her life, in spite of what amounted to a handicap all these years. He knew it couldn't have been easy, having no support from her family, nobody to talk to about what had happened. He had read his mother's copy of Carrie's book, *Winter's End,* the other night, staying up far too late, but unable to put it down. It struck him that Carrie felt the way he did about a lot of things: about injustice and the way people seemed to become more and more desensitized to each other, even as the world grew supposedly more civilized. Too much "News at Eleven," seeing people crash, burn and die in their living rooms every night.

He liked, too, the combination of vulnerability and strength he had seen in Carrie, and he thought they could become friends. Whether or not they could ever be more, he would only know when this was over.

He wondered if she was in a relationship with anyone now, and somehow, he didn't think so. Or at least not anyone important, or wouldn't the guy be here? Wouldn't she have shared what she was going through with him and asked for his help?

Probably not. Carrie, he guessed, was in and out of

shock now. Whatever had happened to open all this up
after so many years, for her there were times when the
molestation was happening all over again. The way she
related to anyone now would not be the way she would
relate later, if she had the right help.

Nicky admitted to himself that he was anxious for
this to happen, anxious to see what Carrie would be
like without all this pulling her down. And he was glad
it would soon be over, glad Carrie was out of this today, home safe with his mom and the family. When
he'd left the house she'd been there on the lawn, and
he'd asked his mom to make sure she stayed there, to
not let her leave the house alone. He pictured her that
way now, and it felt good, remembering how she had
been this afternoon, laughing and joking with everybody. Those were the first glimpses he had seen of
humor from her since she'd arrived in Holly Beach.

"Nicky." Hal motioned to him, turning up the knobs
on the tape recorder. In the Sunday school room there
were sounds of children talking as they prepared to
leave. Rosemary Lambert said, "Everybody have a ride
home, or someone to walk with?" They heard the children answer and Rosemary say, "Okay, good. See you
all tomorrow, same time."

Footsteps pounded as the children ran out the door
and down the steps to the courtyard. After they were
gone, Rosemary could be heard straightening chairs
and crossing the room. A door closed. In the relative
silence that followed, one of the mikes picked up dripping water from the kitchen. Hal adjusted a knob to
turn it slightly down.

They waited, tuned in to all three mikes now. The
silence on each mike extended so long they were both
raw with tension by the time it began.

A door opened and closed. At the same time a red light flashed on the tape recorder's console. Hal turned up the volume in the small office by the baptismal pool. There were footsteps. A chair squeaked, and a drawer was pulled open. The sound of papers being shuffled was deafening. Hal and Nicky looked at each other. Nicky nodded. Hal adjusted the volume once more, then turned down the other two mikes. They could now hear every sound from the church office as if they were in the same room.

Nicky's stomach twisted with sick excitement. This was it. He knew it more surely than he'd ever known anything in his life.

He swung to his feet and began to pace, the long cord of the headphones trailing behind him. His stomach tightened into knots, and he stretched, trying to ease the discomfort, but every muscle was tense with anticipation. His ears strained to pick up any sound, and he worried, as he always did when these things were coming down, that the mike would go out. Or be found.

Through the headphones, he heard a soft knock. A man's voice said, "Come in."

A door squeaked as it opened. "I'm here."

"Yes, come in, Tess. Come right in."

Nicky heard slow footsteps, and a chair being moved. It sounded as if it caught on something, then was pulled again.

"Here, let me get that for you." Another rustle of footsteps. "Sit here by me, Tess. That's right."

There was silence.

"What did you want to tell me?" Tess said at last.

"In a minute. It's not that important. I'd like to hear about you."

"About me?"

"Yes. What have you been doing, Tess? I haven't seen you for a while."

More silence.

"Tess?"

"I don't know. I went to the boardwalk the other day."

"Oh? With your mother and father?"

"No…with Carrie."

"Carrie? Oh, that's right. I remember."

"She's my friend now."

Nicky could hear a drumming, like that of fingers on a desk. "That's nice. Tess, I'd like to be friends with you, too."

No answer.

"Do you know what I mean?" he said.

Still no answer. Nicky thought he could almost hear Tess swallowing.

"Well, I could meet you here, say, once every week? Like this? We could talk."

"I don't know…." Tess said.

"You look awfully pretty today. I like the way you fixed your hair. The way it curls, here, on your shoulder…"

"Thank you," she said, her tone unsure.

"Your dress…" The man's voice lowered, and Hal fiddled with a knob. The volume went up on the console speaker, and both men removed their headphones. They could hear uneven breathing. "I like your dress. Pretty buttons…but you should open one, here at the top…"

Nicky halted his pacing. His legs seemed to lock.

"There. Isn't that better? So pretty. You're a pretty girl, Tess. Your skin is so white, so pale…."

They heard Tess release a breath, an uneven shudder.

"Don't pull away. I won't hurt you. I like the way you feel."

Nicky flicked a horrified glance at Hal. Hal's face twisted in disgust. "This is it," Nicky mouthed, his voice a bare whisper. *"This is it."*

"Why don't you sit on my lap," they heard.

"I don't..."

"There. That's better, isn't it, now?" The man's voice became thick. "Such a pretty little girl."

"Can I get down now?" Tess said querulously. "I want to get down."

"Not yet, not yet." A soft, seductive whisper.

Bile rose in Nicky's throat. "That's it, Hal! I can't take this shit!" Dropping his headphones, he barreled toward the cellar door.

"No! It's too soon, Nicky! He hasn't said enough yet."

"I don't care! You know goddamned well what he's doing."

His partner shook his head. "One more minute."

Nicky seldom pulled rank, but he was doing it now. "I'm in charge of this operation. We move *now!*" He yanked the cellar door open just as Hal put out a restraining hand.

"Wait!" he growled. "Listen!"

Clearly, over the mike, came the sound of the door in the church office opening once again.

"Somebody else is there, Nicky! Somebody else is fucking there!"

Nicky stood motionless, disbelieving.

"You shouldn't have done this," they heard. The words were said in a voice that was hard as stone, that chilled Nicky with its flat, nearly mad detachment.

"You should not have done this," Carrie Holt said.

29

"Jesus Christ," Nicky said savagely, "What the hell—"

He heard Carrie say, "Tess, get out of here. Go into the church and stay there. Do you hear?"

There was no answer.

"Tess!"

A timid, shocked, "Yes, Miss Holt." There was the sound of Tess's quick, frightened footsteps, and the door closing.

"You slime!"

"Carrie, this is not—"

"Shut up! I know what this is, Ron Devereaux. The monster's apprentice has stepped into his shoes—in every horrible way."

"What the fuck is going on?" Hal said angrily. "Who is that?"

"It's Carrie Holt, dammit!" Nicky shook his head. "Never mind! Turn that thing up!"

"Shit, Nicky, she's ruined the bust!"

"Quiet." Nicky held up a hand. "Listen."

Carrie was speaking, her voice rising. "I can't believe I let you take me in that way. I thought you were good. Innocent. Everything he wasn't."

"Carrie, this thing—it wasn't what it looked like," Devereaux said. "I swear—"

"Don't waste your breath! I saw what you were doing to Tess. You had your hands all over her. On her bare breasts, for God's sake! And how many more have there been?''

Silence.

''Answer me, dammit! How many? And Tess. Have you done this to her before? Is this the first time?''

She was on the move, Nicky thought, her voice fading in and out slightly over the speaker. He strained to hear every word.

When Ron didn't answer, there was a loud clatter, the sound of papers rattling to the floor, a crash of glass.

''Answer me!'' she shouted. ''What about Tess? And her sister? For God's sake—it was you all the time, wasn't it? That's why Breen didn't confess to anything recent. He wasn't molesting kids anymore. *You* were!''

''No! You don't understand. It wasn't like that with Debra, I just tried to help her. Debra was...she was promiscuous, and her parents turned against her. I tried to show her I cared about her, that's all.''

''She was pregnant!'' Carrie's voice began to shake. ''Was it your baby, Ron?''

''I—no, no, I swear. It was some boy's she'd been out with in the spring. She was afraid of what her parents would do, and she and the boy came to me and asked for my help.''

''And you took advantage of that. You molested a girl who had absolutely no support or protection from her family, a girl who was already at the end of her rope.''

Ron's voice rose to a whine. ''I'm telling you, it wasn't like that. I was just a friend to her, that's all. But Chris found us talking together, and he took it all wrong." Drawing a deep breath, he let it out on a sob. "Chris threatened to send me home. I pleaded with him not to, told him I'd never done anything like he said with any of the kids, and I hadn't, I swear. I said I'd die if I didn't get to work with him, it was all I'd ever wanted."

"And your good friend," Carrie said sarcastically, "your idol, Chris, said exactly what?"

"He wouldn't listen to me at first. But then he said he believed me, and he was sorry. But he kept watching me, you know. And half the time he acted like he didn't trust me anymore. He said somebody he knew did those kinds of things to kids years ago, and so maybe he'd leaped to conclusions. But I knew he didn't really believe that, because of the way he acted, you know?"

Carrie was silent a moment. Finally she said, "What about Debra? Tell me about Debra."

"She—Chris talked to her parents and gave them some money to help her go somewhere and have the baby. He wanted to help her, that's all, the way he did a lot of people. Only Debra's father, he kept the money, and she—she didn't know what to do."

"So she killed herself," Carrie said softly. "Oh, God, Ron."

"I didn't do it," he whispered. "I didn't do anything."

There was a sound of movement. Ron's voice rose, becoming louder, yet at the same time remaining uncertain. "I...I'm sorry, I have to go now. I have to write a script for Sunday's show."

Carrie laughter was one of disgust rather than humor. "A script? For Sunday's show? You don't get it, do you? There's not going to be a show on Sunday, Ron. And you're not going anywhere—except to jail."

"No!" he cried. Then, more softly, "I mean, no, please, Carrie. I can't go to jail. I have to carry on Chris's work."

"You won't be carrying on anything here, Ron. You think I'm going to just let you go on molesting little kids, the way you were doing with Tess?"

"I told you," he said, sounding panicked now, "I didn't *do* anything."

"And I told you," Carrie said angrily. "I *saw* you. I saw what you were doing to her, Ron. The only thing I don't know is whether this was the first time. Was it? Was this the first time?"

He was silent.

"Answer me! Or so help me, I will strangle you with my bare hands!"

There was no doubt from Carrie's tone that she would do exactly that. Nicky and Hal glanced at each other uneasily, but then Ron said in a low, resigned voice, "I...yes, yes, it was the first time. I guess I've kind of been crazy since Chris died. He was the only person in my life I cared about, really. He was like a father to me. And all of a sudden he was gone, and everything was falling apart. I...I needed Tess today. I never had any women friends, Carrie. It's like I told you, I don't know how to talk to women. I was lonely. I needed somebody to be close to."

"Close! You call molesting a seven-year-old child being 'close'?"

"I didn't molest her, I tell you—I cared about her! I was her friend. I even encouraged you to be a friend to her."

"That's what I don't get. How could you be sure she wouldn't tell me about you? Oh, no...wait, I do get it. You told her not to tell, of course. It was your secret. Yours and hers. That's what all of you do, isn't it? Force them not to tell.''

"But she *wanted* it," he said, his voice breaking. "I didn't go after her, you know. She came to me first. Carrie, you can't imagine how it was that day her sister died. Tess was so…so pitiful. She came to me sobbing her heart out, and I…I took her in my arms, I held her. She put her arms around my neck, and it felt so good to just comfort her. Her leg, under my hand, felt thin and frail, her waist so tiny, like…like the neck of a bird. She's terribly thin, you know. They don't feed her well at all. And then later she came to me again—''

"I could kill you right here and now," Carrie interrupted in a strangled voice.

But Ron went on as if he hadn't heard. "She's a lot like you, I think, Carrie. Tess has the same problems as you did, a father who drank—''

There was the sound of a sharp, indrawn breath. "What the hell do you know about that?''

"I…Chris told me. He told me everything.''

"Chris?'' Carrie's tone was disbelieving. "He couldn't…''

"He told me everything, Carrie. He said that was why I had to be careful with the kids in my care. Because when you hurt little kids, they don't get over it. He said he was the 'someone' he'd told me about who did that, and he said he'd promised somebody he wouldn't ever do those things again. And he never did, he said. Not once. He spent the rest of his life, in fact, making up for it.''

Carrie sounded horrified. "And even after he told you that, you still did what you did to Tess? You didn't just neglect to give her and her sister the right kind of help—you prevented them from finding it? You used your position as someone they looked up to to destroy them rather than save them!''

"No!"

"God help you, Ron Devereaux. Because no one else will. It's time the children here, and their parents, learned who you really are.''

"What are you doing?'' There was outright fear, now, in Ron's tone.

"I'm calling the police.''

"No! No, please stop. I told you, Carrie, you can't do that.''

"Watch me.''

"But they want me to come back now. They want me to take Chris's place. If you do that, you'll ruin everything!''

There was the sound of a chair scraping loudly on the wooden floor, followed by footsteps and a scuffle.

"Let go of me!'' Carrie said hoarsely. "Get your hands off me.''

"No, you've got to listen to me. You've got to understand. Carrie, people are weak. That's what Chris always said, and he was right. They don't know what's best for them, so we have to show them. That's all I tried to do.''

"You're insane!''

"Don't struggle, Carrie. Look, we can work together. If you don't tell anyone about this, I won't tell that I saw your grandmother kill Chris.''

Carrie's breath came in harsh, angry gasps, and Nicky couldn't stand it. He had to go to her, to stop this right now. He ran for the cellar door.

"Nicky, wait! Listen!'' Hal turned up the volume on the console speaker.

Carrie gave a groan, a soft, brittle cry. "You're hurting me, Ron. I can't breathe."

"I can't let you do this, Carrie. It would be in all the papers, just like it was about him. I'd never be able to work with kids again—"

"Get off me!"

Ron gave a sharp cry and there was the sound of someone stumbling. "No, Carrie!" Ron yelled. "Don't!"

Nicky heard a click—a hard, metallic click that was unmistakable. The hairs on the back of his neck stood on end. He broke out into a cold, drenching sweat.

"Christ, she's got a gun!" Hal yelled. "She's gonna shoot the son-of-a-bitch! Nicky—"

But Nicky was yanking the door open, his own gun out of its holster, his face rigid with terror.

"Stay here!" he ordered. "Don't let anything happen to that tape!"

He tore out of the room and up the cellar stairs, two at a time, then down the hall, his heart pounding wildly, fear pumping adrenaline through his limbs. All the while he could only think *I've got to get to Carrie, I can't let her ruin the rest of her life over a shit like Ron Devereaux, I have to get to her in time.*

"Jesus, Mary—!" The door from the upstairs hall to the main church was locked. He had checked this one when he got there, because it was the shortest route to the church office. All the other routes were clear, to the Sunday school room, the kitchen—

Who had locked the goddamn door?

It was a fire door with a steel core; no chance of breaking it down. Nicky ran outside, through the courtyard and around to the street, pounding up the long, steep flight of steps to the main church doors and yanking at all four of them in turn. They were brown, simulated wood, but steel—and locked. Every one locked.

His imagination ran wild as he pictured Carrie standing before Devereaux pointing a gun—Jesus, where in the hell did she get a gun?—and no, please, no, tell me she didn't already do it! But he would have heard the shot—dear God, stop her, don't let her do it, please God, If you're out there anywhere....

He ran for the far side of the church, the sound of his own footsteps pounding in his ears, too slow, too slow, panic racing through him—*don't let her ruin her life this way. Let me have her, just for a while, I can help her, I know I can help her.* He ran faster, along the hot sidewalk, people staring, he knew—he must be a terrible sight, gun in hand, face an ungodly twisted mess, fear spilling from every pore. But then he was there, at the narrow stone steps leading up to the small office from the sidewalk, the office where Devereaux and Carrie were. He breathed a prayer, *Don't let this door be locked. Please, Saint Jude, Saint Michael, pray for us, pray for us—*

He was shaking, every muscle in his body preparing to do whatever had to be done—break down the door if necessary; he would kick it off its hinges. Then he was there, and the door was locked, *oh, Carrie,* but his shoulder was against it, then all of his weight, a 190-pound battering ram, and the door gave and he was bursting through it, the noise deafening as the old wooden door splintered and flew back against the inside wall.

Carrie turned and screamed. "No!"

Nicky stood there a fatal moment, a huge dark outline against the sun, blinded, the small room invisible to his unaccustomed eyes. In that brief instant he realized that Carrie didn't know who he was, and then he saw her eyes, the only thing he saw, disconnected from reality, full of some distant terror, and he knew he had gotten there just in time. He held out his arms, but Carrie was shaking her head, back and forth, back and forth, her eyes huge with fright, and she screamed once more, *"Don't touch me!"*

The gun went off.

It exploded, one shot after another. Nicky felt the bullets tear into his flesh. There was no pain. Only shock. Then nothing. He felt himself fall.

In the instant before everything went black he thought he saw his mother and Sally, their faces frozen with terror as bullets sprayed the room.

He remembered, too late, his mother's warning: "You care too much, Nico," and fifth grade, Babs Lake, laughing: "You're so silly, Nicky D'Amico, what makes you think I need your help?" Turkey Bowen punching him out, taunting, "If it ain't Saint Nick to the rescue. Fuck off, D'Amico!" And Nicky knew he was dying and he wouldn't be able to help Carrie now—he wouldn't be helping anyone, ever again, and Christ, that was so goddamned bad.

"Mary, Mother of God," he whispered. "Mother of God. Oh, hell."

30

Carrie sat huddled on a cot in a dimly lit holding cell. In a corner, a toilet ran constantly. Water dripped in a sink, making a rust-brown stain on white porcelain. Voices rumbled from other cells.

Carrie noticed none of these things. She was numb, her mind working on another level, unconnected to present reality while immersed in the terrible unreality of the recent past.

She still saw Nicky as he broke through the church office door. Except that it wasn't Nicky then. To her distraught mind it was her father, pounding on the door of the bathroom as she knelt between the toilet and wall, hiding. Her father at the door, saying, "Come on out, Carrie, I won't hurt you, come out," and she thought he had broken in.

But she would not be a victim this time. She had reached, in her mind, for his hunting rifle in the linen closet and—

Nicky. Oh, God, dear God. She moaned, rocking with grief. What have I done? Not just to Nicky, but to the whole D'Amico family.

Helen and Sally were there, she remembered...and someone screaming, blood all over...blood pumping from Nicky, his life's blood—

Then someone called the paramedics, and moments

later it seemed the entire church was filled with uniformed men.

They had placed Nicky's body on a stretcher and taken it away. Someone from the police had searched her, then there were handcuffs.

They had taken her, too. And brought her here.

It had gone all wrong. So wrong.

She had brought pain to good people, people who, in her own inept way, she had come to care about.

She couldn't address it. If she did, she would fly into little pieces. She had already gone partway, she knew. There wasn't much chance that what was lost would ever come together again. She had to hold herself tightly to keep from disintegrating further.

She lay back and stared at the ceiling. Rigid, arms at her sides. Studying the whirls of plaster, as she had in bed as a child. Drifting.

Then, without warning, she was wrenched back in time.

"I'll kill you!" she had screamed at her father one night. "Someday I'll kill you," she had cried. Strange she hadn't remembered till now. The memory came crashing in, stunning her brain, a horrible thing she hadn't known was there.

Voices in her head. Taunting. *Little girl...little girl...impotent, powerless little girl...*

"But guns give people power," she heard Jake Sharley, in Berkeley, say. "They add height and breadth and steel to the voice. Guns can protect you from people who would hurt you."

They can also kill people you love.

And now, the same gun that had killed Breen, the gun she had so thoughtlessly, even criminally, left in her purse—

Nicky. Oh, Nicky.

How would she survive, knowing what she had done?

She wouldn't. A terrible sickness filled her. A black pit of hopelessness yawned at her feet. What did one do when one killed a brother, a much-loved son? Apologize? How does one apologize for such a horrible deed?

"Sorry" would not do.

Of all the words in the English language, *sorry,* she had always felt, was the most misused. It was squandered on everything from burps to spilled milk, from stepping on a dance partner's toes to running down a small child while drunk. The ancient church knew that, and had instituted the practice of striking one's breast while repeating, "*Mea culpa, mea culpa*...my fault, my fault." The words were to be accompanied by fiery repentance, wretchedness and woe. Often the offender lay prostrate on a cold stone floor, in humility and anguish for his sins, until his penance was done. The miscreant would then be lifted up—"resurrected"—though the sin, if of great proportion, might weigh upon the heart for the rest of his life.

There was a Latin phrase, Carrie recalled: *haeret lateri letalis arundo*—the iron entered into the soul.

The ancients knew.

And Carrie knew. "Sorry" would never cover what she had done to Nicky D'Amico. To Helen and Sally. To Mario. She had seen her crime in Helen's terror-stricken face, heard it in Sally's screams. The moment she'd pulled that trigger, iron entered into her soul.

Better to die now than later. Like Debra Stanley. Better to die, what else to do?

She covered her eyes, and doubling over in pain, she wept.

A sound. Scraping of steel on steel. A door opening outside her cell.

Look up. Open eyes. People there...Helen. Sally. Carrie gave a cry of anguish and turned away, facing the wall.

A hand on her shoulder. Helen's fingers turning her face around. Helen's face white, tearstained. "Nicky," she said.

Carrie waited for the blow to be struck for her sin. It never came.

"He sent us," Helen said. She smiled.

Part 3

From *Webster's Dictionary:*

To survive: to continue to live after,
or in spite of.

Epilogue

Holly Beach, New Jersey
January, 2000

Wearing a bright red parka, Carrie walked the hard sand of Holly Beach. She noted that a winter storm was brewing far out at sea. She could see the rain slanting in sheets like great diagonal walls of lead beyond the buoys and waves. A pale sun poked through, but managed only to silver the water as if billions of gasping fish tumbled and clawed in the waves, anxious to get to shore.

She had clawed that way, to get herself well. In the past five months she had become a more-than-determined patient, attacking her therapy, both private and group, with the same perfectionistic tunnel vision she had used to tackle everything else, all her life. The skills that had gotten her through life as an unwell person were put to use in recovery—and if Esther Gordon sometimes lifted an eyebrow at her intensity, she would then shrug and say, "Whatever works…for now."

Carrie knew she wasn't completely well yet. Someone had said that it took fifteen hundred hours of tears to fully recover from sexual abuse as a child. Still, significant changes had taken place. She was less afraid of people and more in control of her life. Further, she knew where to get support for the times she felt unsure.

She had been writing to Tess and sending money from the *Winter's End* royalties to help with her expenses. Tess's parents had separated, and while her mother was finding a job and struggling to set up a new home for herself and Tess, the child was living with the D'Amicos. One of the reasons Carrie had come to Holly Beach was to see her—to keep her promise and to reassure Tess that she cared.

"I'll miss her terribly when she leaves," Helen had said. "When you asked me to take her, I wasn't sure. Now..."

Carrie bent to inspect a large piece of driftwood and found beneath it a perfect conch shell. All the way from the Caribbean, she supposed, on the tide of the latest hurricane. She would take it back to the inn for Tess and teach her how to hold it to her ear and listen to the sea. She wiped it dry on her jeans.

Ron Devereaux was in jail, awaiting trial. That was another reason Carrie was here. To testify. This time, however, it was unlikely there would be other victims coming forward. So far as anyone knew, Tess had indeed been Devereaux's first victim. Carrie thanked God every day that he hadn't had a chance to harm Tess beyond repair. A miracle, she knew. A significant miracle.

As for what would happen to Ron, Carrie had mixed emotions. His lawyer had advised an insanity plea, and no doubt he'd end up in a hospital rather than prison. He'd be on the streets again before anyone knew it, and the question that haunted Carrie nightly was would he start in with children again? If so, and if he were able to cover up his past, few would suspect. That was the hell of it. Molesters didn't always look like monsters. Often they were delightfully charismatic people—people who hid behind engaging masks while performing dark, monstrous deeds.

A deep sadness filled her. When it came right down to it, they were the most evil of all. Who could protect children from the charmers, the beguilers?

Way off down the beach, Carrie saw a figure and recognized it immediately. She stepped up her pace. The figure, tall and solid, grew closer, and Carrie felt a heaviness she had been carrying for six months lift from her shoulders. She began to run.

"Nicky!"

She grabbed him, hugging him. "I'm so glad to see you!"

Pulling back, she flushed, embarrassed at her outburst. But Nicky was grinning.

"Mom said you were down here."

"You...you just look so good," she said.

"No thanks to you, Annie Oakley." He tapped her nose to show he was teasing. "Actually, I feel great. You look great, too. How's the therapy going?"

"Fine. It's going really well."

"You got my letter last month?" There was a hint of uneasiness in his eyes.

"Yes." A fresh gust of wind blew in, and she brushed her hair away from her face. "I couldn't answer it, Nicky. I had to see you and try to say it right." That was the other reason she had come to Holly Beach. It was the most essential reason for her being here.

"C'mon, let's walk." Nicky took her hand and they headed south, away from town. The beach was deserted except for the two of them and a young woman with a dog. The dog chased through the surf after tiny crabs, pawing as they burrowed into the sand.

Carrie tried to sort out what she wanted to say. She

would never forget what Nicky had done, restoring her freedom even while he was lying in the hospital, wounded. Persuading the district attorney not to file charges; convincing him, with the help of Hal and that tape, that the shooting was an accident, a result of the confusion surrounding her having to fight off Ron.

Without that, she might well have ended up in jail along with Ron. Nicky argued, however, that the way he'd handled it was the best use of the judicial system.

"You never meant to shoot me, Carrie," he said now, as if sensing her thoughts. "I saw your face. You'd gone way back into the past."

She knew that now. But not at the time. She had been so full of anger and hate in the church office that she wasn't sure, really. Had it spilled over onto Nicky?

Post-traumatic stress, she had learned. It could go on and on when a woman was abused as a child and hadn't resolved that abuse. Further, it could pop out at the most unexpected times.

Indeed, Carrie had not even remembered having the gun. It was only when faced with Ron's attack that she'd felt the weight of it in her purse. She had pulled it out without thinking.

"You still didn't have to help me that way," she said. "You're a cop, Nicky. It was your job to enforce the law."

"I like to think it's my job to maintain peace. And this wasn't the kind of thing you'd be likely to repeat. So I used the law to protect the innocent, which is, after all, what it's supposed to do. Besides, you were in lousy shape," he reminded her. "You needed protection, not punishment."

The system couldn't let the wounding of a police officer go by unpunished, however. Between them, Nicky and the D.A. had worked out an alternative. Carrie would return to San Francisco for therapy with Esther Gordon, who had already been contacted. Meanwhile, Carrie had agreed to a thousand hours of community service.

"I've been working at two child abuse centers," Carrie said. "One in the city, one in Berkeley."

"A thousand hours is no picnic."

"No, but it's good for me. Sometimes I feel I should pay them to let me do it. Nicky, I never realized what an epidemic of child abuse there is right now. If three out of every four girls, and two out of every four boys are being sexually abused, which is what the statistics tell us...God, Nicky, something needs to be done."

They had come to a small dune, and Nicky made a motion toward it. "Let's sit a minute. Dinner's at five. We've got a while."

Carrie sat beside him on the sand. "I've been keeping in touch with Rosemary Lambert. She says she's taken over with the kids, keeping *The Christopher Show* going under another name, *The Children's Ministry*. She also says she's had the help of several well-known figures from the entertainment world, as well as the new minister at the church. Who, she tells me, is great."

"He is. In fact, they're all doing a great job. We've got a lot to be thankful to them for."

"Them, and the Holly Beach PD forensics department, finding that bodyguard's print on the barrel of the gun I shot you with. If it hadn't been for that, my grandmother might be sitting in jail now."

He shook his head. "I wouldn't have let that happen. Besides, nobody would dare arrest your grandmother. She'd stare them down with that haughty look of hers, and they'd run for cover."

Carrie smiled. "You know, she's remembered everything about that night. She also remembers Petrelli wheeling her out onto the sand and spiking her water.''

"I know, I talked with her just a week ago. She loves that new apartment you moved her to. It's got everything. Light, convenience, comfort…''

"And a view." Carrie's smile widened. "She sure loves her view." Sobering, she said, "So, you think you know, now, why Breen was killed?''

"It's coming together. Once Senator Weiss gave us a statement implicating Congressman Tanner and Petrelli—bodyguard to congressmen and senators, ex-hit man for the mob, by the way—things began to fall into place. Weiss said there were too many people starting to talk about Breen's past, and Tanner's solution, born of panic, was to silence everyone who might know about it, before the President's speech on Sunday. They had bugged the church office and found out about you the day you confronted Breen. That meant that you, and your grandmother, too—since you and Breen had both been visiting her—had to go. When Petrelli's plan to spike Elizabeth's water failed, we think he must have followed her to Anglesea that night to give it another go.''

Nicky shook his head. "Unless Petrelli talks, we can't know why he decided to kill Breen instead. But Weiss says Petrelli isn't the brightest bulb on the Christmas tree, and in fact he's a bit of a wild card, known for not following orders and just going off on his own. He might have decided on the spur of the moment that the more efficient way to save Tanner and everyone else embarrassment would be to just get rid of Breen.''

"But why simply put a gun in my grandmother's hand, hoping she'd be charged? That wouldn't shut her up about Breen.''

Nicky shrugged. "We may never know. Maybe he figured no one would listen to her—an old woman, already known to be confused at times. It's pretty certain he didn't figure on Weiss coming forward."

"We owe Weiss, Nicky. He's left himself open to speculation, as well."

"But not arrest. He managed to escape that by speaking out. Clever, these politicians."

"Oh, yes. And what about Petrelli? Where is he now?"

"Still sitting tight in jail. But I've got a piece of recent news for you. An unlikely witness—Ron Devereaux. We managed to get out of him, just the other day, that he was outside walking in the center gardens when he heard a shot. He ran to a window just in time, he said, to see Petrelli put the gun in your grandmother's hand."

"Well, great. A bit late in the day, though, wouldn't you say?"

"He claims that he was afraid, at first, that Petrelli would come after him if he told anybody what he saw. Apparently, he'd had some sort of meeting with Weiss, Tanner and Petrelli at the Bahia, just a day or so before. They scared the bejeepers out of him. Then, that day in the office, when you threatened to expose Ron, he decided to try a bluff—blaming Breen's death on Elizabeth. He thought it might be a bargaining chip, to get you to let him go."

Carrie shook her head wonderingly. "You know, sometimes I wonder how I could have been so wrong about Ron—and Breen. I feel almost guilty about it. From what Ron said that day, Breen truly wasn't molesting kids anymore. In fact, he apparently wasn't doing anything but good when he died. He even left a whale of a lot of money to the Pines. Nan won't have to worry about closing down, now.''

"He was still responsible for his past, Carrie. He did too much, hurt too many people, and it finally caught up with him.'' A shadow crossed Nicky's face. "I know what you mean, though. I don't feel as certain myself, anymore, about right and wrong, black and white. Or about the proper punishment for any particular crime. I've even…''

"What?'' she prompted.

"Oh, wondered if maybe I shouldn't be a cop anymore.''

She looked at him, aghast. "Not be a cop? Why?''

He shrugged. "I've been wrong about so many things lately. If I'd been more on my toes, I might have caught on to Devereaux earlier. He never would have gotten to Tess at all. And if I hadn't lost it so bad when I heard about Sally, our family wouldn't be having the problems it's having now.''

"Nicky, your family is crazy about you! You can't go on blaming yourself for that. Besides, you're in counseling with them, you're doing everything you can to set things right.'' She put a hand on his arm. "You know, I've been doing a lot of thinking about Sally since I've been working with abused kids. And I think you were right to charge the man with rape. There's something basically wrong with a thirty-five-year-old man who seduces a fifteen-year-old girl, no matter how much she might think she wants it. A kid that age hasn't had the kind of life experience to make that kind of decision. As for Devereaux, none of us caught on to him. And I, of all people, should have. If anyone's to blame…''

Nicky leaned back on one elbow, ready to talk about

something else. He didn't want Carrie to feel she had to keep going over what had happened.

Besides, he couldn't wait any longer to ask her.

"About that letter I sent you..." he began.

He had told her, in a letter, some of the things he'd been thinking as he raced to the church office that day, his heart in his throat, terrified that he was losing her. He had written that he cared about her and always would, no matter how things turned out. Not that he meant to push. But he had to give her the facts, see what she'd do with them.

Carrie pulled out a strand of sea grass and fiddled with it. She sat cross-legged facing him and rubbed nervously at the side of her face, then made herself stop. It was a habit she'd developed in group, like biting nails. She had never been able to talk one-on-one with a man about these things. It was like there was cotton in her mouth—no, not cotton, but lead poured into her jaws, keeping them from moving, her lips from forming words. She plunged on awkwardly.

"Nicky, I'm a whole lot better. Maybe eighty percent. But the other twenty..." Her voice grew hoarse, and she threw her arms wide in an exasperated gesture. "Oh, God, I hate this."

Nicky knew just how she felt. The suspense was driving him nuts.

"The other twenty," Carrie continued, "has to do with relationships. At the strangest times I realize I'm still afraid. Not just of being hurt, but that I'll hurt someone I love in some awful way because I'm not well yet. Esther says...I mean, she knows how grateful I am to you..."

"Grateful." He'd been afraid of that.

"And how much I love your family..."

"My family." Had the sun gone behind a cloud?

"And that's why I'm especially afraid now to admit how I feel."

Nicky was silent a long moment, despairing. Then it struck him that Carrie was blushing. He'd seen her red from anger, and pale before, but he didn't think he'd ever seen her blush.

"How you feel?" he said, hardly daring to hope. "How do you feel?"

Her color deepened. "Like a sixteen-year-old with a crush. I've never really been a teenager before, you know."

A *crush*. God in heaven. It might be a good day, after all.

"I talk about you all the time," Carrie admitted. "Every other word in group, or to Esther, is Nicky, Nicky, Nicky…and Esther says…"

He grinned. "What does Esther say?"

"To take it slow. That anything worth having is worth waiting for. All the irritating clichés."

Nicky felt better, suddenly, than he had in months. "You know what Uncle Mike says about clichés?"

She grinned. "No. What does your uncle Mike say about clichés?"

"That they're truth preserved, like fine old wine."

Carrie laughed. "I think your uncle is right. In fact, I would love to interview him for my new book. It parallels the inner lives of older people and children. Do older people, if single, miss not having had children? What about their relationship to their church and their soul? And are children these days losing out by not having lived through an age that's mostly gone and forgotten, at least in this country? I…" She took a breath, hearing herself and knowing she was rambling, the way she usually did about her work. "Oh, never mind. Nicky, you know something? I feel so good right this minute. It's in my bones, even. A good, solid joy that was never there before.''

He stretched out full-length, his hands locked behind his head on the sand. "Sally says that, too. She's not having the nightmares anymore, you know.''

"She told me.''

"She's starting to date. It's like, when all that happened that night, with Devereaux…when that happened and she and Mom found you there, and took care of you after, she had to call on strengths she didn't even know she had. She's more sure of herself now.''

"She always seemed that way to me.''

"Yeah, but she had to stretch a bit more for you. It was the stretch she needed to get over the hump.''

Carrie leaned back on her elbow and faced him, her hand reaching out hesitantly to touch the navy blue sweater over his abdomen, an inch above the waistband of his jeans and slightly to the right.

"I'm so sorry, Nicky,'' she said softly. "Does it still hurt?'' In her voice was all the sorrow and remorse that words or letters couldn't express. In her hand was the need to heal.

He laced his fingers through hers. The bullets had hit the soft flesh; the most serious problem had been loss of blood. "You can't do too much damage in that area,'' he said. "You might as well have thrown rocks.''

She didn't smile.

"No, really,'' he said, "it only hurts when I laugh. But then, so do my knees. It must be old age. Speaking of which, I finished my house. I'll be moving into it in a couple of weeks.''

"Really? That's great.''

Who would live there with him? she wondered with a twinge of envy, remembering how warm and welcoming that house had been, even in its unfinished state.

He picked a piece of dry sea grass, like straw, from her hair. "Well, I've stayed a little longer at home than I'd planned. But it's time."

"It's good you'll still be close to your family, though."

"That's what I figured. I, uh…I suppose you can live anywhere, being a writer."

"Yes, I do have that freedom."

"But you wouldn't like to leave San Francisco, I guess. I mean, it's your home."

"Well, to tell the truth, I've never felt quite comfortable there—" She broke off, realizing suddenly what he was saying.

"Of course, I don't have to stay here forever, either," he said quickly. "The world I've been living in seems to be shrinking. I figure there's nothing wrong in keeping the options open."

"But now that you've finally got your own house…"

"Yeah. It'd be a shame to leave it."

"I can certainly understand that. I, uh…may I see it?"

His face lit up. "Sure, if you'd like to. We could walk over after dinner. Wait'll you see the new fireplaces I put in, and the greenhouse window in the kitchen."

"I can't wait. I'll bet it looks great."

And maybe, later in the week, she would stop by her grandparents' old house and their farm. It would be difficult, seeing the only places in Holly Beach she had ever known happiness in. Knowing they were no longer part of her life. Or worse, possibly finding them gone—covered over by acres of parking lots.

She glanced at Nicky. After all that had happened, Nicky was still here. She met his eyes and smiled.

He smiled back. "I kind of like you, too." He got to his feet and pulled her up to stand beside him, brushing sand from her hair. "I'm glad you came."

"Me, too." She reached up around his shoulders and he lifted her off the ground for a hug. When he didn't put her back down immediately, she laughed and said, "What time was dinner supposed to be?"

"I don't remember."

"What time is it now?"

"I don't know." He planted a kiss on her nose. "But from where I stand, it's a good time. What do you think, Carrie Holt?"

"The best," she agreed.

A brand-new blockbuster from
bestselling author

R. J. KAISER

The unidentified body of a young woman has washed
up on the shore of the Sacramento River and
everything points to Frank Keegan as the prime
suspect. But Abby Hooper, the police chief, doesn't
want to believe Frank is involved, and she'll risk her
professional reputation to clear his name, identify
their Jane Doe and find out who really murdered
the young woman.

Jane Doe

"...[an] Elmore Leonard-style combo of
good guys and bad...has big screen
written all over it."
—*Publishers Weekly*

On sale mid-May 1999
wherever paperbacks are sold.

ROTTEN TO THE CORE...

When gallery owners James and Victoria Harting plan a dinner party for their star artist, Jack Carey—a man more famous for his philandering than his art—what starts as an innocent gathering becomes an outrageous comedy of bad manners.

Jack is a master at creating chaos, and by the end of the evening he will have set in motion a chain of events that will end in a wickedly delicious conclusion.

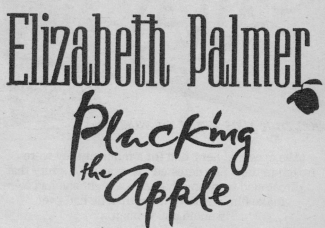

Elizabeth Palmer
Plucking the Apple

"With an impeccable blend of empathy and mocking wit, Palmer delivers a novel of high-society slapstick that is nearly impossible to put down.... A savvy and highly literate romp."
—*Publishers Weekly*

On sale mid-May 1999 wherever paperbacks are sold!

MIRA